Waiting for Aegina

Book Two in The Gift Saga

Effie Kammenou

Printed in the United States of America

First Edition: January 2017

10 9 8 7 6 5 4 3 2

ISBN 13: 978-0-692-82593-8
ISBN 10: 0-692-82593-2

Library of Congress Cataloging-in-Publication Data TXu 2-028-520
Kammenou, Effie. Waiting for Aegina

Cover Design by Deborah Bradseth – www.tugboatdesign.net
Cover Photography by Ioanna Chatzidiakou
Author photo by Daniel Krieger

This book is dedicated to my father, Nicholas Kameno – your memories and inspirational life have given me a wealth of interesting storylines and rich characters to develop. The love and respect your family and friends have for you is a testament to the integrity, warmth and dedication you have lived by your entire life. I love you.

A Note to Readers

Inspiration can come from any number of sources – a life experience, a fleeting yet compelling observation, or perhaps an unforgettable dream. I began writing *Evanthia's Gift* when my mother passed away. It was my way of working through my grief, and at the same time honoring her. Anyone who knows my family can find pieces of my mother throughout the story and in the character of Anastacia.

In 2004 I reluctantly attended my thirtieth high school reunion. The committee chairperson, an old friend I hadn't seen since those school days, contacted me repeatedly until I finally agreed to attend. I ended up having a wonderful time and reconnected with many old friends. We became a close-knit group, and twelve years later, we still get together. Because of this, the idea came to me to write a fictionalized story about a circle of friends who grew up together. Later, when I began writing I decided to bring these characters to life in Anastacia's daughter, Sophia's, world. And so, that is how the 'Honey Hill Girls' came to be.

Although there may be bits and pieces of my friends in the 'Honey Hill Girls,' they are purely a figment of my imagination. At the same time, this was my way of acknowledging all the friendships, old and new, that I'm blessed with. The oldest of friends, with whom I share a history. New friends, who I've been so lucky to cross paths with. The friendships I share with my daughters, husband, sisters, nieces and nephews. The very special friendship with my father. I could go on and on. Each one of these people has touched my life in a meaningful way.

Sadly, the chairperson of the reunion committee passed away a couple of years after we'd all reunited. Jill was the life of the party, the 'social director,' and a huge personality packaged in a 4' 10" frame. What better way to remember her than to portray her real life role in my work of fiction?

And I can't forget you, the readers—my friends of a different sort. We may not have met, but you know me through my words, my thoughts and my emotions. I know some of you through your messages, emails and reviews. I am truly overwhelmed by your outpouring of love.

Acknowledgements

To my husband, Raymond Speyer, and my daughters, Eleni and Alexa for all your support and understanding. You're always there for me when I need you. Ray, you show me every day how proud you are of me. Eleni, you are my biggest cheerleader, and Alexa, you calm me down when I'm having a computer crisis and solve the problem for me as no one else can.

To my unofficial editor and number one beta reader Valerie Gildard – I can't thank you enough for all your diligence and hard work. You missed your calling.

To my beta readers – Beth Farber, Alexa Speyer, and Joanne Manez. Your opinions and input were invaluable to me.

To my critique partner, Merry Freer – I've learned so much from you and I thank you for your input, support, and encouragement along the way.

To my editor, Katie-bree Reeves – you are a talented and remarkable young woman with the insights and maturity of a person beyond your years. It was a pleasure to work with you and I look forward to our next project together.

To Deborah Bradseth of Tugboat Design for another beautiful cover. You are always so accommodating and such a delight to work with. From the inside formatting to all the advertising material you created – your talent is endless.

To Ioanna Chatzidiakou for taking so many beautiful photos for the cover that it was almost impossible to choose one. I knew the first time I saw your breathtaking portfolio that I would someday want your pictures to represent my books.

To the models who graced the cover - Anastasia Argyrou, Anastasia Kovaiou, Mika Leventi, Alexandra Pouliou, Theodora Savvidou. You captured the spirit, love and friendship between Sophia, Demi, Amy, Mindy, and Donna. Thank you.

To my unofficial public relations team – Pam Krieger, Jo Grisafi, Maureen Nolan, Beth Farber, and Liz Fetzer. I believe you've sold as many of my books at MSO as you have eyeglasses. My sister, Kathy Tillchock – how many books have you sold while sitting for manicures? My sister, Jeanine Soregaroli – Scoping out potential readers at the Greek festivals proved to be a talent of yours. Thank you to each of you for having so much faith in me.

To Joanne Manez, *Licensed Mental Health Counselor* – our time power walking around the neighborhood while discussing psychological conditions and therapies was insightful. Thank you for taking the time to read over the manuscript for accuracy in handling some of the situations that arose throughout the story.

To Dr. Matthew Stripp – thank you for taking time out of your busy schedule to discuss trauma and accident injury with me.

To Dr. Jonathan Lown – thank you for answering my many questions on recovery and healing.

Dr. Lown is also our very caring family physician. My mother, who inspired the character of Anastacia in *Evanthia's Gift*, was under his care during the most challenging period of her life. We couldn't have asked for a more dedicated and compassionate doctor.

To Father Elias (Lou) Nicholas of St. Paraskevi Shrine Church – thank you for answering theological and church related questions.

Father Lou was and remains an important part of our family. He visited my mother often during the last days of her life, providing her with comfort and peace.

To Krystina Kalapothakos for trusting me with a very raw and personal life experience. Because of you, one of my character's storyline took an unexpected turn, one that contains a valuable lesson. You are a remarkable young woman.

To Pamela and Dan Krieger – your author photo for *Evanthia's Gift* was so flattering, Dan, that I used it again. Pam, thank you for bringing my books into your store, and for your enthusiasm and encouragement.

To my mother, Eleni Debonera Kameno – without your inspiration, *Evanthia's Gift* and *Waiting for Aegina* would have never been written. I know you are still with me in spirit, cheering me on to continue the saga.

"Dear friends are like rare jewels to be treasured—never underestimate the value or importance they hold in your life."

—Anastacia Fotopoulos Giannakos to the 'Honey Hill Girls' 1968

Chapter 1

Sophia

October 2004

Sophia was seated at the edge of a worn leather chair with her eyes fixed on Dean, tears streaming down her cheeks. Ignoring the sting from the cuts and bruises on her forehead and nose, the soreness on the left side of her body, and the sharp pains coming from her casted arm, she gently gripped her husband's hand, hoping her touch would will him into consciousness.

Not twenty-four hours ago, they were having the time of their lives—reconnecting with old friends, dancing, and maybe drinking a little too much. Which is why Sophia took the keys from Dean and insisted she drive home.

Their joyful night came to a crashing end when a bright light reflecting from her side view mirror blinded Sophia. It was as though everything after that happened in slow motion—the sound of crunching metal and screeching tires, a surreal feeling that the car may have flipped over and over, and the shattering of breaking glass when a car struck theirs, slamming into the passenger door where Dean was seated.

When their vehicle came to a sudden halt, Sophia found that the car had not turned over as she thought, yet somewhere in her confused and disoriented mind, it had registered that they must have spun around.

Clouds of white surrounded Sophia and she screamed out to Dean, afraid he was unconscious or severely injured from the impact the car had taken.

Her door flung open. "Sophia, I have to get you out of the car. Help is on its way."

"Dino! Help Dino!" Sophia desperately pleaded, not sure to whom she was speaking. It was so dark and she was blinded by fear.

Slapping away the airbags obstructing her view, she called out to her husband. "Dino! Talk to me. Say something."

Struggling to open his eyes, Dean groaned, but his lids remained closed.

Michael, who had been following in the car behind, could see that metal from the car had compressed around the lower half of Dean's body and, without help, he would not be able to pull him from the wreckage.

Sophia reached for Dean, but Michael stopped her.

"It's better not to touch him until the EMTs get here."

Panic-stricken after watching the erratic driver crash into her brother's door, Demi helped Sophia out of the car and clung to her.

Within minutes, the dark road was polluted with flashing lights and the sound of blaring sirens. Rescuers came swiftly, assessing the situation quickly deciding to rely on the 'Jaws of Life' to cut Dean out of the car. Another medic came to Sophia's aid, placing her arm in a splint and tending to the open gashes on her face and arm.

"Forget about me! Take care of my husband," she demanded, her voice strained from fear.

"Your husband is in good hands." The female medic looked up after she finished wrapping Sophia's arm. "They're about to load him into the ambulance now, ma'am."

"Take me to him."

"Of course."

The uniformed woman guided Sophia to where Dean was strapped on a stretcher and about to be lifted into the back end of an ambulance. Too many people surrounded him, making it impossible for Sophia to get close.

Movement, noise, lights, and voices shouting commands—it was all happening at lightening speed, yet at the same time the moment seemed to drag on forever. Sophia became agitated. There was too much *fasaria* around her. Her yiayiá would say that when there was too much noise and commotion. It was the first word that came to mind as witnesses dramatically recounted the accident, mangled cars were pulled onto flatbeds, and police officers gave the drunk driver, who had sped across three lanes before hitting them, a breathalyzer test. The son of a bitch didn't look as though he had a scratch on him, and Sophia's Dino was—she didn't want to think about what his condition was. She just needed to get to him, but no one would let her.

"Ma'am, we have another ambulance for you if you'll come with me."

Sophia pushed away from the EMT. "I don't need one. I want to go with my husband."

"That's not possible, ma'am."

"You're hurt," Demi said. "You need to go with them."

"I want to stay with you. Michael, drive me to the hospital. I want to be there when Dino arrives."

"We'll follow along behind the ambulance you're in," Michael said. "You're in shock, Sophia, and you need to be examined. Let's be on the safe side."

Leaning over the hospital bed, Sophia prayed. "Please, God, don't take him from me now," Sophia begged in an inaudible whisper. "Dino, oh, my Dino." She bent over him and caressed his cheek. "Don't leave me. Not after all we've been through. Squeeze my hand. Move your eyes. Give me a sign that you're still with me. Anything."

Comforting arms wrapped around Sophia. "Sweetie, you need to take a break. Get some sleep. I'll stay with my brother."

She turned to look at Demi and, collapsing into sobs she shook her head. "No. What if he wakes up and I'm not here?" Sophia's face grew pale and her lower lip quivered. "Or what if—"

"Don't say it," Demi ordered. "Don't even think it." Demi wrapped her arms around Sophia. "The doctor said he'll be unconscious for a while. If anything changes, I'll call you."

Sophia pulled away and shook her head adamantly. "I can't."

"If you don't, I'll get your doctor in here to order you to go home and rest. Your body took quite a beating also. You can't help Dean if you don't take care of yourself." Turning Sophia by the shoulders to face the entrance to the room, Demi said, "Look. Everyone is here. Any one of them will be happy to take you home. I'll stay with my brother until you get back."

Sophia waved weakly, her heart melting at the sight of them. In the doorway stood Amy, Mindy, and Donna. They were there when she needed them—always at her side without question—her oldest and dearest friends. The Honey Hill Girls were loyal to the core.

Chapter 2

Sophia

January 1999

B arely a hint of light escaped the outer edges of the Roman shade covering the large window in Sophia and Dean's bedroom. It had snowed the day before, continuing far into the night, the ominous black clouds advertising there would be no relief for some time to come.

Dean was asleep; his body spooned into his wife with one hand splayed over her belly as if possessively protecting the child within her. Sophia looked at the time on the clock and began to slip out of the bed, but Dean, roused awake from the feel of her body parting from his, wrapped his arm around her waist and pulled her back toward him.

"Not yet," he mumbled drowsily. Sliding his hands under her nightshirt, he found her breasts—a little fuller now that she was in her fifth month.

Turning to face him, Sophia kissed him good morning, a sensual purr innately rumbling from her throat as she ran her hands through his silky, brown hair. He wore it longer these days, and not in the conservative style he'd worn for years as an executive at a Manhattan-based hedge fund—his ex-father-in-law's hedge fund. To Sophia, Dean's hair was like a symbol signifying that her true Dino had returned to her—her Dino—the teenager with the long, silky mane, sparkling eyes, a smile that made her weak in the knees, and the spirit of a rebel.

"It's cold. You need to keep me warm," Dean said, pulling her on top of him.

"I *need* to? Is that an order?" Sophia asked playfully. "Maybe you should keep me warm."

"I intend to. For the entire morning."

And how could she resist? Why would she want to? The children were at Demi and Michael's home for a sleepover. There was nothing keeping them from making love all day if they chose to.

The children—Sophia loved them more than life itself, but a tiny break from them, even just one day, would restore her strength. The last two years had been trying. The loss of their father left each of her children scarred differently: Nicky more private in his thoughts than before, and seemingly armored in anxiety, and Evvie was mad at the world. Well, maybe not the world—just me, Sophia admitted to herself. It was as though Evvie looked for reasons to blame her mother for anything that didn't go the way she wanted it to—her yiayiá's death, Sophia's marriage to Dean, and now a new baby on the way.

Sophia propped herself up on her pillow and leaned in closer to Dean. "Are you happy, Dino?" she asked.

Dean raised his eyebrows and with an impish grin he asked, "Didn't I spend the better part of last night showing you how happy I am?"

"I'm being serious. The last few months couldn't have been a piece of cake for you."

"I've never been happier." He brushed a stray strand of hair from her face. "Do we need to work out the kinks? Sure. But give it time. And Evvie will come around. The kids have had a lot of changes. Don't worry about me. I can handle it."

Sophia rolled onto her back and rubbed her eyes with her fingertips. "I worry about you, the kids, my dad. Then I think about what I'll do with the dance studio while I'm out on maternity leave. And your commute to Jamesport has got to be brutal in this weather. And—"

"Stop!" Dean rolled on top of her, boring his eyes into hers. "You are going to drive yourself crazy. One thing at a time. Isn't that what you tell everyone when they get overwhelmed? Just deal with one thing at a time. Take your own advice and let me worry about a few things."

Sophia nodded. "You're right. I'll pull a Scarlett and think about it tomorrow," she said in a poor attempt at a Southern drawl.

Later that afternoon, Dean and Sophia turned onto the gravel driveway of the Angelidis Vineyard. Slowly, they passed the rows and rows of grapevines, the twisted branches now plundered of their fruit stood stiffly, waiting for the rebirth of spring. Only three months before, the oak trees surrounding the tasting room and the Carriage House were alive with brilliant shades of gold and orange, the sun forcing its way between the leaves and casting a heavenly glow.

Dean and Sophia were the first couple to celebrate their union on this breathtaking piece of property, riding by horse and carriage from the church down the long path to the beautifully decorated tent adorned with crystals and tulle. Forever, the memory of this place, on that long awaited day where their life together began, would be embedded in their hearts. And knowing this was the place where Dean felt pride in his accomplishments along with a sense of peace and contentment made Sophia treasure this land all the more. Dean drove his Range Rover past the building that housed the oak barrels and steel tanks, then continued through gates that read, 'Private Property.' From the outside view, Demi and Michael's home looked unoccupied. No movement or sound seemed to be coming from the house—until they opened the door that led to the mudroom. Evvie could be heard calling out for Nicky and Paul to shut up, the boys were screaming over a video game, and Stella was looking for her mother, complaining that the boys weren't letting her play with them.

Sophia and Dean looked at each other and they simultaneously had the idea to get out while they could.

"Oh, no you don't," Demi demanded. "Get your asses in here right now."

"Where's Michael?" Dean peeked around the kitchen corner.

"Where's Michael? You want to know where Michael is?" Demi slapped a dishrag over her shoulder. "His mother called. His brother is sick and they needed an extra hand at the restaurant. So whom does she call? My husband. Not one of the other employees. No. My husband who can't say no to her."

"Okay. Relax. Sorry I asked." Dean opened the refrigerator and removed a beer.

"What was he supposed to do if they needed the help? Family helps family," Sophia said. "You would have done the same if your parents needed help."

"Whose side are you on?"

"Yours. I'm just trying to point out—" Sophia widened her eyes when Demi cut her off.

"Oh, you know as well as I do that she tries to control him. And Peter probably isn't sick. I'll bet any amount of money that he's hung over. Why should Michael be taken away from his family on a Sunday, when he works hard all week, because his brother is irresponsible?"

"Mom," Stella whined, as she dragged herself into the kitchen. "Make the boys let me have a turn."

"I'll go see what they're up to in there," Dean said. He headed up stairs where he was sure to find the boys engrossed in video games.

"Why don't you go watch the movie with Kristos and Evvie?" Sophia suggested. She took Stella by the hand and guided her into the family room. The fireplace was warm and inviting, the wood crackling as flickers of flame danced. Kristos and Evvie were settled under a heavy velour blanket, their eyes fixed on the TV screen.

Evvie looked up. "Are the boys giving you a hard time? Come sit next to me. I'll French braid your hair while we watch the movie."

Sophia smiled at her daughter and returned to the kitchen. "You're not in a very good mood. Were the kids too much for you? I can take them next weekend, if you like."

"Can you take my mother-in-law instead?"

"No, thank you. I'll stick to the mother-in-law I have."

Dean took a pull from his beer. "I have a few details I want to run by you about some plans for the opening. Sophia can round up the kids' things and we can talk, or if you have time schedule me in for a meeting tomorrow."

"Tomorrow," Demi said. "I have some things to run by you too. Time is speeding by and I need to firm things up."

"Put the kids to bed and try to relax," Sophia suggested. "I'm sure Michael will be home soon."

Chapter 3

Demetra

January 1999

Demi was seated at the far end of the couch, resting her head on a pillow, her mind trying to stay focused on the television. But right now, she didn't feel 'Touched By an Angel.' She was burning nearly as mad as the devil himself. Once again, Michael's mamá had called, and he went running. The family restaurant and the catering hall had plenty of employees to call upon. It was never Michael's father who called asking for help. It was always his mother insisting he come to help the family.

"What would you do if your parents needed help?" Michael asked each time Demi complained.

What was she supposed to say? She was starting to feel like a bitch. Her husband didn't perceive his mother's behavior as manipulative, and there was nothing she could do to make him see it, or to stop it altogether.

Demi hadn't always played this game of tug of war over Michael with her mother-in-law. At first, Stella Angelidis was ecstatic that her son brought home a Greek girl—especially one she knew from their church.

And when Stella liked someone, everyone knew. Demi and Michael weren't dating three months when she asked the two of them in front of the entire family, "So … when are you going to get married?" She crossed herself repeatedly waiting for their reply as though God would answer her prayer at that very moment.

"Mamá! Come on." Michael stiffened. He pulled his hand from Demi's.

"Your father and I were married four months after we met." She threw her hands to the heavens. "That's all I'm saying."

"People do things a little differently now. Okay, Mamá? This isn't 1950 back at the *horio* in Greece."

At that point, Demi didn't know what to do with herself. The rest of the family seated at the table sat tight-lipped, watching the exchanges between Michael and Stella like spectators at a tennis match shifting their heads back and forth as the ball was being lobbed from one side of the court to the other.

And what did this mean for her and Michael? Demi kept shifting slightly in her chair, hoping to make an escape. And what would she say to him later? She could make light of it and laugh it off. 'Imagine us getting married!' Or she could simply ignore the whole thing as if it never happened. After all, parents embarrassed their children all the time. Besides, clearly it was too soon for Demi to expect Michael to entertain the thought of marriage, although if she were completely honest with herself, it wasn't far from her mind. Heat warmed her cheeks and she began to feel lightheaded as the conversation became more and more cringe-worthy by the second.

"You think the time and place matters? What difference does it make? People don't change." Stella looked at Demi. "A girl needs to think of her eggs."

Demi rubbed her temples. Now she was embarrassed.

Michael jumped from his seat. "Oh for God's sake. Mamá, I love you, but this conversation is over." Michael turned to Demi. "I'll take you home."

"That might be a good idea," Demi agreed. "I feel a headache coming on."

Later, after Stella received her wish and Michael and Demi married, Demi had grown fond of her mother-in-law. Stella was helpful and kind, often bringing food to the house when Demi was busy overseeing a wedding or an event. And she was generous with her offers to watch the children when Demi and Michael were working, switching off with Demi's own mother, Soula.

But it all seemed to change when Demi's brother went into business with her husband. Michael and Dean entertained the idea of partnering with Michael's family for the catering end of the business, but they'd decided against it. Too many chiefs in the mix, they both agreed. Michael grew up in the restaurant business and although his main concern was the vineyard, he would assist in managing the catering staff if Dean managed the rest of the Carriage House business.

Michael's father had no issue with this, but his mother was not pleased, and from that day forth she seemed to crave more of his attention than she ever had before.

Demi heard the thrumming vibration of the garage door.

Michael entered the house through the door that led from the garage to the kitchen. Hearing the clink of keys thrown onto the counter, she pulled a sofa pillow protectively in front of her and hugged it.

"Hey! I'm back," he said as he strode into the family room. "Everyone's gone?"

Demi gave him a disgusted look. "Yes, everyone's gone. How long did you expect them to wait for you?"

"Look. I'm not going to have this fight with you again. I was needed and I went to help."

"You complain that I work too much, and you want me to hire more help so I can cut my hours and spend more time with you, but when your mother calls, you run. You left on the one day we had to spend together as a family."

"I don't know what you would like me to do."

"I want you to acknowledge that your mother has you under her thumb."

Michael gave her an exasperated look.

"Oh, come on! Don't even try to deny it. John runs the business with your dad and he lives on the same street. Peter still lives at home and your mother lets him get away with murder. You're the only one she can't completely control, but she's trying."

He sat down beside her and sighed. "I don't want to fight with you." He reached for a stray hair that had escaped the ponytail she'd tied her hair into, but she flinched.

Michael frowned. "You were right about one thing," he admitted. "Peter was hung over. I stopped by the house to see him and read him the riot act. You would think at thirty-five he would grow up already."

With little warmth, Demi drew her eyes up to meet his. "Talk to your mother. Or your father. Do something. Make them understand you have your own responsibilities and Peter needs to live up to his."

"Okay. I will. I promise."

"That's what you always say. Don't try to appease me and then do nothing. The problem won't solve itself."

"I'll talk to my parents and tell them to make arrangements for back up help that doesn't include me, and I'll have a serious chat with my brother. I'll tell them I'm too busy at the vineyard to bail them out every time they get short staffed. Okay?" Michael's dark brown eyes stared into hers in a way that always told her she was all he thought about.

"Don't look at me that way."

"What way?"

Demi whirled her pointer finger around Michael's face. "That way—like you're seducing me into going along with you."

Michael flashed her a crooked smile. "Is that what I'm doing? Good to know." Suddenly his expression changed. The faux cocky smile left him. "Seriously, Dem. I hear you. Are we good?"

"Yeah." Demi nodded, as she looked into the face she'd crushed over as a young girl and now all these years later, loved with all her being.

"Can we have make-up sex now?" Michael wound his hand around her ponytail, playfully pulling it to bring her face closer to his. "All your pent up anger made me horny." He straddled Demi and smirked.

"You're always horny."

"And that's a problem?"

Demi giggled. "The kids. Stop!"

Michael reached for the discarded blanket on the floor. "I haven't heard a peep from them," he said as he covered their bodies. "I bet they're sound asleep. I love you and I especially love your body." He looked into her large, green eyes and played with the golden wisps of hair that framed her face. He grazed his lips against hers—once, twice, and Demi could feel his hunger for her set in as he kissed her urgently. Reaching under her sweater, Michael found her ample breasts and Demi moaned at the sensation that rocketed through her. His mouth left hers to find her hardened nipples, and she leaned her head back and closed her eyes, enjoying the effect her husband always had on her. Demi reached for Michael's belt buckle …

"Mommy, I can't sleep," Stella complained as she padded her way into the family room. She scrunched her nose. "What are you and Daddy doing under the covers?"

"Nothing that concerns you, young lady. Daddy was just rubbing my sore neck." Demi got up, took her daughter by the hand and began to walk down the hall.

Turning, she pouted, drawing her bottom lip down. "Sorry. Later?"

With all the planning and details that needed attention to complete the Carriage House building, the next few months flew by. Dean and Michael were busy hiring staff, meeting final construction deadlines, and dealing with town inspectors. Michael was also busy with preparing the vineyard for another season, and Demi was organizing a lavish party for their grand opening.

Seated at the desk in her new Carriage House office, Demi sipped a cup of hot cinnamon spice tea. Previously, she'd been working out of the flower shop in Commack, which she had expanded into a full service wedding and special occasion planning business. Now as the catering venue was nearing its grand opening, it made sense to use that as the home base for her business.

Demi had been working tirelessly, advertising and promoting the Carriage House as well as her own services, tending to the children, and preparing for the holidays.

Easter was approaching, and this would be the first one without Sophia's mother, Ana. Demi wasn't sure how they would all get through it. Christmas had been eerie, strained—almost surreal. Everyone tried to pretend all was normal for the children's sake. But a melancholy mood hung in the air. Even Alex, who tried his hardest not to spoil the usually joyous occasion for the rest of the family, could not hide the emptiness in his heart that was reflected in his eyes.

And Sophia, she thought, not realizing she was shaking her head and expelling a large sigh—Sophia was practically manic. Determined not to ruin the day for anyone, she bounced around making sure to engage her father in conversation, help Soula in the kitchen, and have an overly exaggerated smile on her face as the children opened their gifts. It was exhausting to watch.

There was a moment when Demi's father recited the prayer before they ate, when he asked that God keep Ana's soul in his loving arms, that everyone shed a tear on her behalf. But not Sophia. Demi looked at her friend, and it seemed as though she was about to cry. She didn't miss the subtle tightening of Sophia's jaw and neck muscles, or how her eyes glistened.

But then she took a deep breath, swallowed and lifted her glass. "*Kalá Hristouyienna* - Merry Christmas."

Oh, yeah, Demi thought, Easter was not going to be easy. Which was why she and Michael offered to have the Anastasi dinner at their home. It couldn't be at Uncle Alex's. That would be too hard on him and too painful for everyone without Ana. She had lived for this holiday, preparing and cooking for weeks to make it perfect. For as long as Demi could remember they all went to church, came home around one-thirty in the morning and went straight home to Aunt Ana's for an eating fest. Even Mindy, Amy and Donna joined them each year up until the time they graduated high school, and the girls wouldn't have missed it for the world.

Demi hoped that by having the holiday at her home, it would distract the attention away from the loss of Ana.

The ring of the phone interrupted Demi's thoughts. "Good afternoon, *It's Your Day Event Planners*, how may I help you? Hi, Donna! How are you?" Demi pressed the speaker button and placed the receiver down.

"I'm fine. It sounds like you are all set up for business there."

"It's all coming together. I'm tying up the finer details but I already have several weddings booked for the Carriage House."

"I can't wait to see it."

"You'll be at the grand opening party, right? It will be here before I can take my next breath."

"I wouldn't miss it," Donna said. "Listen, I was talking to Sophia and she said you were having Easter night this year."

Demi blew out a breath. "Yes. I thought it would be easier on everyone that way."

"Yes, I think you might be right. I was telling the boys how much fun we had as kids, and how all of us girls spent every Greek Easter together. I was wondering if you had room for three more?"

"Sure," Demi said questioningly. "Only three?"

"Yes, me and the boys. Richie … will be busy that night."

"By the way you mentioned him, it sounds like Richie is in the doghouse." Demi had noticed a bit of frost between Donna and her husband lately. The last time they were all together, Donna had completely ignored him and Richie had drunk beer after beer, barely cracking a smile.

"If he is, he put himself there," Donna said flatly. "Getting the boys away from the tension for a day or two would be good for all of us."

"Well, we'd love for you to join us."

"Thanks. I'd like them to get a taste of what it was like when we were children. I think it would be a good experience for them."

"Yes! It will be like old times," Demi chuckled. "Except we're the parents now. How the hell did that happen? It seems like only a minute ago we were figuring out our own future and suddenly we're knee deep in planning our children's lives."

Donna's deep sigh expressed her anxiety. "I don't know that I'm equipped to guide anyone's life. I feel like I'm traveling on a dark road without a map," Donna said. "Damned if I know where it will lead me."

"A parent's role is to nourish a child's body and soul and encourage him to discover who he is meant to be." — Alexandros Giannakos

Chapter 4

Donna

April 1999

"Boys!" Donna called out from the bottom of the staircase. "Are you ready? It's a long ride to Jamesport and I don't want to make everyone late for church."

"We'll be right down, Ma," Richie Jr. answered. "I'm helping Anthony with his tie."

Donna walked into the kitchen. "Don't forget, we'll be staying at Demi's tonight," she told her husband. "You can join us tomorrow afternoon if you change your mind. Michael's parents are having a big Easter celebration at their restaurant." Donna's tone held indifference.

Richie twisted the cap off a bottle of beer. "I'll pass."

Irritated, she turned and walked away, muttering under her breath, "Why do I even bother?"

This was the main reason she was taking her boys to Jamesport for the weekend—to get them away from this toxic environment. Richie was often in a foul mood, especially with a few beers under his belt. Little by little, the boy she once loved had slipped away, replaced by a bitter and insensitive man.

Occasionally though, the old Richie would show his face, glowing at RJ's athletic prowess.

"My boy made first string," he'd brag. "My boy was named MVP, just like the old man." He'd puff up his chest and flash an obnoxious grin.

But then his smile contorted to an odious glare as he glimpsed his other child—the one immersed in Shakespearean literature and Renaissance art.

In the car, the boys occupied themselves with their Game Boys, while Donna's mind wandered. RJ was now seventeen and a senior in high school. In many ways he took after his father: captain of the football team, homecoming king and a good student. But RJ achieved something his father never had. He had won an athletic scholarship to the University of Virginia in Charlottesville. Richie liked to spout the cliché, *chip off the old block* when it came to his older son, and he never stopped bragging about him.

Donna loved RJ with all her heart, but it irritated her that Richie never boasted about Anthony in the same manner. One too many times, she'd caught the hurt look on her youngest when he'd tried to impress his father, or get any form of approval or praise from him, only to be disappointed.

Anthony was a sweet and gentle boy, and he never blamed his brother for winning all the attention from their father. He instinctively knew it was not his brother's fault.

While RJ was built and muscular and proficient at every sport he played, Anthony was slight in build, and he had no interest at all in sports. He enjoyed the arts—literature, theater, music and dance. This brought great frustration to Richie, who accused his wife of turning their son into a *sissy* by bringing him along to Sophia's studio when Donna taught dance and allowing him to take class.

"There are a lot of boys taking dance class. Especially hip-hop," she argued.

"They're not my sons. My sons play sports."

"Your son doesn't have any interest in sports. He should do what he enjoys."

But there was no winning. Richie was thick and narrow-minded, and nothing would change his mind. Last fall, when Anthony had won the lead in the 8th grade play, his father refused to attend. Donna didn't speak to him for two weeks after that. Not that they spent much time together anyway.

Richie worked at the high school and coached the football team. When he was home, he was either in the garage puttering with an old car he'd been restoring, or sitting on the couch watching a game. Some evenings, he would go to a local bar to grab a beer and catch a game with his buddies.

Donna taught at the elementary school, drove the children back and forth to their activities, and in the summer she taught dance. Now, with Sophia so close to her due date, she worked evenings, taking over Sophia's classes and helping her to run the studio. The more hours she worked, the less she had to deal with her husband, and that was fine with her. Shaking away the thoughts, Donna turned her attention back to the road. It was going to be a long drive.

A little over an hour later, they pulled into Demi's driveway.

Demi came running out. "Don't even get out of the car. We better get going if we want to get a seat."

"I can fit two more in my car. Tell Nicky and Paul to come with me."

A procession of cars drove to the Transfiguration Church in Mattituck. Demi had decorated Anastasi candles for each one of the children. As the large group entered the church, they lit thin, beeswax candles, made their cross and placed the candles in a bed of sand. Reverently, they kissed each icon in the narthex and silently found the pews where they would be seated until it was time to go outside for the Anastasi service. And that's where the quiet ended.

"I want to sit next to Kristos," Evvie said, as she got up and changed her seat.

"Then I want to sit next to Nicky," Stella complained, jumping out of her seat.

And the adults weren't much better. It was like a game of musical chairs, and it wasn't until Michael's mother turned around, gave them all *the look,* and scolded, "*Skasé,*" that they settled down.

"Yiayiá said shut up in church," Paul giggled.

Donna whispered to Sophia and Demi. "Were we this raucous?"

"Close, but not as bad. There are ten of them with Michael's brother's kids," Sophia said.

"And mostly boys. We were much better behaved," Demi added.

Demi felt a tap on her shoulder. She turned around to find her father grinning. "No, you weren't."

Just as Donna predicted, her boys were glad they went to see what their mother had been telling them about all these years. They loved the outdoor service and joining the hundreds of people raising their candles while shouting out a hymn they didn't understand.

It was a beautiful night, clear and brisk; there was always a special feeling in the air on this night, and Donna remembered it well. It was as though the stars in heaven touched the earth, surrounding her with a sense of peace, if only for a brief time.

"I thought you were joking when you said we take lit candles in the car," RJ said.

"No, I wasn't kidding. It's apparently an old tradition where the Orthodox Christians take the holy light from the Easter service to bless their homes," Donna explained to her sons. "Of course we weren't thinking about that. We thought it was fun and different. Before we could drive ourselves to church, we were always getting warned not to drip candle wax on the seats or burn the upholstery."

At two in the morning, they arrived back at Demi's home. An assembly line of practiced women got to work heating up food and putting out platters of *mezethes*. The children cracked red eggs, but not before Stavros said a prayer.

"How's she holding up?" Donna asked Demi and Soula as they ladled *mayiritsa* into soup bowls.

"She's putting up a good front. I don't know how long she can do it without cracking like those eggs." Demi gestured to the children, who were competing for the strongest egg.

"We will all be here when she needs us. It's Alex I'm worried about. He sits in the house alone all day," Soula said.

Sophia walked into the kitchen, her hand resting on her large belly. "The three of you look like you're up to no good. What's going on?"

"Nothing. Come. Give me a hand." As Donna and Sophia served bowls of soup, Donna caught the haunted look in Sophia's expression as she looked around the table. Donna knew what she was thinking. Ana should have been there.

Chapter 5

Sophia

May 1999

As tempting as it was, Sophia resisted the urge to look inside the Carriage House while it was being decorated. She wanted the full impact of what she expected to be an impressive final result, rather than seeing it in stages as the bits and pieces came together. Her reaction when she soaked in her first glimpse reflected the awe and pride she felt at what Dean had accomplished.

As she stepped into the high-ceiling lobby she was struck by the old world charm mingled with a modern day touch. The ceiling, walls, and each doorway were framed with Greek key molding—rich, but not ornate. Large, etched, antique Venetian mirrors adorned the empty entranceway walls, and the modern light fixture that hung above was a welcome and refreshing contrast. Suspended from an oversized sphere of twisted brushed nickel were invisible wires holding delicate orbs, resembling floating bubbles.

"Oh, Dino! It's more beautiful than I imagined."

"You like it then?"

"I love it." Sophia surveyed every inch of the room. "And that staircase—what bride wouldn't dream of walking down that staircase!"

"Your mom had her hand in some of this," Dean said.

The corners of Sophia's mouth curved ever so slightly, but the veil of sadness in her eyes could not be hidden. Yet, a part of her drew comfort from knowing that, even now, Ana was sharing in their future. She walked over to the ebony lacquered banister and ran her hand along it slowly, as if feeling her mother's presence as she touched it.

Dean took Sophia by the shoulders, turning her to face in the other direction. He pointed to the ceiling. "That light fixture was her idea. The decorator had it slated for the main ballroom. But she said putting it in the grand foyer would add just the right amount of edge to make it fresh and not predictably cliché."

"That was my mom. She always had great taste." Sophia sighed. "She should have been here to see this."

"She's here," Dean said as he brushed his fingers across her cheek. "That foyer table was her idea, and she chose the floor to ceiling mirror with the antique frame. There will always be a part of her here."

"Thank you for saying that." She reached up on her toes to kiss him. "I love you so much, and I'm so proud of you."

"And I love you, and this little one, too." Dean gave her belly a pat. "I'm glad we had a few minutes alone before the troops come storming in."

"Me too."

Tonight was an important evening—the grand opening of the Carriage House—the catering venue situated on the property of the Angelidis Vineyard. Family and friends, as well as business contacts and local officials, were invited to attend.

Dean wore his black Armani tux, and at forty-six years old, physically fit and with a full head of rich, brown hair, he looked magnificent. He rarely dressed in anything formal these days, and Sophia liked his easy, casual style, but once in a while, she thought, it was a treat to see him this way. Such a treat, she thought, that despite her bulging belly, she wanted to undress him right then and there and have her way with him.

Sophia was looking quite spectacular herself, and Dean told her so.

She wore an Aegean blue, one-shoulder gown with an empire waist. In spite of the fact that she was eight and a half months pregnant, she wore strappy silver sandals with four-inch heels and, from the back view of her, no one would suspect she was at all. "You're having a boy," Dean's mother, Soula predicted. "When you carry in the front, you are having a boy."

An old wives' tale, Sophia thought, but she kissed her mother-in-law on the cheek. She loved Soula Papadakis and, as long as she could remember, she had always been like a second mother to her.

They made a beautiful couple, Dean looking distinguished with a touch of gray at his temples, and Sophia with her dark mane worn loose with soft waves framing her face.

As the guests arrived, they greeted them at the ballroom entrance and made sure to give each one individual attention. Michael was also in the main lobby representing the management, but Demi was bouncing from room to room, making sure every detail was executed properly. She'd worked tirelessly for months on the planning of this event and she'd outdone herself.

The cocktail hour was set as though it were to be photographed for a trendy culinary magazine. Instead of large buffet trays, neat rows of individual single-serve tableware held a variety of food tastings. Japanese renge spoons held mounds of creamy mushroom polenta, silver cones lined with the Carriage house logo parchment paper were filled with fried *kalamaria*, and shrimp cocktail sat atop horseradish sauce in tiny wide-mouthed glasses. The wait staff walked around offering bite-sized skewered meats, caviar on paper-thin crackers, and mini triangles of *spanakopita*.

After dinner was served, Dean and Michael addressed their guests, thanking everyone for their support in making the Carriage House possible. Soothing, classical dinner music played softly in the background, creating an ideal atmosphere for conversation. But afterwards, the guests were ushered into another room where the party livened up.

The band played everything from jazz to rock and disco. Stavros and Soula danced a cha-cha. Donna's son, Anthony, showed off his break dancing skills when MC Hammer's, 'U Can't Touch This' played and, later, Sophia forced her father onto his feet for a slow dance.

Toward the end of the night, the band began to play lively bouzouki music and the family gave their guests a taste of the Greek spirit. Sophia had been up and down all night, resting between dances, but she couldn't resist and got up to dance the *kalamatianós* with the rest of her family—until a sharp pain stabbed her in the belly.

She took a seat and in less than a minute the pain was gone. But five minutes later, it had returned.

Demi plopped down next to her. "God, I'm tired. Have you seen Michael? Every time I try to get his attention he's either disappeared or on the phone."

"It's a busy night," Sophia grunted through a sharp pain.

"Are you okay?"

"I'm not sure." Sophia cradled her belly and sucked in a slow breath. Attempting to speak over the loud music, she leaned closer to Demi. "I'm getting cramps and I feel a tight pulling that I suspect might be contractions. I think I'm in labor."

"Really?" Demi's eyes widened. "Why didn't you say something right away instead of letting me go on about Michael?" She jumped up from her seat. "Let me get Dean."

"No!" Sophia caught her hand and pulled her down. "I don't want to spoil his night, and if it is labor, it's just the beginning. It could be hours before it's time to go to the hospital." Sophia leaned back and rubbed her belly. She took some slow deep breaths, hoping it would help to relieve the discomfort. "Help me to the ladies' room."

"If you can't get up on your own, then it's time to get my brother."

"Not yet."

Demi helped Sophia from the chair and they walked slowly to the ladies room. As the door swung open, Sophia felt a rush of liquid traveling down her leg. Alarmed, she dug her nails into Demi's arm.

"What's wrong?"

"My water broke!"

"Can I get my brother now?" Demi raised her hand before Sophia could answer. "That was a rhetorical question."

Sophia nodded. "Yes. Hurry!"

"Sit down." Demi helped her over to the powder room sofa. "I'll be right back."

In less than two minutes, Dean was in the ladies' room by Sophia's side.

She saw the look of deep concern on her husband's face and she took his hand in hers. "Don't worry. I'm fine. Just take me to the hospital."

Dean helped her off the sofa and together they walked to the front entrance of the Carriage House. "Demi went to get my car." Dean was trying to stay calm for his wife's sake, but Sophia could see the worry written on his face. "You choose very interesting times to go into labor, Mrs. Papadakis." Dean tried to make light of it, but Sophia heard the nervous undertones in Dean's voice.

Sophia recalled the day she'd given birth to her twins. Her husband, Will, had been out of town and Sophia had spent the day in her parents' backyard. Dean offered her a ride home but halfway there her water broke, leaking fluid all over Dean's expensive sports car.

With no way to get in touch with Will, it was Dean who stood by her during her labor and delivery, refusing to leave her side.

Dean nervously walked back into the birthing room. Sophia had been in labor for four hours and Dean had promised to update the family, all of whom were seated in the waiting room. He hadn't wanted to leave Sophia for even one second, but Dean didn't feel right to leave them all out there without any information.

"Everyone sends their love," Dean told his wife.

"Who's out there?" Sophia asked between deep breaths.

"Everyone," he accentuated, rolling his eyes.

"Demi and Michael?"

"Uh-huh … and my parents, your dad, the kids and Michael's parents."

"Michael's parents? It's so late. They should go home and we'll call them when the baby comes. Your parents and my dad, too."

"Like that's going to happen."

"What time is it?"

"It's almost four in the morning."

"Ooh, hold my hand. Another one's coming." Sophia tried to control her moans, but the contractions were at their peak.

"Okay, it's almost over," Dean told her as he studied the monitor that measured the contractions. "Oh, I forgot," he said, attempting to take her mind off the pain. "Donna and Mindy are here, too."

The fashion world kept Mindy on a hectic schedule and she found herself traveling often. She'd become a well-known and respected clothing designer, but she always made an effort to stay in contact with her closest friends and attend all the events in their lives that were important, just as they had for her. Sophia knew that Mindy must have had to juggle her calendar to stay in town beyond the party. Donna lived fairly locally and it was easier for the friends to run to each other at the drop of a hat when they needed to.

After eight hours of labor, the doctor told Sophia it was time to start pushing when her next contraction began. She was exhausted, having been up for almost twenty-four hours. She was a much younger woman when she had the twins, but just as with the first time, Sophia had her Dino by her side to give her the inner strength to brave through. She pushed with everything she had, and within twenty minutes, Anastacia Tasoula Papadakis was born.

Chapter 6

Mindy

May 1999

I just saw her and she's magnifique!" Mindy exclaimed as she made her entrance into Sophia's hospital room. Mindy looked as though she'd stepped out of a Vogue spread, with her wavy red hair flowing down her back and her waif-like figure.

"Magnifique?" Sophia giggled.

"I was supposed to be on a plane to Paris, but someone changed my plans." Mindy placed a floral arrangement on the windowsill and set down a giant stuffed giraffe on the seat next to Sophia's hospital bed.

"That toy is bigger than she is! She'll be ten-years-old before she'll be able to pick it up," Sophia laughed. She reached her hand out to her friend. "Mindy, you should have gone. I would have had someone call you when she was born."

"Are you kidding? I wouldn't miss this while I was still in town. Aunt Mindy is going to spoil her."

"I'm sure you will. Evvie thinks you walk on water."

"You're a lucky woman, Sophia." An underlying sadness lay below the surface of her compliment.

Mindy couldn't help but wonder what kind of a mother she would have been, if she'd had the opportunity. There was a time when she was certain that she could have juggled it all—the big career, a glamorous social life, and a family.

But time slipped away as quickly as a feather blowing in the wind. In her twenties, Mindy worked endlessly to prove herself and make a name in the fashion industry. She started at the bottom, but she worked long hours, taking on extra responsibility and volunteering for committees and projects. She made sure she was visible to those who could help her, promote her and connect her with the right people in the industry. Naturally, without her talent, she wouldn't have gotten far and would have been relegated to an administrative or marketing position rather than a creative one. But she was talented, and she made sure to make careful, calculated decisions where her career was concerned. If she wasn't noticed or moving up quickly in one design house, she moved on to another until she landed a position assisting the designer of a major label.

Her social life had revolved around work and, occasionally, she met a man who interested her, but it never lasted long. She simply had no time to invest in a relationship.

By the time Mindy was in her early thirties, she had established herself with a designer who specialized in haute couture eveningwear, and whose many famous clients wore his designs during the Hollywood award season. But Mindy was becoming restless and was ready for a change. Ideas were flooding her creative senses, and she was longing to free herself of the limitations that working under another artist's vision put on her, although she adored him and had the utmost respect for him.

Mindy was ready to venture out on her own, and what she wanted to create was not what her current employer was designing. She'd become fond of the older gentleman and, in the years she worked for him, he had become a friend as well as her mentor. Marcello Venezia had not only encouraged her to create her own label, he had offered to back her financially and professionally. And Mindy decided it was time to take him up on his offer.

To celebrate the launch of her new clothing line, Marcello threw her a grand party at a popular nightclub. It was there that Mindy met the love of her life.

"Earth to Mindy." Sophia gave her a puzzled look. "Where did your mind wander? You were a million miles away."

"Nowhere," Mindy answered, plastering an unconvincing smile on her face as she straightened her posture. "I was just thinking about what might have been."

Chapter 7

Mindy

1989

Marcello escorted Mindy through the doors of Club Moore. The Tribeca hotspot was *the place* where anyone who was anybody with power and money in the art or fashion industry was sure to be seen. Tonight, the massive, converted ground floor warehouse was overflowing with fashion industry trendsetters dressed in excessively ornate costumes to match the whimsical theme the space was decorated in.

When Marcello offered to throw her a party, he asked Mindy what kind of event she'd prefer. "You can have anything you desire. As long as it's fun. Nothing stuffy."

"And when have I ever been stuffy?" Mindy pointed to her eclectic outfit, a mixture of several trends that the average person wouldn't conceive of combining.

"I'm sure you'll throw a fabulous party. You always do. I should be throwing you a party—not the other way around. I've dreamed of my own line since I was a child and now, thanks to you, that dream will come true. I feel as though I've stepped into a fairy tale."

"Now that's an idea."

"What is?"

"Fairy tales. For the theme of your party."

"Fairy tales? For an adult party?"

Marcello nodded, satisfied. He clapped his hands together. "Fairy tales it is." He cupped Mindy's chin in his hand. "But, mia amore, the princess needs a prince."

Mindy kissed her mentor on the cheek. "I don't need a prince. I have a fairy godfather."

Marcello, known to wear only the finest fashions, carried himself regally dressed in King Arthur's attire, while Mindy took slow careful steps in her confining mermaid costume.

Ariel, the red-haired animated Disney character was the first princess to resemble Mindy, and she claimed her as her very own. The costume she designed for herself was covered with thousands of turquoise Swarovski crystals, hugging her from waist to ankles and glimmering like the rays of the sun dancing on gentle ocean waves. A violet seed pearl bra, scalloped to simulate seashells covered her ample breasts, and her naturally red hair hung past her shoulders, the wavy tips grazing the arch of her back.

As Marcello and Mindy walked toward the platform above the dance floor, the DJ stopped the music and a sea of bodies parted to make a path for the guest of honor and her host. The crowd began to murmur their admiration and clap as they passed, but when they reached the top of the steps, all noise ceased as Marcello raised his hand.

"Tonight, we are here to celebrate the achievement of our Mindy Bloom. Mindy has worked tirelessly for La Casa di Venezia, and her talent and dedication is unsurpassed. But it is time for my Mindy to bloom—to open like a flower and let the sun shine on her talent. Thank you all for coming tonight to celebrate Mindy's new line—Bloom."

Behind them, a large backdrop fell, revealing the logo for Mindy's new line. Bloom was written in curvy black letters, but the O's were replaced by a pair of pink peonies. The crowd murmured their approval.

Marcello raised a glass of champagne that was offered to him by an oddly perverse looking fairy-costumed waiter. *"Salute!"*

Mindy mingled with coworkers and spoke to business contacts. Champagne in hand, she soaked in the imaginative way the theme was woven into the party. Stations of food were set up under colorful displays. Sleeping Beauty's bed held towers of French food—mini quiches, boeuf with béarnaise, and escargot in white wine.

Lady and the Tramp's doghouse was filled with tomato and basil focaccia, antipasto and arancini.

But Hansel and Gretel's house was the most impressive. Made of actual gingerbread, within the edible walls were overflowing displays filled with sweets. Garlands of colorful marshmallow ropes adorned the inside walls, sugared marzipan were stacked in pyramids, and life size candy topiaries looked too beautiful to eat.

But that didn't stop partygoers from indulging. A beautifully handsome man with corn silk hair sashayed in a pink satin dress as Little Bo Peep, treating himself to butterfly shaped chocolates. A bikini-clad Cleopatra wrapped her tongue around a gummy snake, and a whimsically dressed Queen of Hearts sipped on a cotton candy martini.

Mindy turned her attention away from the gluttonous guests when she heard Marcello's voice calling her. Glancing around, she sought him out through the crowd. Beside him stood a man dressed in stark contradiction to the party's atmosphere.

"Ah, there you are," Marcello called to Mindy over the loud music. "I want to introduce you to a friend. This is Tyler Moore, the owner of Club Moore."

"Hence the name," Mindy said. "And I thought it was named after the street."

"Both. It's one of the reasons I chose the location." Tyler waved his hand around the club. "That and this amazing space."

Mindy's chest tightened when her eyes met Tyler's. He was gorgeous. Probably the most attractive man she'd ever laid eyes on. Extending her hand, he gently reached for it and held it between both of his. Her breath became hitched as their skin made contact, but her eyes never left his. They were mesmerizing—the pale blue color of aquamarine stones.

But it wasn't only the color that drew her in. There was understanding in his eyes. No, she corrected herself. It was … recognition. It was as though she had been looking into those eyes her whole life, and he had seen through hers and into her soul.

Her hand tingled as she pulled it from his, and Mindy had an unexplainable feeling of loss as her skin lost contact with his.

"Can I refresh your drink?" Tyler asked.

"Um," she looked at her empty glass. "Sure."

"Come with me." Tyler turned to Marcello. "Would you excuse us?"

"Of course!" Marcello replied with a hopeful smile.

Tyler took Mindy by the hand and led her through the crowd. He was tall, and he was built. His defined arm muscles were unmistakable even through his dress shirt. And he had one fine ass. The man was hot.

"Where are you taking me?" Mindy shouted over the music.

"Someplace where I can have a conversation with you without shouting." He led her to a door and held it open for her.

Mindy looked around as they stepped into a plush office. It was almost completely decorated in black, but it was sleek and masculine. Instinctively she knew it was perfect for this man, with who she hadn't exchanged more than ten words.

"Your office, I presume?"

He nodded. "Much quieter in here. Please, take a seat." Tyler motioned toward the black leather couch, and she complied.

She smiled at him. "You look too young to own this club."

"You look too young to have your own designer label."

35

"Touché," Mindy laughed, and she began to relax a bit.

Tyler stared intensely at her, and she nervously averted her eyes to the turquoise crystals on her costume that mimicked fish scales. When she dared to look up at this man who made her heart race, she found his eyes still fixed on her.

"What?" Mindy asked. It wasn't the first time a man had stared at her or admired her beauty, but she felt his gaze penetrating her soul— prodding, analyzing.

Tyler shook his head. "Nothing," he said nearly inaudibly. Standing, he walked over to a cabinet bar, removed two glasses and poured an Argentinean red blend. Three strides back to the couch, he handed Mindy a glass and claimed the seat beside her. "No. Let me correct myself. Everything. Tell me everything there is to know about Mindy Bloom."

The more she told him, the more relaxed she became. She leaned back against the couch and stretched her legs as much as she could in her constricting fishtail. They talked about Marcello, and the many ways he'd helped her, and he in turn explained that Marcello was a close family friend who had always been a guiding force in his life, more so than his own parents.

Mindy couldn't take her eyes off him as she reminisced her childhood and acquainted him with her friends. As he listened, she examined his chiseled jaw, the spiked, gold-tipped hair and bow-shaped lips that were too pretty to be male but somehow made him all the more handsome. She noticed that he sported tiny gold-hooped earrings in both ears, but wore no other jewelry.

"So if you had to describe each with one word, what would that word be?" Tyler asked. It was apparent he was amused by the history she shared with these women.

"Hmmm. One word. Let me think." She nibbled on a thumbnail as she pondered how to reply. "Sophia ... loyal, nurturing, sensible."

"That's three words."

Mindy laughed. "You ask tough questions. It's nearly impossible to narrow a person down to one trait." She decided to challenge him at his own game. "So tell me," Mindy began, as she drank in his imposing good looks, "what word epitomizes Tyler Moore?"

His answer was immediate. "Enigmatic."

"That doesn't tell me anything."

"That's what makes me enigmatic." He raised his eyebrows and smirked. "Back to you. Who's next?"

"Demi. Okay, she's ... honest to a fault."

"That's four words. Do you have trouble following directions? Warn me now. It may be important to know this later on."

"Do you want to hear about my friends or not?"

Tyler's hand gesture urged her to continue.

"Donna is ..." She blew out a breath, "simple yet complicated. Her situation is hard to explain."

"She's the teacher?"

Mindy nodded.

"Who's next?"

"Amy. Opinionated."

"One word!" Tyler clapped.

His smile was captivating, his face breathtaking. She wanted to reach out and touch him, as a sculptor would—feel the nuances of his bone structure, the softness of his skin, the flutter of his eyelashes as she brushed her fingertips over them.

"Your turn," she said. "What's your story?"

The smile faded from Tyler's face. Clasping his hands together on top of his head, he breathed out a sardonic laugh. "My childhood was nothing like yours." He jumped to his feet and poured himself another glass of wine.

The air had suddenly chilled and Mindy was fearful that she had upset him with her question. She rose to her feet, preparing to excuse herself and rejoin her party. "I'm sorry. I've taken too much of your time."

He caught her hand as she began to walk toward the door. "Don't go." Standing, he placed his hands on either side of her waist, turning her to face him. "Don't go," he repeated. He drew up his hands to cup her face, and a shiver traveled down her spine as he closed the space between them. His lips were so close to hers, his breath warm against her face, and he hypnotized her with his pleading blue eyes. "I've never wanted anyone as much as I want you at this moment," he whispered huskily. "I don't want to dredge up my past, but if you must kn—"

Mindy touched a finger to his lips. "Later. You can tell me later."

Wrapping his arms around her waist, Tyler pressed her body against his. The moment his lips touched hers, she knew this was a man she would not easily forget. Heat and electricity filled the air around them as they consumed each other with deep kisses that were ignited with passion.

When the kiss broke, they stared questioningly at one another for a brief moment, until the answer was evident in their eyes. Mindy pulled his shirt off, while Tyler flicked the clasp of her seed pearl bra open.

Guiding her to the sofa, he unzipped the back of her fish scale skirt, removing it, and sat down dragging her to his lap. He cupped her breasts, running the pads of his thumbs over them as they hardened.

The way he touched her, and held her breasts in his hands, and with the intensity his eyes bore into hers, it was as though he worshiped her. Never had she felt this way before and she moaned in pleasure and ran her lips across his muscled chest. Desperately, she shed him of his jeans, discarding them on the floor.

As her body straddled his, she could feel his arousal, and he slid out of his briefs in one swift move. The man was perfect in every sense, and as she touched him a growl escaped his lips.

"What are you doing to me?" Tyler grunted. He could barely speak. "I need—"

He took hold of her arms and pulled her up, guiding himself into her. "I need to be inside you," he said urgently. "Now."

When he entered her, she closed her eyes and threw her head back.

Mindy pushed as far into his lap as she could, taking him in deep. There were no words for this kind of gratification. It was new for her and not born of lust as it had with her other lovers. There was a celestial pull between them. A desperation and need born from having waited centuries to unite. For Mindy, a sense of familiarity, only possible when two souls staked their claim for one another took hold—rooted from the first moment they laid eyes on one another—and she knew he felt it too.

Three days later, Mindy called Sophia. "I have news!"

"You do? You've had a lot of exciting things to share lately. How was your party?"

"Magnificent. Marcello outdid himself. I wish you had been there."

"Me too. I'm sorry. I couldn't, but I really wanted to. So …"

"So," Mindy shrieked, "I met my Dean."

"Your what?"

"My Dean. Remember how Donna and I envied what the two of you had together? How you were so connected and how you knew he was your soul mate? All these years I've never really understood how you felt. I wanted to, but I never had those emotions for anyone, and I was starting to think I was incapable of feeling them." Mindy waited for a response. "Hello? Are you still there, Sophia?"

"I'm here," Sophia sighed. "I'm having a difficult time getting past your comment."

"Which one?"

"The one where you called Dean my soul mate. If we were soul mates we would have ended up together. Anyway, I came to terms with that whole part of my life long ago."

"So you're saying Will is your soul mate?" Mindy thought the guy was okay, but she just didn't see it. But they were married—with children, no less, so what did she know?

"Not everyone gets a soul mate," Sophia said defensively. "But tell me about yours."

Mindy told Sophia about the party and how they met. "And we've spent just about every minute of the last couple of days together. When I'm away from him, I feel as though a part of me is missing. He's sweet and attentive, and hot. Very hot. And we can't get enough of each other. And did I mention he's very, very hot? He's the one."

"Mindy … be careful," Sophia advised. "You've only known him three days."

"I'm not a child, Sophia. I'm thirty-three. At my age, you just know when it's right."

"Okay. I love you. You know that. I want the best for you and I don't want you to get hurt. Take your time and get to really know him."

"I will. And I want you to meet him. You're going to love him."

Chapter 8

Sophia

July 1999

Baby Anastacia cooed to her father, her tiny hands wrapping around his fingers. Dean and Sophia were seated in the first pew of the church, their many guests behind them, gathered to witness the baptism of their daughter.

Today was a joyous occasion, and Sophia did her best to forget, if only for an hour, that a little less than a year ago, this was where her mother had lain in repose. Finding it impossible to stay focused, she paid little attention to the priest's words.

"Today, we celebrate life," Father John began. "A life in Christ's light, and the relationship little Anastacia will begin with his church ..."

Thirteen years ago, when the sacrament had been performed for Nicky and Evvie, it was her mother who had changed the twins into their baptismal gowns after the priest had immersed them in the font and wrapped their naked bodies in a white towel. Her mother's absence was all the more palpable at times like this and it stung knowing her mother had been robbed of the privilege of this age-old tradition.

As Dean's mother, Soula, returned the child to Sophia's arms, she caught the sorrow in her daughter-in-law's expression and took the seat beside her. Soula wrapped her arm around Sophia's shoulder, pulling her close in support. "Ana's hands were guiding mine," Soula whispered. "I could feel her. Your mother is with us."

Sophia swallowed and shut her eyes to avoid the tears from flowing. Returning the gesture, she tenderly wrapped her hand around Soula's. "Yes, I believe she is."

When the priest finished speaking, Alex was the first to approach Sophia and Dean. "*Egoní mou*—my granddaughter," he said, motioning for his daughter to hand the child over to him.

A renewed sense of joy had breathed life into Alex on the day Anastacia, or Cia as they had come to call her, was born—a reason to live and to carry on as the head of the family, fulfilling the promise he'd made to his beloved.

Sophia wasn't sure whether her father would be saddened each time he heard her mother's name, however the opposite seemed true. No longer did he sit alone at home, refusing invitations for dinner or family outings. There would always be a part of him that would be forever lost without his Ana—a piece of him that could never heal. But now Alex was ready to do what Ana had asked of him—to be strong for his family as he had always been for her. He was ready to heed her words, and he found any excuse to spoil his new granddaughter and rebuild the relationships he had with the twins when Ana was alive.

"She's all yours, Dad." Sophia looked over his shoulder to the pews behind him. "I'm going to say hi to my friends." Sophia walked up the aisle.

"I am so happy you made it!" Sophia opened her arms to Amy, one of her oldest friends, a congresswoman who spent much of her time in Washington, DC.

"I wouldn't miss it. You look incredible for a woman who recently gave birth."

"I don't know about incredible, but I can tell you what I am— exhausted." Sophia examined her friend from head to toe. "But look at you! I hardly recognize you these days. What happened to my favorite anti-establishment activist?" Sophia asked.

"Oh she's still in there. But what I've established is that I need to pay my bills." Amy had shed herself of her ragged jeans and peace sign t-shirt, which she had worn braless. Her wavy, sandy brown hair had once framed her face, which had always been free of make-up. But now, dressed in a St. John suit and her hair cut in a neatly tamed bob, she looked professional and conservative.

"Let's talk more at the house. I want to hear everything you're up to," Sophia told her.

The baptismal party was held at Sophia's home—the one she had lived in and raised her children with her first husband. Will had been tragically killed in a plane crash almost three years prior when Flight 800 exploded into the Atlantic Ocean. Not wanting to uproot the children too quickly, Dean had moved into Sophia's home, however the plan to move elsewhere was constantly a sensitive subject.

"Well, what do you think?" Demi asked Sophia.

"You've outdone yourself once again."

With the twins, a newborn, and a dance studio to run, Sophia was too inundated to think about party details. She knew Demi would want complete creative control anyway. After all, event planning was her business.

Demi looped her arm around Sophia's. "Come! I have to show you the candy bar."

Glass jars, in various shapes and heights, were arranged on a pale pistachio green wooden planked table. An enticing assortment of pink and green candy teased the children waiting eagerly to indulge. Clear bags and ribbon sat in a small, pink crate on one side of the table, while the other side held a three-tiered display with tulle wrapped *koufeta*. The clusters of candy-coated almonds tied with Anastacia's name and baptismal date was a traditional Greek party favor.

"I don't know how you're going to keep the children off this table until dessert," Sophia laughed. "It almost looks too pretty to eat."

Like the candy, the round tables and chairs Demi had ordered were also pink and green. Baby pink roses with pale green porcelain vases decorated each table, matching the linens and the dinnerware.

Children played on the lawn with Nerf balls and Frisbees that Demi provided for them in the thematic colors. Demi had thought of everything, and Sophia was grateful for all she'd done.

"Great job, Dem," Dean complimented his sister as he walked over to them. Wrapping one arm around Sophia's waist, he pulled her close. In his other hand was a small, triangular spinach pie. "I'm starving. Did you make these, Dem?"

Demi nodded.

"They taste just like Mom's."

"I'm glad you like them." Her words were laced with annoyance. "Michael's mother said they were too salty."

All three of them rolled their eyes and laughed.

"Ignore her. She means no harm. She thinks she's helping you," Sophia said.

"You don't have to put up with her the way I do."

"Taste this," Dean said. He brought the last bite of the *spanakopita* up to Sophia's lips.

"Hmm, delicious."

Dean held her gaze, enjoying the expression her face made as she ate. He bushed his fingers across her lips, wiping away a flake of crispy phyllo. Sophia kissed the tips of his fingers. It was a tender moment, like many others they'd shared. He bent down and grazed her lips with his. "I love you."

"And I, you. More than I can express," Sophia replied. He'd always had a visceral effect on her, and it was no different now, the flutter in her stomach and the goose bumps on her flesh were proof of that.

"Should I send everyone home so you two can be alone," Demi said sarcastically.

"No, but I may send the kids home with you later," Dean teased, shooting his sister a devilish grin. He turned to his wife. "I want you to go sit with your girlfriends. It's not often you're all together. You too, Dem. The wait staff have everything under control for now."

All five women were seated at a table engrossed in chatter not too dissimilar to the way they had conversed when they were younger. Time and distance were no obstacles for them—it never was where true friendship reigned.

"So, what's up and coming in the fashion world?" Demi asked Mindy.

"If you only knew." Mindy had a look of disgust on her face. "Pink velour track suits and ballet shrugs."

"To go out in?" Sophia had a skeptical look on her face.

"Workout clothing as dress wear." Mindy raised her eyebrows. "Not my style, but I added some pieces into my collection to stay with the current trends." Mindy extended her fork into Demi's plate. "Let me have a taste of that."

"Get your own," Demi told her. "You're like a scavenger."

Donna plucked a shrimp from a small glass bowl and dipped it in cocktail sauce. "Sounds comfortable. I'd wear the track suit." She bit the shrimp off the end of the tail and instantly dunked another shrimp in the red sauce.

"What about you, Amy?" Mindy asked.

"Me? I don't think they suit my style."

"No, I mean what's new with you. What's shaking in Washington?"

"Do you really want me to go into it?"

"No. Just tell me when you're up for re-election and I'll vote," Mindy said.

She shook her head, but then turned her attention to Sophia. "Your dad looks good."

"He's doing better, thanks to little Cia. I try to keep him busy. I hate that he lives alone, but thank goodness he has Aunt Soula and Uncle Stavros next door."

"You still call them aunt and uncle? Are they okay with that?" Mindy wondered.

"It's what I've called them my whole life. They know I love them like my own parents. I haven't been able to get the word 'mom' out. Not yet."

"My mom understands," Demi said. "She loved Aunt Ana like a sister."

"I am going to mingle with some of the other guests and then maybe we can get the men to join us," Sophia said.

"They're playing with the kids. Leave them. How often do we get to do this?" Donna asked.

Amy rose with Sophia. "Before I leave tomorrow afternoon, I thought you and I could have lunch together. Alone," Amy said, discreetly pulling her aside.

"Sure," Sophia agreed. "Is everything okay?"

"Yes, for now. But I'd like to speak to you, uninterrupted."

~Spanakopita~

2 pounds fresh spinach
1 teaspoon kosher salt
6 finely sliced scallions
¼ cup olive oil
½ cup loosely packed fresh parsley and mint combination, chopped
¼ cup fresh dill, chopped
1½ pounds imported Greek feta cheese, crumbled
¼ cup breadcrumbs
2 eggs, lightly beaten
Pepper to taste
1 pound packaged phyllo
1 cup unsalted butter, melted

Preheat oven to 350°

Sauté the scallions until tender. Normally, what most people do, and what I'd always watched my mother do, was to sauté the spinach, and then squeeze out the excess liquid. This is where I decided to cheat a bit. I saved myself the aggravation of all that pressing and draining, and … it paid off. It was a risk, but it was worth the try. In a huge bowl, I toss the spinach, sautéed scallions, parsley and mint, dill, breadcrumbs, salt, pepper, eggs and feta together. The spinach wilts as it cooks in the oven and, by not sautéing it, it seems to be less wilted and has a fresher taste.

Grease a large baking pan and lay 8-10 phyllo leaves down, brushing each layer with butter. Spread the filling over the buttered pastry leaves. Lay another 8-10 leaves on top, brushing each leaf with butter. Tuck in any overhanging phyllo edges. Score the spanakopita with a sharp knife into square pieces. Pour any remaining butter evenly over the top. Bake for 45-55 minutes until golden.

Chapter 9

Amy

July 1999

Of the five women, Amy had kept in touch with everyone the least over the years. However, she never lost contact with Sophia and to this day relied on her as her most trusted confidant. The summer after college graduation had cemented their already strong bond, and the secret between them was never shared with the other girls or ever spoken of again. Only Sophia's mother knew the truth, having given the girls permission to spend the remainder of the summer in Greece with Ana's parents.

For Amy, it was a period in time that had changed her as the events sent her down a path she never predicted. This reality separated her from her friends, causing her to shy away from the other girls, using law school and, later, her career as an excuse. But in truth, there was no need to justify the absence in her friends' lives because it took every ounce of her energy and time to achieve what she had.

Graduating at the top of her class from Cornell Law School, she had visions of becoming a defense attorney. But after working at the public defender's office, she became frustrated and disenchanted. When the senior attorney she worked for fought and won to get the charges dropped on an armed robbery suspect, she was in awe of his litigation skills.

Three days after his release, the former defendant shot and killed a pharmacist at a local drug store, taking with him two hundred and thirty-four dollars and a few bottles of a controlled narcotic.

Dispirited and disillusioned, Amy couldn't do it anymore. She changed her focus and applied for a position as an ADA. After eight years of hard work and long hours, Amy ran for district attorney and, because of her volunteer work in the community and her dedication to her position, she won.

But Amy's aspirations went beyond the district attorney's office, and within four years she was elected to the New York State Senate. Her husband, Ezra Rosenfeld, was her biggest champion, and he encouraged and supported her ambition.

A partner in a prestigious law firm, Ezra was tough as nails in the courtroom, but kind and loving at home. When Amy made a bid for the United States Congress, she was concerned with the effect it would have on their son, Adam, but Ezra reassured her he would be fine.

Now with almost two years serving as a congresswoman, re-election time was approaching fast.

Sophia smiled warmly when Amy approached her and took a seat in the café booth.

"I hope you weren't waiting long. I forgot about the Long Island traffic," Amy said.

"No, I just got here myself."

They made small talk for a while, discussing the children's homework loads, their husbands, and Sophia's dilemma with what to do about the house.

"Ideally, Dino wants to move to Jamesport. His commute now is over an hour and a half. But the dance studio is here. I couldn't possibly commute back and forth."

"Somewhere in the middle might be a solution," Amy suggested.

"It's a consideration, but then there's the children. Nicky might be okay with moving, but Evvie … Evvie fights me on everything these days. At first I thought she was adjusting. She seemed excited about the wedding and was beginning to accept Dino, but suddenly her attitude turned again."

"What do you think changed?"

Sophia sighed. "I think it might have been Demi's toast at the reception."

Amy stared at Sophia in confusion.

Sophia ran her hand through her hair, brushing the ends away from her face. "Demi said that Dino and I were always meant to be together, and that we had loved each other since we were children, even before we understood the kind of love we had for each other."

"Oh, I remember that speech. It was definitely one of Demi's finer moments." The smile left Amy's face. "Oh, no. Evvie wondered where that left her father, didn't she?"

"Exactly. As Demi spoke, I caught Evvie's expression. Devastation was written all over her face. I tried to speak to her, but she wouldn't listen to what I had to say."

"And all these months later?" Amy asked. "Is it any better?"

"She runs hot and cold."

"It takes time. She'll come around."

Sophia exhaled. "I hope so."

The waitress came over to take their orders. When she walked away, Sophia asked, "What's on your mind, Amy?"

"I feel that I should tell Ezra what only you and I know, but I'm not sure I have the courage."

Sophia opened her mouth to speak, but said nothing. A line formed between her brows as she frowned. "You've been married for fifteen years and you've never told him any of it?"

"No."

"Why have you chosen now to tell him?"

"I've been carrying it a long time and I need to make it right. For all parties involved."

"I don't disagree, but I don't know why you've waited this long. Ezra would have understood the decision you made at the time. You've always stood by your conviction to be pro-choice, and the important word here is choice. Ezra supports and loves you. I'm certain that he would be accepting of any decision you made. But … the thing he may have trouble with is why you kept this from him all these years."

"It's not only Ezra I had to consider."

"I know. But I would wait until after the election. You have enough on your plate right now."

"You're right. But when I'm ready, will you be by my side when I have to explain what happened back then?"

"Of course," Sophia said.

Chapter 10

Sophia

August 1999

Mom!" Evvie called out to her mother. "Can I stay at Aunt Demi's house this weekend? Uncle Michael promised to let me help him at the vineyard."

"I think that's fine. Did you ask first?"

"I just told you, Uncle Michael said I could come," Evvie answered in an impatient, snippy tone.

"Do not speak to me that way. There is no excuse for you to be disrespectful."

Pivoting to walk away, Evvie rolled her eyes.

"Before you storm upstairs and I change my mind, would you please go out and get the mail for me?"

A minute later, Evvie walked in and handed Sophia a pile of letters, circulars and magazines.

"Does Nicky plan on going also?"

Evvie nodded without saying a word and retreated up to her bedroom.

Seated at the kitchen table, Sophia rifled through a pile of bills and junk mail sorting out what needed to be discarded. A letter, addressed to Sophia and handwritten in a penmanship she did not recognize, piqued her interest. Nor was the name on the return label familiar. Ripping open the envelope, she removed the contents, stiffening as she began to read.

When she finished, she slipped the letter back into the envelope and stared out her back window, unconsciously gnawing on the inside of her cheek.

Startled by the sound of her baby's cry, she rose from her chair, dropped the letter in the wastebasket by the corner desk nestled between the kitchen and hallway, and climbed the stairs to Cia's room.

Sophia drove the twins to Jamesport. Nicky went to find Paul, but Evvie dropped off her overnight bag at the house and ran straight to the vineyard to find her Uncle Michael.

Sophia thought it was odd that her daughter would seek out Michael rather than her cousins. With Cia in her arms, she walked through the long rows of grape vines, searching for her daughter to see what had caught her interest.

When she found her, Sophia was struck by the change in her daughter's attitude. In the car she'd been quiet and unwilling to engage in conversation. One-word answers were all Sophia could pull from Evvie. But even from the distance she stood, Sophia could see an exuberance emanate from her daughter as bright as the sun that was shining on them. Evvie's curiosity of each step of the winemaking process seemed to have captivated her attention as she asked her uncle dozens of questions.

His own children hadn't shown any interest at all, and Sophia could see that he welcomed her enthusiasm to learn as he bent down, taking a fistful of soil in his hand and urging Evvie to do the same. She stood and observed them as Michael showed Evvie how to examine the grapes. Plucking one from the vine, she held it between her fingers and squeezed, nodding while Michael explained what to feel for. She popped the grape in her mouth as he went into great detail about the soil and irrigation, and Evvie listened as though it were the most important information she'd ever been given.

A feeling of anxiety washed over Sophia and it left her feeling conflicted. Naturally she wanted Evvie to have a close relationship with her uncle, and shouldn't she be relieved to see her daughter smile for a change? There was a time when she had the same look on her face when she saw her 'Uncle Dean.' When he was her 'Uncle Dean,' perfect in her eyes—before—when Evvie's father was alive. Now that he was her stepfather and threatened all she thought true, well ...

It was a beautiful sunny day, but Sophia remained in a pensive mood in spite of it. She thought of the day before when Dean, once again, made an effort with Evvie only to get rejected and disrespected.

She hadn't caught the whole conversation, but Dean had offered to help Evvie with something or maybe to take her somewhere, and the venom in Evvie's answer distressed Sophia.

"I don't want anything from you. Not your help or your advice. You're not my father!"

Sophia briskly strode toward the room where they argued, but Dean put his hand up, signaling for her not to interfere. She wasn't sure how he could keep his composure, but he did.

"I am not trying to replace your father. But I'm here and someday you may need me. But, suit yourself. Ignore me. Silently hate me if you like. But do not disrespect your mother or me. Especially your mother."

Evvie stormed into her room and had barely uttered a word to either of them since.

Walking back toward the house, she put Cia in the stroller, wheeled her down to the Carriage House and slipped into Dean's office, hoping to find him there.

"What a nice surprise!" Dean said, jumping to his feet. Two quick strides had him lifting his daughter from the stroller and kissing

Sophia. His hazel eyes sparkled green as he looked at her.

"I dropped the twins off for the weekend. I couldn't leave without saying hi to my favorite man."

"Everything okay?" Dean examined her. "Your smile isn't fooling what I'm reading in your eyes."

"It's nothing. Let's have a nice quiet evening after I put this little one to bed."

Dean narrowed his eyes. Kissing his daughter's cheek, he set her back down into the stroller, handed her a toy from the diaper bag, and turned his focus to his wife. He tugged on the belt loops of her jeans and pulled her close to him, waiting.

Sophia groaned. She didn't want to talk about how she was feeling. Ignoring it might make it disappear. Lately, that's how she dealt with everything—she simply didn't deal with it at all. This wasn't typical for her, but too much had happened in the past year, and she was doing her best to think only of the good aspects of her life and all she had to be grateful for.

"Sophia *mou*, talk to me."

She pulled out of his embrace and walked over to his desk. She fiddled with the paperweight, examined the picture of the two of them by his computer and turned back around to face Dean.

"Did you ever feel as though something was gnawing at you, but you couldn't pinpoint exactly what it was?" She didn't wait for him to answer. "I feel that way often lately. Sometimes I wish I could crawl out of my own skin."

Dean furrowed his brow. "Are you ... unhappy?"

"God, no! Not with you. I guess I'm feeling a little overwhelmed, that's all."

"Your whole world was turned upside down. You need to let it all settle." Dean took Sophia's hands in his. The look of concern across his face did not escape her. "I'm about done here for today," Dean said. "How about I follow you home and we get an early start on that quiet evening you are hoping for."

"Don't cut your day short for me. I'll be fine."

Dean grabbed hold of the stroller, wheeling it out the door. "Let's go."

When they arrived home, Cia was fussing. Sophia started up the staircase and asked Dean to bring up a warm bottle. She rocked the child in her arms, seated in the violet upholstered chair by the corner of the nursery room.

"Here. I checked the temperature. It's lukewarm," Dean said.

Sophia took the bottle, cooing to the child as she placed the nipple in her mouth. "Thank you," she said with a weary smile that didn't reach her eyes.

"I'm going to order take-out while you put Cia to bed." Dean kissed his daughter's forehead before exiting the room.

Downstairs, Dean rifled through some menus he found in the kitchen desk drawer. Making his choice, he set aside the rest of the menus, punched a phone number into his cell phone, and placed his order. One of the menus fell into the wastepaper basket and when Dean reached in to retrieve it, he noticed the discarded letter.

Plucking it from the basket, his instincts told him this might have been the key to Sophia's frame of mind this afternoon. But did he have the right to read it? He held it between his fingers for a few moments, trying to justify a motive for invading her privacy. Concern, he thought. He was very concerned for her. The letter was left in plain sight. And that was how Dean assuaged himself from guilt at reading what was meant only for his wife.

The next morning, before Dean drove to work, he stopped by his parents' home to speak to his mother.

"*Katse*," Soula told her son, motioning for him to have a seat. "Did you have breakfast? I can make you an omelet or some pancakes."

"I didn't come to eat Mom, but thank you. I'll take a cup of coffee though."

Soula poured him the coffee, set it down in front of him, and then went to the refrigerator for a container of milk. "So, what's on your mind, *agori mou?*"

"This." Dean reached in the back pocket of his trousers and showed his mother a folded paper. He handed it to her and as she took it from him, a puzzled look crossed her face. Dean answered his mother's wordless question. "Just read it."

Soula's eyes squinted in concentration, her lips tightening as she read. "What did Sophia say about this?"

"Nothing. I found it in the garbage. She didn't tell me a thing." His voice was blended with a mixture of worry and insult. "Not so much as a mention."

"Well, I think she made it clear last year that she wanted nothing to do with him. Leave it alone."

"Mom, I'm not sure that I can. It's just one more thing to pile on her that she's pushing aside. At some point, she needs to address certain realities and deal with them. I'm afraid if she doesn't it will come back to haunt her."

"And letting that man back into her life won't haunt her?" Soula challenged.

"I think if Jimmy dies and she never makes peace with him and what happened in the past, it will hurt her. She needs to know who he is and hear his story."

Soula huffed. "His story." She groaned. "Let's do this," Soula suggested. "Alex is home. We can discuss this with him. If he thinks Sophia should see that man, then we'll speak to her about it."

Dean and Soula found Alex in his backyard tending the flower garden that his Ana had been so proud of. Dean suggested they take a seat on the patio. He felt awful about stirring this up and putting him in the middle of it, especially since he knew how much Alex was still grieving, but he was a pragmatic and fair man, so Dean filled him in on the contents of the letter.

"So, what do you think we should do?" Dean asked.

Alex scratched his forehead and sighed. "I'm not sure there is too much we can do right now. You said she threw the letter in the garbage. She didn't share it with you, or any of us. You know as well as I do that Sophia does not like to have her hand forced. She also doesn't like anyone going behind her back and making decisions for her."

"How do you feel about this?" Soula asked.

Alex clasped his hand over hers. "How do you think I feel? I have very mixed emotions. Sophia is my daughter in every way that counts. But now she knows the truth and it must be dealt with. It is not something she should ignore as she has been doing. Do I want him near her? No. Like I said, I have very mixed feelings."

"So, we do nothing for now?" Dean asked.

"What if you contacted this friend that wrote the letter? Find out a little more about the situation. If Jimmy is as ill as the letter states, then we may have to persuade Sophia to see him. For *her* sake."

"Alex, I'm so sorry. We shouldn't have put this on you," Soula said.

"She's my daughter. I'll do what's best for her. Even if it means contacting *that* man."

For Sophia, the days seemed to drag as she anticipated what Sunday would bring. Dressed in black, she sat in the first pew of the church. Family and friends surrounded her, praying for her mother's soul during Ana's one-year memorial service. As the priest finished liturgy, he reverently walked down the altar steps and stopped in front of a table that held her mother's picture, several glass-encased seven-day candles and a large tray of *kollyva*. The blessing of the boiled wheat berries, nuts and raisins blanketed in powdered sugar and adorned with edible silver dragees was an ancient tradition and done in remembrance of the departed soul.

Soula held the baby, and Dean held tightly onto Sophia's hand. Alex gripped Sophia's other hand for strength, but as the priest sang the memorial hymn, her fortitude vanished. Her throat tightened and her face grew warm, yet her body shivered. *A year without my mother. A year without my mother.* She heard it play over and over in her head, and still she could not comprehend it. Sometimes she'd fool herself into thinking her mother had been away on a long trip and any day she would call. But here she stood as the priest chanted prayers for her mother's memory to be eternal. The sound of the bells and the aromatic odor emanating from the censer he used to bless the congregation gave her little comfort. Mesmerized by the swirls of smoke that rose from the golden thurible, Sophia imagined it ascending to the heavens, sending a message of remembrance to her mother's soul.

She got through the *makaria*—the memorial luncheon—but when she arrived home, she handed the baby to Dean and went to bed—it was still daylight, but she was so very tired.

Chapter 11

Demi

September 1999

Demi knocked on the open door to her brother's office announcing her arrival but refrained from speaking when she noticed his ear to the phone. Dean glanced up, raising a finger for her to wait a minute. Lifting the white deli bag, Demi shook it to indicate she was armed with food and stepped into the room, taking a seat on the other side of his desk.

Dean ended the call and placed the receiver back in its cradle. "Hi. Thanks for picking up lunch."

Demi handed him a sandwich. "Roast beef on garlic bread with melted mozzarella."

"How did you know?" A faded smile crossed his face.

"I know you well. Enough to know something's up. What's on your mind?" Demi asked.

He rested his elbows on the desk and leaned in. "I'm worried about Sophia. She hasn't been herself. Have you noticed?"

"To tell you the truth, we haven't had a chance to see each other much. With the school year just beginning and all the after school activities, it's been hectic. That, on top of a busy wedding season here.

And I'm sure Sophia must have a full schedule with the new year of dance classes beginning." She ate a forkful of her salad and thought for a moment. Circling her fork in the air, she said, "Come to think of it, I've been so wrapped up, I didn't realize that I haven't spoken to her in a couple of weeks. Huh! That's not typical of us at all."

Frustrated, Dean raked a hand through his hair and leaned back in his chair. "She's been very withdrawn the last couple of weeks."

"Since Aunt Ana's *mnimosino?* That's understandable. It's hard to believe it's been a year." Demi frowned. "Anniversary dates are bound to dredge up those last painful days."

"No, I don't think it was only because of the memorial. Did Mom tell you about the letter Sophia received regarding Jimmy?"

"No?" Demi looked puzzled.

"Apparently, Jimmy is very ill. His neighbor checks in on him and takes him to the doctor and his treatment sessions. He found our address and contacted Sophia to let her know."

"Holy shit! How did Sophia react? She said she wanted nothing to do with him, but I know her. She has a soft heart and I bet she's feeling bad for him."

"I wouldn't know. I found the letter in the trash. She hasn't discussed it with me." Restlessly, Dean stood. "I'm worried, Dem. Evvie's testing her patience and Sophia is still grieving over her mother. I could see it in her face at the memorial, but she won't talk about it. When I try, she changes the subject."

"It's only natural for it to come to the surface at an anniversary date." Demi rested her hand over her brother's in comfort.

"And pretending Jimmy doesn't exist? Is that healthy? It was bound to come back to haunt her. I was hoping not so soon though. She's not dealing with anything. She's not doing anything!" Dean emphasized. "She's not even teaching at her studio. She said she's not up to it yet so she's hired another ballet teacher instead."

"Hmm, that's not like her." Demi looked at her brother with concern. "How has this affected the two of you? I mean ... on an intimate level?" Awkwardly, she waved her hand at him, dismissively. "Sorry. None of my business. I shouldn't have asked."

"It's okay. Let's just say that the last two weeks I feel like I am living with someone else. I'm trying to be understanding and supportive. I love her. I'll do anything to help her. But I'm at a loss. I think she should see someone."

"Have you suggested it?"

"No. I'm not sure how she'll take it. You know how she is. She believes everyone should be able to handle their own problems."

"She loves you. She knows that you are always thinking of her first."

"I'm not sure she will feel that way in her current state," Dean said.

"How about if I go speak to her and see what I can do—feel out the situation and pave the way for you."

"That would be helpful. She listens to you, and when she doesn't, you force her to listen."

"It's a gift." Demi rose from her seat, chucked the remnants of her salad in the trashcan and planted a kiss on her brother's cheek. "I'm on it," she said, before scooting off.

As Demi turned the corner into Sophia's neighborhood she thought about her brother's concerns and wondered how she hadn't noticed the decline in Sophia's tenor herself. Was she so wrapped up in her own life that she had stopped paying attention to her dearest friend? Maybe she thought that she and her brother were finally settled and happy. It certainly seemed that way when they'd married. She'd never seen two happier people.

Demi parked the car in the driveway. She hoped that Sophia would open up to her. The more she thought of it, she realized that anytime they had spoken recently, it was herself that had initiated the call, not Sophia.

She rang Sophia's doorbell several times. Peeking in the window,

Demi saw no sign of life, but she knew her sister-in-law was home—her car was in the driveway. Fishing in her oversize bag, she hunted until she found the spare key that Sophia had given her and opened the door.

"Hello!" Demi called out. "Anyone home?" Gingerly, she climbed the stairs and peeked her head into Cia's room. The baby was fast asleep, so she continued to the master bedroom. The shades were drawn and the lights were off, but curled up in a corner chair was Sophia, clothed in sweatpants and a t-shirt, her hair tied back in a messy ponytail.

Sophia looked up at Demi and rubbed her eyes. "Hi."

"Hi," Demi repeated back, questioningly. "What are you doing in here?"

"Nothing. The baby is taking a nap. I'm so tired … so tired."

Demi seated herself on the ottoman across from Sophia and softly patted her leg. "Talk to me," Demi urged. "This isn't like you to be holed up here by yourself."

Sophia looked away. She said nothing. Silence hung between them for several minutes until Demi could stay quiet no longer. Nervously, she swung her crossed leg back and forth, while contemplating an approach to ferret out the root of Sophia's anguish. One part of her wanted to pick her up by her tangled hair and tell her to cut the shit and deal with whatever she had to like the strong woman she knew she could be. But in her heart, she knew that if her friend was in this state there was a good reason and she would not respond well right now to that tactic. Demi leaned in and took Sophia's hands in hers.

"If you're not going to tell me what's bothering you, and you don't plan on talking it out with your husband, then you need to speak to someone," Demi said, trying to sound sympathetic. "Bottling it up will not solve anything."

"I need to escape the world for a while," Sophia said practically inaudibly. A tear fell from the corner of her eye and Demi gently wiped it away for her. "I don't want to think about how unfair it is that my mom is gone, or have to deal with a father I never knew I had, or pre-teen moodiness, or uprooting my whole life and moving, or coming up with new choreography for class when I have zero inspiration."

As Sophia went on, the pitch of her voice rose and her breath became ragged. Demi slid off the ottoman and squeezed herself onto the upholstered lounge chair beside Sophia. She began to massage her shoulders, attempting to calm her. "You need someone objective to speak to. Someone who can give you the tools to cope when you become overwhelmed."

"I'm not crazy. I don't need a therapist."

"No one said you were crazy. You just need someone objective to give you a little perspective. You can't do this for much longer." Demi motioned to Sophia, reproving her current state. "If you love your children, if you love my brother, you'll do something to help yourself."

That got Sophia's attention, as Demi knew it would. Demi saw the resignation in Sophia's eyes and she was certain she'd won a small battle.

"Here." Demi pulled a business card from her bag and handed it to Sophia. "She's a client of mine. I recently booked her daughter's wedding. I think she could help you."

Sophia reluctantly took the card and nodded imperceptibly. "I'll make an appointment," she sighed.

Chapter 12

Sophia

October 1999

Adverse to the idea of discussing her innermost thoughts with a stranger, it took Sophia three sessions with Dr. Grace Whitman to become somewhat comfortable with the idea.

Sophia was seated in a well worn, but cozy, microfiber loveseat. Across from her, the gray haired, fifty-something psychologist with the kind blue eyes began to speak. "This is our third appointment and you've been fairly forthcoming, but what you haven't shared with me is what you expect to achieve from these sessions."

"I'm not sure I know what you mean."

"What are your goals?"

"To feel like me again. Isn't that why I'm here?"

"But how can we work together to make that happen?" Dr. Whitman asked.

"I don't know. If I knew, I wouldn't be here."

"Let me start by explaining my goal. And that is for you to become self aware of what you need to do to reach your goals. I am only a guide—merely someone to bring to the surface what you've been trying to suppress. Clearly, you have quite a few issues to come to terms

66

with. Nothing that can't be dealt with if we break them down one at a time. We'll need to spend a session or two dissecting each concern. Together, we will work through it and I'll give you the tools to either resolve the dilemma or cope with your reality."

"How will any of that matter if I'm suffering from postpartum depression? Isn't it a matter of my hormones settling back to normal?"

"Mrs. Papadakis—"

"Sophia," she interrupted. "If I'm going to share my most personal thoughts with you, the least you can do is call me Sophia."

"Very well. Sophia, what makes you think you suffer postpartum?"

"That's why I'm here, isn't it? Haven't I been talking about how unlike myself I've been feeling since the baby was born? My friends and family urged me to find help for this temporary problem. Postpartum, that's what they all said I'm suffering from."

"I can assure you, Sophia. You do not have postpartum depression." The expression on Dr. Whitman's face was an oath of gentle confidence.

Sophia knitted her brow. "I'm confused."

"Let me explain. Often, actually almost always, in order to be diagnosed with postpartum, there must be some indication that there is a history of depression. You are clearly not bi-polar, I have no sense whatsoever that you have ever suffered from depression, and there is no history of it in your family. Correct?"

Sophia nodded in agreement.

"What I believe you have is depression caused by anxiety adjustment disorder."

Sophia sighed deeply and shrugged her shoulders. The woman may as well have been speaking Russian. "Dr. Whitman—"

"Grace," the doctor said. "If I'm to call you Sophia, then you are to call me Grace. I know it sounds ominous, but it isn't, really. It's a temporary condition caused by a stress or anxiety in your life that you are having difficulty coping with. For example, a new job, a move or a divorce could cause this. Terrible loss—a house fire for instance, or worse—the death of a loved one. Happy events can cause anxiety also. A marriage, a baby, even winning the lottery." The corners of Grace's mouth turned up in a smile, her eyes sparkling with compassion. "You haven't had one trigger for anxiety, you've had multiple triggers."

"When you lay it out like that, I suppose it's true."

"I don't suppose. I'm sure. In the last three years, you've lost your husband, your mother, remarried, and had a third child. Your daughter is testing your patience, your new husband wants you to move from your home, and you're juggling a family and a business. And we haven't scratched the surface regarding your paternity. Any of these can cause anxiety or depression. It's no wonder you suffer both anxiety and depression being bombarded with all of these issues. "

"None of this is anything I can do something about so I chose not to discuss it," Sophia said. She wondered how any of this was helping. If anything, she was more agitated than before. Sophia could feel the muscles on her shoulder blades tighten as she crossed her arms over her chest.

"Did you see what you just did?"

Looking down at her feet, Sophia pursed her lips.

"Your whole body language changed. When you crossed your arms, you closed yourself off to me. Choosing to set matters that bother you aside will not make them go away or fix them. For this to work, we have to be open with each other. I can help you, but only if you want to be helped. And only if you do the work."

"Okay," Sophia whispered skeptically.

"Before anything else, you need to put order in your home. I want you to keep a journal. Write down the changes you are making as you go through the week and the progress you think you are making. During each session, we can discuss what is working and what you are struggling with. This is what I suggest. For the time being, you should table any discussion of moving. If your husband has a problem with this, we may want to try a few additional sessions in couple counseling, but only if both of you agree. I also think you should consider exercising. I don't need to lecture you on the health benefits for the body and the mind. No more sitting around, and since you're a dance teacher, what better way to accomplish this than to get back to tending to your business. You'll feel stronger and more able to cope with the care of your baby and the discipline of your older daughter."

"Everything you are telling me to do, I can tell myself to do, but I can't seem to do it."

"That's because you are thinking of everything at once and it's weighing you down. Exercise, dance studio, Eva. That's all you concentrate on for now. Nothing else."

"Evvie. My daughter's name is Evvie."

"Forgive me. It's an unusual name."

"It's short for Evanthia. It was my grandmother's name. I guess she's not really my grandmother though," Sophia said, disappointment coating her words.

"Eh! What did I just say? You are not to dwell on that right now. We will address that at a later date. One thing at a time." Grace had been jotting down notes on and off during the session. Now, she laid the pad and pen down on a side table by her seat. She glanced at Sophia. "I want you to spend some time alone with Evvie. She needs reassurance that her family was solid, and that you cared for her father. Pull out a photo album. Talk about the good times the four of you had together. Tell her you haven't forgotten him just because you've remarried. She needs to understand that one life can never replace another."

"She resents Dean because she's under the impression that I've only loved him and not her father."

"It's up to you to make her understand that the time you were with her father belonged to him, and that the past teenage relationship you had didn't take away from that."

"But what if it did?"

The doctor looked Sophia square in the eye. "We are all entitled to our own private and deeply personal feelings. You needn't explain the different forms of love you had for each of these men. You only need to confirm that her father was loved and she was a result of that."

When the hour with Grace Whitman was over, Sophia called Soula and asked if she could babysit a while longer. She decided she would take the first step in following the doctor's orders—to the best of her ability anyway. She drove to her dance studio, changed into a black leotard, a sheer chiffon wrap skirt and her battered ballet shoes. It was time to dance.

"Men can be difficult. A woman must learn to ignore their shortcomings."
—Stella Angelidis (Mother to Michael, Peter and John)

Chapter 13

Donna

November 1999

Gray skies mirrored Donna's frame of mind. She hurried from her car, running across the parking lot and swung open the door to Sophia's dance studio. Shivering, she rubbed her hands together in a mock attempt at warming herself.

It was mid-November and it seemed as though the cold bitter dampness had swept in overnight. It was only last week that she had gone to Demi and Michael's home where a group of friends had gathered together for an autumn backyard party.

Hanging her coat in the office closet, she called out for Sophia.

"In here!" Sophia answered. "You're early."

Donna shrugged her shoulders. "No one's home. Football season, you know," she said, rolling her eyes. "I am so sick of football. Richie acts as though RJ is going to be the biggest star to hit the NFL one day."

"Where's Anthony?" Sophia asked as she began her pre-class warm-ups.

"Rehearsals for the play. I'll pick him up when I have a break and bring him back for class."

Sophia motioned for Donna to join her. "Come. Stretch with me."

Sophia positioned herself seated upright on the floor, her legs spread wide. She reached both arms over her left leg, touching her toes with her fingers, sat up, and repeated the movements on her right side. "Why can't Richie drop him off?"

"Pul-ease," Donna said in exasperation. "He doesn't support Anthony dancing or being in the play. It's sports or nothing with him. He won't lift a finger to get him here."

"Does he have any idea how physical dance is? I'd like to see his football players in one of our leaps and turns classes."

"Now that's a visual!" Donna laughed. The smile left her face and she examined her friend. "How are you feeling?" Donna asked, laying a compassionate hand on hers.

"I'm hanging in there. I still feel all churned up inside, but I'm making progress. Dino and Demi were right to suggest—strongly suggest—I speak to someone who can help me work it all out. I'm taking it one step at a time. Evvie is getting a little more cooperative, so that helps, and with Cia for my dad to focus on, he seems to be less lonely these days. The rest?" Sophia lifted her palms upward. "The rest will come in time."

"How about you and Dean? Everything okay there?"

"You know I love him madly. But I just haven't been myself and it's not his fault. My mom was alive when we first got back together. She wasn't even sick. Not that we knew anyway. And after all I'd been through after Will's death, having Dino back in my life—the way it once was—well, let's just say I felt like I was walking on air. Until my world collapsed."

"I know losing your mom was hard on you, but she wouldn't want you to drudge along in sadness day after day. Don't be so demanding of yourself. That's half your problem. You're too busy worrying about everyone else. Eventually the grief will change into memories and become a little easier each day."

"I hope so. It's hard for me to feel anything right now. I'm barely getting by."

"We're all barely getting by. We play with the cards we're dealt and make the best of it." Donna told her.

"That's glum. It doesn't sound very hopeful."

Donna averted her eyes from Sophia. "Hopeful is for teenagers. I wish I knew then what I know now."

Sophia flashed her a look of concern. "Come," she said, urging Donna up off the dance floor, "let's get our heart rate pumping and release some endorphins."

Donna taught two classes before leaving to pick up her son. When she arrived back at the studio, she found Dean with Sophia in the office with his arms wrapped around her and his face buried in her neck.

"Break it up you two." Donna smiled. "There's a pack of kids out there waiting for you." She made light of it, but Donna didn't remember the last time her husband held her that way, or looked at her with so much love in his eyes.

"I dropped Evvie off for class. I wasn't about to leave without a proper good-bye," Dean said. He gave Sophia one last peck on the lips before walking toward the door. "Say hi to Richie for me. Tell him we missed him last week."

"I'll be sure to tell him," Donna muttered.

After classes were done for the night, Donna and Anthony drove home, chatting about school, the play he was in and the paper he had to finish writing by the end of the week. Anthony had always been a happy well-adjusted child. But lately there was a quiet, pensive side to him. Donna noticed this more when he was in the company of his father, whom he'd never been able to please. Richie was a big part of the change in Anthony's demeanor, but there was something more lurking below the surface that Donna could not decipher. "Is everything okay at school?" Donna asked Anthony.

"Fine, Mom," He answered back in a tone that told her he was annoyed with the question and not willing to talk.

"Did you have a fight with Dad? Something seems wrong."

"Mom! Stop. Just 'cause I'm not in the mood to talk, it doesn't mean anything is wrong."

"Okay. I just worry about you."

"You don't need to. I'm fine."

Donna was irritatingly aware that Anthony did not meet up to Richie's expectations, but she thought her son was perfect just as he was. The last thing she needed was another sports-crazed man in the house. Anthony's sensitive nature and his creative interests were refreshing and Donna loved the fact that her son had an identity all his own and one that wasn't instigated by his father's limited standards.

When they arrived home, the house was empty. Donna threw her keys on the kitchen counter and noticed a note left from RJ telling his mother that he was having dinner at his girlfriend, Emily's home. Donna had no idea where her husband was. And somehow, that was okay with her.

As Donna straightened the house from the trail of clothing, shoes, newspapers, and beer cans that Richie left behind, she thought of how her marriage had traveled in the direction it had.

By the time they had both graduated college and found steady employment, they'd been going out for six years. They were in their early twenties and the future was mapped out before them. No pressure, no worries. With their combined salaries they were able to live comfortably and buy a home.

Even when the children came along, their lives seemed to fall into place just as they hoped and planned. But somewhere along the way, with anticipation and excitement for the future gone, life became a routine. Eventually, communication between them tapered to a near halt—and so had their sex life.

Richie found interests independent from Donna—a classic car to restore, a team to coach, or a buddy to get drunk with. At first, Donna saw nothing wrong with this. It was healthy to have separate hobbies and time spent with individual friends. But their time spent with each other grew less and less and, after a while neither of them seemed to care.

Donna showered and slid on a pair of sweat pants and a chenille pullover top. She was about to pour herself a cup of tea when the sound of heavy, clumsy footsteps caught her attention. Turning, she looked at her drunken husband with disdain.

"You're drunk."

"I'm fine," Richie snapped. "I had a few beers."

"More than a few." She observed the keys in his hand. "Did you drive in that condition? You're going to kill someone someday."

"Don't fucking lecture me. You're not my mother."

"Screw you," Donna spat, walking past him.

Richie caught her arm and angrily tugged her close to him. "I'd like to screw you, but you're a frigid bitch."

Donna wrenched her arm from his grasp. "No, you bastard. I'm an adult. Someone needs to be." She walked up the stairs, slamming the bedroom door shut. Throwing herself onto the mattress, she sank her face into her pillow.

Chapter 14

Mindy

Hanukkah 1999

New York City in December was vibrant with lights, decorations and warmly clad visitors shopping for the holidays. For many New Yorkers, the additional foot traffic was annoying, and some wished the season was over and hassle-free from tourists. But not Mindy. She loved the energy and the magical atmosphere that filled the air.

Before dashing into Penn Station to catch a train to Long Island, Mindy couldn't help but take one more peek into Macy's windows. Ornate depictions of fashions long past were extraordinary to view—the glamour of the twenties, the romance of the forties, the madcap mod styles of the sixties. Red ropes lined the sidewalks, keeping the crowd moving as hundreds stopped to gape at the displays and to snap photos.

The temperature had dropped below zero, so Mindy quickly scurried from window to window before crossing the busy intersection where she and her frozen toes made a dash for the train.

Tonight was the third night of Hanukkah, and she was spending the rest of the weekend with her parents. An only child, Mindy had no nieces or nephews and her mother had given up hope that Mindy would have a child by her age.

"I had a thought," Mrs. Bloom announced to Mindy over the phone two weeks prior. "What if we made a real celebration of Hanukkah like we did when you were a girl? We could have everyone over like the old days."

"Mom … it's not like the old days. Everyone has husbands and children. We're not little girls anymore."

"I know!" Mrs. Bloom exclaimed. "That's what makes the idea so delightful. To have children about again."

"Do you have any idea what you're in for?"

"I do, and it's settled." When Edna Bloom was determined to have her way, it was all but done—in the most well intentioned way, of course.

Mindy fought her way through the crowd and onto the train as she scanned the rows looking for a seat. When she settled in, a whisper of a smile crossed Mindy's face as she imagined her mother's exuberance preparing for the holiday.

Commuters were still finding seats on the train while Mindy busied herself with the latest copy of Harper's Bazaar.

"Mindy?"

Looking up when she heard her name, Mindy tried to conceal her reaction. Could he tell that her heart was about to jump out of her throat? "Tyler?"

"Mind if I sit here?"

"Yes—I mean, no," she stuttered. *Yes, I mind, damn it. What am I supposed to do now?*

"It's been a long time. You look …" he paused for a second, examining her, "… beautiful."

Uncomfortable, Mindy nervously ruffled the edges of her magazine. "You look very well yourself, Tyler." It took great effort for her voice to stay even. "What brings you out this way?"

"I live in Brookville now."

"Really? Somehow I thought you'd always stay in the city."

He looked into her eyes as though searching for answers. "No. I thought that was clear. I always wanted a home—I wanted more."

Mindy looked away. Facing the grimy train window, she caught a dulled version of her reflection—the face of regret. She sucked in a deep breath, fearful she might shed a tear or worse—her body stiffened as her stomach churned.

She turned back to Tyler and forced a smile. "I did too," she said, her words barely a whisper.

"Not enough."

She wasn't prepared for this, she thought. To be chastised for a choice she'd made long ago—one she'd questioned every day for the last eight years. Mindy's heart was racing. She dared to look up into the face she'd never forgotten, and wondered if she could undo the damage of the past, given the chance.

"Tyler," she started, but she abruptly stopped when he brushed his hand across his face. A gold band on his left hand ring finger glared at her like a lighthouse beacon. "You're married." The statement flew from her lips with an alarm she feared announced her desolation.

"Yes," he brightened. "Five years now," he said, aiming his hand in front of himself, admiring his symbol of commitment.

"That's wonderful." Mindy could feel the heat rising to her cheeks and pain shooting through her temples. Suddenly, she felt as though her head would explode.

"We have two little girls."

Of course you do. Why not? "Hence, the house?" she asked.

Tyler nodded. "Yes. We wanted room for the children to spread out … have a backyard, a pool. The schools are excellent. Paige is only three; she's not in school yet, but before you know it …" He pulled out a photo from his wallet.

Mindy thought she was going to be sick. Searing pain burned in the back of her eyes and she knew a headache was on its way. Naturally, they were blonde and adorable like their father and their stunningly gorgeous mother. "You have a beautiful family. I'm very happy for you."

Tyler looked up as the train stopped. "This is where I get off. It was great to see you." He looked at her quizzically for a moment. "It looks like we both got what we truly were looking for. You've become a great success in your industry and I'm happy for you."

Mindy forced a smile, trying her hardest not to let him see how difficult this was for her. "Thank you, Tyler. It was good to see you."

He looked earnestly into her eyes and laid a hand on hers. "Yes, it was. Take care." Turning, Tyler exited the train.

"Goodbye, Tyler," Mindy whispered for her ears only. She swallowed a sob thinking of what his last look conveyed. Regret? Nostalgia? Pity? Oh God! Please, not pity.

By the time Mindy arrived at her mother's home, she had a full-blown migraine.

"Oh, dear. Go on up to bed. You need a dark room and a good night's sleep," her mother said.

When Mindy awoke the next day, she was determined to put on a cheerful face and help her mother. Mrs. Bloom had been looking forward to this evening for weeks and she didn't want to spoil it for her.

That evening, as the house filled with conversation and laughter, Mindy looked over at her mother. She was in such high spirits that she thought the woman might explode with joy. Then it occurred to her. Her mother had been lonely. Her father was a good husband and they spent much of their time together, but she missed the energy of the happy chaos that children brought to a home. She thought of Tyler and his two little girls. Not only had she lost her chance with him, but she had also robbed Edna of her only chance to become a grandmother.

Dean, Michael and Richie were taking bets on who would be in the Super Bowl.

"My money is on St. Louis," Michael said.

"Not a chance," Richie argued, after taking a pull from his beer.

Amy's husband, Ezra, and Mindy's father, Harold Bloom, had the youngsters engaged on the other side of the room. Remembering when she was a child, of how her father told the story of the Festival of Lights to the five of them year after year, warmed Mindy's heart. Now, she listened as he told her friends' children of the ancient miracle.

Edna passed out dreidels for the children to play with and promised them another surprise after dinner.

"Mom, why don't you sit and relax for a bit and we'll get the food onto the table."

"Are you sure?"

"Yes. You've done enough. I think we can handle it from here."

Edna took a seat by Soula, Stavros and Alex, and Mindy was grateful that her mother listened. She'd worked for days to pull the holiday together and she wanted her to have a chance to enjoy it.

Demi and Sophia followed Mindy into the kitchen. Amy and Donna joined them a few minutes later, asking how they could help. Abruptly, Demi turned and looked at Mindy.

"Everyone stop!" Demi ordered. They all looked at her in puzzled amazement. "We are all here now, Mindy. What's the deal?"

"Huh?"

"Don't 'huh' me. Cut the shit and get to the chase. Something is wrong and this food is not going out until you tell us what it is," Demi insisted.

Sophia laid her hand on Demi's back. "Maybe it's private. Back off just a little," she whispered.

"No." Demi shook a finger at Mindy. "You've been dragging around all night. Your shoulders are slumped and you've barely said anything the whole evening."

"You might feel better if you talk through it," Donna said.

Mindy inhaled, closed her eyes and exhaled slowly. "I ran into Tyler on the train."

Amy took two quick strides and was at her side in an instant. "I'm sure that wasn't easy. Did you speak to him?"

Mindy nodded.

"What did he have to say?"

Tears rolled down Mindy's cheeks in streams. "He's married." She tried to hold it together, but she couldn't any longer. Crying turned into sobbing. Gasping for air, she thought she might hyperventilate. She tried to calm herself before she continued. "He has two children—girls—blonde, and a beautiful wife."

"Oh, Mindy. That must have been hard for you to hear," Sophia said sympathetically.

"And to see," Mindy cried. "He showed me pictures."

"Don't cry." Sophia handed Mindy a napkin.

"It's been eight years. He was bound to get married at some point," Demi said.

"I didn't need it thrown in my face."

"It wasn't intentional. You met by coincidence. You've both moved on with your lives," Amy told her.

"At least you finally have closure." Donna added. "Move on without regrets. It wasn't meant to be."

"Maybe not. But I'm the only one here without children, or even one very important person in my life. Seeing him, being reminded of what I gave up and knowing someone filled my spot in his life, hurts."

"Mindy, look at me," Amy ordered as she clasped her hands on Mindy's shoulders and forced her to listen. "We have all made choices. Some of them were more difficult to make than others." Amy glanced over at Sophia, who in turn nodded her head as though to give Amy the strength to continue. "But the decisions we made were based on what our instincts told us. You made the right choice for your life at that time. Had you done it differently, you might have been miserable and it could have ended with greater heartbreak."

"We're all here for you," Sophia said. "You'll never be alone."

"You may not have one important person in your life, but you have the four of us. And like it or not, you're stuck with us until we can't walk and our teeth fall out," Demi joked.

The five friends huddled in a circle and put their heads together.

"What's going on in here?" Edna asked as she entered the kitchen. "Just like when you were girls," she shook her head. "I'd ask you to help me with one chore and you'd get distracted and I'd have to get after you to finish."

Mindy smiled. "We're on it Mom. Everything is ready to go on the table."

They brought out platters of brisket and gravy, vegetables, and challah bread. A ceramic baking dish held noodle kugel with bits of caramelized apples bubbling to the surface covered with cinnamon. Two large trays with crisp potato latkes were layered in a mound, and Edna had even made her own homemade apple relish.

For dessert, there were jelly donuts dusted with sugar and *rugelach* filled with apple butter and walnuts. But Edna had something else for the children. Cradling a glass bowl in her arm, she passed around pouches of chocolate gelt to the youngsters. The gold coin wrappers were emptied and the chocolate devoured with great enthusiasm.

When it was time to leave, Amy asked Mindy if she would like to come to Washington for a few days.

"Thanks. Maybe another time," Mindy replied. "I have a few things to wrap up in the city and then I think I'm going to get away for the rest of the holidays."

"When did you decide that?" Donna asked.

"This very minute, I think." Mindy was surprised by her own impulsiveness.

"If you're up for a trip to Europe, you can stay at our place in Chios."

"That's such a generous offer, Sophia. You wouldn't mind?"

"Of course not. I'd offer you my grandmother's beach house in Aegina, but it needs some renovation."

Mindy looked around her. "I wish you could all come with me."

"That sounds like heaven." Donna put her arms around her friend.

"Maybe someday we will finally take that trip together."

"We've been saying that since we were twelve," Demi rolled her eyes. "Somehow, we've never been able to make that happen."

"Well, I think a quiet vacation alone sounds in order right now," Amy said.

"And you really don't mind, Sophia?

"Not at all. That's what the house is there for. For family to enjoy."

Family. Yes, Mindy thought as she scanned her surroundings, this spirited clan was her family.

Chapter 15

Mindy

1991

Mindy lifted her arms above her head to stretch out her back. She looked up at the wall clock in her office and groaned. She'd promised Tyler that she would be home no later than seven. His club was closed on Mondays and he'd suggested they have a cozy night at home, just the two of them.

He was going to be angry, she worried. It was after eight and by the time she got downtown to the Tribeca apartment they shared, it would be close to nine. Lately, between his work schedule and hers, social commitments and her need to travel for business, they spent little time together.

In those first few months after they met, Mindy and Tyler couldn't stay away from each other, and nothing else seemed to matter. It was an all-consuming relationship, like no other she had before and, without a doubt, Mindy knew she was in love.

Tyler was sexy, attentive and considerate. He knew what he wanted and planned for it, yet he had an impulsive side that always surprised her—impromptu weekend trips where he packed her bag and announced they were off to … wherever, a surprise birthday party for her at his club, or a picnic lunch in the middle of her workday. It was fun and manageable for a while, but as her label grew, the price of success possessed her, and the more in demand she became, the less time she had for play.

For Tyler, from the moment he laid eyes on her, he knew she was the one he wanted—the one he had waited for, and it didn't take him long to tell her as much. Mindy was gorgeous and smart, talented and sweet. She didn't possess the obnoxious awareness that some women had knowing men were attracted to them. It was as though she was oblivious to her looks and charm. And she was normal. Not like some of the crazy girls that flung themselves at him simply because his looks and money appealed to them.

Tyler wished his childhood had been like hers, with attentive parents and close friends. He constantly prodded her for stories, and Mindy complied.

"That's what I want," he told Mindy. "It's too late for me, but my children will have parents to come home to every day. And holidays at home, not in a hotel."

Mindy didn't push Tyler for answers, but she knew there was resentment eating away at him and wished she knew the source of his pain. One night at her apartment, after making love several times—against the wall, on the ottoman in her walk-in closet, and finally sprawled across the bed—she leaned her chin on his chest and looked up at him when he began to speak.

"I want to live inside your world, Mindy Bloom." Her heart melted as he looked at her with eyes as light as a soft blue sky, but deep with old wounds. He flipped her over so that she was underneath him. "I want to live inside you."

He kissed her and she giggled. "That's where you've been most of the night," Mindy said.

Tyler rolled onto his side; his elbow propped to lift his head. "I spent most of my childhood alone," he said quietly.

Mindy rolled to face him. She waited. They were nose to nose, and she stared into his eyes. Lifting her hand, she brushed the back of her fingers across his cheek. "Talk to me. Why were you alone?"

"I was an only child—like you—but not like you. My parents ignored me. My father went away on business … a lot. Sometimes, if it suited her, my mother would go with him and they would lengthen their trip. They traveled overseas for extended periods."

"And they didn't take you?"

"No. We had a live-in nanny and I stayed with her. But the nannies changed many times over the years and I never formed a real attachment to any of them. Skiing in Gstaad, sailing in Capri—you name it, they went there. And when they were home, they were always out at social events and charity dinners."

"Did they spend any time with you at all?"

"A little. When it suited them. I was always vying for their attention and I started to misbehave. I broke an expensive floor lamp playing ball in the living room. I spilled my mother's wine on her precious Kashan-Persian rug—things like that. I'd get punished and sent to my room. As I got older, I gave the teachers in school a hard time. That would get my parents to notice me, right?"

Mindy nodded in agreement.

"Wrong. One time they were too busy to bother so they sent the nanny to deal with the principal."

Mindy didn't want to interrupt him while he was willing to continue, but she had no understanding of this kind of parenting. Her parents and the parents of her friends were completely wrapped up in their children's lives.

"Did it ever make you wonder why they decided to have a child?"

"All the time," Tyler scoffed out in disgust. "I started giving the nannies a hard time. I thought if they couldn't keep one, they would stop hiring them. That backfired. They sat me down one night and told me I was going to boarding school, and I would love it there because I would have friends around all the time. Friends, but no parents. Not that I ever really had them to begin with. So, you see why I prefer to hear about your childhood? It's the one I'd hoped for."

"What's your relationship with them now?"

"Non-existent with my mother. When I was twelve, she left my father for some guy she'd been fucking. She sat me down for a brief talk the day after Christmas. 'A boy needs his dad,' she told me. 'That's why I can't take you with me.' After that, I got an occasional postcard or a gift in the mail, but eventually that stopped too."

"Oh, baby, I'm so sorry." She kissed him. "I love you." She didn't want to be the first one to say it, but she instinctively knew it was what he needed to hear. "I can't do anything about your past, but I hope I can make your present brighter."

Tyler wrapped his arms around her. "My present and my future," he said. He sighed. "I am so crazy in love with you."

Goosebumps pricked the surface of her skin when Mindy heard the words she longed to hear. She had never felt this strongly about any man before.

Mindy scurried into the lobby of her building. As she rode the elevator, she thought of those first months together. She'd felt so secure in Tyler's love, and he could count on hers, but lately she was always on edge around him and suspected that she wasn't living up to his expectations.

"I'm home," Mindy called out, tentatively. "Sorry I'm late. I lost track of time."

Mindy looked about the room, which served as a combination living and dining room area. The table was set and candles lit, but the room was eerily quiet. "Tyler," she called out, as she walked down the narrow hallway that led to the bedroom. "What are you doing?" she asked. Clothes were strewn on the bed and a suitcase lay on the floor.

Tyler turned to look at her with hard eyes. "What does it look like? You're an intelligent woman. I'm moving out."

Mindy thought her heart would drop to the floor. Panic pervaded her and she began to shake. "Tyler, please," she pleaded. "Let's talk this through."

"I'm done talking," he said coldly. "Nothing ever changes. This isn't what I signed up for. You knew what I wanted from the beginning, and it isn't an absentee girlfriend. You're never home, and when you are, you're preoccupied."

"When we met I was just starting my own label. You knew this. It's a huge undertaking and commitment to make it succeed. Was I supposed to neglect it to play with you?"

"Play! You think I'm playing? Do you even know what today is?" Tyler asked.

Mindy crinkled her brow. "Today?"

"Yes, today. It's the two-year anniversary of the night we met. I ordered in a special dinner. You promised you'd be home," he raised his voice, pointing at her. "Tonight was supposed to be a special night, but if this is any indication of what our future would be like together, I don't want it. It's not enough for me."

"I love you, you know that. But I'm not about to throw everything I worked for away. I'm doing the best I can to fit in all the parts of my life. I don't want you to go. Please."

Tyler shook his head. "No." Zipping up his suitcase, he took his anger out on the luggage, slamming it down on the hardwood floor. "I spent half my life being ignored. I don't intend to spend the rest of my days that way. I don't want to be *fit* into your life! I want to be the love of your life."

"You are." Tears were trickling down Mindy's cheeks. She reached for him but he pushed her arm away.

"Good-bye Mindy." Tyler walked past her and he was gone. She thought she detected a hint of sadness and regret in his face, but it didn't matter because he chose to leave her. The finality of the door slamming made her crumble to her knees. Desolation paralyzed her as she stared at the empty closet, disbelieving at what had just happened.

Time eluded Mindy. It must have been hours that she sat on the floor, her back up against the bed, staring at nothingness. She was lost in her thoughts—replaying his abandonment. How could he leave her when she loved him so?

Mindy was numb—no tears left to shed. She closed her eyes and pictured her long hours at work, the broken dates, and her constant preoccupation. She had no one to blame but herself.

Eventually, she swept herself off the floor and dragged herself over to the dining table. She blew out what little was left of the taper candles and began to remove the place settings from the table when she noticed a small red box from Cartier. Her hands flew to her mouth and she gasped. Reaching for the box, she pulled back, fearful that the contents would cause her pain.

Slowly, she lifted it off the table and carefully pried it open. Nestled in velvet was an emerald cut diamond, which at her estimation looked to be about three carats. The ring was stunning, but dulled by the reality that it would never sit on her finger.

Devastated, she picked up the phone. "Soph?" Mindy cried. "I need you."

Chapter 16

Amy

1999

"That was a pleasant evening," Amy said to Ezra in the car ride after they left the Blooms' home. "They're such kind people."

"And tomorrow we get to see your mother. That's always an experience," Ezra said.

"That's an understatement. Do you think she has any realization whatsoever that we've heard her rants over my dad more times than we care to?"

"I'm not sure she cares. I think she wants to reinforce how horrible he was to her, just in case you didn't already know," he laughed.

"Laugh now," Amy said, poking his side. "But you didn't live with the constant fighting. I would escape to Mindy's house and Mrs. Bloom would talk the tears away. After a while I became indifferent to their fighting and tried not to let it affect me, but I would hustle my brothers out of the house and ask Dean or Vinny to distract them."

"Speaking of your brothers, are we going to see Joel and Aaron tomorrow?"

"No," Amy answered. "Joel can't fly across the country for just a day or two. He's spending the holidays with his wife's family. Aaron broke his leg skiing, so he's staying put."

"You didn't tell me. When did that happen?"

"Last week. I've been busy wrapping things up before the holiday break. I forgot to mention it."

The next day, when their plane landed in West Palm Beach, they rented a car, and drove to Amy's mother's condo.

"Are you ready?" Ezra asked.

"As ready as I'll ever be," Amy replied sucking in a deep breath and squaring her shoulders. She rang the doorbell and Mrs. Jacobs promptly answered it.

"Hi all! Come in." She seemed excited to see them. "Boys, come give your grandmother a kiss. You've grown so big." She turned to her daughter. "You really need to visit me more often. Before you know it the boys will be grown men."

"We'll try Mother. It's hard to get away. You can visit us anytime you want."

"Not in that cold climate!" she exclaimed. "I left that behind long ago. Just like your father left me. Cheating bastard!"

"And here we go," Ezra leaned over, whispering in Amy's ear.

"Mom, can we not do this today? We all know Dad was awful to you, but it's Hanukkah. Can we talk about something pleasant?"

"You don't know what it was like. You didn't live your life every day knowing your husband was off with other women."

"Boys, why don't we take a walk around the neighborhood," Ezra suggested. Ezra rounded up the boys and scooted out the door, leaving Amy to contend with her mother.

"I do know what it was like, Mother. You know why I know? Because I spent the better part of my childhood listening to your fights." Amy closed her eyes and pinched the bridge of her nose. "Can I have one day—just one day with you—where I don't have to listen to you complain about what you went through with Dad?" Amy was raising her voice, and her mother's eyes grew wide as she spoke. "I went through it, too. And so did Joel and Aaron."

"Well, I'm sorry," Mrs. Jacobs huffed, and Amy knew she had insulted her mother but, at that moment, she didn't care. "You'd think a mother could confide in her grown daughter."

"You've been confiding in me for years. What Dad did was horrible and I don't know why you didn't divorce him sooner. You never got along. But it's done. Move on, Mother. You've been festering this hate for years and it's not healthy."

"It's easy for you. You have everything—your career, your family —I'm left here alone with nothing."

"You made your choices, Mother. You could have stayed in New York to be close to us. When we moved to Washington, I offered for you to come along." Amy stared at her mother. She was about to blast her with more truths than the woman could handle. She had held back for too many years. "You say I have everything. Would you like to know the one thing I never had?"

Mrs. Jacobs looked at her daughter quizzically.

"I never had a mother. Or at least a relationship with one. Over the years I've had my own problems to deal with. Were you ever there for me? Did you ever ask me if I needed you? You have no clue of some of the shit I've been through because you were too self-absorbed." Everything Amy had held in since she was a teenager came boiling to the surface. "Both you and Dad seemed to thrive on yelling at each other and you paid no attention to what was happening with your own children."

"That isn't true. Why are you being so cruel?"

"I'm tired, Mother. You started this when you began complaining the minute we got here. I've got some things weighing on my mind and I needed a peaceful visit. I didn't want this."

"What things are weighing on your mind? Tell me. I'll listen to you now."

"It's too late," Amy conceded. "Let's gather Ezra and the boys and go out to dinner."

"I can do better. I'll try," Mrs. Jacobs promised, her shoulders crumbling forward. "Really, I will try."

Amy shook her head, admonishing herself for losing her temper. "Me too, Mother. Me too."

"If you stumble on a rock, steady yourself and continue on. You may arrive late and be a bit weary, but open hearts will be waiting for you."
—Litsa Fotopoulos to Ana 1956

Chapter 17

Amy

Summer 1978

Amy nervously looked out the window, waiting for Sophia to arrive at her home. Despite graduating at the top of her class and being accepted into law school at Cornell, Amy felt like a failure. Worse than that, she'd been rejected, thrown aside and had been very, very careless.

Instinctively, she knew she could trust Sophia, but when she'd called and asked her to come over, she made her promise not to breathe a word of what she was about to tell to their other friends.

Amy flung the front door open the minute she saw Sophia's car pull up on the driveway. Waving Sophia over, she demanded she pick up her step.

"I'm coming," Sophia exclaimed, as Amy tugged her by the arm, dragged her upstairs to her bedroom, and shut the door behind them.

"You're making me very nervous. Sit down and stop pacing," Sophia ordered. "Whatever it is, we'll deal with it. Oh, God, you're not ill or anything?"

"No, I'm not ill … but I'm more like the *anything*," Amy said cryptically.

"What? Anything? What are you saying?"

"I'm … I'm … shit—pregnant."

Sophia didn't move, but her eyes met Amy's, and then drifted down to her stomach. "How pregnant are you?"

"How pregnant? You either are or you aren't."

Sophia put her hands on her hips and rolled her eyes. "How far along?"

"Oh, about ten weeks. So listen, no one knows, nobody—only you. And I was hoping … what I'm asking is, would you come with me to get an abortion?"

"Amy!" Sophia said in surprise. "You need to think this through. This is a big shock to you. It's a big decision, and I'm not sure it's the right one."

"It is for me." Amy couldn't imagine having a child. Not now, at twenty-two. She had plans, and having a child was a long way off. She wasn't sure if she even wanted to have a child at all. It wasn't something that crossed her mind, especially at this point in her life.

"Why me?" Sophia asked. "You know how I feel about abortion. How many arguments have we had on that subject?"

"This isn't the time to get all 'judgy' on me. I need you. I know I can trust you. Do you remember that time you asked me to support your decision to sneak around with Dean, even though I was dead against it? You told me that someday I might do something you didn't agree with, and you would be there to support me. Today is someday."

"You're right. Okay. Under one condition: you take a couple of days to think about it, and I mean *really* think about it. And about all the ramifications. Just because you have the right to choose doesn't mean the choice is easy. You will have to live with this decision the rest of your life. If this is what you want, I will take you there, and I'll do what I can to help you afterwards."

A week later, Amy was nervously seated in Sophia's metallic blue Camaro as Sophia drove her to her appointment. After pulling into the parking lot of a brick building and finding a vacant spot, neither girl made an attempt to exit the car.

"I wish you would say something—anything," Amy said softly. "Sprinkle me with your Sophia magic and make me feel better."

"You have your own magic and your own mind. You made your decision and you need to make peace with it. I can turn the car around if you've changed your mind."

"No." Amy shook her head. "I thought it through like you asked me to. This is the right thing for me. For my future. I'm not equipped to raise a child right now. But ..." Amy cast her eyes downward and played with the strap of her shoulder bag.

Sophia shifted her position and eyed Amy. "But, what? We are not going inside until I know what's on your mind."

Amy sucked in a deep breath and sighed. "I'm scared," she blurted out. "There! I said it. Me, Amy, who pretends to be afraid of absolutely nothing, is scared shitless."

"Anyone would be scared," Sophia smiled sympathetically. She took Amy's hand in hers and gave it a reassuring squeeze. "It's perfectly normal to feel that way, but you'll be asleep and it will be over in no time."

After a moment of silence, Amy exhaled nervously. "I've never been in a hospital or had an operation."

"I know. This isn't the same. You're not ill."

"But I've never had anything done. I don't even remember having a blood test."

"I'm sure you've had a blood test," Sophia said. "Who hasn't had blood drawn by the time they're our age?" She rubbed Amy's arm. "You don't have to do this."

Amy sucked in a deep breath. "Yes, I do." In resignation, she sighed. "I have to do this. I can't have this baby."

Steeling herself, Amy opened the car door, stood up and squared her shoulders, trying to build up her courage.

Sophia came around to her side of the car, wrapped her arm around her in comfort, and together they walked through the glass doorway.

After filling out the paperwork the receptionist had handed her, Amy was asked to follow her in order to speak with a counselor.

"Can my friend come in with me?"

"Oh, no. I'm sorry. Your friend will have to wait out here."

"I'll be right here, waiting for you," Sophia said, as she rose to embrace Amy.

Once Amy was seated in the counselor's office, they discussed her reasons for wanting to have the procedure and the woman asked her to confirm whether she was sure of her decision. When the counselor was satisfied, she called out for the nurse who would be prepping Amy.

Her immediate appearance unnerved Amy and a wave of anxiety ran through her knowing the moment she feared had come.

"My name is Leanne. I will be with you the whole time. Let's get you into a gown." Leanne led her through the doors, handed her a gown and pointed to a dressing room.

As Amy removed her clothing, she began to shake. It wasn't that she was cold, but she was frightened. Leanne seemed kind and had tried to put her at ease, but suddenly she felt alone and abandoned. The father of the life she carried wanted no part of it. He'd thrown her some cash and begged her to quietly abort. It devastated her to think he could dismiss her so easily when she needed him the most.

Her own parents knew nothing and she wondered how they would have reacted had she told them. But their own drama always took precedence over the children they'd brought into the world. Amy vowed she would never be that kind of a parent. She would not mother a child without giving them all that she had of herself.

"Are you ready?" Leanne called to Amy through the door.

"Yes," Amy replied, her voice cracking through her tears. Amy's heart began to race. This was really happening, she thought. A cold sweat chilled her body.

"Oh, honey … let's sit a minute here." Leanne held Amy's hand, observing her compassionately. Leanne was a tall, full-figured woman in her late forties. The wedge haircut and the perm indicated that Leanne made an attempt to stay current with the trends, but the way she applied her bright blue eye shadow and heavy black eyeliner exposed her age. "Now, I know you signed the papers, but we are obligated to ask you again. Are you sure this is what you want?"

"Yes. I'm just scared."

"That's understandable, but it's a routine procedure. You have nothing to worry about."

Leanne escorted Amy into the surgical room where the procedure would be performed. The room looked similar to ones that she'd only seen on television medical shows and the smell that permeated the air reminded her of walking into a high school biology class. There were all kinds of instruments near the operating table—instruments she didn't want within ten feet of her body.

Leanne instructed Amy to lie down on the operating table and told her the anesthesiologist would be in shortly.

Alcohol and another unidentifiable odor lingered in the air, making the already intimidating atmosphere even more threatening. The instruments arranged on the cart to her left did not help to calm her. The bright overhead light reflecting off the stainless steel scalpels, scissors and clamps advertised a perilous warning. Amy wiped away the beads of sweat that had formed above her lip.

"What is that for?" she asked, pointing to a long sharp object. "Is the doctor going to use that on me?" Panic thickened her voice.

"You lie down and don't look at anything. We will be giving you something to put you to sleep in a minute."

Amy's breathing became rapid. She didn't want to lie down. "If I'm asleep I won't know what's going on."

The nurse patted Amy's hand. "That's the idea. You lie back and relax now."

Amy tried. She really did. The bright lights overhead were blinding and reminded her of a torture scene from an old movie. The instruments looked barbaric and antiquated. She tried to tell herself this was done every day—that these were modern times and the doctors knew what they were doing.

But fear attacked every part of Amy's body and mind. Every muscle in her body stiffened and a heat from within her caused her face to flush. Sweat seeped from her pores and her throat tightened. She tried to take slow deep breaths to calm herself. *I'll be asleep. I won't feel a thing.*

Leanne took her by the hand when the anesthesiologist came in.

"Hello, Amy. I'm Dr. Stern. I'm going to administer your anesthetic."

Amy reluctantly nodded. The doctor was about to administer it when Amy stopped him. "No, wait! I'm not ready." Amy began breathing rapidly. She'd never had one before, but she knew she was having a panic attack. The walls were closing in on her and her eyes saw gray. Trapped and out of breath, Amy wanted out. "I can't do this!" she said, alarm coating her words. "I've changed my mind. I have to get out of here."

"Okay, okay," Leanne said calmly. "No one is going to force you to do anything you don't want." She rubbed Amy's shoulders. "If you're sure, I'll take you to get your clothing. But if you don't calm yourself you are going to hyperventilate."

When Amy emerged from the double swinging doors, Sophia jumped from her seat.

"That was faster than I expected," Sophia said.

Amy threw herself into Sophia's arms.

"Don't cry. I'll take care of you. Are you in pain?"

"No. I didn't go through with it."

Sophia pulled Amy away enough to see her face. "You didn't?" Sophia asked, puzzled. "What happened?"

"I got scared. Really terrified. I think I panicked when the doctor was about to put me to sleep. I just couldn't do it."

"Come on. Let's get you home." Sophia supported Amy by the waist and walked her to the car.

"What am I going to do now?" Amy's words were racked with fear and uncertainty.

"We'll work it out. Let's go home."

Amy cried all the way back to Honey Hill Circle. Instead of taking Amy home, Sophia took her two doors down to her own home.

"You can always try again next week. You'll be more prepared and you'll know what to expect," Sophia said.

"No. I'm never going back there. I can't do it. I'm a chicken. Nothing but a big coward! I didn't back out because I changed my mind. I backed out because I was scared to death. The worst thing I've ever been through was vaccine shots. I was terrified! I just can't do it!"

"So ... what now?" Sophia asked.

"I have no idea."

"You're going to have to tell your parents."

"No."

"What about the father?" Sophia asked. "Now that there will be a baby, the father should know. Did you tell him you were pregnant?"

Leaning against Sophia's headboard, Amy hugged a pillow. Her eyes were filled with a mixture of anger and hurt. "I told him. He told me to get rid of it. He threw some money at me to make sure I did."

"Who is this jerk?"

"I'd rather not say. It's not important anymore."

"You need to think about what to do next."

"I need to run away from my life," Amy said.

Sophia jumped off the bed. "That's a great idea! Let's go to Greece."

"Greece? This is no time for a vacation."

"It's the perfect place to clear your head and think about what you want to do. We can go to my family home there."

"I was supposed to leave next week for Africa to work with the relief organization I signed up with."

"That's out now. You can't go there while you're pregnant. Let me confide in my mom—"

"No!"

"Amy, hear me out. Let me talk to my mom about going to Greece. I think one adult should know what's going on. She would never tell anyone, but if we are going to stay at one of my family's homes we have to tell her. You need a solid plan and right now your only choices are to keep the baby or give it up for adoption."

Covering her face in her hands, Amy let out a frustrated scream. "This wasn't supposed to happen. My life is ruined!"

"Your life is not ruined. You'll just have to alter your plans a bit," Sophia said.

There was a rap on the door. "I thought I heard someone scream," Sophia's mother said as she opened the door and stepped inside. "Is everything okay in here?"

Amy looked up at Sophia. She knew her friend's eyes were begging her to confide in Sophia's mother. Amy closed her eyes and nodded slowly.

"No, Mom. Everything is not okay. Amy needs our help."

The girls discussed the situation with Ana, and she was very understanding.

"I do think Sophia is correct. A trip to our home in Greece will give you time to think. But Amy, don't you think you should speak to your parents?"

"Please Mrs. G, please don't say anything. I really can't deal with my parents right now. They'll end up making it about themselves and blaming each other. They think I'm going to Africa to volunteer, and they've showed little interest in my plans. Let them think that's where I'm going."

"You're their child. They should know where you are," Ana told her.

"I'm an adult. I'm twenty-two. I don't think I need their permission to do anything anymore."

"It doesn't matter if you are two or ninety-two, you will always be their daughter and they will always worry about you." Ana brushed her hand down the length of Amy's hair. "I will respect your wishes, with hesitation. But only because I want you to know that you can always come to me."

"Thank you, Mrs. G." She was truly thankful to have Sophia's mom to help her through this, yet at the same time, she felt empty inside. She knew her own mother would not stroke her hair and comfort her, and the man who had made her pregnant all but threw her away like the trash. If only he had been some random stranger it wouldn't have mattered to her. But he was far from a stranger and she had loved him.

Chapter 18

Amy

Summer 1978

For Amy, the three weeks that she and Sophia had spent in Greece together proved to be a perfect escape, and a place where she made some very important decisions.

They were in Aegina, seated on the elevated front porch of the Fotopoulos beach house overlooking the clear blue water as sunbeams reflected off its gentle waves. Fuchsia bougainvillea spilled over the sides of the whitewashed walls and down the stone steps that led to the golden sand. Amy picked a flower off the vine and brought it up to her nose. For all its delicate, paper-like beauty, it did not have a determinable scent. But the vibrant color and the abundance in which they grew were stunning in contrast to the white homes and the blue sky.

They sat contemplatively and ate a simple lunch. Plump red tomatoes, chunks of cucumber and slabs of feta cheese filled their plates. Sophia ripped a small piece of bread from a crusty loaf and spooned some *melitzanosalata* onto it. The eggplant dip was one of her favorites, and her yiayiá had given her some to take back to the beach house when they visited her in Athens the day before.

The girls spent most of their time on the island, exploring the tiny shops, tavernas and markets on the main street of the waterfront. They'd wander ancient ruins and sometimes offer to take a photo or two for a group of tourists. And Sophia even took Amy to Agios Nektarios, the holy monastery where tens of thousands went each year to pray to the patron saint for a miracle.

But they often took the ferry to Athens and spent the night at Sophia's yiayiá and pappou's home. Three days a week, Sophia went to the mainland to take ballet class. Amy would often join her for the ride and explore the streets of Athens. Other times, she'd stay back, using the time alone to reflect on her life and weigh her options.

"What would you like to do today?" Sophia asked.

"I don't know." Amy popped a quartered tomato in her mouth. "Mmm, why don't tomatoes taste like this in the States?"

"They do when you grow them yourself and eat them right off the vine. Do you want to go into town?"

"Yeah. Maybe we should. My clothes are starting to get tight. I'll look for some new things to wear."

Just beginning her second trimester, Amy was still slim and not yet showing the signs of carrying a child. But she had filled out just enough to make her clothing uncomfortable to wear.

Soon, they would be traveling up to Thessaloniki with Sophia's grandparents to meet with Father Vasili, Sophia's great uncle. It would be there, with the help of the elderly priest, that Amy would have her child. He'd found a family to adopt the newborn, and he thought it best for all parties that they get acquainted before the birth. The woman who would become the child's mother was a trained midwife and she had requested to deliver the baby. The only stipulation Amy had was that the child be raised in a Jewish home.

"When we return to Athens, I will have to leave a few days later," Sophia informed Amy. "I wish I could stay with you until you have the baby, but I can't."

"I know. I can't expect you to put your life on hold for me."

"Yiayiá and Pappou will take care of you and, if it's possible, I'll come back near your due date. Okay?"

"I'll be so bored here without you. I was thinking I might take a couple of classes at the university in Athens while I'm staying with your grandparents."

"We can get some information," Sophia said. "You don't want to waste your time though. What if the credits don't transfer? Doesn't each law school have a specific program?"

Amy shrugged. "Just something to look into. Let's go." She pushed away from the patio table. "I could use a walk around town."

A few days later after the long drive up to Thessaloniki, Spyro, Sophia's pappou, pulled into the parking lot of the hotel, got out of the car and stretched his legs. It was late and they were all hungry and tired. They checked into their rooms and went to get a bite to eat. They would meet with Father Vasili in the morning, and Amy was beginning to feel a bit anxious.

"Hey, is something wrong?" Sophia asked, gently rubbing circles on her back.

"This is all beginning to feel too real. What if I'm making a mistake? What if the family doesn't like me? Are they going to ask me embarrassing questions like how I got into this predicament? What if they change their minds and they don't want my baby?" Amy was shooting off questions and beginning to panic.

"Amy, Amy!" Sophia raised her hand. "You're getting ahead of yourself. You need to calm down and take this one step at a time. No one is going to judge you, and I'm sure this family wants your baby very much. And … if at any time *you* change your mind and feel giving up the baby is a mistake, then that is your right. You will know what to do when the time comes."

They were back in their hotel room and Amy sat down at the edge of the bed, resting her elbows on her knees and rubbing her face with her palms. "You're right. I'm just nervous."

The next morning, they drove to St. Demetrios Church to meet with Father Vasili. At first, Amy felt like an outsider, observing a reunion that emanated warmth and love beyond anything she'd ever witnessed. These people truly cared about each other, enjoyed each other's company, and there was an evident unspoken respect for the elderly priest. Kindness shone from his eyes and she had the sense that he held within him infinite wisdom.

Father Vasili extended his arms to welcome Amy. "Come. You may not have met me before, but I have known you since you were a little girl. Sophia has told me all about her friends back home."

He was so warm and compelling. Amy stepped into his arms, and when he hugged her she began to cry. She could feel his compassion and his understanding. He would keep her safe—she knew that instinctively. She had never felt so much love, and she knew that this man loved all of humanity in this way. She had heard the stories from the war, about how he risked his life to save people from torture and death, but it was more than that. There was something about him that radiated goodness.

"Are you ready to meet the family that will raise your child?" Father Vasili asked.

"Yes, I think so. I asked that they be Jewish. Are they? Not that I have anything against your faith, Father," Amy said, hoping she didn't insult this kind man who offered to help her.

"Not to worry," Father laughed. "I'm not offended. I fully understand."

"It's just that if I can't raise him ... or her, I would at least like to know he or she will be raised the way I was. Jewish."

"Of course. That is very important. Amy, during the war, we raised Jewish children and had to pretend they were Christian to protect them. But once the war was over, all efforts were made to reunite them with their Jewish relatives. We understand all too well because there have been many times in our own history when we were not allowed to practice our Christianity."

"Thank you for arranging this for me," Amy said.

"These are very good people. I think you will be pleased." Father Vasili turned to Spyro and nodded, "*Eíne kaíros ya mas na páme* —it is time for us to go," he repeated for Amy.

Amy sat silently in the car during the short ride to the home of the couple that would adopt her child. She paid little attention to the landscape or the neighborhood until they stopped in front of a modest but charming home.

As they got out of the car, Sophia looped her arm in Amy's and nodded her head encouragingly. After that, everything seemed to happen so quickly. Amy was welcomed by Revekka and David, who wanted to know all about her, but never once asked about her circumstances. In turn, they gave her a brief history on their lives and why they were in need of adoption.

The young couple had been married for seven years. They were ready to start a family and had been trying for several years, but the only time Revekka was able to conceive, she'd had a miscarriage, and had not been able to fall pregnant since.

"I can promise you, we will be good parents. Father Vasili can vouch for us. He's known me my entire life," Revekka said to Amy.

With a hint of trepidation, Amy looked directly into Revekka's hopeful dark brown eyes. "You must be wondering why I would give up my own baby. We can't be more than a few years apart in age."

Revekka reached out and clasped her hands in Amy's. With a gentle smile, she assuaged Amy's fear of judgment. "I am certain you have thought this through and want what is best for your child and I am grateful that you are trusting me to care for him … or her."

By the time they left, Amy was confident that David and Revekka were the right choice in parents to raise her baby. They were loving and kind, and she knew that she would feel comfortable with them when she returned to Thessaloniki to have her child. *Her child.* She had to stop thinking of this baby as hers. It would be theirs, and the sooner she trained her mind to understand this concept, the easier it would be to hand the baby over. This wasn't in her plan. She didn't want a baby. The only reason it existed at all was because she had been foolishly in love with a man who didn't give two shits about her, and she was too scared to have an abortion. So giving this baby to someone who would want it and raise it properly would be easy. It was the right thing to do. Or at least that's what she told herself.

~ Melitzanosalata ~

3 large eggplants
1 head of garlic
¼ cup seasoned breadcrumbs
½ cup extra virgin olive oil
1 teaspoon balsamic vinegar
Juice from ½ of a large lemon
3 tablespoons freshly snipped dill
1 teaspoon sugar
1 tablespoon paprika
Dash of cayenne pepper
Salt & pepper to taste

Pre-heat oven to 400°

Place the eggplant on a rack in a baking dish. Puncture each eggplant in several places so that excess water will drain as it roasts.

Place a head of garlic on aluminum foil. Slice off the top and drizzle with olive oil. Wrap the foil around the garlic and place it in the same baking pan as the eggplant.

Roast for 1 hour. Remove from the oven and cool for 45 minutes to an hour.

Peel away the skin of the eggplant and remove as much of the seeds as possible. Squeeze the roasted garlic from the skin.

In a food processor pulse together the eggplant, garlic, breadcrumbs, olive oil, balsamic vinegar, lemon, dill, sugar, cayenne, paprika, salt and pepper until fully blended.

*Keep in mind that each eggplant is different in size and water content. You may need to adjust the amount of oil or breadcrumbs to achieve the consistency you desire.

Serve on crostini, with crackers, pita, or with crusty bread.

"There will always be evil around us and we must be on our guard at all times."
—Evanthia to her brother Vasili 1931

Chapter 19

Sophia

Summer 1978

Although Sophia was pleased to see her great uncle, and to know that he had been instrumental in finding parents for her dear friend's newborn, she was glad when they returned to Athens. Sophia only had a few days left before she had to return to the States and she wanted to make sure Amy would be comfortable in Greece without her. Additionally, she wanted the opportunity to have one last heart to heart with her friend before returning home.

Amy had made some very important decisions during this stay in Greece, and although Sophia knew her grandparents would be good to her friend, Sophia needed to be reassured that Amy was confident with the decisions she'd made. And until she left, Sophia was determined to give Amy nothing less than her undivided attention.

But unfortunately, that wasn't to be.

When they arrived back at the Fotopoulos home, they were greeted by ear-splitting music. Yiayiá and Pappou looked at each other, alarmed.

"I don't remember leaving the radio on, Yiayiá," Sophia said.

"No, *kouklitsa*, you didn't. Spyro, take the valises and I'll shut off the radio."

"No. Let me go in first." The sound of Spyro's shoes tapping on the tiles as he walked down the foyer could barely be heard over the loud music.

From behind the walls leading to the kitchen, a figure emerged. "There you are! I've been wondering about you. I come to visit and no one is here to greet me."

Irini! What was she doing here? Sophia wondered. She could feel the blood drain from her face, and the expression of irritation on her grandparents' faces also showed their displeasure with her.

Irini stood, scantily clad in a lime green Norma Kamali one-piece ruched bathing suit that mimicked a bikini. In her hand was a glass of champagne.

Sophia had only met her briefly once before, and if she thought her to be flashy and tasteless then, well now she looked downright cheap and tawdry. A twenty-year-old super-model could wear that suit, not a forty-five-year-old wannabe sex symbol.

"We weren't expecting you. Why didn't you call to let us know you were coming?"

Sophia heard a hint of nervousness in her yiayiá's voice.

Irini waved her champagne in the air as she spoke. "Eh! A last minute thought. I needed a vacation."

"Where is your husband?" Spyro asked.

Irini's laugh was a low rumble. "That's who I need a vacation from. Why all the questions? If I didn't know better, I would think you weren't happy to see me."

"Of course we're glad to see you," Yiayiá Sophia said as she walked toward her daughter and embraced her. "We were just taken by surprise, that's all. Spyro. Come give your daughter a proper hello."

Spyro walked over to Irini and pecked her on the cheek. "Go put some clothes on," he huffed. Turning to his wife he said, "I'll take the bags upstairs."

"Let's go to my room," Sophia whispered to Amy. She wanted to get as far away from her aunt as possible.

"Sophia, darling," Irini called out in her best movie star imitation, "aren't you going to greet your Theiá Irini?"

Sophia made no move to approach her aunt. She lifted her hand and waved. "Hi."

"Didn't my sister teach you better than that?" She walked over to her, grabbed Sophia's face in her hands and kissed both of her cheeks. "That's more like it."

Sophia used the back of her hand to wipe off the orange lipstick that she was sure had smeared her face. "This is my friend, Amy."

"Amy." Irini examined her from head to toe. "What are you girls up to?"

"Nothing special," Sophia said. She turned toward her yiayiá. "We're going to change our clothes and come down to help with dinner."

The girls disappeared, climbing the staircase and retreating to their room.

"I can't believe she's here," Sophia said incredulously. "If my mother knew, she would make me get on the next plane home."

"That bad, huh?" Amy asked.

"Worse. You saw her. I only have to put up with her for three days. I'm not sure how long she'll be here or how much you will have to deal with her. Don't tell her anything and stay away from her. She's a demon."

"What do you think she would do to me? She doesn't even know me."

"Trust me. My mom told me stories that I won't repeat. Let's just say she seems to hurt everyone she meets."

"Your grandmother seemed conflicted about having her here but your grandfather looked pissed."

"I've never told anyone this before," Sophia whispered, "but I'll tell you if you promise to lock it away and never repeat it."

"Okay, but why are you whispering?"

"I don't trust her. She could be listening."

"Right. Sex bomb out there has nothing better to do than to eavesdrop on the two of us."

"Well, if you don't want to hear about how my aunt almost got my Pappou charged with murder, then I won't tell you."

"What?"

"You heard me. She was always a problem child. So, this is what I've been told. Irini was a nasty girl who got along better with the boys than with the girls, if you get my drift. Pappou was super strict—too much so— according to my mom, but my aunt never listened anyway. By the time she was in her teens, she knew how to string boys along, and men for that matter. She would use them until she was done with them."

Amy moved closer to Sophia. "Done how?"

"My mom said the talk around town was embarrassing, but there was nothing they could do. She was uncontrollable. When she was around twenty this guy had been pursuing her for months. She would go out with him and let him buy her things and then the next week she would make sure he would see her with someone else."

"She liked to play games," Amy said.

"Hmmm. It was more than that. She liked to screw with their heads to the point that they became obsessed with her. Word got around that she would have sex with him, tell him she loved him and that he was the one she wanted. Then it would make him nuts when he saw her with someone else. He told her he wanted to marry her and she said someday when they were older. He showered her with gifts and wanted to be with her every free minute he could. She used her father's rules as a way of keeping him away."

"Sneaky. So, why did she do this? Did she like the guy or not?" Amy asked.

"I got this story from my mom. She's never been able to figure out my aunt's motives. How would she know why someone would do something so mean? She guessed it was for power—to see how far she could take him before his breaking point, I suppose."

"What do you mean by 'breaking point?' Like, he couldn't be bothered anymore, or that he was completely crushed?"

"Considering what happened," Sophia pondered, "I'd say until he was completely crushed and heartbroken."

"Crap! So what happened?"

"He killed himself. He shot himself right through the heart."

"Oh my God!"

"He did it in his back yard and at first they thought he was murdered."

"And they thought your grandfather did it?"

"They questioned him because the police had interviewed friends and neighbors and you know how it is, people love to gossip. They were more than happy to tell what they knew about the guy—Taki—I think that was his name."

"Taki?" Amy covered her mouth, stifling a laugh. "That's a stupid name."

Sophia waved her off. "It's a common nickname. Anyway, everyone saw what she was doing to him. She tormented him. But they figured my Pappou found out he had sex with his daughter and killed him."

"Really? If there was a murder for every time a father found out about a man having sex with his daughter, there would be a lot fewer men in the world. Something more must have happened to make the authorities suspect him," Amy said.

"When the police came to speak to Irini, she said she broke up with him because he was stalking her. She lied and said he got rough with her when she told him she didn't want him anymore."

"Didn't she worry that story might implicate your grandfather? Any father might want to protect his daughter if she were in danger."

"I think in her sick mind her story justified what he did to himself— as though it proved he was guilty of hurting her. They were trying to find evidence to arrest my Pappou, but then the police found a suicide note hidden away in his desk drawer."

"Man, this is better than my mother's soap opera."

"Glad my family can provide you with entertainment," Sophia said sardonically.

"What did the note say?"

"It revealed all the games my aunt had played. On the night he took his life, she'd asked him to meet her at a certain time in the park. He asked her to marry him and she promised she would give him her answer that evening. When he arrived, she was not alone. As he put it, another man had his hands all over her. She laughed at him and told him that was her answer. She wouldn't be marrying him or anyone else. His letter said she'd humiliated him and he was heartbroken. He didn't want to live anymore."

"So she fucked with his head for months and drove him insane, literally. Why would anyone do that?"

Sophia blew out a loud breath. "It wasn't months. I think it was closer to a year. I have no answer. I think some people are just born mean. After the whole mess, my mom told me that Pappou called his brother and asked if he could send her to New York to live with them."

"They got rid of the scandalous daughter," Amy joked. "Smart move."

"Well, from the little I heard about it at that time, Uncle Tasso had his hands full. But it wasn't long before she took up with some man and moved in with him. No one ever saw her after that until I met her at Aunt Litsa's funeral."

"Is this her first time back here?"

"I don't think so. I think she's been back once or twice. We don't really talk about her."

The girls changed their clothes and went down to help with dinner. Yiayiá was peeling potatoes while Irini read a magazine. When they finished preparing the meal and setting the table, they sat down to eat on the patio.

Irini tried to impress the girls with her travels and bragged about the money she spent in the exclusive stores she shopped in, but Amy and Sophia refused to gush over her.

"Amy, darling, I must ask. How is it that a skinny girl like yourself is so full in the tummy?" Irini eyed her closely. "Pregnant?"

"Um, yes." Sophia kicked her under the table. She could see that Irini had taken Amy by surprise.

"And where is the father of this baby?" Irini pried.

"He's not in the picture."

"Hmm. Because he doesn't want to be, or because you haven't told him?"

"Irini, leave the girl alone," her mother insisted.

"I'm asking a simple question, Mamá. What's the harm?" Irini turned her attention back to Amy. "You have to be careful when you hide the truth. You never know what the consequences will be down the road." Irini sipped her wine and eyed Sophia over her glass. "When you don't tell a man he's fathered a child, it can come back to haunt you. Do you agree, Sophia?"

Sophia did not understand why her aunt was staring at her so intently. "I—"

"That's enough!" Spyro demanded. "This discussion is over."

"Calm down, Spyro." His wife laid her hands on his. "Let's not argue at the table, especially in front of our guest."

"Tell that to your daughter! Always looking to stir up trouble."

"You're always looking to silence me, Babá. I was only trying to make conversation with my niece and her friend." Irini narrowed her eyes, challenging her father.

"You don't fool me for one second. I know what you're up to." Spyro slapped his napkin onto his plate and rose from the table. "Watch your words."

A sly smile crossed Irini's face. "What words?"

"Irini, please," Yiayiá Sophia pleaded. "No more."

Sophia looked at Amy and shrugged her shoulders. She was confused. Something more was going on here than she understood.

"Eh, I'm bored, anyway. I'm going out," Irini said, pushing her seat away from the table.

"And where are you going?" Spyro asked.

Sophia twisted her face in disgust when Irini cackled with evil laughter.

"I'm a grown woman, not a child. I don't answer to anyone." She got up and began to walk from the room. Halting, she pivoted, turning toward her father. "I have a date." Irini's lip curled upward in satisfaction.

Spyro's nostrils flared. "You're a married woman."

Irini looked at her father blankly and walked away.

"Okay, you were right. She's something. I'm not sure what, but she's something else all right." Amy shook her head in disbelief. "Two more days and you'll be gone. It won't be the same here without you and I'll be stuck here with witchy woman."

Sophia slapped her hand over her mouth and giggled. "Do you think The Eagles know her?"

"If the song fits …"

"I don't think she will stay long. I asked Yiayiá and she said she didn't know but Irini tends to get bored fast, or she picks a fight and leaves. I feel bad for my grandparents. Yiayiá tried to defend her and say that she's not all bad. She still has hopes that her daughters will make up someday. I didn't have the heart to tell her that from the way my mother reacted when she saw Irini at Aunt Litsa's funeral, there is a zero chance of that ever happening."

Chapter 20

Amy

November 1978

The months flew by surprisingly fast considering Sophia had gone back to the States to tour with her ballet troupe. Amy stayed in Athens at the home of Spyro and Sophia Fotopoulos, Sophia's grandparents, and they doted on her. But her pregnancy didn't stop her sense of independence, so she insisted on helping out with the meals and chores. She also enrolled in two international law classes that although she knew wouldn't count toward her degree could only aid her when she entered into law school as she'd planned to before her unexpected detour.

In an odd way, Greece, even under these circumstances, had been good for her. The lifestyle was far different from what she was accustomed to. The people had an appreciation for their surroundings, and nothing was taken for granted. Hours could be spent over a cup of coffee, debating or catching up on news while the sun warmed their skin.

Family came first. She'd never seen her mother's eyes light up the way these mothers' and grandmothers' eyes brightened when speaking of their children. She hadn't spoken to her own mother in months.

Of course, her mother thought she was in Africa tending to the under-privileged. To get around her lie, she sent the letters she'd written to her mother via a friend working in Africa and asked her to mail them for her.

Sophia's grandparents, who she now referred to as Yiayiá and Pappou, were so warm and wonderful to her that she didn't want to leave their protective cocoon. But in early November, it was time to head back to Thessaloniki as the time drew near for the baby's due date.

Reality had Amy shaking in fear the night before they left, and Yiayiá took Amy into her arms to comfort her.

"You have nothing to fear," Yiayiá cooed, taking Amy's face in her hands. "It's all perfectly natural."

"I'm afraid it will hurt or something will go wrong."

"Oh, *koukla*, it will hurt, but nothing will go wrong. You are a strong, healthy girl. Everything has gone as it should so far. There is no need for concern."

"How can you be so sure?" Amy asked.

"Nothing is certain in this life. But I did bear two children of my own and, at that time, the conditions weren't as advanced. I was also a lot younger than you. I had witnessed births, so I knew what to expect, but still ... I was only fifteen."

"Fifteen!?" Amy was not easily shocked. But fifteen!? At fifteen she couldn't imagine the responsibility of a child. The biggest decision she and her friends made at that age was which movie to see on a Friday night.

"That's a story for another day," Yiayiá said. "But the point is that I was young, still a newlywed, and had little experience in life, and I was fine. I had people with me who loved me and that made all the difference."

Amy drew her eyes to the floor. Lifting Amy's chin with her gentle fingers, Yiayiá's kind eyes held her gaze. "You will have loved ones with you. I love you."

Amy had never felt so vulnerable or sentimental. She'd never had this before in a parent—warmth, kindness, and acceptance.

"When I tell you to push, lean forward and push as hard as you can," Revekka instructed Amy.

It was late November and Amy had gone into labor the evening before. The contractions were mild at first—just a tightening in her stomach every seven minutes or so. But as the night went into the early morning hours, she could no longer ignore what felt like a tourniquet around her stomach—until it ceased—and then came back again.

Ten hours later, Amy was ready to push. With Yiayiá on one side of the hospital bed and Revekka on the other, they encouraged her and gave her the strength and support to fight through. Her hair was matted with sweat and her face pale from the intense pain of the last few contractions, which felt as though they lasted an eternity, but she mustered the energy to push with all she had as she grunted and leaned forward.

"That was terrific! Rest a minute and you'll know when to push again," Revekka instructed.

Amy turned to look at Yiayiá with questioning eyes. "It's all going very well. This is how it is," Yiayiá reassured her. She wiped the beads of sweat from Amy's brow with a white cotton towel.

After an hour, Amy grunted as she pushed, knowing it felt different this time.

"Push again! Now!" Revekka called out as a head appeared. Another push and shoulders emerged. Amy screamed. One last push and the tiny human being that occupied Amy's womb was no longer a mystery.

"It's a boy!" Revekka cried out with joy. Her eyes glistened with unshed tears of happiness for the child that she would call her son.

Amy fell back in exhaustion. Tears streamed down the corners of her eyes, dripping onto the pillow. Thousands of emotions ran through her. The ordeal she'd been through for the last twelve hours, not to mention the past nine months, and now the reality of seeing what had been inside her all this time, was overwhelming. Somehow, it had never been real. She knew the baby was there intellectually, but it had never fully sunk in.

Now she was expected to hand over this tiny life to another woman—this life she had inside her only minutes ago—and walk out of the hospital as if the whole ordeal had never happened. But could she do that?

From the corner of her eye, Amy watched as Revekka washed the child and wrapped him in a swaddling blanket.

"Would you like to hold him?" Revekka asked.

The words caught in Amy's dry throat. Her answer came in a shake of her head and a regretful tear.

"*Dóse mou to moró*," Yiayiá said. "Give me the baby," she repeated in English, turning to Amy. "Look at him. Hold him. You love him enough to make sure he goes to a good home. Love him enough to embrace him."

"I can't. I just can't." Turning her head, she couldn't bear to look at him.

Two days later, Amy and the baby were ready to be released from the hospital. Amy would be going back to Athens with Yiayiá and Pappou. The baby would be going home with his parents, Revekka and David.

Amy walked by the nursery window. Inside, Revekka held the baby in her arms, David by her side. The child was dressed and ready to go home—home with somebody else.

He had been inside her for nine months—kicking and moving about, reminding her everyday of the life that she had created. And as much as she tried to separate herself from him, she couldn't. He was her son and she loved him. Amy's chest tightened and, in a split second decision she entered the nursery and approached them.

"I've changed my mind."

Revekka was stricken with a look of terror. "What?" she squeaked out.

"I've changed my mind. Can I hold him before you go?"

Revekka's sigh was loud and breathy. Her relief was evident. "Of course." She placed the baby in Amy's arms.

"What's his name?"

"Samuouél."

"Is that Greek for Samuel?"

"Yes."

"I like it. Would it be okay if I checked in on him once in a while? Maybe find out how he's doing?"

Revekka gave her husband an ambivalent look. With a serious expression, David nodded imperceptibly. Turning back to Amy, she said, "I think that would be fine."

Amy handed Samuouél back to his mother. "Good-bye little Sam," she said, his name catching in her throat. "Have a beautiful life." Abruptly she darted for the door before anyone could witness the tears she was about to shed.

Chapter 21

Sophia

January 2000

Sophia sat on Grace Whitman's office couch, waiting for her to enter and for their session to begin. Although originally she was opposed to the idea of counseling, Sophia had to admit that Grace helped her tackle the challenges she'd avoided facing over the last year.

Dean was completely understanding and supportive when Sophia explained why they needed to put the idea of moving on hold for the time being, and made it clear that she was his first priority and was willing to do whatever it took to take the pressure off her.

Evvie had become somewhat more cooperative, thanks to Grace's suggestion to look through old photo albums with the twins. Sophia had sat between the two of them on her bed, examining each page and reminiscing the days when their father was alive. Together, they laughed at some of the memories they shared with him, but cried at others knowing that he was lost to them forever.

Sophia was beginning to feel better and she knew it was due to the assistance Grace was giving her. Grace never forced or insisted, but she made herself clear that if Sophia wanted to regain happiness in her life, then she must be willing to do the work. Grace suggested that Sophia resume dancing. It wasn't until she'd gotten back into the studio that she remembered how good it felt for her body and her soul. Stepping onto the dance floor took a Herculean effort at first, but once Sophia took that first step, the familiar comfort of the movement combined with the music transported her to a state where nothing existed in her mind but the creative process that had been absent for so long.

"Thank you for waiting," Grace said, as she entered her office. "I had an urgent matter to discuss and it couldn't wait."

"It's not a problem," Sophia smiled.

"Well, I'm going to get right to the point, Sophia. You've made great progress these past few months from what I can see. I think you have become comfortable with the suggestions I've given you so far, and they seem to be working for you."

Sophia nodded in agreement

"I think it's time for you to take the next step."

A nervous shiver traveled up Sophia's spine.

"It's time we talk about your biological father."

Sophia sighed. "Why? He's nothing to me."

"Isn't he, though? Like it or not, he is something to you, and you need to find a place for him and make peace with it."

"His place is not with me. That was the choice he made long ago, and now I am making mine."

"Sophia," Grace began, "that is not entirely true and you know it. You told me yourself that your mother never told him you existed."

"But there's more to the story, and Aunt Soula told me everything." The Kleenex in Sophia's hand was twisted around her finger. Unraveling it, she smoothed it out and then began twisting it tightly again. "He suspected that I might be his and he took money from my uncle to promise to stay out of our lives. Do I want a father like that?" Sophia lashed out bitterly.

"I'm not saying this for him. He's not my patient. You are. The man is dying. If you don't go to see him, you will never get the full story—his story. It might be your only chance to get to know who he is beyond what you've been told." Grace leaned back in her chair. "You also can tell him how you feel. Try to get a dialogue going. You owe it to yourself."

"I don't know if I can bring myself to do that. I may have no feelings for him, but I'm not cruel. How could I tell this man on his deathbed how I feel about him?"

"Let's take a different approach. I'm going to say that this man did you and your mother a favor." Grace waited for Sophia's reaction.

"A favor!?"

"If your parents hadn't split up, you would have been raised by the two of them, correct?"

"I suppose. Although I can't imagine my mother staying with him." "But if they had, how different would your life be?" Grace leaned forward, waiting for Sophia's answer.

"Very different, I guess."

"Your mother wouldn't have met and married Alex. He wouldn't have raised you. Would she have been happy with a man who cheated on her continuously?"

"No. That's why she divorced him."

"Would you have been the same woman you are today if you had been raised by him?"

Sophia shook her head, narrowing her eyes. She knew what Grace was doing. "I don't want to betray my father by seeing *that* man."

"Ah. Now we're getting somewhere. Talk to your father and see what he says. From everything you've told me about him, I suspect he'll be okay with it. Alex knows how much you love him." Grace steepled her fingers, then tapped the tip of her nose. "Are you at all curious about Jimmy?"

"Sure. It's only natural. But I know a little bit about him from when I met him in Chicago. Before I knew who he really was."

"Go see him. Time is running out. You received that letter months ago."

Sophia sighed heavily and sat silently. Grace kept her eyes fixed on her, waiting patiently for a response.

"You're asking too much of me. There was a reason my mother kept him away from me, and never even told me about him. I need to respect that and trust her reasons for taking such an extreme position."

"You need to consider yourself first. No one else. What is healthy for Sophia? Whatever you decide, you will have to live with it. There are no second chances here."

Sophia rolled her eyes. "I won't make any promises, but I'll give it some thought, and discuss it with Dino and my dad."

Almost a week later, Sophia had yet to make a decision or address the issue with her father or husband. What she did do was drive herself crazy with worry. What was expected of her, and who was she to consider? Would her father feel betrayed if she went to her birth father's side in his last moments? Did she even owe Jimmy her presence? He had never been a part of her life and she had not even known he'd existed until recently. And what would her mother want her to do? Ana had done everything in her power to keep Sophia away from a man she considered unworthy of knowing he had fathered a child.

But if Sophia refused to go, and ignored a dying man's plea, would she be able to live with herself? The internal storm in her head was clouding her judgment.

Sitting on the rug by the fireplace, her feet tucked under her, Sophia stared trance-like at the flames jumping between the logs. Lost in thought, she failed to hear the hum of the garage door, or the tapping of heels across the tile.

Dean seated himself behind Sophia, wrapping his arms and legs around her and resting his chin on her shoulder. Wordlessly, she shifted her position to look at him solemnly, noticing the sadness in his eyes. Turning, she re-focused her attention back on the sparks crackling within the wood.

"Do you still love me?" Dean asked quietly.

Sophia's lip quivered and a stream of tears rolled down her face, landing on the arms that desperately bound Sophia to Dean.

"I've never loved you more," she told him. "It hurts that you would ask."

"I feel like you're slipping away from me, and I don't know what to do to stop it."

"Some things have nothing to do with you, and as much as I know you want to, you can't fix them."

"Just don't shut me out," Dean pleaded.

"It's not intentional."

"I hope not, because I'm staying right here until you let me in." Dean hugged Sophia tightly, caressing her. "Two bodies; one soul. Don't forget that. When you hurt, I hurt."

The conflict within her was consuming, and Sophia grew frustrated with her inability to take a stand one way or another. But an unexpected phone call from Amy shifted her perspective.

"Do you have a few minutes?" Amy asked Sophia.

"Yes, of course."

"I did it. I contacted Samuel's parents to find out if they thought he might be interested in meeting me."

"And what did they say? Were they surprised to hear from you after all these years?" Sophia was genuinely concerned for her friend. For several years Amy had kept in touch with Revekka and David. Occasionally, the couple would send her a photo and assure her that she need not worry about the child she left for them to raise. He was a happy, well-adjusted child with a kind spirit and a sharp mind.

But after Amy gave birth to Adam, it felt wrong to continue contact. Omission was deception and deception bred guilt. Her sons would never know one another—or be aware of the other's existence.

She would have to let Samuel go in order for him to live the life he was meant to have.

But there would not be a single day that Amy wouldn't think of him. Sophia was sure of that, and she'd been correct. She made it a point to call Amy each year on his birthday. More to check on Amy's frame of mind, and often she'd been quiet, contemplative or lost in thought.

"They hadn't expected to hear from me," Amy explained. "They were curious as to why I'd reached out now."

Cradling the phone between her ear and shoulder, Sophia had been canvassing the house for mislaid items while tidying up. Walking into the kitchen, she planted herself at a counter stool, focusing her full attention on her friend. "I'm curious about that too. Why is it suddenly so important for you to meet him now that he's a grown man?"

"He recently turned twenty-one," Amy said. "And it hit me that I missed it all—his entire life." There was silence between the phone lines until Amy blurted out, "It's because of you. That's why I need to see him."

"Me?"

"Observing you, and the lack of interest you have in knowing your biological father, struck me. The parallel is clear. I'm Jimmy and you are Samuel. No one gave you the choice to make your own conclusions about the circumstances of how you came into this world or about your father. The choice was made for you. You don't know your father's story and I am not sure what Samuel has been told about me."

"I think the situations are very different."

"Not really," Amy argued. "I don't want him to hate me. I think it's important for a child to know that they weren't just tossed to the curb."

Sophia sighed. "Amy, you didn't toss him to the curb. You made sure he had a good home."

"He had remarkable parents. After corresponding back and forth, they told me Samuel had always known that he'd been adopted. They told him at a very young age. Sophia, they gave him my address and this morning I received a letter from him."

"Oh my! That's wonderful." Suddenly uncertain, she asked, "It is wonderful, isn't it?"

"Can I read you the letter?"

"Of course."

Amy cleared her throat. "Dear Ms. Jacobs, My mother said you requested contact with me. I would be interested to meet you. My parents told me long ago that I had a birth mother in the United States. I would like you to know that I have been aware of this for many years and I've wondered about you. I can only imagine what led to the decision you'd made, and I am anxious to hear your story for it is my history as well."

Sophia could hear Amy pause to sip a drink. "It sounds positive so far," Sophia told her. "Go on."

"I would like our meeting to be one of possibilities, not one of regrets. Please be assured that I have had a wonderful life with the best parents any child could wish for. I thank you for that. And I thank you for my life. You brought me into this world and there is no greater gift than life." Amy choked out a strangled sob. "I look forward to hearing from you, Samuouél."

It took a few moments to process, but Sophia's eyes welled up with tears in response to this extraordinary young man, who was, apparently, wise beyond his years. After discussing some preliminary ideas on where and how mother and son should meet, Sophia ended the call.

Amy's son did not shun her. He thanked her. He found it within his heart to find goodness and not to lay blame. Suddenly, Sophia was ashamed of her behavior. Her bitterness and hurt had hardened her heart to a dying man whose only chance at peace may be the hope of redemption. This was not who she wanted to be. Knowing she couldn't live her life with a stone lodged in her heart, she was certain what her next step must be.

"The most moral and just acts can be the most rewarding and the most frightening." —Evanthia 1944

Chapter 22

Sophia

January 2000

By the time Sophia's plane landed at O'Hare Airport in Chicago and she arrived at the hotel, she was a bundle of nerves. She wondered if she had made a mistake by asking Dean not to come with her. At the time, her argument for going alone made perfect sense to her, but now she wasn't so sure. Sophia mulled over their last discussion on the subject, and as adamant as she was to have her way, a wave of uncertainty had passed through her as Dean unexpectedly relented.

"This is something I have to do on my own," she'd said to him. "I'm not sure what to expect. I don't know how bad his condition is, or how I'll feel when I see him, or even what we will say to each other."

"That's exactly why I want to be there. This isn't something you should confront on your own," Dean said.

"I disagree. I need to face him by myself. You tend to be overprotective and I don't want you worrying about me. I won't break, Dino," Sophia told her husband the night before she left.

Sophia rested her hand on his cheek and a twinge of guilt twisted inside her. She'd put him through so much these last few months. And he stood by her and had seen her through every crisis, but it was a lot for a newly married man, even this man whose soul was embedded in hers from the day she was born.

Now, as she gathered the courage to leave the hotel and make her way to the hospital, she wished her Dino was by her side. But if she wanted to be whole again—strong and capable the way she'd been before—she knew she had to get through this on her own.

"I'd like to visit Jimmy Pappas," Sophia told the receptionist at the visitor's desk at University Hospital.

"Hmm. Let's see," the elderly woman said, frowning. "I have a Pappas, but the first name is ..." she hesitated. "I'll spell it out. I-a-k-o-v-o-s."

"Oh, yes. That would be him." Sophia had never thought about what his Greek name would be. *Of course, Iakovos,* she thought.

The woman handed her a blue pass and directed her to the elevators. A few minutes later, Sophia found herself outside Jimmy's room. Frozen, Sophia was unable to take the next step. A chill came over her body. Fighting an overwhelming desire to back away and run, she steadied herself against the wall, closed her eyes and drew in a deep breath to calm her nerves. Turning, she stepped into the room—there was no backing out now!

The man lying in the hospital bed had little resemblance to the man she had met in Chicago when she was touring with her ballet company. More recently, she accidently came across him at her mother's grave a few days after her passing. But the man she saw now had aged considerably in the two years since she had last seen him.

Frightfully thin and sallow in color, the frail stranger lay asleep. Jimmy was held captive by machines that monitored his vital functions and an IV that left a trail of bruises down his arm.

What if it was too late? Was he capable of speech at this point?

Would she ever hear his truth? Taking a seat beside his bed, she let her mind wander. She tried to imagine this man in his twenties when he must have been married to her mother. What did this man have that had drawn her to him? She couldn't envision her mother with anyone other than Alex, and this man was nothing like the father who raised her.

Jimmy, she imagined, had a lifetime of disappointments and heartaches. Triumphs and milestones. It was common to forget this when looking at the elderly. Each person was a stitch woven into a greater tapestry—timeless tales to be retold from generation to generation, in the hope of preserving a heritage and teaching salient lessons.

It seemed natural for Sophia to rest her hand over his. It wasn't out of devotion, but merely a human kindness. The man was alone, and no one deserved that.

Jimmy stirred and slowly opened his eyes. Sleepy confusion stared back at her. "How did you know?" Jimmy asked weakly.

"Your friend, Homer, called me."

"And you came."

Sophia sucked in a breath. "I came."

"I don't want your pity."

"What do you want?" Sophia asked flatly.

A barely imperceptible smile crossed his lips, and for a second there was a light in his eyes that had not been there moments before. "What don't I want? I want my body not to fail me. I want my youth back, a chance to go back and to change … certain circumstances. I want your mother to be alive and I want to know her child … my child."

Sophia gasped at the mention of her mother. Stiffening, she turned away, the tension evident in her posture. She glared out the window, attempting to tamp down her resentment. "We only get one shot in this life," she said, pivoting to face him. "We do the best we can," she added dryly. "What have your doctors told you? Sophia asked, changing the subject.

"There's not much hope for me. I suspect that is why Homer called you. The last wish for the dying."

"I don't know much about cirrhosis of the liver. What are the treatments? Do you know what caused it? I read drinking too much was one way."

"Yes. My vices always seem to pay me back," Jimmy said weakly. "There's not much to be done at this point. I was never one for visiting doctors and I was diagnosed too late. It wasn't until I was too weak to get out of bed or feed myself that Homer insisted I see a doctor. I'd been hemorrhaging from the abdomen and, according to the doctors, my liver was barely functioning."

"Is there anything I can get you?"

"You're here. That's enough."

Sophia nodded. Jimmy closed his eyes, drifting off.

Sophia took a seat in the high-back faux leather chair. Resting her head back, she closed her eyes and contemplated what to do next. She wasn't sure where to go from here—what he expected of her or what she expected of herself. She had come to see him, making the obligatory appearance. Sophia could return home, satisfied that she'd done the right thing, and resume her life without a further thought. But could she, really? She had not even scratched the surface with this man.

Various hospital staff wandered in and out of the room—a custodial team who emptied trash and cleaned the bathroom—nursing aids, checking Jimmy's blood pressure, and finally a nurse who replaced his empty IV bag with a new sack of fluid.

It was an odd situation sitting here with a virtual stranger, and Sophia didn't know what role she was to play or what her responsibility was. Did she leave and come back for a short time tomorrow? Or did she stay until visiting hours were over? In her mother's final days, someone had always been at the hospital with her. A multitude of people cherished Ana and she was never left alone for even a moment. But this man had no one, it seemed, other than a kindly neighbor.

Examining his face for traces of her own features, she couldn't find any. Sophia was the image of her mother—the large brown eyes and dark hair, the delicate features and olive complexion. Jimmy's dirty blonde hair had gone gray and his deep-set green eyes had no resemblance to Sophia's; she found it oddly comforting that she looked nothing like him.

"Hello!" The man walking through the door wore a large grin as he made his way to Sophia. "You must be Sophia." He extended his hand to her.

"Yes, I am. And you are … ?" she asked, looking at him quizzically. The man seemed genuinely excited to see her.

"I'm Homer. I wrote you the letter."

"Of course. It's nice to meet you."

"It's so good of you to come. I didn't want to intrude on your life, but I thought you should know, in case …" Homer didn't finish his sentence. He looked over to Jimmy. "Has he seen you, or has he been sleeping since you arrived?"

"We spoke briefly." Sophia averted her eyes away from Homer.

"Jimmy speaks of you all the time. I'd know you anywhere."

With a look of confusion, Sophia furrowed her brow. Her eyes shot up to Homer looking for an explanation.

"Pictures," he said. "Mostly from newspaper clippings and theater programs."

"Oh."

"Give him a chance. We all have mistakes in our past that we regret. He doesn't have much time left."

"I'm here. But he's not a part of my life. I never knew he existed until recently." Sophia sighed. "It's complicated."

"I'm aware. He told me all of it."

"All of it?" Somehow she doubted that.

Homer nodded, his eyes locking with Sophia's. In an instant she was convinced the man wasn't lying.

Hours later, Sophia was still seated in the chair beside Jimmy. The nurse told her the pain meds left him extremely drowsy and that it was normal for him to sleep for so long.

Slowly, Jimmy opened his eyes. He lit up at the sight of her. "Sophia?" Jimmy croaked out. Years of smoking had changed his once smooth, seductive voice to a gravelly tone with a hard edge.

"I'm here." She didn't know what to call him. Jimmy? Certainly not Dad! Pop? That's what she called him when she met him in Chicago, touring with her ballet company. He'd gotten a job helping out at the theater for the sole purpose of being near her. Everyone called him Pop because he worked with troubled teens and they gave him the nickname. But Pop sounded too much like a dad and she wasn't comfortable calling him either.

Jimmy extended his hand to her and she reluctantly took it.

"I have no family," he said. "My parents are gone. I have no brothers or sisters. Maybe I have cousins in Ikaria. I don't know."

"You have Homer. He's a good friend. The ones we choose to be in our lives can be just as important," Sophia said, thinking of her own friends.

"You are my only blood," he said, squeezing her hand. "I've always been sure of it, even when they all denied it was true."

Sophia's forehead creased in the way it did when she was deep in thought. A tiny groan escaped from her throat. "I think it's about time I hear from you what happened back then." She'd heard it all from Aunt Soula, and as much as she wanted to forget everything she learned that fateful day, Sophia now realized she needed to hear it again from this man's point of view.

"My beautiful Anastacia … she came home and found me with another woman. I know this isn't news to you."

"Her sister," Sophia said flatly.

"She's a devil," he scowled.

"She didn't act alone. Tell me, was she the only one, or were there others?"

Jimmy looked away. "There were others."

"And you dare to call my mother, 'Your Anastacia?'"

"You can't understand this, but what I did with those women had nothing to do with my love for your mother."

"That's disgusting."

"Despicable, maybe. Definitely screwed up. And it cost me her. She wanted nothing to do with me, and her uncle made sure I disappeared. I don't believe your mother knew she was pregnant at the time, but when she found out … well. It would have been the right thing to tell me."

"But if you had already left and were out of my mother's life, how did you find out about me?"

"I saw your mother in church with her new husband at her side. I assumed he was her husband because he was carrying you in his arms. I had never felt so many emotions at once. Anger. Jealousy." Jimmy's words stuck like dry cotton in the back of his throat. "Remorse," he croaked. "Remorse that another man was living the life I wanted."

Sophia examined Jimmy's face as his eyes glazed over and his expression took on a faraway look.

"But later that night, I figured out that you had to be mine, judging from how old I thought you were."

Sophia detected a hint of resentment and anger in his voice.

"So, you tried to extort money from my family in exchange for leaving us alone?"

"No," he said wearily. "I went to your mother's uncle to confront him and make him admit you were mine. He claimed you weren't mine and I should leave his niece in peace. That's when he gave me the money."

"And you took it. How much money was I traded for?"

"It wasn't like that. I was caught off guard. I was stupid, and I reverted to old habits and took the money. They weren't going to let me near you or your mother."

"They?"

"Your mother's Uncle Tasso, Stavros and your … father."

Sophia shook her head. "They were only trying to protect me."

"I have regretted this every day of my life. But in my heart, I knew I didn't deserve you or your mother."

A smile crossed Sophia's lips. "But Alex did. And he gave us both the best life. I couldn't have asked for a better father." And with those words, Sophia's burden was lifted, softening her heart to this broken man.

Everything happened for a reason. Even when hurtful revelations were unearthed, from the ashes came rebirth, creating an existence more harmonious than the one before.

"I didn't mean to hurt you. I should actually thank you for the life I was able to have. I wouldn't have changed a day of it."

"I understand. And when I finally got past my self absorption, all I wanted was for you to be raised a happy child."

"Tell me what happened to you after you left New York."

"Oh, if you don't hate me by now, I'm ashamed to say you will." Jimmy tried to pull himself up.

Reaching behind him, Sophia lifted his pillow to give him better support.

"I got into more trouble—running scams and gambling, until I owed a loan shark money, more money than I could pay back, and was threatened with my life. I robbed a store in hopes of paying off my debt, but I got arrested and ended up in prison for seven years. It was the best thing that could have happened to me."

"Going to jail was the best thing that ever happened to you?" Sophia asked, surprised.

"I straightened my ass out and worked on a college degree. That's how I ended up working with children."

"That makes sense to me. You wanted to stop kids from making the same mistakes."

"That's right. The experience changed me and I felt like I was finally making my father proud."

"I'm sure he was very proud."

"He'd been gone for years, but I'd like to think he somehow knows."

"I believe he does." She thought of her mother at that moment because she knew in her heart her mother was always watching over her. She looked at her wristwatch. "It's late and you should rest. I'll come back tomorrow and we can talk some more." She took his frail hand in hers compassionately and smiled. "Okay?"

"I'd like that."

Sophia had to admit to herself that she was curious about this man. But she was emotionally drained and she'd heard enough of Jimmy's story for one day.

Chapter 23

Sophia

January 2000

It had been a long day, and Sophia was tired. Having only eaten tasteless bites of stale hospital food, the noisy protest of her stomach competed with the icy pelts hitting the window of the cab.

A gust of wind nearly slammed the passenger door on her as she exited the taxi, and by the time she walked the few steps to the revolving doors, Sophia was soaked. Her body could take the arctic assault, as much as she despised the cold, but her mind and her heart were battered with conflict and upheaval.

She had wanted to go in, do the 'right' thing and get out, free of guilt. Sophia could then say she was there for this man in his last hours and, although she didn't owe him consideration, she had acted as any individual with a conscience would.

But during the course of the day, Sophia concluded that coming to Chicago was less about her own frame of mind and more to do with the dying man she had spent the day with. This was about a human being hoping to take his last breath with dignity and redemption. This was a plea for mercy.

Sophia was, after all, her mother's daughter, and aspired to be a compassionate soul who had the capacity for infinite love, as her mother had. And what would her mother have done if she were here, she wondered? Ana had cooked for the homeless, and visited the sick in the hospital—all strangers. Would her kindness have stretched to the man who hurt her so? And would she have granted him forgiveness? It was hard to know for sure, but Sophia was fairly certain that she would have.

Sophia was weary, and had little patience left for the unruly child in the elevator making demands on his parents. A young couple huddled in the corner whispered 'sweet nothings' to each other, and watching them filled her with loneliness and longing for her husband. Sophia was wrong to think she should do this on her own, and she missed the strength she drew from Dean simply by having him by her side.

She made her way to her room, shed her sodden garments, and called for room service as she perused the menu.

The hot shower was soothing, and Sophia could feel the stress rolling off her as quickly as the lavender scented suds slid down the drain. After ensconcing herself in the velvety white hotel robe and wrapping a towel around her hair to help it dry, Sophia was about to turn on the television when there was a knock at the door. *Food!* she thought.

Sophia opened the door, prepared to offer a gratuity in exchange for her dinner, but her eyes widened as she stood immobilized with disbelief.

Dean opened his arms and, without hesitation, she jumped into them. "You're here. I needed you and you knew that." Sophia buried her face in his chest. "I regretted coming without you the minute I landed."

"I had a feeling that once you got here, you might need some back up."

"What I need, is you," she said, grabbing his face in her hands and pulling him down for a kiss.

"Sweetest words I've ever heard," Dean said as he kicked the door closed.

"Really? You told me the sweetest words were, 'let's have sex.'"

"Okay."

"Okay what?" Sophia asked.

"Let's have sex." Dean untied the belt to her robe and slid it off her shoulders, letting it fall to the floor.

As he kissed his way down her body, Sophia felt as though she were an ice statue beginning to thaw. She could feel again. The prickles on her skin and the shivers up her spine attested to merely a trace of the need she had for her husband. She had just about closed herself off from everything and everyone she loved. It was as though Sophia had built an impenetrable glass wall around herself where she could view the outside world without engaging it. It was easier that way, or so she thought, to live in a state of numbness.

But Sophia had been fooling herself. And her denial to face certain truths and realities only caused more harm than good. She understood that now.

Dean's touch lit a flame in her heart—one that was always there, but suppressed by grief and hurt, anger and confusion. Sophia's spirit was being restored as her body responded to her husband's. He kissed her with longing, pressing his body to hers—skin-to-skin—heat-to-heat. Sophia could feel Dean's desperate need to explore and feed his desire, and she in turn never wanted her Dino more than she did at that moment.

Dean scooped her up and carried her to the bed. With her arms around his neck, she fixed her vulnerable brown eyes on his compelling green ones.

He had come to her, and it meant everything knowing that Dean instinctively understood how much she needed him. But he always did.

Urgency built up inside her and she needed, more than ever, to feel what their lovemaking did for her—making her feel completely connected to him—body and soul.

Dean entered her, groaning his pleasure as their bodies joined. He relished every inch of her, and she moaned her satisfaction through long kisses, each blissful thrust and every stroke. Dean rolled onto his back, taking Sophia with him so she was on top of him. He pulled himself up against the headboard and brought her down onto his lap.

Sophia braced her hands on Dean's shoulders and stared deep into his eyes as she moved up and down the length of him, taking him in as deep as she could. She wanted all of him. She wanted to stay like this for a long time. It felt so good—she felt so good. Like floating on a cloud.

Her orgasm began to peak, overtaking her. One by one, each wave of pleasure released the tension and burdens she'd been carrying for far too long. It was all drifting away. There was nothing in her mind or heart but the man who moved inside her, the man she would love until the day she died, and the man who would lay his life down for her.

The next morning, as they lay in bed sated after several rounds of lovemaking, Sophia was prepared for whatever the day would bring. Dean agreed to drop her off at the hospital, give her some time with Jimmy, and then later join her to meet the man who was her birth father.

"This is not only a kindness to him," Dean told Sophia before she exited the car in front of the hospital entrance, "this is a kindness to yourself—to your own peace of mind. I know you, and you'd never forgive yourself if you ignored his need to see you."

Sophia cupped Dean's cheek in her hand and brushed her lips across his. "You're right. Have I told you how happy I am that you're here?"

"Not with words." Dean's face brightened. "Maybe you could express those sentiments again tonight."

"That can be arranged." Sophia held his gaze, finding it difficult to walk away from him now that she felt so alive again—as if she'd awoken from a long slumber. One last kiss and Sophia dashed from the car and disappeared through the hospital entrance doors before another gust of wind or blast of cold air froze her.

Chapter 24

Sophia

January 2000

Before Sophia took the elevator to the fourth floor, she stopped at the hospital gift shop. She chose a floral arrangement with a low-sitting vase that could easily be placed on Jimmy's bedside table or the windowsill. His dreary hospital room cried for some cheer and Sophia thought it was the least she could do.

Jimmy was asleep when she entered his room, but today he seemed a bit paler and his breathing was labored. She'd been somewhat harsh with him the day before. She was angered by some of the things he told her, and she had a right to be. Sophia's response was direct, refusing to sugarcoat the resentment she held on her mother's behalf.

Now, looking at him, she felt awful. She hoped she wasn't the cause of his worsened condition. Sophia stared at Jimmy as she replayed their conversation in her mind. Yes, she was a little hard on him, but she had to admit to herself that, by the time she left that evening, she'd softened, and she thought he had sensed it.

The floral arrangement tapped against the worn side dresser by Jimmy's bed when she set it down, announcing to him that someone had entered. "You're back." His lips curved slightly, forming a weak smile, and the expression in his eyes signaled to Sophia that he was both relieved and elated to see her.

"I told you I would be back." With a cheerful smile on her face that was partly forced, Sophia told Jimmy that her husband had surprised her by arriving in Chicago the night before, and that Dean would be visiting him later that evening.

Jimmy wanted to hear about her life, her husband, and her children. They spoke for a while until she brought the subject back to him.

"Enough about me," Sophia said, her tone light. "You promised to tell me more about your family."

"It wasn't much of a family," he said. "I was an only child and, other than my parents, whatever relatives we had were in Ikaria."

"Ah, yes. I remember that you told me you were from there."

"My parents were, although they never knew each other there. They met in New York City. Their marriage was arranged."

Sophia's eyes widened. "Really? But did they love each other? I couldn't imagine being married to someone who was chosen for me whether I liked it or not."

"Same here. But I think it may have been common back then," Jimmy answered before coughing.

Sophia poured him some ice water from a pink plastic pitcher and handed it to him. "Maybe you should rest awhile."

"That's all I've done since I've been here. I want you to know your ..." Jimmy paused. "... your family history."

The wince was imperceptible, but Sophia couldn't stop it. She knew logically that he was her family, yet ... he wasn't. After placing the water pitcher back in its place, she dragged the same chair she was seated in the day before closer to the bed and made herself comfortable.

"So, I remember that you told me your grandparents had a farm and they were struggling. Your father came to America to help them financially."

"Yes. But that wasn't the only reason. His parents wanted to keep him from serving in the Turkish army. Greece hadn't been liberated at that time."

"Right. So, your dad came to New York to look for work. Did he know anyone there?"

"Not a soul. He wandered the streets of New York City, lost and searching for anyone who could speak Greek. It took two days before he happened to run across an agent who found immigrant factory workers to do menial jobs." Jimmy coughed several times and motioned for Sophia to pass him the cup of water that was on his tray table.

"Maybe we should do this another time. I don't want to tire you."

"There's no time left." He gulped the water down. "Andreas. That was my father's name. The agent helped him find a cheap boarding house and several months later he met a fruit stand owner—an older man who was more established in the immigrant community—who introduced him to other Greeks." Jimmy smiled. "Dad said after he proved to be a hard worker and had solid plans to improve his future, the older man introduced his daughter to him, hoping to arrange a marriage. My father worked from early morning until late at night. He had no spare time for courtships, so he made the practical choice and agreed to marry her.

"So the fruit stand owner was your grandfather?"

"He was. But I never met him. They went back to Greece after he retired."

"I'm surprised they went back and left their daughter behind. I don't think I could do that," Sophia said. "So your parents got married, and ... ?"

"And my father used the dowry money to open a tiny luncheonette that would provide immigrant factory workers with inexpensive meals. Business boomed. More and more immigrants came for jobs and my dad expanded the luncheonette. He built a thriving and successful business, hired more grill men and dishwashers, and after a while he was able to supervise and leave the labor to the employees." Jimmy seemed lost in the memory.

"Do you remember the luncheonette?"

"Only through my father's eyes. He lost it when I was very little."

"How? You said he was doing so well."

"The crash of 1929. With so many people out of work, business at the luncheonette died and he couldn't pay the rent. He told me it broke his heart taking his last look at the place before he walked away from it for good. Like so many others at that time, he lost everything."

Sophia sighed. Jimmy tried to pull himself up and Sophia popped up from her seat to help him. She told him to lean forward as she fluffed his pillow and helped him to position his body more comfortably. He looked at his estranged daughter appreciatively.

"My dad was a good man. I looked up to him. My mother, Maria, she was not the easiest woman. But my dad always defended her."

"He did love her then?" Sophia asked.

"Yes, but I don't think it started out that way. It was more a mutual respect at first. He had a gentle manner, and I suppose my mother saw that in him and realized how lucky she was. He was a simple man, and as long as she kept a clean house and had food on the table when he came home, that satisfied him." Jimmy shook his head. "I don't know. When you work fourteen hours a day, maybe that's all you want out of marriage."

"Times were different—more difficult. Maybe love was a luxury that gave way to practicality," Sophia pondered.

"My mother had a miscarriage before I was born, and it seemed to change everything for them. Naturally my dad was sad she lost the baby, but he was terrified of losing her. That's when he realized how much he loved her. And when they had me, they were very happy. Dad would do anything for us. I was just about four when he lost the business, but he was determined to make sure we had what we needed."

"You look tired," Sophia interrupted him. "Do you want to continue later?"

"No, please. I'm fine."

Sophia nodded.

"My mother was not accustomed to hardship of any kind. Her

father had always provided well for her. Dad went back to working the kitchen of whichever restaurant was hiring, often working two jobs back to back. I hardly saw him and I'd wait for him to come home so I could listen to his stories from his childhood in Ikaria." Jimmy smiled pensively at the fond memory. "God, I admired him, but it pained me to watch my father killing himself day after day, and as much as I wanted to be like him—the kind of man he was—I never wanted to live his life. My father deserved better than what he got. My mother was a pain in the ass."

Sophia met his eyes, startled.

"I'm telling you like it is. I think complaining was her favorite pastime."

"But you said they had a mutual respect and grew to love one another. Was she always like that?"

Jimmy shook his head. "No. Everything changed after Dad lost the business. My mother nagged my father constantly, claiming that he was never home to spend time with us, but in her next breath she would demand something she needed that we'd been doing without. 'Andreas, I want an icebox. Andreas, we need new furniture. Andreas, I haven't bought any new clothes this year.' Nag, nag, nag."

Sophia detected resentment, even after all these years. As she listened, she thought of how everyone's life experience molded them. There was so much more to a person than what could be seen on the surface. "What about you? Did you feel as though your dad wasn't around enough?"

"He always worked too many hours. As I got older, I found myself getting irritated with the way my mother treated my father. I could see how exhausted he was at the end of each day. So I got a job bussing tables at the restaurant where my father cooked. It was one way for me to help out financially and be able to spend time with him." Jimmy closed his eyes. "I didn't get as much time with him as I'd hoped. One afternoon, as I carried a tray of dirty dishes into the kitchen, I found my father clutching his chest. Without thinking, I dropped the tray and ran to my father's side as he collapsed to the floor."

Empathetically listening, Sophia handed Jimmy a tissue when she noticed a tear spill from the corner of his eye.

"I screamed for help, holding my father in my shaking arms and begging him to stay conscious. But by the time the ambulance arrived, he was gone."

"I'm so sorry," was all Sophia could say. It didn't matter if it was two years ago, or fifty—a loss was a loss, and the pain of it never ceased.

"My dad worked himself to death. My mother? She was a piece of work. After the funeral, all she could worry about was how this affected her financially. God forgive me, but I remember wishing it were she, not he, who died."

"I know you were grieving, but she was too. You probably didn't see it. She had you to think about, and times were different. It wasn't easy for a woman to support herself back then. She had to think practically," Sophia said, trying to outlay a different perspective for Jimmy to consider.

"My father's voice played in my head, as though he were whispering in my ear, so I did what he would have wanted me to. I took care of my mother and fulfilled all my obligations as the head of the household. I was still in my teens. I hated stifling obligations, and I felt trapped by a dependent, incapable mother who was always crying that her husband abandoned her, and that someone must have given her *to mati*, the evil eye because life was too hard on her. Hard on her!" he hacked. "I was saddled with her and a hell of a lot more responsibility than I wanted."

It was evident to Sophia that he'd been coughing from the strain of speaking too much. "I think you should rest now. I can ask the nurse for something to ease the cough."

Jimmy shook his head and labored out, "Chain smoker."

She nodded, pursing her lips. She'd never understood what the rush was from inhaling smoke into your lungs. And if this was the result, was it really worth it? She thought of Demi taking her first puff on a cigarette at a party in tenth grade. She wanted to be cool and grown up, but she had all but embarrassed herself in front of an upper-classman she was trying to impress.

"I have more to say."

"Tomorrow. You can tell me tomorrow. But later I'll stop by with my husband if you are up to it."

Seated in a booth situated near a window at the Capital Grille, Sophia told Dean what she learned that day from Jimmy. The opaque curtains blocked the activity of the busy street as well as the mounds of snow on the sidewalk that had turned a grimy black. It was a welcome setting after having spent most of the day sitting in a hospital room. Wearing a tan cashmere cowl neck sweater, Sophia was cozy sharing a meal and a glass of wine with her husband.

Dean grinned as he watched her devour an aged strip steak and a side order of potatoes gratin.

"What?" she asked when she caught him laughing at her.

"It's good to see you eating ... and smiling," Dean said, and he reached across the table to take her hand.

"I'm happy you're with me."

"It's more than that. So much more," Dean said, relief coating his words.

Sophia set down her utensils. Leaning in, she rested her elbows on the table and fisted her hands under her chin. "I'm starting to feel like myself again. Or at least I'm getting there." She couldn't remember the last time she'd felt this relaxed. No knots in her stomach. No tension in her shoulders. The veil of darkness that had enshrouded her was lifting and a glimmer of light had begun to shine through, giving her the strength and perspective she needed.

Dean reached his hand across the table and Sophia placed her hand in his. "You're a remarkable woman."

"You're a patient man."

"You've had a lot to work through."

"And I'm learning to accept that life keeps moving and changing and it often throws in a surprise or two, even when we wish it wouldn't."

After dinner, Sophia and Dean drove back to the hospital. Jimmy was awake and speaking to a nurse who was administering his nightly dose of medicine. They hovered by the door until the nurse finished checking his monitors and changing his IV fluids.

"It's fine," the nurse waved them over when she spotted them. "Come right in."

"You're back," Jimmy said.

"You seem surprised," Sophia said. "I told you I would come. I'd like you to meet my husband, Dean."

Jimmy lifted his hand and Dean shook it gently.

"So, you're the one who captured Sophia's heart?"

"Yes, sir. I'm a lucky man."

"Dean is Stavros and Soula's son," Sophia told him.

"Huh, is that so?" Jimmy narrowed his eyes at Dean. "I can see it. You look like your father."

"Maybe a little," Dean agreed. Is there anything we can do for you?"

"No." Jimmy shook his head. "Sophia being here was more than I could hope for."

The mention of Dean's father made Sophia nervous. There was no love loss between Jimmy and Stavros, and she worried that this acknowledgment would incite tension between the two men. "Dino and I just came from dinner. I hope you don't mind that I shared your stories with him," Sophia said.

"No, it's fine. I'm ready to tell you more if you want to hear it."

"You must be tired. It can wait until tomorrow," Sophia told him.

"I'm not sure how many tomorrows I have left. Stay a while," Jimmy said through his hoarse voice.

Dean pulled another chair next to the one Sophia had sat in earlier that day.

"Where was I?"

"Your father had passed away and your mother had come to depend on you," Sophia reminded him.

"Yes. I had to do something. I was going crazy. So I enlisted in the Army. After the attack on Pearl Harbor, the United States declared war on Japan, and men of all ages were enlisting. When I turned seventeen, I convinced my mother to sign the papers and let me go. She was devastated until I promised to send her a good portion of my earnings. It was my escape from a life I didn't want."

"Did you see combat?" Dean asked.

"Nope. I could have been sent anywhere, but I hit the jackpot. Hawaii—paradise even at wartime. And because of my restaurant experience I was put on kitchen patrol."

"Sure," Sophia joked. "Put the Greek guy in the kitchen."

He tried to chuckle along with her, but it threw him into a coughing fit. "It was no picnic at first. Cleaning mess halls and scrubbing the kitchen grease was no fun, but once they discovered that I could cook, I got the cushy job. It was better than having my head blown off on a battlefield."

"Your dad taught you well," Sophia said.

"I should have taken more of his lessons to heart," Jimmy said, contrition in his words. "He was the best of them. A man of integrity. It was better he was gone before he could see how I turned out. He would have been disappointed."

"We react to our circumstances at the time," Dean interjected. "You were dealt a bad hand and you did the best you could."

"Did I? When I counseled with the boys at the youth center, you know one of the first things I told them?" He didn't wait for an answer. "Don't let your current situation dictate the rest of your life or use it as an excuse not to do better. That was a lesson I learned the hard way."

"Did something happen in Hawaii?" Dean asked.

"Well … a lot of things happened. Let's just say that four years in the military can change a man, for better or worse. Me? I picked up the bad habits rather than the noble ones. By the time the war had ended, I had learnt how to drink, gamble and scam my way out of any situation. Women were drawn to a man in uniform, and I had more than my share of them falling all over me. I was a good looking little shit and I knew it."

Sophia and Dean laughed.

"This one over here," Sophia pointed her finger at Dean, "was the same way. Girls were throwing themselves at him."

"But I only had eyes for you." Dean wrapped his arms around her. Sophia pushed him playfully and pulled a face. "Liar. You never looked at me until you'd gone through dozens of girls first."

"Were you counting?" He turned to Jimmy. "Truth is I was always crazy about her, but that's another story."

Jimmy's weary eyes sparkled with delight as he witnessed the banter between his daughter and her husband.

"Let's get back to you. What did you do after the war?" Dean asked.

"I kept the promise I made to my mother and she managed fine in my absence. I sent her enough money each month to live on, but the thought of going back to that life was unbearable. I put up with her for a while before suggesting that she would be happier with her parents who had long since retired to their village in Ikaria. When she agreed to go for a long visit, I was relieved to be rid of the responsibility of caring for her."

Plus, I had my own worries. Jobs were not easy to come by. Some soldiers came back with marketable skills, but not me," he said with sarcasm, "unless you could make a living playing poker. 'I'll be damned if I'd work in a kitchen again.' That's what I told myself, and so I found a job in the stockroom at McCains Five and Dime to get me by."

"Is that where you worked when you were …" Sophia hesitated. She didn't think she'd ever get used to the idea of her mother being married to this man. "… were married to my mother?"

"No, I'd left there by then. Like I said, I wasn't a person of integrity like my father. I used my charm on women to earn a living as an escort. You may as well hear this from me before someone else tells you."

A tiny gasp escaped Sophia's lips. She suddenly felt very warm and lightheaded. This was one thing she would have rather not known.

"Are you okay?" Dean asked, laying his hand across her back.

"No, I'm not okay," Sophia snapped. "This is what you were doing when you cheated on my mother?" Her voice was laced with a mixture of desolation and anger.

"No! I loved your mother. I left all that behind me when I met her. It was a means to an end, and it was only meant to give me a jump-start in life until I met the girl of my dreams. I know that's not a good excuse. But I was crazy about your mother. I hated how my parents were thrown together, and I vowed that I would never marry under the circumstances that my father had. I always said that I would have to be head over heels or I would never marry at all. And then I met Anastacia."

"But you cheated on her," she said harshly.

"I did. It was the worst mistake of my life."

Chapter 25

Sophia

January 2000

Are you sure?" Dean asked Sophia.

She nodded her head adamantly. "Yes. I came. I did my duty, whatever that was, and now I want to go home."

With renewed disgust for the man to whom she wanted no connection, and clinging to a fierce loyalty on her mother's behalf, Sophia left the hospital the night before wishing she hadn't come at all. Had Jimmy been a well man, and had he not been living out his last days, she might have told him what she thought of him, but her harsh tone when she ended their conversation said it all.

"This visit was more for you than it was for his sake. At least your reason for coming was." Dean had ordered breakfast in their room, but while he ravenously ate a three-egg western omelet, Sophia picked dejectedly at an English muffin. "Now you can finally put this to rest. You did right by him and you should feel free of guilt."

Glaring at him, she scoffed. "What? How do I put this to rest? My biological father and the man my mother was married to was an escort. Which is just a nice way of saying—"

"Hold it! Don't go there. Young people do all kinds of dumb ass things." Dean blew out a breath. "It couldn't have been easy for him to come clean with you, knowing he'd risk losing any shred of respect he might have gained."

"I was starting to think he wasn't too horrible, and then he has to tell me ..." Sophia cringed, "... that."

"Instead of focusing on his mistakes, try giving him credit for how he turned his life around."

Sophia composed herself and got up from her chair. She refused to slide backward by letting circumstances beyond her control dictate her moods. Coming around to the other side of the small breakfast table, she straddled Dean's lap. "You're right," she agreed, running her fingers through his hair. "I refuse to let this affect me. It's me and you and our children," she said with determination.

They kissed and Dean slid his hand under her shirt, but before he could make his way to her breasts, the ringtone on Sophia's cell phone interrupted them. "Ignore it," he mumbled while running his lips down her shoulders.

Breaking away, she rose and reached for the phone in her bag. "What if it's the kids?" But when Sophia flipped her phone open, she discovered it was Homer on the other end. "Hello?" Sophia furrowed her brow. "When?" she asked after what seemed like a long minute. "No. I'd rather not come to the hospital. Is there anything I need to do?"

Dean, who had been watching Sophia closely, came to stand by her side.

"Thank you, Homer. Yes, I'll meet you there in two hours." Flipping shut the phone to end the call, Sophia sighed as she placed it back in her bag. "Jimmy passed away early this morning." She didn't weep as she said it, but there was burden and regret in her tone. Dean wrapped his arms around her and they stood together, still as two blocks of stone, wordlessly, until Sophia finally broke the silence. "If I wasn't so damn self-righteous, my last words to that man would not have been so mean."

Dean cupped her chin in his hands, his eyes piercing through hers. "Don't. You did nothing wrong. You reacted naturally to information that would have upset anyone. You came to him when he needed you. You gave him a chance to make peace with himself before he died. I believe seeing you was enough for him."

"Homer was with him when he passed. At least he wasn't alone."

"He was a good friend to Jimmy." Dean stroked the length of Sophia's arms. "What now? Should I change our flights?"

"You go home. You must be needed at the Carriage House, and the children have been without us long enough. I can handle this and I'll be home in a few days."

Tilting his head to one side, Dean pressed his lips together. "Whatever you go through, I go through with you. That's the deal."

"The deal?" She laughed.

"Yeah. You know, for better or worse."

"We never actually said those words," Sophia teased.

Dean caught her arm and playfully dragged her to him. "It's understood. No words are necessary."

"No words needed," she agreed.

Two hours later, Dean and Sophia pulled up in front of the address Homer had given her over the phone. Homer had a key to Jimmy's apartment and was waiting for them at the front door. As the three of them entered together a chill crawled up Sophia's spine.

The apartment was small and bare in décor but tidy. It was an odd feeling to poke around when it was all so unfamiliar to her. She had never sat on the weathered old couch, or put up a pot of tea on the stove in the tiny kitchenette. Yet here she was, expected to go through Jimmy's belongings simply because he had a biological connection to her.

"Jimmy had his funeral details pre-arranged, but he owned two suits and didn't make mention of which one to use. Would you like to choose one?" Homer asked Sophia.

"Sure," she said awkwardly. When she'd gone through her mother's things, it had saddened her, yet it seemed natural. Anastacia's clothing and personal items held memories for Sophia. She'd picked up her mother's perfume, dabbed it on her wrist and breathed in the scent. Closing her eyes, it had felt as though her mother was next to her for a brief second.

But Jimmy's possessions meant nothing to her and it seemed odd to be rummaging through his personal items. They walked into the bedroom and removed the suits from the closet. Turning to lay the clothing onto the bed, Sophia felt the blood drain from her head when she spotted a picture frame on his nightstand. In it held a worn, wrinkled photo of her mother and Jimmy on their wedding day. Picking it up, she stared blankly at it.

Dean came up behind her, wrapping his arms around her waist. "It's in the past Sophia *mou*. It's all the man had left—one picture," Dean whispered.

Even after all she'd heard from Aunt Soula, her father, and Jimmy, she found it unnerving to absorb this photo documentation of a time that existed before her.

"He talked about her often," Homer said, interrupting her private thoughts. Sophia turned to look at him. "He was remorseful. It took him years, but he changed his ways. He said there were only three people in the world whose opinion mattered to him—his father's, Anastacia's … and yours." He handed her a scrapbook.

She took it from him and sat down at the edge of the bed, Dean coming up beside her. As she flipped through the pages, Dean draped an arm around her shoulders. Sophia was astonished. Reflected back to her, she saw herself. Page after page—photos from ballet tours, newspaper articles and programs with her name highlighted in yellow marker.

"The only side of you he could have was the public one. He was grateful to have that. In the end, all he wanted was redemption and acceptance. The last few days you spent with him did that."

"Thank you, Homer. Thank you for saying that."

Tears she didn't know existed for this man spilled from her eyes. Although she wouldn't change one moment of her life with Alex, the only father she'd known until recently, there was a sadness brewing inside her for Jimmy's self-induced tragedy. Sophia prayed his moments of happiness were not limited to an old photo and a few news clippings.

The funeral was simple and not well attended. Naturally, Homer was there, along with a few past co-workers who Jimmy had worked with, and a couple of the boys—now grown to adulthood—whose lives Jimmy had steered in the right direction through his counseling. Devoid of allegiance to Jimmy, Stavros and Soula arrived to pay their respects to support Sophia. Demi wanted to be by her side, but Sophia asked that she stay with the children.

Smoke filled the air in the tiny church as the priest censored the body lying in the casket. "May his memory be eternal," the priest chanted. Would it? Sophia wondered, since she had no memories to keep him alive in her thoughts. A tap on her shoulder startled her and she turned. Her eyes widened. Sitting in the pew behind her were Amy and Donna.

"Who told you?" Sophia asked.

"Who do you think?" Amy replied.

"Demi said if she couldn't be here someone had to," Donna said.

"You shouldn't have come all this way."

"We want to be here. You should have called us yourself," Amy said.

Sophia kissed both of them on the cheek. "Thank you."

With the scant number of mourners, Sophia spared herself the agony of eulogizing a man she hardly knew. Instead, she spoke to each person with interest as they approached Sophia in consolation. Sad, she thought. It's all so sad that these strangers knew Jimmy better than she did.

At the gravesite, Sophia solemnly stepped forward. A myriad of confusing emotions ran through her—anger, sadness, loss, regret, and maybe a bit of something she was ashamed to admit—relief.

She laid her rose upon the casket and silently bid good-bye to the man who'd given her life but had never had the chance to be a part of it.

"Never cry over a man. There's always another waiting at your door."
—Irini Fotopoulos

Chapter 26

Mindy

January 2000

When Mindy first arrived at the Fotopoulos home on the island of Chios, her sole purpose was to isolate herself from the world. Content to be on her own with no distractions, she re-examined her life. What Mindy needed more than anything was to process what she'd discovered and get past it—Tyler was a happily married man with children.

As she pondered her own circumstances, Mindy's thoughts swung from one extreme to another. One day she would think to herself, 'I am a successful woman, fulfilling my dreams every day.'

But then, the next day, Mindy would sink into a depressing abyss convinced that she had nothing to look forward to in life and that she was destined to spend it alone—until the fateful night when she met Apollo.

One evening after spending the day binging on *frappés* and *loukou-mathes*, Mindy slipped on a body-hugging dress and went into Chios Town. She had to do something to get out of her funk and she thought experiencing the local nightlife might be the cure.

The time had come for her pity party to end and she planned to dance like the locals. She came upon a taverna with a large stone patio and strands of white lights strung between the trees. Weaving between the empty tables, Mindy crossed to the entranceway. Music filled the air and as she approached she smiled, watching people of all ages dance as though nothing was as important as what they were doing at that very moment.

Spotting a table with a prime view of the entertainment, she asked to be seated. And that's when she saw him. With a voice dripping of seduction and a face that matched, the singer locked eyes with Mindy. She'd learned a few sentences to get her by, but the words that rolled off his tongue were, well, Greek to her—but sexy as hell.

Every part of her burned. Heat rose to her cheeks causing them to flush and her heart quickened as he moved closer to the table where she was seated. His velvety voice captivated and the hint of cologne he wore mixed with the scent of the salty sea tantalized her. But as the sexy singer continued to work the room, Mindy could see that he had the same effect on every woman in the taverna and he, in turn, looked at each one as though he wanted them.

Sipping her Skinos Mastiha cocktail, a liquor made from the sap of a tree indigenous to Chios alone, Mindy watched the joy emanating from the villagers around her. Given her current state of mind, she could not relate to their exuberant joviality. Staring into her glass as she stirred, causing a mini whirlpool to form, she hadn't noticed that the music had stopped.

"May I join you?" Mindy looked up to see who had spoken to her in heavily accented English.

She tilted her head, looking at him inquisitively. "How did you know I speak English?"

"American? I am wrong?"

"No," Mindy laughed. "You're not wrong."

"I am Apollo."

"Ah! That explains it," she said wryly.

"Explains what?" he asked as he seated himself in the empty chair beside her.

"You know," Mindy said, gesturing to the sky. "Greek God. Son of Zeus. God of music."

"You are very amusing beautiful American woman who is nameless."

"Oh! I'm Mindy. No Greek goddess name for me."

"You should be the goddess of fire." Apollo reached for a lock of her red mane, wrapping it around his finger. "I will call you *Fotiá*."

She shrugged her shoulders. "Then katalavaíno."

His eyes sparkling with amusement, Apollo laughed. "You say that well."

"I say it a lot. I don't understand anything people say, so I let them know."

"*Fotiá* means fire. My break is over in a minute, but promise me a dance."

A shiver crawled up her spine with the thought of her body pressed up against his on the dance floor. Her answer came out a breathy whisper. "Yes, I'd like that."

She eyed him as he began the song. Commanding and strong; male yet beautiful, Apollo mesmerized her. Casually dressed in black slacks and a white shirt, his sleeves were rolled just below the elbows and he'd left enough buttons undone to show a tease of hair across his tanned chest.

He curled a finger in her direction, inviting her to join him, but she shook her head. Apollo's deep brown eyes bore into Mindy's emerald green ones, as he extended his hand to her and pulled her out of her seat.

Microphone in hand and his other at her waist, Apollo drew her close and began to dance as he continued his love ballad. She reveled in the feel of scruff from his manicured beard against her delicate face. She looped her arms around his neck and they slowly rocked back and forth to the music. Escorting her back to her seat when the song had ended, he said, "I sang those lyrics for you alone."

"*Then kat—*" Apollo pressed a finger to Mindy's lips.

"I know, I know" he bantered. "You don't understand. In the song, the man is telling the woman he will go crazy if he can't see her again soon." He motioned for the band to play. "Wait for me until I finish this set."

It had all begun so perfectly. They talked out on the patio, ignoring the chill in the air, and when it was time for her to go, he pressed her up against the stone wall outside the taverna and kissed her with a passion so deep that every part of her body was tingling. Even when she broke the kiss, he kept his lips so close to hers that Mindy could feel his breath breezing across her face and it intoxicated her. Staring into her eyes, he kissed her again, devouring her, leaving her lip swollen from the sensual assault when he finally pulled away.

Desire built up inside her but, although she'd been tempted, Mindy resisted his seduction. She thought of her first night with Tyler. Adamant that she would not repeat the same mistake, Mindy was careful not to rush into anything. The days of one-night stands and affairs that amounted to nothing but heartache and emptiness were over.

Staring at her with an intensity that made Mindy nervous, Apollo made his intentions clear as he pressed his body to hers. What was the root of the uneasiness within her? The demand in his eyes? Or the fear of jumping into deep waters, unknown?

Mindy steeled herself and ducked out beneath his arms. The tightness in her chest and her rising panic gave her the strength to break away from him where he had her pinned against the wall. "I have to go," she insisted.

Gripping her wrist before she was out of his reach, he held onto it with unyielding determination. "I will make you mine."

Mindy tried to read Apollo's eyes before walking away. Had she seen passion or intimidation? There was no way to be certain.

The next morning, Mindy was seated in a sunny yellow upholstered chair that was nearly as bright as the rays of light shining through the window. The mornings were cold in January, but the afternoons became pleasant enough for a stroll through town.

She was about to take her first bite of crusty bread that she'd spread with a thick layer of marmalade when she heard a rap on the door. No one had come to call on her since she'd been here, and why would they? She didn't know a soul in this corner of the world. Peeking out the window, Mindy was stunned to see Apollo on the landing, armed with two cups of coffee and a pastry bag.

"How did you know where to find me?" she asked the moment she opened the door. Wearing nothing but the satin sleep shorts and tank top she'd slept in, Apollo raked his eyes over her.

"You can find out anything in a small village," he grinned. "May I come in?"

"Oh, sure. Sorry. You caught me by surprise."

"A good one I hope."

Mindy directed him to the kitchen table. They eased into a friendly conversation as they shared a pastry and sipped coffee together. She told him about her work and he spoke of the tours his band had taken and the ones they were planning. A little while later, convincing Mindy to allow him to be her tour guide, the two of them hopped onto his Vespa.

He was a perfect gentleman the entire day and, although a part of her was burning for him, she was comforted that he didn't make an improper move. They stayed out late into the evening, and when he delivered her to her front door, he simply kissed her hand before chastely grazing his lips across hers.

"I'll see you tomorrow," he said, turning toward the gravel driveway.

He had gained her trust, though she found him confounding. The night before, she'd read sex and passion in his smoldering eyes, and it had taken great restraint for Mindy to combat the storm within her. Finding him at her door this morning unnerved her at first, but he'd put her at ease. Apollo made no attempt at seduction. She assumed that somehow he sensed her reluctance, and he had behaved like nothing more than a friendly companion for the day. It was as though she'd met two completely different men.

With only two days left before leaving the island, Mindy was treated to a guided tour by Apollo once again. In the medieval town of Pyrgi, they walked the narrow streets, admiring its unique buildings painted in geometric designs. They climbed one of the many watchtowers, used in days gone past to protect the island from the stream of invaders who attempted to control this jewel of the Aegean. And although the weather was far from warm enough to swim, they went to Mavra Volia, a black sand beach that Apollo insisted she must see.

"Change your plans. Stay longer." Apollo requested when the couple returned to Mindy's doorstep.

Mindy tilted her head and took his hands in hers. She shook her head. "No, I can't," she said regretfully. "I have obligations and a business that needs my attention. It will be hard to leave this beautiful place, but—"

"And what about me? Will you miss me?"

He was looking at her in that way he had the night she met him. "Of course," she said, her lips curving upward.

Apollo cradled Mindy's head in the palm of his hand and pulled her in for a toe-curling kiss. She could feel his raw sexuality whirl around them and it left her breathless. "Do you want to come in?" Her voice was barely audible, and his answer was all the seduction she needed.

With only one day left, Apollo never left her side. He stayed the night, exploring every creamy white inch of her, and she in turn worshiped his body until they fell asleep in each other's arms.

"Where will you take me today?" Mindy inquired the next morning.

"To bed," Apollo chuckled. "I want you to myself."

"The whole day? I haven't seen where you live yet."

He brushed the thought off with a wave of his hand. "Maybe next time. Today, I want you here, underneath me, above me," he lifted an eyebrow, "in the bathtub."

Mindy giggled like a schoolgirl. "Sex fiend."

"Of course I am. I'm a Greek man, after all."

"Demi warned me about men like you. Will you at least tell me about your town?"

Mindy wrapped herself in an Aegean blue satin robe. "I'm going to make breakfast."

Slipping into his faded jeans, Apollo followed her.

Turning, Mindy asked, "What would you like?" Seeing he was shirtless, she fisted her hands on her hips. "How am I supposed to make breakfast with you tempting me like that?"

Apollo snaked his hands under her robe. "No panties? How am I supposed to eat breakfast knowing there's nothing under this?"

Playfully, she nibbled on his bottom lip before pulling away.

"I'll have cinnamon toast and coffee."

"That's it?"

"That's it. I don't often eat breakfast. Coffee and cigarettes—that's all."

"First thing in the morning?"

"Since I was sixteen."

"What did your parents think of that?" Mindy set the plate of cinnamon brushed toast down in front of Apollo.

"By the time I was that age, they had given up on trying to get me to listen to them."

"So you were one of those kids. I should have known."

Apollo wore an impish grin. "My poor mamá. But she gave me plenty of whacks on my ass with her *koutali*. For as long as I can remember, she always had that wooden spoon in her hand." He laughed at the memory.

"Tell me more about your family," Mindy said, as she poured Apollo a cup of coffee.

"Nothing much to tell. They live in Mesta on a mastiha farm. It's been in our family for generations."

"Your parents are farmers?" Mindy seemed surprised.

"Not quite. They inherited the house and the trees. When they were younger they would harvest the mastiha themselves but, for many years now, they've hired workers to do that. They handle the business end only."

"Did you ever help them?"

"A little when I was a teenager. It's not for me. My brother handles most of the business now. He's built up the company making products like soaps and lotions, and liquors."

"I thought mastic came only in gum. My friend Demi's mother chews it. I tried it once." Mindy contorted her face. "It was vile."

"It's an acquired taste. But mastiha is not only used as chewing gum. It's used in baking and liquors … and it's known to heal stomach ailments."

"I would like to have seen your farm."

With an imperceptible tightening of his jaw, Apollo responded. "Maybe someday."

Mindy narrowed her eyes. She caught the change in his mood and she wondered what provoked it. Never had she met a man whose mood could go from playful to dour within minutes. Mindy shifted the subject, asking Apollo about his upcoming tour. As though she had snapped her fingers and ordered it, Apollo was once again the lighthearted man who was quickly claiming a space in her heart.

The next day, Mindy was seated in first class on a plane headed for New York City. She looked out the window and sighed. The plane would take off in a few minutes and her feet would no longer be planted on the same part of the earth as Apollo's. She felt this loss deep within her core. Glumly, she nursed a glass of white wine. Apollo had made her promise to come back, and he vowed he would visit New York to be with her, but at that moment her insecurities vanquished her assurance that she would ever see him again. He would travel with his band, meet other women, and she'd be long forgotten, remembered only as a weeklong dalliance.

~Loukoumathes~

2 pounds flour (approx)
1 teaspoon salt
1 envelope of dry yeast
1 cup water, lukewarm
3-4 cups vegetable oil for frying

In a large bowl, mix together the flour and salt. Set aside.

In a smaller bowl, stir the water and yeast together until dissolved. Add the yeast mixture to the flour. Mix together and add as much water as needed to make a thin batter similar in consistency to a loose yogurt.

Set the batter aside in a warm area until it bubbles and swells.

In the meantime, start the syrup.
2 cups honey
1 cup sugar
1 cup water
2 cinnamon sticks
Bring the ingredients to a boil and lower to a simmer for 10 minutes.

Heat the oil. Forming the honey balls expertly takes experience. I watched my mother and my yiayiá do it my entire life. They squeeze the batter through their fist and control the size of each pastry with their thumb and forefinger as it falls into the boiling oil. I have not been able to master this as well as they did. I try, but often I resort to using a mini ice cream scooper.

Remove when puffs are light golden brown and place on paper towels to absorb the excess oil.

To serve, drizzle with honey syrup and sprinkle with cinnamon. Best if served immediately.

Optional – top with crushed walnuts.

Chapter 27

Demi

Summer 2000

June. Height of the wedding season. But Demi was long since over the frantic brides and their intrusive mothers, who tried to control everything from the color of linens to the volume of the music. Last minute head count changes and seating arrangements created double the work for her, and the arguments between brides and grooms, mothers and daughters, and even siblings, had her mentally exhausted.

She never understood why an event that should hold nothing but beautiful memories could get so ugly at times. What she was sure of was that she had to take a break from the chaos or she would lose her mind. So she summoned her best gal-pals for a leisurely lunch. Amy was in D.C. wrapping things up before the summer recess next month, and Mindy was back in Greece visiting Apollo, the man she couldn't stop talking about, but it had always been difficult to round up all five of them at one time.

Seated in the Love Lane Kitchen, a local, well-known informal restaurant in Mattituck, Demi sipped a glass of lemon-garnished ice water. Waving when she spotted Sophia and Donna, they smiled back at her and claimed a seat across from Demi.

"Sorry we're late," Sophia said. "We got stuck behind a huge tractor that was moving so slowly he may as well have been parked."

Demi grinned. "I've gotten used to that around here. I needed this," she said. "Thanks for coming out."

"I love the summers out here," Donna said. "With school finished for the year, I'm looking forward to some down time." She turned to Sophia. "Except for dance classes, that is. But that never feels like work."

"I'm dying for some down time. These June weddings are sucking the life out of me. Too many personalities to buffer in one month," Demi sighed.

"It sounds like you're ready for a vacation and you've been barely open a year," Sophia noted.

"Well that's out of the question, unless I go without Michael. It's the height of the wine tasting season. The vineyard is packed with tourists all week long and twice as busy on the weekends."

"So your down time is his busy season. That's got to be hard on both of you," Donna commented.

"I wouldn't say that. July and August are slower wedding months, but still pretty busy, so it's fine. We'll try to plan something in January. If, that is, I can get him alone for five minutes to discuss it."

The server came over and asked if they were ready to order.

"Oh, give us a few more minutes please," Sophia told her. "We haven't looked at the menus yet."

"I don't need to look," Demi said. "I'll have the lobster roll."

"Sounds good," Donna said.

"Make it three," Sophia said, nodding to the server to return to their table.

"What was that comment about? Are you and Michael having problems?" Sophia asked.

"Aside from our arguments over his mother and trying to get time alone between our work and the kids?" Demi frowned. "Yeah, something seems off. If I didn't know better, I'd say he was having an affair."

"But you do know better. Michael would never do that to you," Sophia said emphatically.

"That's true," Donna agreed. "Now if we were talking about Richie, I'd believe anything. But the only affair I think he's having is with his beer bottle."

"Oh, Donna. What on earth has happened to him over the years?" Sophia asked.

"I think he found out he had to grow up and he didn't like the idea," Donna replied, her bitterness seeping through her words. "How exactly is Michael acting strange?"

"I don't know. I want to say it's just my imagination, but sometimes when he's on the phone and I ask him who he's speaking to, he avoids telling me." She thought for a moment. Shaking a pointed finger, she asked Sophia, "You know that bartender he hired? She's always gawking at him and uses any excuse to speak to him or move in closer to him than she should."

"That's not his fault," Sophia said.

"Maybe not," Demi conceded, taking a bite out of the overstuffed lobster roll the server had set down in front of her moments ago. "But he should discourage it."

"Maybe he hasn't noticed," Sophia defended Michael.

"What red blooded male doesn't notice when a woman is falling all over him? I may have to straighten her out myself."

"Oh, Demi. Don't do anything rash," Sophia warned.

Later that evening, after having spent the rest of the day fielding questions from prospective brides, Demi went home to prepare dinner, gather the children from their activities, and then finally collapsed on the couch.

Michael strolled in at ten o'clock after another summon from his mother to help her through her latest crisis.

"You could have called." Demi glared at him.

"Time got away from me. I didn't think I'd be that long."

"You can serve yourself dinner. We finished two hours ago," she said, angrily spitting out the words.

"I ate at my mother's."

"Of course you did," she said with sarcasm. Rising, she crossed her arms. "It would have been nice for you to let me know."

Michael's lips pressed tightly together. "I'm not arguing tonight. I'm going up to shower."

Grunting, she threw a shoe at him as he climbed the stairs.

"Very mature, Dem."

Frustrated, Demi picked up the phone and called Sophia. Earlier, Sophia attempted to talk Demi down, as Sophia had done many times over the years. Demi had a fiery temper and, normally, as fast as she'd blow-up, she'd calm down and behave rationally once again.

Sophia suggested Demi try a different tactic and begged her not to make accusations based on unwarranted suspicions. Demi and Michael had a solid marriage and they were crazy about each other. There was no need for Demi to let her imagination run away with her.

"He just got home a few minutes ago," she said into the phone. "Yup," she answered. "His mother's again."

Demi felt better after speaking to her friend and went upstairs to apologize to Michael.

"I'm sorry I snapped at you," she said, leaning on the bathroom counter.

Steam filled the room, the condensation on the shower door preventing Demi from glimpsing her husband's naked body.

"I'm afraid you and I are losing each other and it upsets me," she confessed.

"It's a busy time of year. I'd like more of your time too."

"Let's make the time then. We should plan a trip. Just the two of us. Maybe after the grape harvest?" Demi asked.

"I don't know. We'll see. I still have so much to do at that time."

"Don't you want to be alone with me, or is something else occupying your time?" Or *someone,* she wanted to ask.

"Of course I want to be alone with you." He slid open the glass door, just enough to pop his head out. "We could start now." Michael lifted his brows. "Join me," he invited.

"I can't! The kids are home."

Pulling her by the arm, he dragged Demi, still fully clothed, into the shower. Demi shrieked. "They're not paying attention to us," he said, peeling off the layers of wet clothing sticking to her body. "Now kiss me," he demanded, and her lips, greedy for his, complied.

Chapter 28

Sophia

Fall 2000

I've made a decision about something," Sophia told Dean late one evening as they sat side-by-side on the family room sofa watching the popular law drama, *The Practice*.

Turning to face him, she lifted her legs across his lap. Dean looked at her with curiosity. He pointed the remote toward the television, lowering the volume.

"I'm ready to do what you've been hoping for. Move closer to the vineyard."

"Really? I haven't pushed the issue because you had so much to consider. What changed?" Dean asked. An odd mixture of excitement and concern lit up his hazel-green eyes.

"Well, I think it's time you and I had a home we could call our own. One that we can buy together and the history we'd write would be ours alone. Plus, I know how hard it is on you to commute so far every day."

"But then you'll have the long commute."

"Not exactly. Dino, I've decided to sell the dance studio."

Sophia could tell from Dean's expression that he was stunned.

"What? No, no. Why would you do that? I know how much you love that place."

"Yes and no. It was an important part of my life. But situations change and sometimes it's time to move on. As your life progresses, your dreams change."

"As much as I'd like to move out that way, I don't want you to have to sacrifice what you've built for my sake," Dean told her.

"Nothing is a sacrifice when you do it for the one you love. But, it's time for me to do something a bit different. I'm doing this for me, you and the children."

"The children. Have you told them yet?"

"No, of course not. Not before discussing it with you. I ran the idea by them as a possibility for the future, but only as a 'what if' question. Surprisingly, Evvie, who I thought would give me an adamant 'no', jumped at the idea."

"Hmm. I would have expected resistance from her."

"She asked if we could live on the vineyard. I thought that was an odd request, but she does love spending time with her cousins."

"I think there's more to it than that," Dean said. Sophia wasn't sure what he meant. "Sophia *mou*, haven't you noticed how she shadows Michael when he's working? She's constantly peppering him with questions about winemaking and asking if she can help."

"I hadn't really noticed. I mean, I know she likes to see what he's doing, but I hadn't thought much of it."

"You've had a lot going on. But she soaks up everything Michael shows her."

"So she would support the move just to be near the vineyard?"

"I believe so," Dean nodded.

"Cia is too young for it to make a difference to her, and Nicky seemed okay with it. Not enthusiastic like Evvie, but he didn't hate the idea."

"But what about you? How do you really feel about it and what will you do if you sell the studio?"

Sophia wanted to go in a different direction and she explained it all to Dean. Her intent was to solely teach ballet, but when she opened the studio years ago she knew she had to offer all the disciplines in order to compete with the other studios in the area. And it worked out very well financially for her with enrollment growing along with her reputation.

But her heart was not in it anymore. After all that had happened in the last couple of years, it was time for a change, and she was at the point in her life that she only wanted to do things that made her truly happy. And that would be to take on ballet students privately and, in time maybe form a small ballet company out east once she'd settled into her new life there.

It was time for a change.

Chapter 29

Mindy

Fall 2000

"Hi Aunt Mindy," Stella said after opening the door. "Mom!" Stella, now a precocious twelve-year-old, called out, "Aunt Mindy is here with a man!"

Mindy laughed. "This is Apollo. Now give me a kiss, right here." Mindy bent down to hug her. "You've grown. You're almost as tall as I am."

Demi walked into the foyer. "I'm so happy you made it." She extended her hand to the man standing beside Mindy. "You must be Apollo. *Hárika poli*—a pleasure to meet you."

The large great room fed into the kitchen where almost everyone was hovering. Demi led Apollo over to the crowd and introduced him. Mindy had expected him to feel at home with other Greeks, but instead he seemed standoffish. She brushed it off, thinking he might feel like the stranger in the room, and thought he'd warm up to them eventually. But he didn't. In her eyes, he seemed to be brooding, and he held onto her at all times. She'd seen this man work a crowd and charm them, but not tonight. Tonight he was quite the opposite.

"How long are you here for?" Sophia asked at the dinner table.

"Another week. I asked Mindy to come back with me," Apollo said. "But she can't, she claims." His voice held annoyance.

"Apollo sometimes forgets that I'm busy with my own career and I can't follow his band around Europe," Mindy said with a nervous giggle.

"I need another drink." Apollo rose from his seat abruptly and found the butler's pantry where the liquor was set on the counter. Mindy followed him.

"You embarrassed me in front of your friends," he said coldly.

"How? Because I can't drop everything and join you?"

"Forget it." He grabbed her arms, squeezing tightly. "The next time I ask you to do something for me, don't tell your friends you can't. It makes me look weak."

"That's crazy. Ouch! You're hurting me. Let go!"

Michael walked into the kitchen. "Hey, hey! What's going on here?" Dean was on Michael's heels. "Everything okay here?"

Apollo glared at both men. "Speaking to my woman. Not your concern."

"Come again?" Dean threatened. "You treat her with respect!"

"You Americans are a bunch of pussies. You let your women control you."

"The blood that runs through me is as Greek as yours," Michael argued, "but we don't abuse our women."

"It's okay," Mindy assured them. "We just had a difference of opinion."

"As long as he doesn't lay his hands on you," Dean said sternly.

"*Gamísou*—fuck off!" Turning his back on Dean and Michael, Apollo barked at Mindy. "It's time for us to leave." His sharp tone could have cut diamonds.

"I'm not ready to—"

Apollo cut her off. "We're going," he shouted, grabbing her by the elbow.

Mindy looked around the room. "I think it's best," she said apologetically.

Sophia and Demi rushed over to her and begged her not to leave. Mindy saw the concern in their eyes, but she assured them she knew what she was doing.

The ride back to Mindy's New York City apartment was silent. She was afraid to rile Apollo up again. On only one other occasion had she seen him behave this way, but not to this extent. Her friends were important to her and she didn't want to jeopardize those relationships. It was her hope he would be accepted into their circle, but she feared that was no longer possible. When they pulled into the parking garage by her building, she finally spoke.

"Why did you behave like that in front of my friends? I was very embarrassed."

"You embarrassed me," Apollo spat. "You made me look weak."

"How?" She was on the verge of tears.

"A man expects his woman to drop everything to be with him. You made me seem unimportant in front of those people."

"That's ridiculous. And you knew when you met me that I was busy with my career."

They exited the car and took the elevator to Mindy's floor. Disturbed by what he said, she waited until they were within the privacy of her apartment before she confronted him again.

"This relationship isn't going to work if you stifle me," she told him.

Apollo shot his arm out, unexpectedly seizing her throat with his strong hands. "I decide when we're over! Not you."

Mindy shrieked, punching and pushing at his chest trying to free herself from his grip. When he released her from the chokehold, he took a swing at her, the punch landing on the apple of her cheek. Her reaction was swift, lifting her knee to slam his crotch. Letting go to cup his injured area, Mindy was able to break free of Apollo and run to her bedroom.

While Mindy tended to her aching cheek, tears filled her eyes as she wondered how and why this had happened. The man had a temper and a possessive side that she wasn't sure she could live with, even if she loved him.

"Mindy, *Fotiá mou*, please come out," Mindy heard him from behind the door. "I'm sorry. I don't know what came over me. I love you so much … I went crazy when you said we might be over. *Agapi mou*, talk to me. I need you."

Mindy opened the door slowly. She stood at the threshold and looked at Apollo with wounded eyes. He ran his fingers through his hair, cupping the crown of his head in his hands. Mindy saw that he was genuinely upset and remorseful.

"I'll get some ice for you." A bruise was beginning to bloom on her cheek. Apollo came back seconds later holding an ice-filled dishtowel. He kissed her gently on the affected area and pressed the ice to her cheek. They stared at one another, Mindy scared and confused, and Apollo seemingly bearing the weight of what he'd done.

"It will never happen again," he promised. "I love you so much. I lost my mind. You know I would never hurt you."

"But you did," Mindy whispered. "Not only my face, but also my heart."

Apollo kissed her softly on the lips. "I can't live without you."

The next morning, Mindy was at her desk when she overheard her assistant arguing outside the office doorway. Mindy had specifically told him she didn't want to be disturbed and asked that he cancel all her meetings and hold her calls.

She and Apollo had made up the night before, but the incident at Demi's home and what followed after disturbed her.

"I don't give a damn what she said. I'm going in and don't even think of trying to stop me."

Mindy knew that voice only too well. Demi. She was wondering how long it would take for her to call. She didn't expect her to actually show up and, right now, it was the last thing Mindy needed.

Demi barreled through the doorway with Sophia following behind, stopping only to apologize to Mindy's assistant.

"What's this crap that you won't let anyone see you today?" Demi asked.

"Well, thanks for respecting my wishes."

"You will not barricade yourself from us."

Sophia laid her hand on Demi's arm, a signal for her to pull back a bit. "We're concerned for you, Mindy," Sophia told her. "Your boyfriend's behavior was very aggressive."

Demi moved closer to Mindy, eyeing her suspiciously. "What in hell is that on your cheek?"

Mindy brushed her fingers over the bruise that she had tried to conceal with makeup. "It's nothing. I was clumsy in the shower. I slipped when I opened the glass door and it hit me in the face."

"Is that the truth?" Sophia said gently.

"Of course."

"Apollo didn't do that? He seemed to have quite a temper last night," Demi pointed out.

"I know he was a little rude, but he's not a bad guy. He was nervous meeting all of you. He knows how much you mean to me."

"Well, he made a lousy impression."

"Maybe he's not the right man for you if he has such a bad temper," Sophia suggested.

"I didn't come here to tiptoe around the facts," Demi said. "We don't like him and we think he's wrong for you."

"Who I date is my decision. I don't need your consent."

"We're afraid for you," Sophia added. "He might hurt you."

"He won't. He loves me." She rose from her office chair and walked over to the large window, turning her back on them. Staring down onto the crowed street, she crossed her arms over her chest.

"That's not love." Demi raised her voice. "Obsession, maybe.

Definitely domination. Not love."

Mindy swung back around to face them, her eyes blazing. She fisted her hands on her hips. "I'll be fine. I won't bring him around if you hate him, but I'm not going to stop seeing him because you tell me to." She went back to her desk, clicked on the mouse to her computer and shuffled a stack of papers. "Now if you'll excuse me, I have a lot of work to do," she said without looking up.

Demi looked as though she was ready for a fight. Sophia tugged on her jacket sleeve. "Let's go." She turned to Mindy. "Please don't let this come between us. We love you. You can call me anytime you need me, okay?"

Mindy nodded. Sophia hugged Mindy goodbye, but Demi just stood there, waiting for Sophia.

"Bye, Dem," Mindy said, but Demi turned her back on her and walked out the door.

*"I love you. I hate that my weaknesses won over my love for you.
I never meant to hurt you."* —Jimmy Pappas to Anastacia 1958

Chapter 30

Mindy

Summer 2001

The months that followed the disastrous evening at Demi's home were relatively peaceful. Mindy and Apollo traveled between New York and Chios in order to spend time together. There was one other occasion, when they were out having dinner with his band, that Apollo's violent tendency emerged.

Mindy had done nothing to instigate it. She made a purely innocent remark that, for some reason, raised Apollo's ire. She could see the tightness in his jaw and the imperceptible flare of his nostrils, and it made Mindy's stomach clench in response.

She excused herself and set off for the ladies' room, wishing she could stay in there until she was sure Apollo's temper had calmed. Telling herself that she was making more of it than she should, she wet a towel with cold water, wrung it out and placed it on the back of her neck. Mindy then re-applied her lipstick, ran her hands through her hair and straightened out her skirt. Yes, she was definitely overreacting. She merely suggested that since they were gaining international popularity, the band should think about hiring someone to refine their brand and market them properly.

Dropping the wet towel into the trash can, she opened the door and was startled to find Apollo waiting for her to emerge. When their eyes met, he pushed her up against the wall and grabbed a fistful of her red locks, tugging until she thought he would pull the hairs from her scalp.

"Shut the fuck up and stay out of my business," he spewed. "I bring you along to look pretty, not to make me look like an asshole."

Mindy was scared speechless. She was frightened of this Apollo. How could this be the same man who'd made beautiful, tender love to her just hours before?

"I won't embarrass you further. I'll leave," Mindy said, searching for the strength and courage to be defiant, but her words were too tremulous.

"You'll do no such thing. No woman walks out on me." His hand was like a vice around her arm, cutting off the circulation. Mindy was sure she'd have a ring of bruises around her arm in the morning.

Later on the way home, Apollo apologized and explained he was under a lot of pressure. Mindy accepted his excuse and told herself it had been her fault in the first place. She wouldn't like it any better if Apollo had interfered in her business, which he never had. Although he occasionally made snide remarks, dismissing her 'dressmaking' as nothing to take seriously.

By the next day, all had been forgotten and Mindy was enjoying the warm summer weather on the beautiful island. She felt content and at peace as she walked along the beach, gazing up at the sky as the shoreline swallowed the colorful sunset.

But Mindy's tranquility was short lived. That evening, Apollo and she went to dinner at one of his favorite tavernas. Inside, Apollo met several friends and they joined the jovial group at their table. The men began to drink pretty heavily and when the song changed from a ballad to *zembetiko*, they all got up to dance. Mindy clapped and cheered as they each took the dance floor, slapping their shoes and jumping in the air. Soon it had become a competition and they only stopped briefly to pour themselves another shot of ouzo.

When they finally sat down, one of the men squeezed Mindy's shoulders and ran his hand down the length of her back. "Did you enjoy that?" he asked. "Maybe Apollo will let me borrow you for a dance."

Mindy didn't respond. She smiled politely and ignored the question.

"It's time to go," Apollo said abruptly.

"But it's still early." Mindy was enjoying herself and she wasn't ready to call it a night.

Lifting Mindy from the chair by her arm, Apollo demanded she follow him.

It was nearing ten o'clock in the evening, the sky was dark, but from the reflection of the full moon, Mindy could tell a storm was brewing—although the one about to erupt from above was nothing compared to the tempest that had resulted from Apollo's jealousy.

Accusing Mindy of flirting with his friend and allowing him to put his hands on her, Apollo demeaningly reprimanded her.

"I didn't know you were a whore. How many men are you fucking behind my back in New York?"

He had that wild look in his eyes. Afraid to argue, she attempted to calm him, reassuring him that she only had eyes for him. But he was too enraged and beyond rational thought. They began to drive away, but Apollo was driving erratically and when she asked him to stop and let her drive, another argument ensued.

But this time, he'd gone too far. Throwing her off his Vespa he spat, "Find your own way home if you don't like my driving."

Frightened, Mindy pulled her cell phone out, but Apollo grabbed it from her hands and shoved her, knocking her into a row of thorny bushes. "Serves you right," he shouted as he sped off, leaving her stranded on the side of the road alone, abandoned, and bruised.

Mindy walked along the main road. She assumed that eventually she would find a public place to make a call. But who was there to call upon? Mindy didn't know a soul in Chios except for Apollo. She had never felt so alone and unloved.

Turning when the glare of a headlight lit up the pavement, Mindy began to walk faster when she realized Apollo had returned for her.

"Go away," she shouted.

"Hold on. You'll get lost in the dark."

"I'd rather get lost than go anywhere with you."

"*Fotiá mou—*"

"Stop calling me that. I'm not your anything."

Apollo caught up with Mindy and blocked her from walking away. "I'm sorry. You made me crazy with jealousy. I love you so much … I can't stand another man touching you. Let me take you home." He led her to his bike and helped her onto it.

"Take me to a hotel. I'm not staying with you." Mindy reluctantly mounted the Vespa.

"No, please. I'll make it up to you." Once again Mindy gave in. She wasn't sure why. Maybe it was the pleading look in his expression. Or simply that she couldn't resist him. Even when he was at his worst.

The next day, Apollo was sweet and attentive. He cooked for her, applied ointment on her arms and legs to heal the scratches from the bush she'd fallen into, and announced he'd be taking her to meet his family that evening.

Why would he take her now? she wondered. "I need some air. I'm going to take a walk on the beach."

"Do you want me to come with you?"

"Why don't you rest and I'll be back in a while." She kissed him lightly on the lips and left his apartment.

Savoring the bit of solitude, Mindy let her mind wander as she planted her toes in the sand at the shoreline. Seawater ebbed and flowed, gently slapping against her ankles and in those brief moments she was at peace. Later, she would fret over meeting Apollo's family.

When Mindy returned, he met her at the front door and showered her with kisses. "I missed you *fotiá mou*," Apollo said as he took her in his arms. Relief washed over her when she saw the gleam in his eyes. Apollo could be moody. He was not a man who could handle pressure or disappointment, and Mindy was still discovering how to reel him in from his darkness. But he had a sweet side as well, and could be very romantic when he chose to be. It was those times Mindy waited for and treasured.

When the hour came and they left for Apollo's family home, Mindy was nervous. She hoped they'd be receptive to her and the idea of a relationship between her and Apollo. They had known each other over a year now, but he always seemed reluctant to introduce her to them and she couldn't help but wonder why.

The house they rode up to was not what Mindy expected. He described the rows and rows of mastic trees, but not the beautiful landscape and the home itself. She noticed field workers cutting into the barks of trees. Below each base was a circle of sand, and Apollo explained that when the tear-shaped drops of sap fell into the sand it crystallized. The fieldworkers would later harvest those crystals.

Apollo's family had owned this land for generations and they'd become quite prosperous, a fact that was evident as they stepped inside a house far more grand than she'd imagined. His younger sister, Athena greeted them at the door, giving Mindy an enthusiastic kiss on both cheeks. She looked very much like her brother, with eyes that mirrored his chocolate brown ones and the silky, dark hair that grazed her shoulders the same color as his.

Athena led them through the large foyer, halting when they reached the great room where the rest of the family sat sipping wine.

A stocky gray-haired man with tanned, weathered skin rose from the sofa to greet them.

Trapping Mindy in a bear hug, Apollo's father introduced himself. Warmth and acceptance emanated from this man, his eyes dancing with delight. In contrast, when she made her way to his mother, who remained in her seat, the chill from her icy stare as she raked Mindy from head to toe unnerved her.

At the dinner table, Athena peppered Mindy with questions with Mrs. Stathis interjecting to interrogate further.

"How do you plan to continue this relationship from such a distance?" she asked.

"Mamá," Apollo warned.

Glaring at him with raised eyebrows, she stated, "It's a reasonable question."

"We do the best we can," Mindy answered, patting Apollo's hand to let him know it was fine. "We both travel often, but we make it work."

Mrs. Stathis gulped her last sip of wine and gestured for her husband to pour her another glass. "How old are you Mindy?"

Caught off guard by the question, Mindy answered with a defensive tone. "Forty-five. And you?" she challenged.

"We're not talking about me. It's you I need to know about. Are you aware that my son is thirty-six?"

"What of it? We are both mature, successful adults."

No one dared say a word. This was a battle of the wills, and Mindy refused to let herself be bullied by this woman.

"You have a big career and no children. I'd say it was doubtful that you could have any now. My son deserves children, he—"

"Olympia!" Mr. Stathis barked.

She ignored him. "You are too old for my son. You cannot give him children. You live in another country. Have your fun, go home and leave my son to marry who he's meant to."

Mindy could feel the tears welling and catching between her lashes. Turning to Apollo, she asked in a low voice if there was someone else.

"Don't pay attention," Athena said. "Mamá thinks anyone from another *horio eínai énas xénos.*" Mindy furrowed her brow in confusion. "Unless you come from our village, she considers you a stranger," Athena clarified.

"That doesn't leave too many options," Mindy said sardonically.

"He only needs one option. Aphrodite is waiting for Apollo to settle down," Olympia insisted.

"Who Apollo settles down with would be his decision." Mindy turned toward Apollo. "And what do you have to say? Who is this woman to you? And why are you sitting here not saying one word while your mother insults me?"

Apollo didn't answer Mindy. He drew his eyes downward, staring at the food on his plate.

Mindy looked around the table. She was about to lose it. "Damn it! Does everyone in your family carry the name of a Greek God? Is that why Aphrodite fits into your mother's plan?" With each sentence her voice grew louder and shriller. She stood up and threw her napkin on the table. "It's time to leave," she said, glaring at Apollo. "Mr. Stathis, Athena, it was a pleasure to meet you. Mrs. Stathis," she said, trying to contain her fury, "it's been enlightening."

"I'm sorry," Apollo addressed his family. Marching behind Mindy, he caught up with her at the front door, grasping her arm tightly.

"Your behavior was inexcusable."

"Mine?! What about yours? You let that woman insult and humiliate me. And you sat there without saying a word." She wrenched her arm from his grasp.

"What would you like me to say? She's my mother. You could have overlooked the comments. She only wants what's best for me."

They reached the car and got in. "And I'm not what's best for you in her eyes. Well, I'm sorry. I'm not Greek, I don't come from your village, and I wasn't named after a damned mythical God like the rest of you. I'm completely unworthy of you," Mindy barked out contemptuously.

They rode the rest of the way home in silence, Mindy only breaking it once to ask Apollo to slow down. When he answered her request by picking up speed, Mindy prayed she'd get home in one piece, and thankfully she did.

"I'm leaving in the morning, even if I have to find a hotel until I can book a flight home," she told him as she walked through his front door. When she met his stare, a chill crawled up her spine. It was as if the devil had crawled inside his body. The stern, flushed face, the dilated pupils, and the clenched fists at his side—the transformation from the charming man she loved to the uncontrollable beast who frightened her was about to happen.

Before she could duck, he swung his arm and punched her in the face. She fell backward, slamming against the wall before she fell to the floor.

"That's for embarrassing me in front of my family." Lifting her off the ground, Apollo kicked her in the stomach. "That's for being rude to my mother." He ignored her squeals of pain and her fearful pleas to stop. "This one is because you asked for it." He yanked her by the hair, then slapped her so hard across the cheek his ring cut her face. "You're not worth it," he spat as he threw her into the wall and walked away.

Mindy grabbed her bag while his back was turned and ran into the bathroom—the only door in his home with a lock on it. She heard a door slam. Thinking Apollo might have left the house, she debated whether to run or stay where she was. Reaching in her bag she retrieved her mobile phone to make a call.

Chapter 31

Sophia

Summer 2001

Sophia groaned when she heard the ringtone of her cell phone. Sunrise peeked through the window shades, casting a golden hue in the darkened bedroom. Who could be calling at this hour?

With eyes still closed, Sophia felt around her side table until she found what she was looking for and flipped it open. "Hello," she said, her voice grainy. "Mindy? Is that you? Where are you? What's wrong?"

Alarmed by the sound of Mindy's panicked cries, Sophia sat up against the headboard. "He did what?" Sophia said, louder than she meant to. Dean, who'd been sleeping beside Sophia, awoke when he heard the distress in his wife's voice.

Dean looked at her with concern. "Mindy," she mouthed. "Apollo hit her."

"Is she hurt?" Dean seethed. "I'm going to kill the son of a bitch!"

Sophia lifted her hand to quiet him. "Where is he right now? Okay. You can't trust that he won't come back. Stay there with the door locked. What's happening?" Sophia asked. "What's that banging? Listen to me. I don't care if he's sorry or how many times he tells you he loves you. Do not open the door."

"Where are they? I'm calling the police and I'll head over there," Dean said.

Sophia shook her head. "She's at his apartment in Chios."

"Fuck! Give me the phone," Dean demanded. "Mindy, where in his house are you? The bathroom. Is there a window? Good. Do you think you can climb out of it? Do you know how far it is to get to the town? Perfect. Walk to the nearest café and call a taxi to take you to our home. The key is under the clay flowerpot near the side entrance. Call the police when you get there and I'll be on the next plane out."

Sophia took the phone from Dean. "Call me when you get to the house."

"I'm coming with you," Sophia told Dean.

"The hell you are! You're staying put with the kids where you'll be safe."

"I don't want you to approach him. Let the police handle it," Sophia said.

"I'd take Michael with me but I don't want to bother him. He's at the height of his season. I'll call my dad to go with me. I'll deal with the police and make sure she gets checked by a doctor before I bring her home."

Sophia nodded. "Okay. I think that's a good idea."

Dean called his father and Sophia made the travel arrangements. There was a plane to Athens that evening and from there they would fly to Chios.

Two hours later, Mindy called to let Sophia know she was at their house. Apollo knew where the house was and would figure out where to find her. Sophia was relieved to know the police were on their way to take Mindy's statement.

After several hours had gone by, Mindy called back to say she was at the hospital. The police had insisted she get examined and, once there, the x-rays showed that Mindy had a cracked rib. She also needed four stitches where Apollo's ring had cut her cheek, but she was safe and had been assured he would not be allowed in her room. She learned from the authorities that this was not the first complaint that had been made against Apollo, and although he was from a prominent family, he would not be able to skirt assault charges this time. Apollo would be behind bars when Dean arrived, and for that Mindy was very grateful.

Less than a week later, Dean and Stavros returned home with Mindy. Sophia was shocked to see the condition of Mindy's face, but at least Sophia's fears for her safety were assuaged.

"You'll stay with us until you're fully healed," Sophia suggested.

"My body might heal, but I'm not sure about my heart."

"You'll put it behind you and eventually it will be a distant memory."

"I should have dumped him after his horrible behavior with all of you. Or after the first time he hit me."

"Why didn't you?"

Mindy stared into nothingness as the tears began to fall. "I convinced myself that it was my fault and that I shouldn't have challenged him when he was under stress. He would tell me he loved me and couldn't live without me. And I believed him. Each time he hit me and later apologized, I thought it would be the last time."

"Why would you let him have that kind of power over you?"

"I wanted to believe he really loved me." Mindy closed her eyes. She shrugged her shoulders. "I thought I had finally found who I've been searching for. But I guess not everyone experiences true love. Maybe I'm not meant for it. I should give up on the idea and concentrate on my career. That was always my priority anyway. If it wasn't, I'd still have Tyler."

"Love finds us at different times. You can't force it. Tyler wasn't meant for you. That was a long time ago and you shouldn't beat yourself up over the choices you made."

"I give up," Mindy shook her head. "It's too painful. I'm not going to go through this again. And honestly, I'm not sure I'll ever be able to trust anyone."

"Life is full of heartaches and triumphs. Don't close off that beautiful spirit of yours over someone who wasn't worth a minute of your time much less a piece of your heart."

Sophia motioned for Mindy to follow her into the TV room. She fluffed the sofa pillows and instructed Mindy to shed her shoes and sprawl out on the couch. Turning on the television, Sophia handed her the remote.

"I'm going to call Demi and Donna. We'll have a girl's night like the old days—movies, chocolate and ice cream."

"And wine. Plenty of wine," Mindy added.

"I was so young during the war. I didn't fully absorb the gravity of what was happening in my country and the rest of Europe." —Anastacia to Sophia 1972

Chapter 32

Sophia

September 2001

It was unusually early in the day for Sophia to be out in Jamesport, but she had an appointment with the contractor to run through the house she and Dean were building on the vineyard property. She had expected to move in before the school year began, but all hope of that had been dashed. It had been a full year since Sophia made the decision to sell the home she'd shared with Will and raised her children in, and she was beginning to grow impatient.

The contractor had not yet arrived, so she decided to peek into Demi's office to say hello. Cia was at her side, donning a sundress that emulated a large sunflower. It was a beautiful, sunny day. The weather was warm and the sky a clear blue. Sophia hoped to convince Demi to play hooky with her and have lunch in East Hampton. She might even twist her arm to do a little shopping afterward.

She found Demi staring out the window of her office. An uncharacteristically worrisome look framed her face as she played with the eternity band Michael had given her for their twentieth wedding anniversary.

"Hi."

Demi swiveled around. "Hi. What are you doing here at this time of the morning?" Before Sophia could answer, Demi stretched her arms out. "Come to me, *koukla*." She bent down and wrapped her arms around the child, who giggled while Demi showered her with kisses."

"You had a serious look on your face," Sophia commented.

The phone rang and Demi lifted her finger, gesturing for Sophia to wait. "No, I don't have the TV on. Why? What? I'll call you back later."

"What's going on?" Sophia was alarmed by Demi's expression.

"That was my manager at the Commack store. She said a plane hit the World Trade Center and the building is on fire."

"My God! How could something like that happen? It's such a clear day."

"I'm not sure," Demi said as she pointed the remote to the TV mounted on her office wall. "Maybe the pilot had a heart attack."

As the commentator reported what little he knew, the two women stood, their eyes glued to the screen. But while he spoke, the live footage behind him shocked the world. A second plane hit the other tower.

The blood drained from Sophia's face. "Dino is in the city this morning. He had a meeting with a distributor. This was deliberate. Two planes—two. They won't admit it yet until it's confirmed, but what else could it be?"

Sophia tried not to panic. Reaching in her bag, she drew out her phone. "I don't know where you are, but something is going on in the city. Terrorist attack maybe. Get back on the train and come home." Sophia's voice cracked. She'd only reached his voicemail.

"Sit down." Demi escorted her to the chair across from her desk. "It's a big city. He's nowhere near there, I'm sure. He probably isn't aware anything is going on."

"That's not the point. What if they don't stop at the towers? Is the Empire State Building next? Or the Chrysler building? Why isn't he answering?" she asked, punching in his number again.

"My God! How many people are trapped on those floors?" Demi was thinking aloud as she watched in horror.

The gravity of the situation was beginning to take root. "And the planes, Demi. There must have been several hundred people on each plane."

"Michael is out in the field. Stay here." Demi poured Sophia a glass of ice water. "Sit. I'm going to fill him in and I'll be right back."

Sophia tried calling Dean obsessively, but to no avail. She wasn't even reaching his voicemail anymore. It was as though all service had been completely cut off.

The city was on lockdown. The commentator reported the bridges and tunnels closed, airports grounded and train service ceased.

Demi returned with Michael.

"Even if I could get in touch with him, he won't be able to get out of the city," Sophia said. "I want him home. I wish I knew where he was."

"He'll be fine," Michael assured her. "He's in Chelsea. He's not that far downtown." Michael turned up the volume.

"It has just been confirmed that a plane has crashed into the western side of the Pentagon," Peter Jennings of ABC news announced.

"Holy shit!" Michael cursed. "What the fuck?"

Sophia retrieved a sippy cup filled with juice and a few toys from her bag when Cia began to get restless. Watching intently for any bit of news regarding rescue and survivors, what they saw from their screens looked grim. Sophia couldn't begin to imagine what it must be like to be trapped there and she silently prayed that the first responders were able to get everyone out. And then it hit her. "Amy is in Washington."

"I'm sure all the government buildings are on lockdown already," Michael said.

"I'll try her," Demi offered. Grimly, she flipped her phone shut and shook her head.

"There's probably no use in attempting to contact Mindy. She's uptown, so I'm sure she's fine, but we should keep trying her, anyway." How many mothers, husbands and wives must be frantic, Sophia thought—families who are certain their loved ones were in those buildings, and are praying they were able to evacuate.

And then she knew their fears would be realized as she watched, before her eyes, the south tower crumble to the ground as if it were made of cardboard. A bellowing sound came from deep within them, as they watched in shock. Demi and Sophia burst into tears and Michael put his protective arms around both of them, but nothing could assuage the sick grief that was building in their hearts. It was a tragedy of epic proportions only to be multiplied as they witnessed the destruction of the second tower.

People fled, running from the clouds of white debris chasing them through the streets of downtown New York City. Reporters covered from head to toe in remnants of what used to be the Twin Towers, held microphones attempting to give the public a rundown of what was happening.

The phone rang and Demi picked it up. "Oh, thank God. Sophia has been frantically calling you."

Sophia snapped her head around. Her eyes widened.

"He wants to talk to you." Sophia grabbed the phone from Demi.

"Dino," Sophia cried. "Where are you?" She listened to what he had to say. "Well, keep trying. They have to let people out of the city eventually. I'll feel better when you're home. Love you too."

"He's safe. The cell calls must have been overloaded. He couldn't get through. He called from a landline and even that took a while. There's no way for him to get out of the city right now. He's going to Penn Station to wait and see if they open up service."

With Sophia's phone still in hand, the ringtone sounded. "Evvie? I know. Really? That's awful. No. Stay where you are. Lend some support where you can. There's no need to leave school. I'm at the Carriage House with Aunt Demi if anything changes. No, 'but Mom.' Please don't give me an argument. You're in a safe place."

While Sophia had been speaking with Evvie, Demi had taken a call from Kristos, her oldest.

"That was Kristos. He's asking to be picked up also."

"I don't know why," Sophia said. "What is coming home going to accomplish?"

"I think some of the students are in a panic. Kristos said the principal put the TV on in the cafeteria."

Sophia exhaled. "I know. Evvie said some of her classmates have relatives that worked in those buildings. I can only pray that most people got out before the building collapsed."

Michael shook his head, his expression grim. "Not from what is being reported. It looks bad."

"Yes, Evvie?" Sophia answered the phone in annoyance. "Alright. We'll be there in a few minutes to get all of you, and then we will swing by the middle school to get Stella."

"You caved?" Demi asked rhetorically. "You never cave."

"She argued that they'll be the only kids left in school if we didn't pick them up."

"Let's go then."

Dean jumped on the first train out when he learned that the Long Island Railroad was running a limited service. When he arrived home, Sophia could see he was visibly shaken. The minute he walked through the door, she threw her arms around him.

Before he had arrived home, Sophia had spoken to the children and assured them Dean was safe, but they had a long discussion about the horrific events that had taken place that day. Her children had seen too much tragedy in their short lives, with their own father dying in a much publicized plane crash. Now they would have to console friends who might have lost their own parents.

Evvie and Nicky came down from their rooms when they heard their stepfather enter the foyer. When Sophia broke her embrace with Dean, Evvie lunged forward, giving him an unexpected hug. "You're home," is all she said.

Sophia and Dean exchanged a quizzical glance. Up to this point, Evvie had kept her distance from him after he married her mother. Before that, Dean had always been like a much-loved uncle to her, but after the wedding that all changed. Now their relationship seemed forced and Evvie made it clear she resented Dean, even with the little progress they'd made lately.

But Sophia understood her daughter. Evvie could feign a tough exterior but, in truth, she was fragile, and another loss would have surely shattered her.

Nicky hung back, planted on the bottom step, his hands deep in the pockets of his khaki cargo shorts. He was a teen who shared little of what he felt inside, but his thoughts couldn't be hidden from his expressive gray eyes—at least not from Sophia. She extended her arms out and waved Nicky over.

"I need to tell you something," Dean told Sophia after the children had retreated to their rooms for the night. His voice was husky as though tears might come to the surface.

"I knew something was very wrong when you came home. Something more than what is obviously going on."

They took a seat on the sofa, Dean cupping his hands over Sophia's.

"It's related to that. It's Elizabeth," he said gravely. "I'm not sure she and her father, or anyone else in their firm, made it out of the towers."

Sophia gasped. Elizabeth was Dean's manipulative ex-wife. She had never liked her, and Dean's marriage to her ended bitterly, but this was devastating news. "How do you know? People were evacuating. Maybe they got out as soon as the plane hit the tower."

"I've tried calling her number, and her father's as well." Dean shook his head somberly. "When I couldn't get a connection, I tried some of my old colleagues. Nothing."

"Did you call her mother?"

"No. I don't know what to do. I don't want to add to her stress, and hearing from me—well, you know how that went in the end."

"I'm not going to tell you what to do. That's your decision," Sophia told him. "But this is no time for old feuds. She may not have anyone to rely on if the worst has happened. Can you imagine losing your husband and your daughter? I don't know how I would get through it."

How many more friends and acquaintances would be touched by this tragedy? Sophia wondered. People commuted from Long Island and Westchester, New Jersey and Connecticut to work in the city. Too many lives lost. So many families left to grieve their loved ones. The number of people presumed dead was staggering. Not to mention the fire fighters who came from every town in the tri-state area and beyond and lost their lives to save others. The country was grieving and there wasn't a soul who wasn't affected in some way.

It took more than twenty-four hours to hear from Amy. Sophia tried her phone several times. Donna called her to see if she had any information on Amy. She had not been able to get through to her either. Mindy fled the city the minute the lockdown was lifted. She was frightened for her friend who she also tried to contact. Demi was relentless, punching in Amy's number over and over again. She and Sophia viewed the news clips from every channel, searching for Amy in the crowd as they watched the evacuation of the capital building.

Sophia lunged for her cell phone when she heard it ring, exhaling loudly. "Thank God! Amy, where are you?"

"Put her on speaker," Demi said.

"I'm home. At the Washington house. Communications were completely down here. I just got service back."

"We were worried sick about you," Sophia said.

"The reports said a plane was circling the capital and the one that went down in Pennsylvania was headed there," Demi said.

"Yes. It was all quite frightening. They evacuated us quickly, but with the news of the towers and the Pentagon and the threat to Washington, we knew we had to stay composed, but it was difficult."

"Are you staying in Washington for now?" Sophia asked.

"No. I'm about to get into a limo. It's imperative that I come back to New York immediately. Ezra and Adam are with me. I have to go. Another call is coming in, but I'll talk to you soon."

The days that followed were surreal. It was as though the country was in an alternate universe. No one spoke of anything else—at work, school or the stores—and the networks replayed the devastation over and over. All airports in the country were shut down, and the quieted skies mimicked the morose mood of the people.

Yet from the rubble, a glimmer of light shone through. A new sense of patriotism was reborn. Flags were raised on the front porches of just about every home and even some miniature stars and stripes were attached to vehicles, flapping in victory as they drove through the streets of America. Footage of strangers aiding other strangers during the destruction was the only silver lining in that carnage of flesh and concrete. There was no distinction between black or white, Asian or Hispanic. Everyone was American, and they pulled together as a united people to help one another.

Even conscious minded children contributed. Piggy banks were broken for donations and lemonade stands collected their profits for the Red Cross. Nicky and Evvie put their heads together, gathering Kristos, Paul and Stella to paint USA t-shirts and create red, white and blue jewelry. They set up a table outside the vineyard tasting room, dragging a large chalkboard from the basement to advertise their fundraiser and selling the products they created.

Patrons of the vineyard were impressed. "Your parents must be very proud of you," a well dressed middle-aged woman complimented the children. Sophia had been supervising them, although they were perfectly capable on their own.

"Are you their mother?" the woman asked.

"These two," Sophia answered, pointing out Evvie and Nicky. "The other three are my niece and nephews. And this little one," referring to Cia resting on her shoulder, "is my youngest."

"Well, it looks like you've done a good job with them. Nice to see. Very nice to see."

Later, an old frail man with wrinkled, spotty skin and faded eyes the shade of pale aquamarines stopped by the fundraising table. He was wearing a ball cap with a World War II veterans' logo.

"You kids giving this money to the Red Cross? Good for you. Good for you," he said before they could answer.

The man looked to be about eighty in Sophia's estimation. He walked without a cane and his voice was strong, but he leaned both hands on the table for extra support.

"Damn shame this business. I never thought I'd live to see the day this would happen. When we fought in the big one, we hoped to protect our children from the enemy coming to destroy us." He shook his head. "Never thought I'd see this day." He dug into his back pocket and took out a thick, black wallet. Pulling out a fifty-dollar bill, he handed it to Kristos. "You donate this to the Red Cross for me. Keep up the good work kids."

The whole day went the same—people complimenting the children, giving their opinions on the situation and telling their own stories. By the time the tasting room closed for the evening, they had sold out of everything they made.

After days of conflict running through his mind, Dean decided to stop by Mrs. Whitaker's home to pay his respects and see if there was anything he could do for her. Sophia agreed that was the right thing to do. The realization struck Dean that along with Elizabeth and Mr. Whitaker, every colleague he'd worked with over the years who was in the building that morning was presumed dead. This was not the time for old resentments and, from all accounts, his ex-mother-in-law may have lost her husband and her daughter. Survival lists were posted every day but so far their names were not among the lists' survivors or of the bodies recovered—they had all perished in a toxic cloud of dust.

Sophia was worried for Dean. Unsure of the frame of mind he'd come home with after his visit, she put Cia to sleep early so they could have a quiet evening and talk.

"When she first saw me in her foyer, I was sure she was going to throw me out. The hate and resentment on her face made me wish I was the one who died."

Squeezing Dean's hand, Sophia closed her eyes shut. The thought was unbearable.

"But then she collected herself, as she always did, and told me it was nice of me to come. I asked her if there was anything I could help her with and she said the lawyers were taking care of business. Mrs. Whitaker was always able to maintain that calm veneer, but for the first time I saw vulnerability in her, and when she looked at me and said she had no one left in the world, my heart broke for her."

"What is she going to do? What do you do when you're grieving and suddenly responsible for an entire business? One that physically doesn't exist any longer but the information must be somewhere. How can it be retrieved?"

"I'm not sure," Dean answered. "With financials, there are always back up files. I'm sure that's the last thing on her mind right now." Dean played with the wedding rings on Sophia's fingers. "Elizabeth was with someone. It was getting serious, Mrs. Whitaker told me. Enough so that they took him into the business." Dean fixed his eyes on Sophia's.

"He's missing too?"

Dean nodded. "Had I still been married to her, it would have been me in those towers."

If Dean had remained married to Elizabeth and perished with the thousands of souls on that fateful day, Sophia knew in her heart that she would have been destroyed even though he was married to someone else. It may have actually been worse, never to have had the opportunity to see how their love could have flourished or to be able to express the depth of their feelings for one another.

"It wasn't your time. You were meant to grow old and gray with me." Sophia tried to put a smile on his face and help him get past the gravity of the situation. But these days, it seemed that everyone carried the weight of the world's evils on their shoulders, and no one person could predict when life would go back to normal, or if it ever would at all.

Chapter 33

Demi

November 2001

I'm so sorry to have kept you waiting," Mindy told Sophia, Demi and Donna. They'd been seated on a white leather sofa for over half an hour, each of them nursing a cup of tea that Mindy's assistant had offered them.

The décor in Mindy's office consisted of stark white walls and furnishings. The larger than life bright pink peony *Bloom* logo painted on the wall behind her asymmetrical Lucite desk was the only splash of color accenting the room.

"My meeting went later than I'd expected and now I'm running behind schedule."

"It's okay. We understand. No need to worry," Sophia assured her.

"You came all the way into the city and now I don't have time to go out for lunch. Are you sure you don't mind eating here at the office? You can go without me if you—"

"Shut up already. You do realize how much time you're wasting?" Demi asked wryly.

"Come, follow me," Mindy waved. Turning, Mindy looked over to Demi. "You haven't gained a drop of grace since high school, you know?"

Demi raised her pinky and pretended to drink from an invisible teacup as though she were the Queen of England.

They followed Mindy into a small conference room where her assistant had set the table and laid out platters of food.

"This is impressive on such short notice," Donna said, admiring the spread before her. "I need an assistant."

"I like this better than a restaurant. We won't have to shout over the noise," Sophia added.

"I'm starved. Let's eat before I start biting my nails off," Demi joked sarcastically.

"Too bad we couldn't do this at the end of the week. Amy will be in New York by then," Sophia said.

"But I'll be out of town," Mindy replied.

"Is she coming in to campaign?" Donna asked.

Sophia nodded.

"How are all the kids faring since 9/11?" Mindy asked.

"If they'd stop talking about anthrax and possible future attacks in school, they might be a little less nervous. Honestly, I know they have to be informed on current events, but they're still children," Sophia complained.

"You can't shield them from the world, Sophia," Donna defended, pointing her fork.

"No, but each child is different. Evvie seems to be fine, but Nicky is afraid of everything. If a plane flies overhead, he flinches as though it will crash directly on him."

Demi knew Sophia wasn't exaggerating. Driving on the Long Island Expressway only days before, a plane had flown overhead, positioning to land at Long Island McArthur Airport. The shadow of the aircraft seemed to engulf Demi's car in its grasp, like a hawk zoning in on its prey. Nicky began to scream. "It's going to crash on us." By the time Demi told him it wasn't so, the plane was out of view.

"I haven't noticed any lasting negative effect on Kristos and Paul, but Stella is anxious. She didn't want me to come into the city today."

Demi had assured her it was safe and that life had to go on as usual without fear.

"Mine haven't said too much one way or another." Donna sipped her orange-infused ice water.

"Demi," Mindy started. "when are you going to tell us what's on your mind?"

"What makes you think there is something on my mind?"

Mindy leaned back in her chair and folded her arms. "How long have we known each other?"

Sophia and Donna tried to conceal the smirk on their faces.

"Battle of the wills. Glad to see you back on your game. You didn't lose your Chutzpah, as your mother would say." Sophia tugged on a lock of Mindy's long, red hair, which she'd straightened. Gone were the natural waves she'd always boasted in the past.

"Therapy will do wonders." Mindy scrunched her nose and tugged Sophia's hair in return. "Anyway ... back to Demi."

Demi sat silently. For once in her life, words eluded her. She couldn't explain how she felt. If she tried she thought she might cry, and that was the last thing she wanted to do. After all the horrific events of the past few weeks, she had convinced herself that her little problems were inconsequential. Or maybe her emotions had gotten the best of her and it was all in her mind. But as the entire world seemed to be in chaos, Demi thought her own tiny corner of it was falling apart.

"Oh, for heaven's sake, Demi. If you don't say it, then I will," Sophia scolded. "She thinks Michael is having an affair, which is ridiculous and not true."

"Why would you think that?" Mindy asked as though it were an impossibility.

"What would you think if your husband was on the phone and hung up as soon as you walked in the room?"

"Um ... he was done with the call?"

"Funny, Mindy. More than once? And on top of it, this pretty bartender makes every excuse to be near him. And a few times when he was gone for a stretch of time, I asked him where he went and he made up some lame excuse."

"It sounds like you're looking for something that isn't there," Donna said. "Michael is a gem. Now if you want to see an asshole for a husband, come to my house. I have one on display."

"My advice to you," Mindy said, "is to go shopping and buy the sexiest lingerie you can find. Then go home and seduce your husband, because there's no way that man is cheating on you. But, if you really think he is, just rip off the Band-aid and ask him straight out. But whatever you do, be the Demi we know and love—not this mopey person I don't recognize."

"Didn't he buy you that beautiful ring you're wearing for your anniversary?" Donna pointed out.

"Big shit," Demi replied dryly. "Anyone can go to the store and pick something out. It was our twentieth."

"Now you're being a sulky brat," Sophia berated her. "I went with him to pick out that ring. He was very specific about what he wanted. Are you looking for an argument? Because you're not justified. He told me that as beautiful as the ring was, in his eyes, nothing could compete with your beauty. Does that sound like a husband who doesn't love you?"

"My gut tells me something is off, that's all I know for sure."

Sophia could vouch for Michael all she wanted, but Michael's behavior was not typical of him and Demi worried he was falling out of love with her. The token anniversary ring felt as though it was something he did out of obligation. He knew she would have expected something, but what she really wanted was more of him and lately his mind seemed to be elsewhere.

That evening when Demi returned home from the city, the house was unusually quiet. She'd promised the children they could stay over at Sophia and Dean's new home. Situated on the same piece of land, the children bounced from house to house, but tonight they'd planned a sleepover.

"Michael," Demi called out, but the house was silent. The TV was not on as it often was in the evening. She heard no footsteps and no shower running. *Where the hell could he be?* Just when they could finally have some time alone, Michael was nowhere to be found. It was as Demi suspected. He wasn't interested in being alone with her at all.

Demi drudged up the staircase and shuffled into her bedroom. Without paying attention, she flung her bag onto the bed, hitting Michael with it. She hadn't noticed him when she entered the room. She screamed when he cursed on impact.

"You almost gave me a heart attack," Demi screeched.

"Me? Why did you hit me?"

"I didn't know you were there."

"I had a busy day. I'm beat, so I thought I'd I doze off until you got home. Did you have a good day with the girls?" Michael asked.

"Yeah, it was okay." Demi sat on the bed and faced Michael who pulled himself up against the maple headboard. Demi sucked in a deep breath and exhaled nervously.

"Just okay?" Michael furrowed his brow. "You were looking forward to going and it was just okay?"

Demi bit her bottom lip. The long strand of pearls she wore were being wrapped and unwrapped around her finger as she toyed with it. She ran her hand through her hair and picked at a pill of fuzz on her sweater.

"What's on your mind, Demi?"

Steeling herself, she took the advice Mindy had given her earlier that day. She would lose her mind if she didn't know for sure. "Michael, are you having an affair?"

He pulled himself up straighter, looking incredulously into her eyes. "For fuck sake, Demi! Why would you ask me something like that?"

"That's not an answer to my question."

Michael balled his fists to his side. Demi could see he was furious with her. "What have I ever done to make you suspicious of me? Huh? What? Have you ever seen me touch another woman or even flirt with one?"

"No but—"

"No buts!"

"Don't yell at me! I'm not the one acting weird and secretive. You're hiding something. I know you are. You're on the phone more than usual and when I catch you on it you hang up quickly."

"I'm running a business. Calls come in all day for me."

"What about the women that hang on you?"

"What women?"

"Don't play me for a fool. That new bartender in your tasting room just to name one. The little tart looks like she's ready to jump your bones." Demi moved away from the bed and tuned her back on Michael. "If you don't love me anymore, just tell me."

Michael angrily strode over to Demi and turned her to face him. "Maybe it's you, Demi. Are you having an affair? Are you looking for a guilt free way out of our marriage by accusing me of something you're doing? Were you *really* with the girls today?"

"You son of a bitch!" Demi shoved him. "How dare you make this my fault?"

"How does it feel?" Michael asked. There was bitterness in his tone. "You don't like having the tables turned on you, do you? I know you are not having an affair any more than I am. You know how I know that?"

Demi shook her head.

"Because I trust you, and your love for me. I thought your trust in me was equal."

His stare seared through her. He was hurt. She could see it and she didn't know what to do to fix it. But he still hadn't explained his uncharacteristic behavior. And Demi hadn't imagined the feeling clawing at her gut. Was she simply paranoid? She thought not, yet looking at her husband he seemed wounded and sincere in his feelings for her.

"Michael," Demi whispered. She reached for him but he pulled away. Bereft, she stared down at her rejected hands. "I love you so much that when something seems off to me my mind goes crazy. The thought of ever possibly losing you ..." Emotion constricted her throat.

"You can worry about losing me to an illness or an accident, that's beyond our control. But for you to entertain for even one second that I would cheat on you or leave you for someone else ..." Michael stood up and turned his back to her. "That hurts. Really hurts." He began to walk away.

"Where are you going?"

"I need some space." Michael waved her off. "Just give me some space."

Demi kicked off her shoes. Sliding onto Michael's side of the bed she hugged his pillow, pressing her nose to it and breathing in his scent. If there was a moment in time she could take back and change, it was that. Michael had been acting odd and she was justified in asking the question, or so she thought at the time. Maybe she shouldn't have been so blunt. She could have simply started off by asking him why he had been acting so oddly. But no, she didn't know how to gently glide into a subject. Demi went full throttle, accusing Michael of the worst.

She wondered how much time he'd need to blow off steam before going down to apologize—and ask the questions she should have asked in the first place.

Killing time, Demi touched up her makeup, windexed the mirrors and picked up dirty clothing from her children's bedroom floors. Finally, when she couldn't wait any longer, she crept quietly down the steps.

Michael had the TV on, but from the annoyed look on his face, Demi could see his mind was not on the screen. He looked up at her blankly when she entered the room.

Swallowing nervously, she looked straight at him. "I need you to forgive me," she begged, walking to him and kneeling by his side. "You have to forgive me. Please." She rested her head on his lap. When he ran his hand through her hair, she lifted her head. "I never meant to hurt you. I love you so much I go a little crazy when I don't understand what's going on. I know you've been busy and I shouldn't have taken it personally."

Michael's expression gave nothing away. "Trust is everything in a marriage. If we don't have that, then we have nothing." He sighed. "But the truth is that I haven't been completely honest with you. I never was any good at keeping secrets."

Demi rose to her feet. "What? You're confusing me." Her voice became shrill. "One minute you swear you're faithful and the next you admit you're hiding something?" She felt as though her heart had sunk to her knees.

She began to run but Michael caught Demi's arm. "Wait. Enough already. Sit down and I'm going to settle this once and for all. But hell, Dem, I have to tell you—you can be damned infuriating."

"Me? I'm not the one with the secrets."

"Can you be quiet for one minute? Please." Michael pulled Demi onto the couch beside him. "The night of our anniversary I gave you this ring." He held Demi's hand and grazed his fingertips over the diamonds set into the band. "It was a week night, but I didn't want the evening to pass without doing something special."

"I remember," Demi said. "You took me to the Jamesport Manor Inn for dinner."

"Yes. A very nice restaurant, but not what I had in mind for a milestone anniversary."

"Well, there wasn't much more we could have done on a week night, I suppose." Demi shrugged her shoulders. "Why are you bringing this up now? That was months ago."

"I know. And if you recall, we were both working extended hours. It was the height of our busy season and, although it was all I could do at the moment, I made more elaborate arrangements for when our schedules allowed."

Demi looked at Michael blankly.

"I made reservations to take you to lunch tomorrow, so I could tell you that we were leaving that evening for Atlantis Paradise Island. Just the two of us."

"Get out of here!" Demi shoved his chest with her hands.

"I've been planning this for months. I had your assistant clear your schedule and I've been on the phone making travel arrangements."

Demi cursed under her breath. "I feel like the biggest idiot." She covered her mouth with both hands.

"You should. You spoiled my surprise."

"You should learn how to hide secrets better." Demi threw her arms around Michael and kissed him.

"Happy?"

"I'm so happy, and so sorry I ever doubted you. Michael?"

"Yes?"

"Did you say we're leaving tomorrow?"

"Uh huh. I did say that."

"How could you give me such little notice? I have to pack."

"No you don't. Didn't I tell you? We're staying in the nudist section. That's your present to me."

"Keep dreaming, buddy! There's no nudist section at Atlantis."

Chapter 34

Amy

November 2001

Well over a year had passed since Samuouél had first written Amy. Reclined in the office chair at her Westchester home, Amy's eyes seemed to hold a faraway look, but behind them was deep concern.

More than anything, she wanted to meet her son face to face, but so far they'd only managed emails and occasional phone calls. But now she feared any reunion she had with him would be marred by publicity. How unfair would it be to have Sam's privacy compromised, even before she had her own chance to explain the circumstances of his birth?

She meant to meet with him sooner, but between her obligations and his studies, they could never find the time. Instead, they settled for cards and letters. Amy admonished herself for her procrastination—it was about to cost her everything she held dear.

The image of floorboards crumbling beneath her feet was the vision in Amy's mind's eye when her assistant informed her that the press had a lead on a story involving the congresswoman and an illegitimate child. There were a select few who knew about Amy's firstborn, and not even those people knew who the father was.

And in an age when it seemed as though more people had children first and married later, why would anyone care?

"Amy," Sophia announced. "I got here as fast as I could."

Amy bolted from her seat and met Sophia in three quick strides. She was not a particularly demonstrative person, but she hugged Sophia, latching on to her as though she was her lifeline.

"Hey," Sophia said, patting her back, "it can't be all that bad."

"It's worse."

"Come. Sit down and tell me everything."

"My assistant is trying to find out the source. I don't know much yet, but I'm about to be exposed at any hour."

Sophia shook her head and scoffed. "What is there to expose? You were a young college student and you gave up a baby for adoption. Not much of a scandal."

"It is when they start questioning me as to why I came to that decision since I'm a pro-choice defender. It is when I haven't reunited with my son or warned him this could happen. He may not wish to be brought into the public eye. And it is a scandal when my husband doesn't know he exists and my son doesn't have any idea that he has a brother."

With widened eyes and her mouth slightly open, Sophia looked at her friend dumfounded. "You still haven't told Ezra?" She planted her hands over her eyes. "You promised me you would tell him. What were you waiting for?"

"The right time and ... courage."

"But don't you see that it would have been so much easier had you done this long ago? Ezra is your husband. He loves you, but now it won't be about a child you had before you met him. Now it becomes a lie. A secret. And he's going to want to know what's behind it all."

Amy huffed. "Don't you think I know that? I have to talk to Ezra and Adam before the press leaks it. And I have to consider Samuouél. I need to go to him as well. Anything he learns should be from me, not from strangers or newspapers."

"Where will you find the time to go to him with the election coming up?"

"I don't know. I'm trying to figure this all out."

"Stay calm," Sophia told her. "Maybe we're getting ahead of ourselves. There's always the possibility the story isn't newsworthy. More importantly, your husband is the most understanding man I know. He may realize you put the past behind you and never wanted to speak of it again."

"Stop trying to put a positive spin on this."

"Isn't that what I'm here for?" Sophia looked at her compassionately. "You need to get out of here. Get some air and a change of scenery. Let's go out to lunch and we can talk more about this later. You need a break from the stress."

"Okay."

"Good. But when we get back, we will make a plan to clear this up with all parties involved."

Together, they walked to the foyer and Amy drew out a camel-colored wool coat. A quiet lunch would clear her head and then she would deal with the matters at hand.

But that was not to be. When she opened her door she was barraged with questions from reporters standing on her walkway. Cameras flashed and cars were blocking her driveway.

"Congresswoman Jacobs, is it true you had a baby out of wedlock?"

"Congresswoman, has the child contacted you? How old would he be?"

"It's rumored that the father is a prominent politician. What can you tell us?"

The blood drained from Amy's face. It was all going to come out. What information did they have on the father, or were their comments merely speculation and a ruse to get her to speak? She was about to say something, but Sophia stopped her.

"The congresswoman will not be making any statements. She will announce a press conference at a later time," Sophia announced.

"Can we have your name for our records? Who are you to Amy Jacobs?"

Sophia waved her hand and began to turn back toward the door.

"I'll find out, you know," the persistent reporter called out.

Amy and Sophia disappeared into the house. "Call Ezra and tell him to come home now."

Amy nodded. "Thanks, Sophia, for handling that. I should hire you as my press secretary."

"You may need one now with all of this. And no thanks needed, but my knees felt like jelly. I'm surprised they held me up."

Two hours later, Ezra Rosenfeld walked through the front door. With an expression on his face somewhere between bewilderment and hurt, he entered the office where he found Amy and Sophia seated on the burgundy leather Chesterfield sofa situated by the fireplace.

"Is there something you need to tell me?" Ezra asked harshly.

"I think I'll leave the two of you alone." Sophia rose but Amy caught her hand.

"No. Stay, please." Sophia had been with her from the beginning and she needed her now more than ever.

Amy told her husband everything—the failed attempt at an abortion, her stay in Greece, the lovely family who raised her son. An important piece of the puzzle was left out—the paternity—but Ezra listened without interjection, his lips pressed together in a hard line.

How many times would she be forced to recount these events? Her son would be home soon and he would have to be told. Then there was her attorney, the press, and God knows who else.

Silence filled the room, casting an air of tension between them. Ezra, as though in a trance, remained reticent.

"Say something," Amy pleaded. "Just don't shut me out."

Ezra turned his head slowly toward Amy, his mouth curling up in an unpleasant smile. "Interesting words coming from you."

Sophia cleared her throat and rose. "I'm going to give the two of you some time." Amy's eyes begged her to stay but Sophia shook her head. Squeezing her hand in encouragement as she passed, Sophia walked through the double doors of the home office leaving Amy and Ezra to speak in private.

"I have been a patient man. I've given you everything I have to offer of myself and I've always loved you, even though I've known deep down that you didn't love me the same way."

Amy began to protest, but Ezra raised his palm to her. "It's my belief that you only withheld this part of your life from me to protect someone—someone you love."

"No. That's not the reason. It was so long ago. I wanted to put it behind me."

"If that is so, then tell me who the father is."

"Ezra, what difference does it make now? It's in the past."

"The boy exists. It's about to explode all over the press." Supporting himself on the chair arms, he rose and walked over to the large window that showcased the many shades of orange and gold on the fall leaves in the woods surrounding their property. Staring out the window, he asked, "Do you still love him? The father?"

Amy hurried to his side and placed her hand on his shoulder. Ezra flinched. "Of course not. I love you."

"I'm not a fool. Don't lie to me. Who is he?"

"I'd rather not say. It's irrelevant."

"And still you hide the truth and claim you love me. Love and trust go hand in hand."

"It not about trust. I don't want anything to come between us."

"But it has. You will hold a press conference today. Before the rumors fly. I will be by your side, but after that ... I'll need some time."

"Time to think?" Amy asked.

"No, my dear. Time to live separately from you."

Chapter 35

Amy

November 2001

The splendor of the harvest moon casting a glow around the Rosenfeld's hundred-year-old colonial was in sharp contrast to the harsh lighting set up for the brief press conference to be held at the front steps of their home.

Amy's attorney introduced the congresswoman, making it clear she would make a brief statement and then answer one or two questions. By Amy's side stood her husband, Ezra Rosenfeld, and their son, Adam, who had been briefed on the situation. On her left, Sophia held her hand until she took the podium.

"In light of some personal information that has come to the attention of the press, I will give you the facts and set the record straight. Shortly after my graduation from college, I discovered I was pregnant. Most of my gestational months were spent in Greece where I gave the child up to a family of my choosing. At the time I was not equipped to properly care for the child and I did what was in his best interest. These past events have no bearing on my ability to serve my constituents and I would expect consideration and respect for my family's privacy in this matter. Thank you."

Reporters competed to ask questions, all of them shouting over one another and edging their way closer to the podium.

"Please. One at a time." Amy pointed to a rail-thin blond, clad in black with large thick eyewear to match.

"Congresswoman, when did you take the leap from pro-life to pro-choice, and do you think these new developments will paint you as a flip-flopper in the eyes of voters?"

"I am not nor have I ever been a flip-flopper. I have always been pro-choice. I have spent my political career fighting for the many rights of women." Amy pointed to another reporter.

"My question is for Mrs. Papadakis."

By the looks on their faces, both Amy and Sophia were baffled. They turned to Amy's counsel and he motioned for Sophia to approach him. He whispered in her ear before she stepped near the microphone.

"My sources say that you accompanied Congresswoman Jacobs to Greece where she stayed at your family home."

"That's right," Sophia responded.

"And it was your uncle who arranged for the adoption."

"That's true. It wasn't uncommon. He's a priest."

"You're not registered to the same political party as the congress-woman. In fact, is it true that you are pro-life and you don't support your friend's beliefs? Did you convince her not to have an abortion and to give up the child? And will you be voting against her in the election?"

Amy's counsel stepped beside Sophia. "Mrs. Papadakis is not required to answer."

"No, it's fine," Sophia said, resolved not to allow herself or Amy to be bullied.

"To answer your first question, no, I'm not registered in the same political party. If pro-life means that I'd love to see an abortion never to be necessary or for a life never to be taken, then yes, I am pro-life. Amy has always been pro-choice, but don't forget the word 'choice.' She made a choice—a difficult one. Personally, in light of the tragic events these past months, aren't there more important issues to focus political campaigns on? To answer your other question—if anyone knows Amy Jacobs, they know she cannot be convinced to do anything she doesn't want to do. My friend always has and always will make up her own mind. Lastly, I vote for a candidate, not a party, and no one is more honest and hardworking than Amy Jacobs. I support her wholeheartedly."

"We'll take one last question," Amy's attorney announced.

"Congresswoman Jacobs, sources say that the paternity of your child is rumored to be Lieutenant Governor Roth."

Amy gripped the podium to steady herself. She forced composure, not allowing facial expressions or voice inflection to give her away. But her head felt as though it would explode into smithereens.

"Since I'd only become acquainted with Mr. Roth years later, I'd say that is quite impossible."

As the questions shot toward Amy like cannon balls aimed and fired, she was whisked behind the safety of her front door.

"I need to lie down." Amy started for the staircase.

"It's true. Roth is the father, isn't he?" Ezra asked.

The nod was imperceptible, but it was the confirmation her husband was looking for.

Ezra raised his eyebrows and huffed. "And it all falls into place."

"What does that mean?" she snapped.

"I've seen the way you look at him."

"You're imagining things. He's a bastard." Amy lumbered up the stairs.

Ezra packed his bags and moved out the next morning. Amy had tried every tactic to make him stay. When deferring to his gentle side didn't work, she argued her case as though they were two opposing attorneys in a courtroom. In the end she capitulated, uncertain whether the time and distance between them would eventually lead him back to her, or away from her for good.

Chapter 36

Amy

November 2001

Sipping a cup of steaming black coffee, Amy was seated at the desk in her home office. Sleep had eluded her the night before, which in a warped sense was almost funny because she could have sworn she was trapped in the middle of a nightmare.

Ezra was gone. She had no idea what her son, Adam was really thinking, the media was relentless, and to top it off she had to take a scathing call from the last person on earth she wanted to deal with— Bradley Roth.

There was a time when Amy waited for his calls and hung on his every word. She was willing to take the crumbs he had to offer and he behaved as though he was laying the world at her feet. That was when she was young and stupid.

Political circles reunited them and when she first spotted Bradley across the room at a charity fundraiser, she thought her heart would stop. She avoided him all evening, hoping he wouldn't see her, but that wasn't to be.

"Amy!" Bradley Roth signaled to her as he made his way through the crowd. Before she could pull away, Bradley had his arm around her waist and pulled her in for a hug. "It's been way too long." He raked her from head to toe. "I've been following your career. I hope I can take a little credit for your success."

"No, no credit to you. I did it on my own." The gall of him to think he was helpful to me in any way. She stepped back, attempting to widen the space between them, but he bent down to whisper in her ear.

"I see the feistiness hasn't left you." There was a nefarious glint in his eyes. "I wouldn't mind revisiting that."

She wanted to slap him, but she kept her composure—or at least she tried. There was still a part of her that was drawn to him and it sickened her to admit that to herself. So she laughed it off and hoped he wouldn't bother her again.

But the next time she ran into him he tried again. And each time after it was always the same.

"For the last time, I'm married. You're married and you need to stop."

"Oh, but I don't want to."

Amy jumped when the phone rang. She'd been far, far away, lost in her thoughts, wondering how and why she had ever fallen for Bradley Roth.

"Hello?" Amy reluctantly answered the phone, wincing when she saw who was calling. "Mother, stop screaming in my ear."

"Bradley Roth! You had an affair with Bradley? And a child resulted? One I never knew of?" Mrs. Jacobs was furious.

"Mother, if you let me explain."

"Explain? What is there to explain? My teenage daughter has an illicit relationship with one of my closest friend's older son and I never knew about it? Or a baby? My God, Amy! How could you? What am I going to say to Sylvia Roth?"

"Why don't you ask her why she raised a prick for a son who used my crush on him as a way of seducing me? Why is everything always my fault in your eyes?"

"Oh, don't you throw this on me. Did you or did you not willingly have sex with that man?"

"Yes, Mother, I did. Are you happy? And he broke my heart. And yes, I had his baby. Maybe if for one second you could think about someone other than yourself, you would ask me about your grandson."

"But Amy, our family's reputation is at stake."

"I didn't murder anyone. Goodbye, Mother. I have more important things to worry about than what your friends will think." Amy hung up the phone and rubbed her temples.

Two hours and three cups of coffee later, Amy managed to go through all her important emails and get a little work done. "Come in," she said wearily when she heard the rapping on her office door.

"I didn't want to disturb you and Ezra this morning," Sophia said. "I imagine the two of you had a lot to discuss."

"Not as much as you'd think apparently. He's gone. Ezra left early this morning with no plans to return any time soon."

"Oh, Amy, I am so sorry." Sophia came around to Amy's side of the desk and hugged her.

"This is your moment to tell me 'I told you so,'" Amy said.

"You know I'd never do that, but now that I have you alone, maybe we can discuss what you'll do from here."

A humorless laugh escaped Amy's lips. "The question is, what do I do first? Patch up this campaign? Try to get my husband back? Contact the son I abandoned?"

"You didn't abandon him. You left him with a family who love him as their own." Sophia sighed. "I'm afraid you will need to give Ezra time. But you need to examine your depth of feeling for him and your motives for concealing such an important segment of your life."

"I can't think about that now. What's done is done and I can't take it back. I have enough to worry about. I received a nasty call from Bradley Roth."

"So it's true? He's the one?"

"Yes." Amy picked up the morning edition of the newspaper. "And he's fuming mad." She slid the paper to Sophia's side of the desk.

"'*Power Couple's Secret Love Affair Resulted in Illegitimate Child,*'"

Sophia read aloud. Underneath the headline was an old photo of Amy standing beside Roth, apparently in conversation, her expression revealing awe in the more experienced statesman.

Sophia's eyes flew up to Amy's. "He called early this morning," Amy answered Sophia's question before she asked.

"What did he say?"

"'So there's a child?' That's how he greeted me. Then he asked what I did with the money he gave me for the abortion. I told him I'd give him a refund."

Sophia pressed her lips together, trying to suppress a giggle.

"Then he began to yell at me. I told him I never revealed the father to anyone, but he just kept ranting that I was going to ruin his marriage and mar his reputation."

"You?" Sophia rolled her eyes. "Because he had no part in it," she said sardonically. "Can I ask you something?"

Amy gestured for Sophia to continue.

"All those years ago when I asked you who the father was, you wouldn't tell me. You were protecting him." Sophia stated it as if speaking out loud a revelation she'd just discovered. "Were you in love with him? Are you still in love with him?"

The answer lay behind brown eyes muddied by sadness and memories. Amy did not have the words to sufficiently articulate her complicated emotions. "I've loved him and I've hated him—sometimes both at the same time. I thought I loved the man I was infatuated with until the bastard he actually was showed his face and woke me up."

"Where did that leave Ezra?"

"I was never unfaithful." Amy was adamant.

"There are many ways to be unfaithful."

"Sophia, when the election is over, I will put my personal life in order." She wanted to change the subject and, thankfully, Sophia did just that.

"Why do you think the press is all over you for choosing to have the child? Shouldn't that be a positive and not a negative?"

"Not when your platform is to fight to keep abortion legal in this country and to allow the woman the right to make that choice. I'm being painted a hypocrite."

"It sounds like a weak and desperate ploy from the opposition. What we need to do is find out is how the information was leaked. Aside from my parents, grandparents, uncle and the adoptive family, no one else knew about your pregnancy. Not even your own parents."

"There has to be someone who would know enough to give a reporter a lead." Amy was thinking aloud. "It would have to be someone close enough to one of us or your family to learn of my condition, yet—"

"She wouldn't!" Sophia broke Amy's thought.

"Who?"

"My aunt. That's who. Irini. She was there. In Athens. Remember? She came to visit my yiayiá and pappou."

"Yes, I do remember," she answered, dragging out her words. She narrowed her eyes. "She made some odd statements at the time when she asked if I was pregnant."

"It had to be her. Who else would do such a thing?"

"She tried to make it sound as though not telling the father was a crime."

"No," Sophia corrected. "Her moral compass doesn't spin that far around. God, it was such a long time ago. Do you remember exactly what she said?"

"Yes. 'There would be consequences to pay,'" Amy recalled. "Now that I think of it, it almost sounded like a warning."

"Or a threat. But how could she have found out about Roth?"

"A little digging and deduction. These pictures. The way I'm looking at him. If she dug a little further, she'd find out my father mentored him and he'd been to our home many times. What did she have to gain? Why would she do this?"

"Because she can and because she hates me. I can't tell you how sorry I am."

"This is not your fault," Amy assured her. "Are you going to confront her?"

"I want to, but I think that's what she's waiting for. I won't give her that satisfaction."

"There's something else I need to do right away. I need to meet Samuouél in person. It can't wait any longer. As soon as the election is over, I want to fly to Thessaloniki. Will you come with me?"

"Oh, Amy. I think the time has come for you to go. It's imperative for you to speak with him as soon as possible, but I'm not sure I can get away. My children need me at home and Dino is too busy right now. I don't want to throw the full responsibility on him."

"I know it's a lot to ask. Please, just think about it."

"I will. I'll talk it over with Dino and if I can get away I'll be there with you."

"Admitting your shortcomings might be a sting to the ego, but at the same time it could ease the soul." —Father Vasili to Dean 1971

Chapter 37

Sophia

December 2001

I am a fraud," Amy declared to Sophia after a long period of silence. They had just settled into their first class seats on a plane bound for Thessaloniki.

Sophia turned to Amy, her brow creased from confusion. Amy was the most upfront and honest person she knew.

"I am, or at least I was. And all this," Amy waved her hand around, "would never have happened."

"You're not making any sense," Sophia told her. "You're exhausted. You ran a great campaign, you won, and now you need to sleep."

"No! I'm not tired. I'm serious. None of this would have happened if I hadn't tried to behave like someone I wasn't."

"When have you ever been anyone other than your true self?"

"When we were fourteen."

"What?" Sophia asked in disbelief.

"I bragged about being the first to have sex and acted as though it was no big deal. I tried to behave like I was someone much older and more mature. I was in charge of my body and my destiny. The hell I was! What an ass I was."

"No you weren't. It was what you believed at the time."

"No!" Amy said a little too loudly. She lowered her voice. "I may have believed some of it, but I was trying to impress Bradley. I was fourteen and he was a twenty-two-year old law student. I wanted him to think I was old enough for him."

"But he knew your family. He knew how old you were."

"I thought if I acted more grown up, I could make him forget. I didn't want him think of me as a kid. Don't you see? I had sex with those other guys as practice. I wanted to have experience before I had Bradley. When nothing happened with him, I made it seem like I was having sex all the time."

"You weren't?"

"No. Not as much as I let on."

"So you think this made you a fraud?"

"That and the hard time I gave you over sneaking around with Dean. What did I do but turn around and do the same thing?"

"When did it begin?"

"I started getting bolder by the time I was sixteen. I could tell he was attracted to me. He would look at me a certain way and I'd get goose bumps. A couple of times when I caught him alone we talked and there was this sexual tension between us. Several times I thought we'd kiss but he never touched me. I was a minor after all and he was much older." Amy began to get lost in the story as she sipped on a glass of chardonnay.

"Anyway, he was invited to my graduation party and, by that time, as you are aware, I was already eighteen."

"I remember your party. Your parents invited so many friends and business contacts."

"And Bradley. Everyone was in the backyard. I told him I wanted to show him an award I received and he followed me right up to my room." Amy purred a sigh. "That was our first time."

"With your family downstairs?" Sophia gaped at Amy.

Amy chuckled. "Still a bit puritanical, aren't you?"

"You became pregnant right before college graduation. This went on for four years?"

Amy nodded. "On and off. I was at school and he was building his career. I would see him on holidays and sometimes he'd come to see me at school."

"Why weren't the two of you open with your parents?"

"He said it wasn't good for his position. I was too young and we would have to wait until the age gap closed a bit. And I did. Waited and waited, until I found out he was engaged to someone he'd been involved with for six years."

"You have got to be kidding me!"

"Oh, I'm not. And to make matters worse, the engagement was announced the very same week that I found out I was pregnant."

By now, Amy was on her third glass of wine. "I was nothing but an occasional fuck to him." She lifted her glass. "Cheers, to me!"

Still, after all these years, the bruises on Amy's heart and pride stung. Sophia could see that now. Her friend had always seemed as strong-minded as granite, never allowing anyone to wound her. Her declarations of, 'no big deal,' or 'I'm over it,' were merely an affectation. No, she wasn't granite, Sophia considered. She was porcelain, and Sophia knew what that felt like. It wasn't long ago that she'd been in a similar state.

"Put the drink down and look at me a minute," Sophia ordered. "You have about ten hours to wallow and then you are going to pull yourself together. This is a happy day. You are going to see your son for the first time since you gave birth to him. Roth's problems are not yours. Whatever his fallout is from this, he deserves it. I say fuck him!"

Amy's eyes widened. "Sophia Giannakos Papadakis! I don't think in all the years I've known you, I've ever heard you curse."

Sophia straightened her back and politely placed her hands on her lap. "After all we've been through and at our age, I think we deserve to say a fuck or two."

The two women giggled like schoolgirls.

"But seriously, my dad always doled out the best advice. Whenever I was going through a tough time he knew just what to say. I'm going to pass some of his wisdom to you. Everything you went through may have been painful at that time, but it led you to this moment. There is a reason for everything. Out from the storm, the sun will shine. You'll see."

After a layover and too many hours aboard the plane, Amy and Sophia exited, waited for their luggage, and stepped outside to hail a taxi.

A tall, young man approached them. In his hands was a bouquet of white lilies. He brushed a mop of golden brown curls from his face and smiled widely. "Amy Jacobs?" he asked.

Amy gasped and dropped her suitcase, her nerves which had been tightening on the plane dissipating as soon as she saw him. "Samuouél?" She opened her arms and they hugged as though they were old friends. "Let me look at you!" Amy's eyes grew misty. "I didn't expect to see you until later. What a lovely surprise."

"I've been waiting a long time to meet you. I wanted to come for you myself."

Sophia covered her mouth with her hands as tears welled in her eyes.

"This is my very best friend, Sophia," Amy said as she pulled out of her son's embrace.

"Oh, yes. Sophia. I've heard much about you from your great-uncle."

"Of course. It's wonderful that your family has kept in touch with him all these years. How is my uncle?"

"I'm afraid he is old and frail. It is good that you are here and can visit him."

"He's eighty-nine, but when I last saw him he was amazingly self-sufficient."

"I think you may find him a bit weaker now."

"It was so nice of you to come for us," Sophia said. "I will go to him right away and you and—" She wanted to say, 'your mother,' but she stopped herself. "The two of you can catch up alone."

Amy reached for Samuouél's hand. "Yes, we have years to catch up on. I want to learn everything about your childhood and your plans for the future."

Samuouél escorted Amy and Sophia to the lot where his car was parked. As he drove them to their hotel, he pointed out landmarks along the way. The three of them chatted like old friends, and it was the first time in over a month Sophia had seen Amy smile. But in the back of her mind, Sophia had her own concerns.

Indeed, Sophia's father was correct, she thought. There was a reason for everything, and from what Samuouél told her regarding her uncle, it was providence that she had accompanied Amy now.

Chapter 38

Sophia

December 2001

Weary from jet lag, plus all that had transpired over the past few weeks, Sophia ignored her need for sleep and pushed on to see her Uncle Vasili, the elder priest at St. Demetrios. When she arrived at his home, a woman answered the door, welcomed her in, and introduced herself as Despina, an old friend of her uncle's. Clad in black from head to toe, she could be mistaken for a nun, but in Greece elderly women often dressed in this manner, especially after they lost a loved one.

Despina spoke no English, however in animated Greek and with eyes that shimmered with delight, she told Sophia how excited she was to meet her. She must have been beautiful as a young woman, Sophia thought. Wrinkles creased the corners of her eyes but the lines hadn't spread to her cheeks. That, along with her smile, could deceive anyone to believe she was decades younger than Sophia estimated she must have been.

Despina waved for Sophia to follow her. "O theíos sou eínai árrostos. Éhei éna krýo."

"Has my uncle's cold been lingering for a long time?"

"Yes, for a while."

"That sounds like more than a cold. Has he seen the doctor?"

"He comes, but your uncle doesn't like a fuss made over him."

Sophia found herself staring at her uncle from the doorway's edge. He looked much older now than the last time she'd seen him and her throat tightened at the sight of his weakening body.

Father Vasili was seated in an upholstered chair, his feet elevated on a worn ottoman. In his hands, he held a tattered-edged, leather-bound book, and a black, knotted, woolen prayer rope that was threaded between his weathered fingers.

"Uncle," Sophia adoringly called to him as she approached him.

He looked up at her and his eyes came to life. "Sophia *mou*." His excitement set off a series of coughs. He reached his hand to her and she bent down to kiss his cheek.

"How can I help? What can I do for you?"

"I'm fine. Just a cold. *Yerásei*—I've gotten old. I don't recover as quickly as I used to."

Kneeling beside him, Sophia declared, "You are the strongest man I know."

Seating herself across from him, Sophia caught him up on news from home. He wanted to know about the children, his nephew, and Dean's business venture.

Despina came in and set a tray down with *fasolakia*—string beans cooked in tomato sauce. She said her goodbyes and promised to return the next day.

"Such a nice lady," Sophia commented. "How nice for her to check on you this way."

"Despina is a very old and dear friend."

Sophia stayed with her uncle until it was time for him to retire for the night. It worried her to leave him alone, but he assured her he would be fine. Up until he was struck with this cold, he had gone about his daily routine as he had for years. Once he was over it, he would be up and about once again. It was just taking longer than usual.

The following day, Sophia and Amy were invited to dinner with Samu-ouél's family. Sophia remembered what lovely people they were and knew that Amy's child was raised in a loving home.

"Don't let him fool you," Revekka said, regarding Father Vasili. "He's not as well as he lets on. We check on him as often as we can."

"That's so kind of you."

"We owe your uncle so much." Revekka planted a kiss on her son's cheek.

Together they poured through photo albums, sharing stories of their son's childhood.

In light of what the press had discovered, Amy apologized in advance for the possibility that the press might approach them.

"I googled him. Bradley Roth," Samuouél uttered quietly.

"What is a google?" his mother asked.

He grinned. "It's a site to search for information on the computer." He looked up at Amy. "I look like him."

"You have his eyes and his chin, but you have my curly hair and fantastic smile," Amy bragged. "You also look like Adam, my son. My other son," she corrected. "His hair is darker though, and his eyes are brown."

"I would like to meet him one day."

"He is looking forward to it. He's lived his life as an only child."

"I understand I am related to two girls as well."

"I'm so sorry." Amy regarded him with regret. "You will not get the acceptance you hope for from Bradley Roth. I'm afraid you will not have the opportunity to meet his daughters."

"Has he always known about me?"

"No, I'm afraid not. He was not very nice to me when he found out I was pregnant. We lost contact after I told him."

"But he knows now?"

"Oh, yes. Thanks to the media. But he's very angry." Amy felt as though a wrench was twisting her insides. "I'm afraid he won't be receptive to meeting you. Bradley Roth is a self-serving politician. He would meet you only if it helped his career in some way."

Sophia and Amy rode back to the hotel in silence, each seeming to be deep in their own thoughts.

"I'm extending my stay," Sophia informed Amy. "I won't be returning with you at the end of the week."

"Why?"

"I'm very concerned for my uncle. I don't have a good feeling and I've called my dad. I think he needs to be here."

"Sophia, I saw him for myself. He's under the weather but do you think it's that dire that you should send for your father?"

"At his age? Yes. And his friend, Despina, says he has been fighting this for a couple of weeks. At the worst of it, Dad makes a visit with him. Dino wants to come too. He's bringing Cia with him, also."

"Do you want me to stay?"

"No, no. You have enough to worry about. I'll keep you informed."

When they returned back to their room, they stayed up and talked for hours. They were so tired, yet their minds were racing—each for a very different reason. It had been quite a day.

Chapter 39

Sophia

December 2001

Sophia poked at the logs in the old stone fireplace, the flames shooting up each time she struck them. Her uncle refused to spend his day in bed, but rather enjoyed looking out his window, or reading his prayers as he sat by the fire.

Sophia went into the kitchen and a few minutes later emerged with a steaming cup of tea infused with lemon and honey and an extra blanket, which she tucked around his legs.

Taking a seat beside him she asked a question she had wondered about for many years. "Uncle, how come you remained a parish priest and you weren't elevated to a bishop?"

"It was never my desire," he answered without hesitation. "Bishops travel from church to church and administer over other priests. I wanted to stay rooted in one place to be part of the people in this community, to hear their confessions, marry them and baptize their babies." Father Vasili coughed and sipped his tea to sooth his throat. "And I've been here to comfort the dying and bury them. Console their families, and see rebirth as another generation is born."

"That's so beautiful. There's such value in all those simple moments and you are in control of each one."

He placed his hand over hers. "Only God is in control. I am simply his humble servant."

"Maybe, but you are a rare breed. There are not too many like you." Sophia had another question. She wasn't sure it was right to ask but they were speaking frankly and she wanted to know more about him. "I'm trying to understand. You chose to be a monastic priest, but never had any ambitions to become a bishop. You could have married. Why didn't you?"

"I didn't choose. Life chose for me."

Sophia didn't understand and looked at him quizzically.

"You see an old priest before you, but I was once a young boy in love."

Sophia had never stopped to consider this. For as long as she could remember her uncle, he was old to her. "Will you tell me about her, Uncle?"

Thessaloniki, 1929

For seventeen-year-old Vasili removing black smoke smudges and candle wax from marble floors was a never-ending job. Yet, despite its monotony, he actually found it very satisfying. The result of his labor was a gleam so pristine, the rays of sun shining through the windows above reflected off of them as though they had never been walked on. Each morning he arrived, recited a series of prayers and began his daily tasks.

Vasili had always been drawn here. It was his place of serenity, and where he knew he belonged. He'd never been taught to attend church, as his parents had rarely attended. His father had been a laborer who worked long hours. What Vasili remembered of him was vague. He'd been only five years old when his father was killed during the disastrous fire in the city's center.

Life had changed drastically after that. Many people were left homeless and it took years to rebuild all that had been destroyed. Now a widow, Vasili's mother had to find work to support her two children. On her feet working in a bakery during the morning hours and taking in sewing at night, she had little energy left to properly tend to her children.

It was his older sister's responsibility to keep an eye on her younger brother. Four years his senior, nine-year-old Evanthia inherited the life of a woman and lost her own privilege of childhood.

But she didn't seem to mind too much. Evanthia adored her little brother, and he was an obedient child, however, as time went on, she found it more and more difficult to keep track of his whereabouts.

"Vasili!" Evanthia frantically called out repeatedly.

Vasili had disappeared from her sight. He was not in the house, nor was he playing with the children outside. Searching the neighborhood, she asked if anyone had seen a seven-year-old boy. Finally, a young girl nodded and pointed to the church.

Vasili turned when he heard the echoing voice of Evanthia reverberate throughout the church.

"I don't think you should shout in God's house," he told his sister.

"Don't you ever leave my sight without telling me! Do you understand?" Evanthia threatened.

The Greeks had regained control of Thessaloniki from Ottoman rule by the time Vasili was born, however Evanthia was old enough to overhear and be frightened by the stories of oppression and torture, and no one could convince her that she was safe. She was a girl born with her guard up, and justifiably so with this city's history.

The walls of the church were covered with mosaic tiles laid in the likeness of various saints. Vasili ran his fingers admiringly over them, examining them with awe as though he could read the stories they told by touching the tiny stone squares.

"I understand, and I'm sorry I worried you. If ever you can't find me, this is where I'll be."

"Why? You should be outside with the other children."

"I feel safe here," he responded.

"Safe," she scoffed. "No one is safe. Come. Let's go home."

Ten years later, Vasili had become an integral servant of his church. Under the supervision of the parish priests, he learned to chant the psalms, prepare for the liturgies, and guide the younger boys who came to serve in the altar.

Above the icons in the church hung red oil lamps, which burned night and day, and it was Vasili's responsibility to check each one—adding oil and changing the wicks as needed.

"Your mamá asked me to bring the *prosforo* for liturgy tomorrow."

Vasili turned to look at the young woman addressing him. He had not heard her footsteps, but there she was before him—like a vision—offering him the communion bread that his mother had baked that morning.

He took the *prosforo* from her. His fingers brushed across hers, causing his heart to leap. "I'm finished here. Would you like to take a walk?" Vasili asked.

"I'd like that," she said shyly. "Where shall we go?"

"I like to go by the waterfront or maybe the beach. Away from what man has built to reflect on what God had created—the sea, the blue skies and the sun shining upon us."

From that day forth, it became a ritual, and the best part of his day— spending time with this girl. For a long time, he had admired her from afar, but after that first day at the beach, he had fallen irrevocably in love with her.

"You've stolen my heart." It didn't take Vasili long to confess his feelings and, from the day he declared the intensity of his love for her, he never again used her proper name. He referred to her as *karthía mou*—my heart.

Together they would walk along the shoreline, picking up asymmetrical pieces of sea glass that caught their eye and sharing parts of themselves never revealed before.

"You have a much deeper soul than I, Vasili *mou*," she told him.

He looked into those round, dark eyes, and twisted a lock of her spiral curls around his finger. "*Karthía mou.* You have a heart as big as this sea. What a gift it is to me."

Vasili brushed his fingers over her tiny rosebud lips, soft as pillows to his touch. Slowly, he bent down and pressed his lips to hers. He could feel her response, and a hum escaped her lips.

"I will love you until the day I die," he vowed.

"And I, you," she said, and he took her face in his hands and kissed her once more.

Later that evening Vasili went to visit his sister. At twenty-one years old, Evanthia was married with three children. The youngest, Alexandros, had just turned three.

As he held Alexandros on his lap, the child fiddled with the gold cross hanging from Vasili's neck. Evanthia set out a plate with feta, bread, tomatoes and olive oil. The aroma of grilled octopus marinated in ouzo filled the air and Vasili asked his sister where it was.

"It's coming," she laughed. "Go tell the boys to come inside for dinner."

"Where's Nicholas?"

"He's working extra hours. He'll be home later."

With three boys to feed, the young couple had to do all they could to survive in those difficult times. At sixteen, Evanthia had not expected to marry, but she'd found herself with child and wed quickly to conceal what would have been thought of as shameful behavior.

"Ev," Vasili started, after putting the children to bed, "I kissed her." Evanthia's smile lit her face. "Finally!"

"I wanted to do more. It was hard to stop," he said shyly, looking down. It was an odd topic to broach with his sister, but he felt she would know what to say to him.

"That's perfectly normal. You are a healthy seventeen-year-old boy."

"Is that what happened to you? You felt that way … you didn't want to stop?" Vasili was bordering the edges of his comfort zone.

"Yes, I suppose. I loved Nicholas very much and maybe at the time I should have had some restraint, but I thought to myself, 'why?' Why should I not act on how I feel? Because someone else made the rules?" She huffed out a little laugh.

"But we can't always act on what we want. We have to think about how it affects others."

"Yes, brother. Or how it affects ourselves. I would have wed Nicholas one way or another. Maybe not so soon, but I married when I did for Mamá's sake." She tilted her head and tried to read her brother's eyes. "What are you thinking?"

"That I'm a man like anyone else, and when I'm near her it's hard to control the urges I feel. But my faith is strong and I don't want to betray that." He stood up and walked over to a lace-covered side table. On it a votive candle flickered near an icon of Saint Demetrios, the patron saint of Thessaloniki. A larger icon of Christ ascending into heaven leaned against the wall. Vasili crossed himself three times and turned back to address his sister. "I want to be a priest," he announced. He assumed it was always understood with the amount of time he spent at the church and the devotion he gave to his prayers, but he had never stated it before.

"Are you sure? It's not an easy life."

"It's not a bad one either," he affirmed. "And the rewards are infinite."

"I wish I had your faith."

"My dear sister. You have the strength and compassion not many possess. It's late. I should be heading home." Vasili started toward the front door.

"Wait! What about the girl?"

"I'm going to marry her, of course," Vasili said happily as he waved goodnight.

Ribbons of color decorated the sky. The setting sun illuminated the rising moon, casting a marigold-colored hue. It held promise—the moon—the incandescent glow assuring a new and bright day would dawn.

He had never been happier. Resting, her head on his shoulder, he knew he was loved with the same intensity with which he loved her. And there was never a more lovely moment to tell her what was on his mind.

"Marry me. I want to be with you always."

"I love you. Of course, I will. I can't imagine my life without you." She wrapped her arms around him and they kissed.

"I would marry you this instant if I could. But we'd never make it on my own. I have to go through my studies first. But before I am made deacon we will have to wed, of course."

"What?"

"We will marry before I am ordained, but it may take a few years, so be patient with me, *karthía mou*."

She became very quiet and Vasili could see her expression change from elation to sorrow.

"Vasili, we never really discussed this." Her tone worried him.

"It was understood. You know how I feel."

"I know you have great faith, but to make it your whole life …"

"Not my whole life." He took her hands. "You are my life."

She released herself from him. "I need time to think. This isn't just a job for you. It affects me. I would become a *presbytera*. Being a priest's wife is not something I ever imagined for myself." Standing, she looked at him with sad eyes. "I will give this the thought you would expect of me, but I expect you to do the same. You may have to choose."

Alone, Vasili ruminated over the events of the evening. It had begun with hope and declarations of love, and ended with doubt and indecision. He looked up. The marigold moon had faded and disappeared behind a dark cloud.

Vasili had taken on a quiet and sullen mood over the next week. She had been avoiding him. Her sister had delivered the *prosforo* to the church, and she was nowhere to be found around town. In a brief moment, he considered giving up his vocation to be with her, but she had not come to him. Could he give up what he needed and wanted for a girl who apparently did not love him as much as he loved her?

In his heart, he knew he had his answer, but he had to hear it from her lips. Marching through town as though on a military mission, he stomped into the bakery. His love was behind the counter handing a bag of *koulouri* to a middle-aged woman draped in black clothing.

"Your mother is in the back," she said nervously.

"I'm not here to see my mother and you know it. I need to speak to you," Vasili demanded.

"But I'm working."

"Take a break."

She nodded and removed her apron. He led her outside and Vasili stared at her, wordless, until he drew some courage. "Avoiding me is not an answer. I want you to tell me to my face that you won't marry me. That you don't love me. I'm suffering. I need to know."

"Are you going into the priesthood?"

"Yes. I don't understand the objection."

"I don't want that life. The life of a poor priest. I want a bigger life, or the hope of one. I don't want to live with the scrutiny of the parish or be an example for the whole community. It's too much to live up to."

"But together we can make a good life."

"Not one that I want. So no, I will not marry you, Vasili. I am very sorry. You asked me to tell you that I don't love you, but I can't. I do love you. You will always be in my heart, but I cannot be who you want me to be."

Taking her hand, he shook his head. "How can you say you love me, and reject me this way?"

"Please, let me go. You have to let me go," she choked out, her tears catching in her throat.

Tears brimmed Sophia's eyes. "How sad for both of you," she said.

"Yes, it was. I imagine you remember what that felt like. Teenage heartache." Weakly, he placed his hand over hers.

"But you never married. There was no one else after her?"

"Not for me. At first I waited for her to change her mind and I suspect she did the same. By the time I came back from the seminary she was involved with another." He closed his eyes. "We each make our choices."

"But surely you may have fallen in love again?"

"My heart belonged to one only and it would have been a lie to be with anyone else. Anyway, I was married to the church. It was enough for me."

"She married the other man?"

"Indeed. It was the first marriage I performed after my ordination."

"Oh, my goodness. How could you? Why would they force you? They must have known."

"I wasn't forced." Lifting himself up, he turned to look her straight in the eye. "I chose to."

Sophia had a look of disbelief on her face.

"Father Raphael was to marry the couple. I asked to do it instead."

"But why would you put yourself through that? It had to be painful."

"It was, but at the same time it helped me to put that chapter in my life to rest. It was behind us and we both chose different lives. I couldn't be a priest of any worth if I held bitterness in my heart."

"You look flush. I'm tiring you out."

"No, not at all."

"Does she still live here? Is she still alive?"

"Oh, yes. I baptized her children and married them off too. And as all priests do, I saw her through some very difficult days. I may not have had her in my life the way I'd hoped, but she had the life she wanted and I had the one I was meant for."

Sophia felt his forehead. She picked up the thermometer and under protest slipped it under his tongue. His fever had climbed and she was concerned. She was right to have called her father to come.

Chapter 40

Sophia

December 2001

P lease, let us take you to the hospital," Alex pleaded. "We can get better care for you there."

"What can they do that can't be done here?" Father Vasili argued. "This is where I am comfortable. You and Sophia are here to help me and Despina comes every day. There is nothing more to be done. My time is coming to leave this world and this is where I want to see my last days."

"Don't say that." Sophia clasped his hand in hers. "You can't give up."

"I am not giving up." He used what little strength he had to squeeze her hand reassuringly. "I am saying what I know to be true. It's my time. Don't look at me with those sad eyes, *koritsi mou*. I've been preparing for the next world my entire life. May God accept me in his loving hands."

The situation had been dire enough for Sophia to call her father, who had not only arrived as quickly as he could book a flight, but had arrived along with Dean, Cia and Dean's parents.

"We love him too," Dean told her. "He's been so good to us over the years."

When the doctor came to check on Father Vasili, he told the family that he was doing all he could for him without admitting him to the hospital. Despite being given antibiotics, his breathing was labored from pneumonia.

"Say what you need to." The doctor's voice caught, and it took a moment for him to continue. He wasn't just a patient. He had known the priest his entire life. "Each of you. Speak from your heart. It may be your last chance."

A whimper came from the hallway. Forlorn, Despina stood in the shadows, her eyes on the doctor. In her hand she held a woven sack and Sophia knew it to be the one she used to transport food back and forth.

"Let me help you with that," Sophia offered.

"I have broth with vegetables. I will take it to him."

"Can I help you?" Soula asked.

"You hold Cia, Mom," Dean said. "I'll help Despina."

Despina held her sack to her chest. "No, I will do it." She looked at the family. "Please let me go to him alone."

"Of course." Sophia placed her arm on Despina's shoulder.

"What was that all about?" Stavros asked.

Wrapping her arms around Dean, Sophia answered her father-in-law in a word. "Devotion."

After some time had passed, Sophia slipped away from her family, making her way to her uncle's bedroom, but she never moved beyond the doorframe. With tears welling in her eyes, she brought her hands up to her lips as though in prayer. She was so moved at the intimacy between the elder pair. It was so simple and pure. Despina spooned broth to Vasili's lips, urging him to drink with loving words. Her uncle's eyes seemed to brighten as they spoke—words that were merely a whisper.

"I'm not ready to live without you," Sophia thought she heard Despina say. Sophia gasped inwardly, as realization came to her.

"*Karthía mou*," she heard him call her. "But I've seen her. I'll be with her soon, and I need you to be strong."

"Who? Who did you see?"

"Evanthia."

"My God," Sophia said inaudibly. "Evanthia," she whispered, brushing her finger over the ring she wore—the one that had belonged to her grandmother. Sophia knew she should turn and leave, but she couldn't pull herself away. She was mesmerized by the elderly couple.

"I have loved you every day of my life." Despina choked out a sob. "I'm sorry."

"Don't be sorry." Weakly, he lifted her hand to his mouth and kissed it. "I told you that I would love you until the day I died. That time is near. But I'm afraid I was wrong."

Despina looked at him, bereft. "I understand."

"No, you don't. I won't love you until the day I die. I will love you for eternity. In this world and the next."

"Vasili *mou*," she cried.

Two days later, Father Vasili slipped peacefully from this world and into the arms of God. The family was deeply moved by the outpouring of support that they received. Priests from the neighboring churches and bishops residing over the district came to celebrate the life of the humble priest. Hundreds of parishioners and town folk lined the streets and followed the casket, many reaching their arms out to touch it as it passed through the town before entering the church.

Sophia held onto Despina—the two women each having their own reasons for their tears. Sophia thought of all the years she had visited him, the advice he had given her and all the time they'd spent together for as long as she could remember. He was a rare gem on Earth that would now sparkle with the stars in the heavens. He would be missed in a way that she could never communicate with words. He would always be in her heart.

Later, when the funeral was over and the house was quiet, Sophia sat down beside Despina.

"Despina?" Sophia asked. "It was you, wasn't it? You were the girl Uncle Vasili loved?"

The tears that rolled down Despina's eyes were the answer to Sophia's question. "You loved him too?"

Despina nodded. "Yes. I loved him very much. I was a stupid girl," she admonished herself, "wanting more than I should have, and giving up what was most important."

"That was a long time ago and you were very young. We all make mistakes at that age. My uncle spoke of you with love and admiration."

"We were never improper, Sophia. After my husband died, we became very close. But as companions and very close friends. Nothing improper."

"Oh, Despina. You don't need to explain. That never crossed my mind."

"My husband was a good man, but he wasn't my Vasili. I would have liked to know him as a husband. But that wasn't possible. We had the relationship we could allow ourselves and that was all."

"We can only do our best and hope we make the right decisions in life." And with that, Sophia's thoughts turned to that of her friend, Amy, back home. Was she making the right decisions?

Chapter 41

Amy

December 2001

T hank you for joining me today, Congresswoman Jacobs and Samuouél," the reporter began her onscreen interview. "May I call you Sam?"

"Of course," he replied in his heavily accented voice.

Tamara Knight wore a pleasant but professional smile as she greeted her guests. Tall and slender with flawless cocoa skin, she'd won first runner up in The Miss America pageant fifteen years earlier, but that defeat did not deter the unstoppable Tamara Knight from reaching her journalistic goals. In an environment that was cutthroat, she aimed for integrity and compassion, making her a favorite interviewer in delicate matters.

Amy answered all her questions, sharing with the public the mistakes she'd made getting involved with the man she had the liaison with, and how it came to be that she decided to have the child in Greece.

"You are one of the biggest supporters of abortion, yet you didn't choose it for yourself. Your critics seem to be making an issue of this."

"I don't know why. I will fight for any woman to have the right to choose, and for that right never to be taken from them. I made a choice."

"I'm sure that was a very difficult choice to make."

"Well, to be perfectly honest, I originally planned to have an abortion. That too, was a difficult decision."

"What made you change your mind?"

Amy chuckled. "It wasn't funny at the time, but I was scared to death. I'd barely had anything more than vaccines at that point in my life. I got on the operating table and panicked."

"How do you feel about this, Sam?"

"Obviously it is not easy to hear. But in the end, I was grateful to be given the gift of life."

"I've come to believe that what is meant to be will come to pass. There must have been a reason greater than my fear and he's sitting next to me." Amy placed her hand over Sam's and smiled at him. "Sam was meant to have a wonderful life and accomplish great things. This, of course, is all thanks to his lovely parents."

"Can we talk about them for a few minutes?" Tamara asked. "It's quite an interesting story how Sam was placed with them. I understand the adoption was arranged by a friend and her family—primarily your friend's uncle, a Greek Orthodox priest."

"Yes, that's correct."

"I can't help but wonder why you would reach out to a priest when you made it clear you wanted your son placed in a Jewish home."

"I spent most of my pregnancy in Athens with Sophia—my friend—at their family home. When I decided to give Sam a better home than I was able to give him, we traveled to Thessaloniki to ask for Father Vasili's help. He knew people. Sophia's grandparents and Father Vasili were instrumental in keeping Jews safe from the Nazis during the war—or at least as safe as they could. One of those families remained close to Father Vasili."

"And this is who adopted you, Sam?"

"Father Vasili's friends are my grandparents," Sam replied. "He hid my grandfather until it was safe for him to be reunited with his family."

"Sam's mother is their daughter, and I am forever grateful to her. Over the years they were kind enough to keep me apprised of his progress growing up and to send me pictures."

"That is quite a story. This priest sounds like a courageous man," Tamara commented.

"He had great wisdom and a heart large enough to embrace all of humanity." Sam's grief was evident. "Sadly, he passed away last week. He was a gift to everyone he encountered and I will miss him tremendously."

"Yes, people with his sense of morality are a rarity. We need more of that. I'd like to ask you about another important male figure. Your birth father."

"There's nothing to tell," Amy interjected. "Sam is not acquainted with him, and he has shown no interest in coming forward."

"There are rumors." Tamara was pushing the limits.

"And that's all they are. Rumors. Sam's father knows who he is. If he doesn't want to be known, that is his loss. I have told you my story. It's not my place to tell someone else's."

Demi had been in the green room waiting for Amy to finish her interview. "You handled that like the pro that you are." Demi looked at Sam. "You too. I hope Sophia was watching. She would be touched by what you said about her great uncle."

"I speak from the heart. He was the best of men."

"When is Sophia getting back?" Amy asked.

Demi looked at her watch. "About ten minutes ago if her flight was on time." She picked up her oversized bag and slung it over her shoulder. "Ready to go? Mindy said she would be waiting for us at Morrell's Wine Bar."

"I'm ready and I need a drink." Amy grabbed her coat.

"After lunch, Sam," Demi said brightly, "we'll take you to see the tree at Rockefeller Center. The restaurant is right across the street, but it still might take a while to push through the crowd to get close enough to appreciate it, and watch the ice skaters too."

Although the skyline of New York City would never again look as it once had, even in the wake of destruction and despair, some of the city's traditions would live on.

"Promise me, you will always stay away from Irini. There's something missing in her. She hurts everyone she touches." —Anastacia to Sophia 1973

Chapter 42

Donna

Spring 2002

Fed up was an understatement. It was one thing for Richie to be rude and inconsiderate to her, but to treat their son as if he was an old rag tossed aside after waxing his car was inexcusable.

Snatching her navy trench coat off the banister as she came down the staircase, Donna pulled it on, yanking the belt a little tighter than needed. At seven in the evening it was still daylight, yet there were remnants of last winter's chill blowing in the breeze.

Loud music was blasting from the garage. Empty beer bottles lined the floor against the wall and a cigarette bobbed up and down from the side of Richie's mouth as he screamed out the words to 'Born in the USA.' Donna watched him, anger increasing by the second as he tinkered with that stupid-ass car he called a classic.

Spotting where he'd placed the boom box, Donna calmly walked over and pulled the plug. Richie looked up to see what had happened and saw his wife holding the disengaged plug in her hand.

"What the fuck?"

"Get your ass out of this garage, change your clothes and be ready to leave in five minutes," Donna demanded.

"For what?"

"We have tickets to your son's play."

"Oh, for fuck's sake! We've been over this. The kid isn't even in the play."

"The kid," she annunciated, "designed and painted the scenery. He's proud of what he accomplished and he'd like to share that with his parents." She walked further into the garage and rested her hand on the old green car. "Anthony wants your acceptance. He needs you to be there for him the way you are for RJ."

"When he takes up a sport, I'll be there for him," Richie said, lowering his head into the hood of the engine.

"You son of a bitch! Don't you dismiss me that way. Get your ignorant head out of that car and look at me." Donna was seething. "You know damn well Anthony's interests are in the arts, not in sports. RJ fulfilled your dream of getting a football scholarship. You're proud and you should be. I am too. But you should be equally proud of Anthony. He's making his mark in a different way."

"I can't be proud of a sissy. When he takes up a hobby or a sport I can relate to, I'll be right behind him."

"Don't. You. Ever—ever use derogatory words to describe our son." The Italian mama was about to unleash her wrath on her husband and if she didn't rein it in, she might split his head open with the sledgehammer she spotted in the corner. "Our son is gay. It does not make him a sissy. He's a better man than you will ever be."

"Gay? I never said he was gay. He just doesn't like manly things."

"Richie. Open your eyes. Your son is gay."

"You're crazy. No son of mine would be like that." A look of disgust crossed his face.

"Why not? Do you have special gay-resistant sperm?"

"He just wouldn't." He slammed the hood of the car closed. "Are you trying to piss me off? Did he tell you he was gay?"

Donna shook her head, the corners of her mouth forming a smile that mocked him. "No. He didn't need to tell me. I've always known.

I'm his mother."

Donna turned her back on him and left for the theater. She didn't need him and at this point she didn't want him to be there. Demi and Sophia were meeting her at the school and, after the show they would take all the children out for a bite to eat.

"Where would you like to go?" Donna asked Anthony. "It's your choice."

"We were all just saying how we haven't been to the Northport Sweet Shop in a while. I'd love an ice cream float."

"Ice cream," Cia repeated.

"When was the last time we split one of those mega sundaes?" Evvie asked Kristos.

"Mr. Panarites always gives me extra cherries," Stella said.

It was a weekday and the season had not begun for the summer crowd to invade the quaint town. Finding a couple of tables to occupy in the legendary local ice cream store was not a problem. The teens and a very enthusiastic three year old sat at one table, while their mothers occupied another.

"What a dick," Demi mouthed.

Sophia scolded her with admonishing eyes.

"What?" she whispered."

"Did he ask you why his dad wasn't here tonight?" Sophia asked.

"No. He's been distracted with the excitement of the play and your kids being here." Donna ran her hands through her hair. "He knows the deal. He's not stupid. I've spoken to him and he knows his father's shortcomings. Still, there are times when I catch him staring out a window or at his computer with a dispirited expression."

"What about you? How are you doing?" Demi sipped her hot cocoa.

"I don't know how much more of this I can take. RJ is settled in college and once Anthony graduates and goes off also, that's it. I'm done."

"Why would you wait two years? It doesn't sound like Richie has much to do with Anthony anyway," Demi asked.

"I don't want to be the one to break up my family. I want Anthony to at least have what little relationship he can with his father until he leaves for school."

"In light of how Richie behaved tonight, I'm not sure that's possible," Sophia added. "I don't know how someone changes that much. He was always such a good guy."

"As long as he was the center of attention and life was going his way. But he didn't factor in that when high school is over, it's over." Donna was frustrated and disillusioned. She wished she'd opened her eyes before the wedding. "Everyone is on the same playing field and no one cares how popular you were when you were seventeen." Donna pressed her fingers to her temples. "We need to change the subject. Please. I'm starting to get a headache."

"Evvie is going to spend the month of July at the American School of Ballet at Lincoln Center," Sophia said proudly.

"That's amazing!" Donna exclaimed. "She's following in your footsteps."

"Hmm. That's to be seen." Demi commented.

"What does that mean?" Sophia seemed annoyed at Demi's comment.

"Dancing was all you thought about. Besides my brother, that is. Evvie has other interests. I'm not sure dancing is her priority."

"She's more talented than I was. She's a natural," Sophia defended.

"Don't get me wrong. She's a beautiful dancer. But she may want to make it simply a hobby."

"A hobby?" Sophia had a look of disgust on her face. "Ballet is not a hobby."

Donna remained quiet. Sophia was getting agitated and Demi was pushing her buttons. Before this went any further, it was time to steer the conversation in another direction.

"Sophia, have you spoken to Amy? Have she and Ezra worked things out?" Donna asked.

"I spoke to her last week, and no. Ezra feels he was deceived and Amy has thrown herself into her work to avoid thinking about him. She's being as stubborn as he is. She says all that transpired happened before she met him, and he's behaving as though she cheated on him."

"Can you blame him? You saw that picture the media keeps flashing. Amy and the lieutenant governor." Demi raised her eyebrows.

"They were at a political fundraiser," Sophia scolded. "Not out on the town together."

"You have to admit, Sophia, she's looking at him like sunbeams are shooting out his every pore." Donna tried to imitate the adoring look.

"She hates him. He was a bastard to her," Sophia said.

"Maybe so, but there was still something there, and Ezra feels like a fool," Demi observed.

"What a mess." Sophia shook her head.

"Talking about a mess. How is Mindy?" Donna asked. "I tried to call her but her assistant said she was out of town."

"She's in South Africa on location for a photo shoot for her new line," Demi told Donna. "She's actually going to be posing with some of the models. I can't wait to see the photos."

"So she's doing okay?"

"She's another one throwing herself into work so she won't have to think. Mindy is fine. A bit jaded about men right now, but that's to be expected," Sophia said.

"Has she dated anyone?" Donna asked. Mindy always had a man on her arm. Over the years some of them had been important and others had been time fillers.

"She's still not ready. But when she is, I think she'll be more selective than she was in the past." Sophia turned to Demi. "It's getting late. I think we should get the kids home."

When Donna and Anthony arrived home, the garage light was still on and the door wide open, which they found odd. Donna called out to Richie. No answer. Walking in to look for him, she stumbled on a cluster of empty beer bottles. Passed out in a folding chair, Richie was slumped over, fast asleep and dead drunk. She had half a mind to let him stay there all night, but she called out for her son to help her get him to bed. *The prom king turned out to be such a prize*, Donna thought, disenchanted.

Chapter 43

Sophia

Fall 2003

I think I like it better out here this time of year than in the summer." Amy sipped her Bloody Mary. "It's more peaceful now without all the summer people and the tourists."

"I like the energy in the summer," Demi disagreed. "It's like a ghost town now. Most of the shops have closed down and many of the restaurants are only open on the weekends."

Seated by a window with a lovely view, Sophia had gathered her friends for a leisurely brunch in Southampton Village. It was rare to get all five of them together unless it was for a major event—a wedding, a graduation—or in the worst of times, a funeral, when you needed your friends the most. So this was a treat to be savored, Sophia thought, as she watched her friends pick at their food as they shifted from one subject to another.

Mindy had just come off Fashion Week NYC and she needed a break from the insanity. Amy was happy to get away. There was nothing pressing in Washington this weekend and she needed her friends. After almost two years separated, Ezra had filed divorce papers. And Donna's marriage was certainly no testament to the institution.

"Have you reached out to him?" Sophia asked.

"What's the point now? He's made up his mind."

"Amy giving up? Who are you? What happened to the girl who made sure she got what she wanted?" Demi motioned for the waiter and asked for another Mimosa for herself and refills of her friends' drinks.

"Isn't that what got me into trouble in the first place?" Amy lowered her voice to a whisper. "I had to have that fucker Bradley Roth, and I wouldn't stop until he was mine. But the bastard never belonged to me. He was playing me the whole time." Pursing her lips in disgust, she added, "And I thought I was such a hot shot."

"At least you didn't get saddled with your bastard." Donna lifted her glass. "A toast to marital bliss," she said sardonically.

Sophia supported her chin in her hands, her elbows on the table as she listened. "How did we get here?" They turned their attention to her. "Five minutes ago we were fourteen, carefree and looking forward to a life of exciting possibilities. That was over thirty years ago. It feels like yesterday yet those teenagers would have never imagined going through all we've been through."

"It feels like a minute ago and, at the same time, a lifetime ago." Mindy sighed.

"You're right," Sophia agreed. "But when I close my eyes and the wind blows a certain way, or I get a whiff of something familiar that evokes the past, it feels like I'm back all those years ago. Whatever I was feeling rushes back. Or I might hear a song and it will remind me of a moment. Sometimes a really insignificant one, but it makes me feel nostalgic."

"I know what you mean." Donna took a bite of her frittata. "I was in the car the other day and I heard that Steely Dan song."

"'Reelin' in the Years?'" Demi asked.

"That's the one. For some reason it reminds me of the drive-thru line at Taco Bell at one in the morning. One night there were like seven or eight cars with our friends all on line at the same time and that's the song I remember playing on the radio for some reason."

"Talking about old friends, did any of you get a call from Jill about the reunion?" Sophia asked.

"Is that who called?" Amy replied. "My assistant gave me a message from a Jill with a phone number to call back."

"So, she's on the committee I assume?" Donna glanced out the window, an unreadable expression crossing her face. "When is it?"

"It's next October. She's trying to get a master list of addresses together to send out invitations and ticket request forms."

"I'll pass. Everyone I want to see is right here." Mindy motioned in her friends' direction.

"I think we should skip the reunion and have our own. We should take that trip to Greece and stay at your grandmother's beach house like we'd planned to when we were in high school," Donna suggested.

"Aegina," Demi said. "That's an idea. We had the best summers of our lives there, right Sophia?"

"We did, but don't any of you want to go to the reunion?" Sophia asked. "I think it will be fun."

"I'm torn. On the one hand I think it will be fun to see everyone after all these years. On the other hand, well, you know, Richie and I are not the golden couple everyone thought we were, and I'm not up for scrutiny on that."

"Leave the *malaka* home," Demi blurted out.

Not expecting that word to come from Demi's mouth—at least not at that moment—Sophia nearly sprayed everyone with the Mimosa she sipped.

"He didn't graduate with our class. Leave him home," Demi added.

"I haven't heard anyone use that word in years. Dean and Vinny would call each other *malaka* instead of their names," Donna laughed.

"What exactly does that mean? I've forgotten, Mindy asked.

Demi sat up in her chair, taking on a mock prim pose. "It's a guy who has jerked off so many times that he went nuts in the brain."

Sophia shook her head, astounded at Demi's laconic and tactless definition. "Basically, it means idiot."

"I used to piss off Dean and call him that every chance I had." Amy smirked at the memory.

"The two of you loved each other to no end." Sophia rolled her eyes.

"Getting back to the reunion," Donna suggested, "Jill left me a message also. But I haven't spoken to her yet. What else did she say?"

"She asked if I was in touch with all of you still, of course. And that we better come because it's going to be a pissa."

The five of them broke out into laughter. "That's Jill!" they all said in unison.

Feeling nostalgic, Sophia's mind wandered as she cut off the tops of the jumbo peppers and tomatoes she was stuffing with meat and rice for the *yemista* she was cooking for dinner. So much had happened in the past thirty years, but for Sophia it had all worked out to a happy end. She had loved with her soul, lost her heart and found it once again with her Dino. Now she wished the same for her friends.

Everything around her was changing. Demi's son, Kristos, had graduated and gone off to college, and now Evvie and Nicky were searching for where they would attend the following year. Donna was on the brink of divorce and Amy was just handed papers to end her marriage. And Mindy. Sigh. Mindy had completely closed herself off to the possibility of personal happiness.

"You look like you've got the problems of the world on your shoulders," Dean observed. "What's wrong?"

"I didn't hear you come in."

"That's because you were on another planet. Did you have a bad day?"

"No. I had a perfect day," Sophia told him as she wrapped her arms around him and played with the hair on the nape of his neck. "And it's about to get even better." She gave Dean a long, lingering kiss—one that evoked more love and appreciation of what they had than words could express.

~Yemista — Stuffed Peppers and Tomatoes~

4 peppers
4 tomatoes
2 pounds lean chopped beef
Extra virgin olive oil
2 cloves chopped garlic
1 large chopped onion
1 cup white wine
1½ cup water
Salt, pepper, parsley
½ cup rice
8 ounces tomato paste
1 large can crushed tomatoes
Breadcrumbs (seasoned)
Potatoes (optional)

Preheat oven to 375°

In a large roasting pan, coat the bottom of the pan with a little olive oil. Prepare the peppers by cutting the tops and removing the seeds and membranes. For the tomatoes, cut the tops and hollow out the middle. Find the largest tomatoes available. Use any peppers you prefer. I like a mixture of red, yellow and orange.

Arrange the peppers and tomatoes in the roasting pan. In a large, deep skillet drizzle 2 tablespoons of olive oil and sauté the onions and garlic for one minute. Add the chopped meat. When the meat is fully browned, add the wine, water, salt, pepper, parsley, tomato paste and the rice. My mom always added the rice by feel. I pour about two handfuls in the skillet, just as she did. I've estimated that to be ½ cup. Let the mixture simmer for about fifteen minutes on medium heat. That will give the rice a chance to begin to cook. If you feel you need more fluid, add a little more water. If the reverse is the case, let the mixture simmer a little longer. Remove from the heat. Fill the peppers and tomatoes. Sprinkle breadcrumbs generously on top and drizzle with olive oil.

Peel the potatoes and cut them into quarters. Place the potatoes between the peppers and tomatoes. The potatoes help to support the tomatoes and peppers, but they serve as a nice side dish as well. Don't forget to season them.

Bake for 1½ hours at 375°. After the tops have browned (about 45min.), you may want to lay a sheet of aluminum foil over pan. Do not cover tightly or seal. You want to bake the peppers, not steam them.

I usually double this recipe. I like finding the leftovers in my fridge on a busy day. They heat up in the microwave easily without compromising the taste, or you can eat them the way I like them—cold.

Chapter 44

Amy

December 31, 2003

With little going on in Washington during the last two weeks of December, Amy had come home to Westchester for the holidays. Ezra had taken Adam to Florida where they spent Hanukkah with Ezra's parents. The Blooms invited Amy to come with Mindy and celebrate at their home. Celebrate. She'd hardly call it that. Christmas and Hanukkah were separated by five days that year, and happy exuberant families surrounded Amy. She had no one.

Her own mother had passed away earlier that year, leaving her emptier than before. They never had a warm mother/daughter relationship, and that made the loss worse in some ways. For Sophia, losing Ana was devastating, but she had years of loving memories to hold on to. Amy had a lifetime of criticism and disappointment. She never quite measured up to her mother's hopes and dreams. Now with her gone, there would never be the possibility of gaining her approval.

With a new year merely hours away, she longed for new avenues of happiness and contentment, but what she feared was a year of slammed doors and closed books. Amy realized what she took for granted and chased away was what she desired most of all.

At least she would have her son for New Years. Together, she and Adam would spend the evening at the Carriage House New Year's Eve party. Demi, she was sure, would pull out all the stops to make it an unforgettable night.

On Adam's arm, Amy walked into the main ballroom dressed in an elegant, gold, floor length, lace skirt, complimented by a black, three-quarter sleeve, form-fitting top with a conservatively scooped neckline.

Spotting Demi, Amy waved as they entered.

"Oh my God!" Demi exclaimed. "You couldn't look more beautiful if I dressed you myself."

"Thanks? There was a compliment in there somewhere," Amy chided.

"You know what I mean." Demi turned to Adam. "And you! I can't remember the last time I saw you. Give me a hug."

"Amy! Adam!" Michael's mother joined them, her arms outstretched. "Don't you look beautiful," she said in her heavily accented voice. "And so age appropriate. You could give my daughter-in-law lessons on how to dress."

Demi, a good foot taller than her mother-in-law with the heels she had on, towered above her from behind rolling her eyes and sticking out her tongue.

Adam stifled a laugh and excused himself to join the rest of the teens.

"It's nice to see you, Mrs. Angelidis. But I envy Demi. She has a style I could never pull off."

"Thanks," Demi said after her mother-in-law moved on to greet other guests.

"I figured you needed my help before she caught you making faces at her. So, I guess she's still winning the tug of war on who gets more of Michael's attention?"

Demi waved it off and rolled her eyes. "No. Michael made it clear that with the vineyard and now the Carriage House opening he would not be able to help them with their staff shortages. He's got Kristos helping out on the weekend and that seems to have appeased her."

"And you and Michael?" Amy asked.

"Better than ever."

"Good. At least that makes one of us."

Demi took her arm and led her to their table. The room was decorated in black and white with pops of golden orange for a dramatic effect. "This is our table. Leave your bag on your seat and let's get a drink."

"Pushy, aren't we?" Amy admired the floral arrangements. Large, snowball sized, white chrysanthemums were arranged in black, art deco vases. In the center of the white cloud of flowers a single orange poppy shone like the sun. "You really outdid yourself." Amy cocked her head to the side. "This table is set for ten. Did you seat Adam with us?"

"Of course not. I don't think those kids will be sitting at all tonight, but they are all together."

"Then who's the tenth?"

"Don't worry about it."

"Oh, Demi. I know that look in your eye. If you are trying to set me up with a blind date, I'm not interested."

"I'm the tenth guest," Amy heard from behind her. She shivered at the sound of his voice and turned quickly.

"Ezra," came from her lips in a breathy whisper. They stared at one another, neither knowing what to say.

"Demi invited me. Actually, invited is not the right word."

"Damn straight," Demi interrupted. "We had a little chat and then I told him to get his ass over here or I would kick it into next year. And with that, I'll leave the two of you to talk."

"If this is uncomfortable for you—"

"No, Ezra. I'm surprised though. I've tried to speak to you many times."

"I know. Can we find a quiet place to talk? I can't hear over the music."

"Follow me." Amy led Ezra out of the ballroom and into Demi's office.

"Two years, Ezra. We've been separated two years and all that time you'd never talk it out with me."

"I need you to look at it from my side. I'm willing to talk now because we are about to sign the papers ... and Demi convinced me that neither of us would forgive ourselves if we didn't at least try to understand each other."

"You've always been the most rational and reasonable man I know. I didn't expect this from you."

"What did you expect? I was played for a fool all these years. You had a whole life that I didn't know about. God damn it! You were in love with another man the whole time we were married."

Furiously, Amy shook her head. "No, no, that's not true."

"I saw the picture of the two of you. I could see the look in your eye. Don't lie to me!" he shouted.

"I swear, there was never anything between us since I got pregnant with Sam. He didn't want me. He was engaged to someone else."

Ezra took a seat and buried his face in his hands. "When did you stop wanting him?" His voice was calmer, now. Almost resigned.

"That's not an easy question to answer."

He looked up at her. "Try." His blue eyes appeared frosty. They held none of the warmth she was used to seeing.

"I had an infatuation for him since I was in my early teens. When I finally had him, I thought he loved me. It took me a long time to get over the pain I felt. And love turned to anger and then hate. But it's a fine line—love and hate. And those feelings I had would creep back." Amy pulled a chair close to Ezra and seated herself directly across from him. "And then you came along. You were everything he wasn't. Kind and gentle; affectionate and caring. Because of you, I gave love another chance."

"Did those feelings for Roth creep back while we were married?"

"Oh, Ezra. You hold me to a standard I can't live up to. Every woman has someone she wonders about. And when she does, old feelings come to the surface."

"Did you sleep with him?"

"Never!" Amy was reluctant to go on, but she had nothing to lose at this point. "I won't lie, he asked me more than once if I'd like to pick up where we left off."

"When?" he asked gruffly.

"Several times over the years, but I finally put an end to that. They say a picture is worth a thousand words, however, the story can be completely misconstrued."

"I don't understand."

"The picture you referred to? The one the media got a hold of? That picture was very deceiving. When the photo was snapped it was right after Bradley told me how beautiful he thought I had become and he asked me if I'd like to go to his hotel room later that evening. I was aware of the cameras. I looked up at him adoringly, giving him the impression I was interested. I didn't want the cameras to pick up on what I was really feeling inside, so I continued to smile while I told him that if he ever came near me with that teeny-tiny dick of his, I'd take a page from Lorena Bobbitt's handbook on how to handle bastards like him."

They looked at one another and broke out into laughter. The sound was like a symphony. She missed him. Amy took Ezra's hands in hers. She looked up at him earnestly. "I am sorry. Sorry I didn't tell you about Bradley or the baby. Sorry I felt the need to keep it buried. But most of all, I am sorry for not truly appreciating what I had in you. You made everything so easy for me, and I took you for granted." She sucked in a deep breath. "I never allowed myself to love you as deeply as I did. I never wanted to chance that kind of hurt again. A part of me was closed forever. Until I lost you. And that pain was greater than any other. I love you so much, and I'm sorry if I slighted you and never fully showed you what you meant to me."

Amy wasn't a woman to shed a tear, but as the words spilled from her lips so did the tears. "It took losing you to know how deeply I love you. Only you. I know it's too late and you're not in love with me anymore, but I—"

Ezra leaned in and pulled her to him, crushing his lips to hers. "It's not too late. I've been miserable without you." He kissed her again. "I will always love you."

Hand in hand, they walked back into the ballroom. The music was pumping and they noticed Adam dancing with a large group of teens his age. Demi was giving instructions to one of the wait staff, but when she spotted Amy and Ezra, her smile brightened. Rushing over to them she asked, "Am I seeing what I think I'm seeing?"

They each took a cheek and planted a kiss on her. "Thanks," they both said.

"I knew you belonged together. My work is done. Now I have to do something about Mindy."

"Is she a party planner or a matchmaker?" Ezra joked.

Later, when they rang in the New Year and kissed at midnight, they toasted the days to come. "To new beginnings," Amy lifted her glass.

"To the best damn year of our lives," Ezra responded.

Chapter 45

Donna

Summer 2004

Lounging on a deck chair in her backyard, Donna sipped a tall glass of freshly brewed ice tea garnished with a lemon wedge. At ten in the morning, the sun was shining in her direction, and with a rare day of low humidity on a July Long Island day, she was in bliss, peacefully relaxing.

RJ had been home since the middle of May, and it was nice to have her family together. These moments were rare and she savored them, although a sense of impending doom always hung over her. Richie had been relatively quiet over the past few months. Donna interacted with him as little as possible. If he was home for dinner, fine. If not, he could eat leftovers from the fridge. It was no longer her concern. With both their sons home for the summer, Richie was on his best behavior and, more often than not, he came home to complete the pretense of a tight family unit. Donna imagined that was for RJ's benefit. He hardly acknowledged Anthony's presence.

"Where's Anthony?" Richie asked, popping his head through the sliding glass door.

She pointed to the far end of the property where Anthony was set up with an easel and paints. Earlier, she'd gone over to see what he was working on and her son showed her the way the light illuminated the dewdrops on the leaves on an oak tree, the sunbeam shining down to cast a glow on a perfect peony that had bloomed the day before.

"I want to capture the beauty of how it looks this very minute," Anthony told his mother. "The dewdrops will fall, the sun will change its position and the peony will wither and die. Nothing stays forever and I want to immortalize the moment."

Her son was so correct. More than he knew.

"Anthony!" Richie called and waved him over. "RJ and I are going out for a round of golf. Join us."

"Thanks Dad. I'm in the middle of something and I need to see it through."

"Your brother is hoping you will come."

"I'll catch up with him later. I'm not hyped on golf anyway."

"What are you hyped on?" Richie put his hands on his hips, annoyed.

Anthony stammered a bit and Donna reached for his hand in a gesture of support. She recognized the look on her husband's face and his aggressive stance. A tempest was brewing and there wasn't much she could do to stop it.

"Painting, music, art. Not sports. I like to swim though." Donna knew Anthony was looking for his father's approval. "And I don't mind tennis once in a while," he added.

"You should have been a girl," Richie muttered under his breath, and Donna watched her son's body language change. He had been so content a few minutes ago. Now he was crushed.

"Richie! Enough," Donna scolded.

Timidly, Anthony defended himself. "The greatest artists in history were men."

"Pff," was Richie's response.

"I am a man. I have no desire to be a girl."

"A man," Richie mocked. "Do you even like girls?"

"Of course. I have many friends. Girls and guys."

"Leave," Donna ordered. "Go play golf and leave him alone."

"You didn't really answer my question. I'll ask another way. "Would you fuck a girl?"

"You're disgusting," Donna spat. "He's only sixteen."

"And a mama's boy. I fucked you when you were younger than that."

"You're a pig to talk like that in front of the children."

Anthony clenched his fists and his face turned red from anger. "No, I wouldn't." He looked his father in the eye. "I'm gay."

It happened so quickly—too quickly for Donna to shield her son. She cried out when she heard the sound of Richie's fist crack across Anthony's face. Richie hit his son for being honest.

Richie slammed the glass door and disappeared. Donna took her son into her embrace. "It's going to be okay," she soothed.

An hour later, she and Anthony were in their car headed to Jamesport. Donna had called Sophia and, in a nutshell, told her what had transpired. They would stay out east indefinitely.

"I'm very concerned," Donna told Sophia and Demi. "At times he seems perfectly content and other times withdrawn. He's spending less and less time with friends. Part of it must be that Richie is chipping away at his self-esteem with the way he treats him. But I wonder if I'm missing something more."

"Come to Greece with us," Sophia suggested. RJ can come too if he likes. I think the change of scenery will be healthy for all of you."

"I don't know."

"What's holding you back? School is out for the summer. It will be fun. And think of the inspiration Anthony will have to paint."

"I'm booking your flights right now," Demi said enthusiastically.

"Hold on. Give me a minute to think." Donna chewed on the inside of her cheek.

"What's to think about?" Demi was persistent.

"We're staying in Chios for the whole month. My yiayiá will travel from Athens to join us. I know she'd love to see you." Sophia refilled Donna's wineglass.

"Are you plying me with liquor to convince me?"

"You need to be convinced to spend a month in Greece?" Demi raised her eyebrows.

For the first time today, Donna was amused. "You're right. I'm going to Greece! Opa!"

"Don't go too fast!" Sophia shouted. The kids were riding jet skis at Karfas Beach, one of the most popular and crowded beaches on the island of Chios.

"They can't hear you," Dean said, wrapping his arms around Sophia's bare waist.

"But if I warn them, I feel like nothing bad will happen."

Dean let out a hearty laugh. "Now you sound like your mother. Do you realize the only time I saw you get annoyed at her was when she 'warned' you of all the bad things that could happen?"

"True." Sophia smiled at the thought. "I'm still in one piece though. Maybe thanks to her."

"I'm sure that's it." Dean nuzzled his face in her neck.

"Get a room," Donna teased. She was her lighter self these days.

"We have one, but the house is crawling with teenagers." Dean turned his wife to face him, drawing her in for a passionate kiss.

Donna looked away as sadness crept over her. She was happy for her friends. Watching them, she realized they were the real deal, and she and Richie never were. They were just an illusion, caught up in being crowned the golden couple. He had been a star football player and she was the head cheerleader. On the surface, they were perfect together.

And that was the problem, she thought. They looked good together and seemingly had the same interests, both going on to become teachers, but beyond that, what did they have but a reputation and the expectation that they would last? Had she ever looked under his layers? Did he even have layers, or was he just a one-note personality the entire time?

Dean and Sophia, with all they'd been through, had what everyone strived for in a relationship. They were considerate and caring of each other, putting the one they loved first.

Richie assumed whatever he wanted was good enough for Donna also. She could have chosen to continue on, both of them living separate lives, cohabitating in the same house simply for convenience. Donna felt completely indifferent to him. But this last outburst, calling his son names and slapping him for telling the truth, was the last straw.

It was so good to see her son having fun, and Donna had noticed that for the first time in months, Anthony was happy. He apparently left all his troubles behind when they came to this beautiful, peaceful island.

"Mom!" Anthony called out, running toward her. "Did you see me? That was a blast."

"I'm glad you're enjoying yourself." It made her heart soar to see her son this way. He'd been so sullen, and she hurt for him.

"Round up everyone and tell them to dry off." Dean began to gather up the beach chairs. "We're going to grab a bite to eat at the taverna."

Anthony tore off toward the water, kicking up tiny pebbles as he ran.

"Do we have to go back home?" Donna leaned back in her seat, appreciating the view. At Pelakanos Taverna near the beach, they were seated at a long outdoor table, large enough to accommodate their entire group.

Donna admired the natural quaintness of the restaurant, the blue sky that was fading into a light pink on the horizon, and the carefree attitudes of locals and tourists alike.

"You have to go home if you want to keep your job."

"Thanks for stating the obvious, Demi. But I can dream."

"We have another week. Let's make the most of it," Sophia said. "I know going home will be unpleasant, but with us at your side you'll face it head on."

"Do you know he hasn't even called to see how our son is?" Donna drained her wineglass. "He's a pathetic excuse for a father."

"He's having a hard time accepting what he doesn't want to be the truth." Cia's eyes grew heavy as Sophia rocked the child in her arms.

"He'll have no choice if he wants a relationship with his son." Demi looked over to Anthony. "He's a great kid."

"Yeah, and he's having the time of his life. I just want him to be happy."

"Dino, take Cia from me. I have to go to the restroom."

"I'll go with you," Donna said.

They got up and climbed the stone stairs to the main building. "The food is so good here," Donna commented.

"That's why it's always packed. Oh, excuse me," Sophia apologized. She looked up at the man she bumped into and froze.

"Sophia."

"Apollo," she said with disdain.

He looked at Donna, and she could tell there was recognition in his eyes. "Is Mindy here also?"

"No." Sophia began to walk away. Apollo grabbed her arm.

Sophia wrenched it from him. "Don't you ever lay a hand on me."

Donna had never heard Sophia speak so harshly, or see a look on her face so hateful. But considering what this man had put Mindy through, she didn't blame her.

Apollo called to her as she rushed away. "I only wanted to know how she is."

Sophia snapped her head around. "How is she? Better off without you."

"Calm down. I've never seen you like this." Donna put an arm around her shoulder.

"He's a savage," Sophia said as she pushed open the door to the restroom. "Even paradise breeds monsters."

The next day, Michael suggested they rent a boat and take the kids fishing.

"Count me out," Demi announced. "Let's go shopping," she suggested to Sophia and Donna. "I bet Stella and Evvie would rather come with us."

Later, they each came home with a custom pair of sandals they'd designed themselves, as well as fresh ingredients they had picked up at the market for dinner. By the end of the week, they were packed and on their way home. Donna waved goodbye to Chios as they boarded the plane and silently thanked the island for the temporary respite.

Chapter 46

September 2004

T he situation at home grew worse by the day. Asking Richie to move out incited his anger to the point where he would do anything to purposely irritate Donna.

"This is my home. If you want out of this marriage then you leave, bitch," he told her.

She filed separation papers, but to no avail. He wouldn't leave and Donna, hesitant to uproot her sons from their home, suffered his verbal attacks and unreasonable behavior. She imagined RJ would graduate from college and move out on his own, but Anthony needed the stability, and he wasn't getting it in this current environment.

Anthony kept as far away from his father as possible and Donna could see Richie made no effort to mend his relationship with his son. It made her hate him just a little more.

"Mom?" Anthony found his mother bundled under a blanket in an Adirondack chair on the back patio deck, a glass of red wine in hand.

Donna looked up and patted the seat beside her, indicating he should sit down.

"What's on your mind?"

"Is it my fault?" he asked.

"Is what your fault?"

"Dad and you. Fighting. Splitting up."

Donna had such love for this sweet boy. "Oh, no. Anthony, people change, and sometimes what worked once, doesn't anymore. We were very young when we married. That shouldn't matter when you love someone, but sometimes a person becomes someone you don't recognize and can't live with." She took her son's face in her hands. "These are not your burdens."

"But you and Dad fight over me."

"Yes and no. The fights are not because of you. It's his behavior toward you and who he's become that's disappointing to me. And you're only one of many issues we fight over."

"I could have made more of an effort to like the things that Dad and RJ like. I'm a disappointment to him. Maybe if I take an interest in his hobbies—"

"Anthony. It's a parent's job to cultivate a child's interests and talents, not to force them into activities or careers they care nothing about."

"But you always say that relationships go both ways. Maybe I need to take the first step."

"You are a very tolerant and mature young man. Have I told you lately how proud I am of you?"

Getting up, Anthony bent down and kissed his mother's cheek.

"Where are you off to?" she asked.

"To take the first step."

Fall had chilled the night air, warning Donna of colder weather to come. She collected her blanket, neatly folded it and carried it into the house. It was as if no one was at home. The house was silent—too silent—no TV on, or showers running, or any voices echoing through the house.

"Anthony!" Donna called. No response. "Anthony!" She wondered where he could be.

Peeking her head out the front door, she noticed the garage light was on. *That's nothing new.* But where was her son. Surely not in there with his father. "The first step," she said under her breath, as she walked toward the garage.

Despite her feelings for Richie, a tiny smile crossed her lips as father and son talked about engine parts over the open hood of Richie's classic car.

"When these cars were made, it was easy to do your own tune-ups," Richie told his son. "Oil changes, spark plugs. You name it. I've even changed a carburetor or two. These new cars today are a whole different animal." Richie wiped grease off his hands with an old terry-cloth rag. "Everything's computerized. You need hundreds of thousands of dollars worth of equipment to fix anything."

"That's why you like these old cars?"

Donna listened in without making her presence known. Maybe this was the first step. Maybe, in turn, Richie will take an interest in what appeals to Anthony.

"Not old. Classic. They don't make them like this anymore. You want to get your hands in the engine and I'll show you how to do an old fashioned tune-up?"

"I don't know. What if I screw something up?"

Richie took a pull on his beer. Donna watched him as Richie eyed Anthony up and down.

"What's the matter? You afraid of getting your hands dirty? Or is it the clothes? I know you homos like to look picture perfect at all times."

Donna could see the look on Anthony's face. The man was such a bastard. But this was her fault. She allowed Richie to do this to their son, because she was foolish enough to stay in a house that had not been a home for a very long time.

"Why do I try?" Anthony said, the venom in his voice concealing the hurt he could no longer bear. Only a mother could decipher the nuances in his voice and the pain in his eyes.

Anthony threw down the wrench that Richie had handed him earlier and stormed off.

Clap. Clap. Clap. "Good job. Let me get you your Father of the Year Award." Donna didn't wait for his insult to fly. She turned her back and left him to the only things he seemed to love—his beer and that damned car.

"Anthony." Donna knocked on his locked door.

"Not now, Mom."

"I only want to help."

"I know, but you can't. I need to be alone right now."

"Okay. I'm here if you want to talk."

There was a knot in the pit of Donna's stomach. There was no way to alleviate her feelings of uselessness and the inability to make her child's world happy and safe from anguish and emotional torture.

Tomorrow, she would pack their clothing and find a new place to live. Donna was done. Richie could have the house and everything that went with it. All she wanted was a happy teenager.

The next morning, Donna was awakened by a bellowing wail. Still disoriented from sleep, it took her mind a few moments to register the cries coming from a distance. The guttural moans were so distressing, she knew in her bones something was terribly wrong.

Leaping out of bed, she shrugged into her robe and ran down the stairs, flying out the front door, following the sounds of her husband's screams.

"Anthony!" Donna cried out. "No!" His body half dragged from the old car, the door swung wide open, Richie had his arms around Anthony's lifeless torso. He was screaming desperately for him to wake up.

Donna ran to her son and beat Richie with her fists. "Get away from him." She pushed him until she had her son in her arms. "Call

911!" Her panicked shrill was high-pitched and constrained. "Call!" Tears spilled on Anthony as she rained kisses on him. "Wake up! Mommy is here. Wake up," Donna cried. "You're going to be okay. We're getting help."

Feeling Richie's hand on her shoulder, she shrugged him away.

"Donna, he's gone," he cried. "Our son is gone."

"No, he's not. No, he's not. My beautiful boy. Don't leave me." She rocked him, holding onto him for dear life.

Squad cars and an ambulance pulled up in front of the house, but Donna seemed unaware. She'd been speaking non-stop to her son, willing him to life, begging him to breathe.

"Ma'am, we'll take it from here." Donna turned to look at the entourage behind her.

"You'll help him?"

The officers and EMT glanced at one another. "I'll check him out. Let me take him from you."

The paramedics examined Anthony and placed him on a stretcher. The police officer tried to step out of earshot of Donna but she heard him say, "We have a DOA."

"No! No!" Donna turned to her husband. "You did this." She laced into Richie. "This is your fault. You killed our son! I hate you!" She began to beat on his chest. Richie stood with no resistance in him to fight or argue. He just stood there and let her pound him. "I hate you!" she repeated.

In the days that followed, Donna felt as if she were in an alternate universe. Her mind, her heart and her womb could not absorb the loss of her child. One moment her son had been a vibrant, living teenager with plans and the rest of his life ahead of him, and now her mind was being filled with what could only be untruths. Her son was gone. Impossible. How could he be here one minute and gone the next as though he never existed at all?

Yet everyone around her believed Anthony was gone. Piles of flowers were left at her doorstep. Students at the high school and neighbors gathered in front of her home, paying tribute to her son with a candlelight memorial.

Well-meaning friends and acquaintances dropped off casseroles, but Donna barely ate. Richie dared not come home again. She had no idea where he was, but she didn't care. She never wanted to see him again.

"Let me help you, Mom," RJ pleaded. "I can take the semester off. We need each other right now."

"No. Nothing will change by you staying here. I will not have both of my son's lives destroyed. You have so much ahead of you and I don't want it stalled."

"That's what family does, Mom. You taught me that. We take care of each other. We make sacrifices."

"I won't have you making sacrifices for me. I don't need a babysitter." Donna looked lovingly at her son. "Go. Live your life. I'm very proud of the man you are becoming. I'll call you if I need you. Please, listen to me."

Donna was alone, and right now it was what she wanted. RJ reluctantly went back to school a few days after the funeral. The sadness in his eyes darkened his spirit as it had Donna's, but she could only deal with her own pain and she thought it was in her son's best interest to get back to his own life.

Donna couldn't face the outside world. Holed up in Anthony's room, she laid on his bed torturing herself with reminders of him. This was all that was left of her baby. His schoolbooks strewn where he left them next to his computer, various drawings and paintings scattered about, and pictures of his brother and closest friends wedged into a mirror frame.

A lamentation hymn from Good Friday came to mind and what she couldn't fully grasp as a teenager, she wished she didn't comprehend now. She'd sometimes attend Holy Week services with Sophia when they were younger. Donna remembered Sophia's mother being overcome with emotion over the hymns that were sung—particularly one section. Of course, Donna thought it was because Ana had lost a child once. Ana understood that kind of pain as only a mother could. Now she too, could understand the Virgin Mother's cries as her child died before her eyes.

O my sweet springtime, my most beloved child, whither has thy beauty sunk down?

O light of my eyes, my beloved child, how art thou now hidden in the grave?

Clutching a paper containing the last words her son had written, Donna held it to her breast, crying for the most unbearable loss a woman can endure.

Donna heard voices calling to her. But she was in her tomb. Unreachable and no one would find her.

"Donna," Sophia said sympathetically.

Donna didn't look up or answer. She stared into the pillow she clung to, desperately breathing in the scent she knew would fade with time.

"Sweetie. We're here to help." Sophia gingerly moved to the edge of the bed. Demi stayed by the doorframe.

"Can you bring my son back?" Donna looked up at Sophia.

Sophia shook her head slowly.

"Then you can't help me."

Demi stepped into the room and sat down close to Donna. "I want to say that I can imagine what you are going through, but I can't. I don't think anyone can understand this pain unless they've been through it. But you have another child to think of. Don't throw away your life and the chance to be part of his." Demi embraced Donna. "That wouldn't honor Anthony."

"I don't know how to go on."

"You will," Sophia assured her. "The pain will always be there but it will change. Eventually you will think of Anthony and the special times you shared."

"It kills my soul that my son was in so much pain. Tortured enough to take his own life."

"We live in a highly pressurized time for teenagers." Sophia closed her eyes and shook her head. "Between their peers, their parents' expectations, career decisions, and this new way kids are socializing on the computer—I'm not sure it's such a good thing."

"What are you holding?" Demi wanted to know.

"The note Anthony wrote before—" Donna held on to it tighter as though someone would take it from her.

Frowning, Sophia and Demi looked at each other.

"Did you show this to the police?" Demi asked.

"No. This is between me and my son."

"Okay," Sophia stroked her hair. "But it might make you feel better to discuss it with someone. A therapist perhaps."

"No. The two of you can see it, but no strangers."

"I understand." Sophia took the wrinkled paper from Donna's hand. Demi moved closer to read it alongside Sophia.

Dear Mom,

Forgive me. I need to stop the pain.

Please know that wherever I am, I will always love you and RJ.

I'm so sorry, but I just can't do it anymore.

Eternally your son,

Anthony.

Both Demi and Sophia choked out sobs as they read. The three women huddled together, drawing strength from each other.

"Does Richie know about this?" Demi wondered.

Donna nodded. "He does."

"Where is he?" Sophia asked.

"I don't know."

"Should we be worried?"

"Maybe, but I don't have the strength to be, and I have nothing left in my heart to give him."

"No matter what you do or where you end up,
don't lose sight of the friendship you share."
—Edna Bloom to the 'Honey Hill Girls' Graduation Day 1974

Chapter 47

Sophia

October 2004

You look far, far away," Dean said. He found Sophia sitting by the fireplace, her arms wrapped around her legs.

"Just thinking."

"What's on your mind?" He came up alongside her, sat down and hoisted her legs over his own.

"I was just thinking how many changes we've all been through this year. "I guess I miss the twins." Sophia's eyes grew moist. "We'll have them back home at Thanksgiving. But Donna ..." Sophia couldn't finish the sentence.

"Yeah." Dean blew out a breath. "Only one of her children will be headed home for the holiday."

"I'm so worried about her. She drags through the day, barely eating or speaking to anyone."

"What about Richie? Any news on him?" Dean wondered.

"Donna's attorney informed her that he checked himself into an alcohol rehab."

"He drank, sometimes too much, but I didn't know it was that much of a problem."

"Apparently he landed in the hospital with alcohol poisoning after he found Anthony."

"I hate to say it, but he created the situation with his insensitivity and ignorance. Still, I feel bad for the guy. He was our friend." Dean picked at a designer rip on the knee of the Abercrombie jeans Evvie insisted Sophia had to buy. "Maybe I should visit him."

"Maybe. I'm more worried about Donna right now. My question is how does a parent recover from this? I don't know that I would be able to, but I can't watch my friend wither away anymore. It's been over a month and I haven't seen a glimmer of progress." Sophia took Dean's hand, lightly brushing her fingertips across his palm as she spoke. "Would it be wrong of me to try to convince her to go to the reunion?"

"That depends."

"On what?"

"Your motives."

She thought about that. They had been talking about the reunion for months. Once she and her friends all decided they were on board with the idea, they'd been looking forward to it. But so much had gone wrong since then. So much pain had been inflicted on their lives. Sophia thought it would be nice to shed themselves from burden for one evening and relive the simplicity that youth had to offer.

"It's not for my benefit, if that's what you're thinking. The whole thing is inconsequential in the aftermath of tragedy. But Donna needs to wake up from this nightmare, and what better way to do it than surrounded by the friends who love her?"

Sophia, carrying a shopping bag of homemade soup, unlocked the front door to Donna's home. Following behind her was the rest of their circle. The 'Honey Hill Girls' were back in town and they were on a mission. Demi was armed with a silver-toned traveler's cosmetic case. Mindy carried a garment bag draped over her arm, and Amy was there to plead for the defense.

"Donna!" Sophia called out as she climbed the stairs.

"We're all here and we're coming up," Demi added.

Donna stared blankly at the four of them standing in her doorway.

"When did you last have something to eat?" Sophia asked, concerned.

Donna shrugged. "I don't know. Maybe yesterday afternoon."

"I suspected as much. You can't do this to yourself. I cooked for you. I'll go heat it up." Sophia ran down the stairs, placed a container in the microwave, and returned a few minutes later carrying a bed tray with a bowl of soup and crusty bread.

"We were reminding our friend here what day today is," Amy told Sophia.

"You girls go and have fun." Donna seemed almost listless.

"Here." Sophia brought the tray in front of her. "Let's get some food in you and then we can discuss it."

"You don't expect me to go?"

"Not looking like that!" Demi exclaimed. "You stink! First we shove you in a shower."

"We have everything under control." Mindy picked up the garment bag she'd been holding earlier. "Look what I have here. A one of a kind *Bloom*, especially for you."

"I can't wear that. I'm not going."

"Donna." Amy sat down next to her and took her hand. "You know me. I'm not one to sugarcoat anything. Will it be hard to take the first step into that party? Hell, yes. Will your heart break a little more each time someone says how sorry they are? Damn, right."

"How is this helping?" Demi crossed her arms over her chest.

"I'm getting to it." Amy flashed Demi a sour look and then turned her attention back to Donna. "When Ezra left me, I thought my world had ended and I'd never be happy again. I know this isn't the same. But pain is pain and once he came back to me I knew I never wanted to endure that again."

"What she's trying to say is that you only have one life," Mindy continued. "And so many people who love you. Not to mention a son who needs you more now than ever before."

"You have to join the living again for him, if not for yourself," Demi chimed in.

"Anthony is at peace now. He wasn't before, but he is now." Sophia picked up the spoon off the tray and handed it to Donna.

"I should have done more for him."

"You did everything," Mindy said emphatically. "You're not to blame. I know I'm not a parent, but it seems to me that there is too much guilt when something happens to a child. I know you mothers want to maintain full control over your children, but you can't."

"She's right," Amy agreed. "Stop torturing yourself."

"Now get your skinny ass out of that bed and into the shower." Demi pulled Donna up.

"Skinny? I haven't been skinny in years."

"Have you looked in a mirror?" Mindy asked. "You must be down twenty pounds."

After Donna finished her shower, Sophia blow dried and flat ironed her hair, while Demi applied her make-up.

Rummaging through Donna's jewelry armoire, Mindy pulled out some pieces, deciding which would complement the dress she had laid out on the bed.

"Okay," Mindy announced, "let's get you into this dress." The form-fitting, knee length, black sheath dress was elegant and conservative, but the cinched waist and asymmetrical neckline accentuated her figure.

"You look absolutely gorgeous," Amy told Donna.

"Thanks." Donna's weak smile didn't reach her eyes.

"We're going to slip into our dresses and we'll be ready to go when the men get here." Sophia rummaged through her bag for her cosmetics kit.

"Men?" Donna questioned. "They're coming here?"

"They are," Demi answered. "And an extra guest for you."

"What?" Donna froze.

"Did you find her a date and not me?" Mindy pouted.

"Do you want a date?" Amy asked dryly.

"Actually, no. I don't."

Twenty minutes later, the doorbell rang and Sophia sped down the stairs to answer the door.

"Everyone is just about ready." She planted a quick kiss on Dean and began to dash away.

"Not so fast." Dean caught her by the waist, pulling her toward him to close the space between them. "You look so hot in that dress."

"Hot? What are we, sixteen?" she laughed. "Forty-eight years old and the mother of three and I'm hot?"

"Yes, you are." Dean ran his hands down the length of her. He whispered in her ear. "And I want to do very naughty things to you."

Sophia giggled.

"Enough you two. I haven't even started drinking yet." Dean's old friend loved to rib him.

"Vinny?" Donna was taken aback when she came down the staircase to find her brother standing beside Dean, Michael and Ezra. "What are you doing here?"

Bowing before her in mock formality, he answered, "I'm escorting my lovely sister to the ball."

Donna flew into Vinny's arms as the tears welled in her eyes.

"If you cry off my hard work, I swear, Donna, I'll beat you with the wooden spoon my yiayiá used to threaten us with," Demi warned.

"I love all of you. Thank you for standing by me."

"Where else would we be standing, Sis?" He looked at her admiringly. "I'm always here for you. You can count on me."

Chapter 48

The 'Honey Hill Girls'

October 2004

On the second floor of the Islandia Marriott, a table was set at the entranceway of the main ballroom to check in and greet attending alumni.

"Well, this isn't flattering." Amy made a face at the nametag she was handed. Along with her name was her senior class picture. "Just in case I'm unrecognizable, this 'lovely' photo ought to do it."

"Isn't this fucking amazing!"

Turning, the five of them glanced at each other and laughed. They knew to whom the voice belonged to before they looked.

"Jill!" they said in unison.

"It's like nothing's changed in thirty years. The five of you together like glue."

Jill was a force to be reckoned with. At four foot, ten inches, she had a personality larger than life. There wasn't anyone in their graduating class who hadn't known and loved the pleasantly plump little powerhouse in the clunky platform shoes who'd made all things social at Commack High happen.

"I gotta run, but we rented two rooms tonight for the after party.

297

You have to come. It's gonna be a pissa!"

"She's an interesting character," Ezra commented.

"You have no idea!" Sophia laughed.

"I smoked my first cigarette with her in eighth grade," Demi bragged.

"You make me so proud," Michael joked.

They made their way through the ballroom doors, stopping along the way to hug old classmates. Sophia noticed more than a few women eyed Dean with some getting a little more 'kissy' than she liked.

"How many of my classmates did you go out with?" she asked him, narrowing her eyes.

"I was trying to keep my mind off you." He circled her waist with his arms and kissed the back of her neck.

"Jerk!" Sophia swatted him.

"Get over here you two." Demi motioned from a table the group had claimed as their own for the night. Black and gold balloon centerpieces decorated each table, representing the school colors. An arch in the same color scheme framed the dance floor where music from their era was playing.

"'We May Never Pass This Way Again,'" Mindy repeated the title song from their prom as the music filled the air, adding to the nostalgic mood.

Donna had been quiet and low key, but smiled and said, "Speaking of proms, here comes your date, Sophia." She waved as Matt approached.

"It good to see you, Matt."

Matt took Donna in his arms and hugged her tightly. When he pulled away, he held her hands and looked at her sympathetically. "I would have been there. I wanted to, but I was out of town. What can I say? Sorry for your loss doesn't begin to cover it."

Donna hugged him, resting her head into his chest. "Thank you," Donna said, barely audible.

He kissed Amy and Demi on the cheek, and shook hands with

their husbands. "Sophia." He kissed her hello. "You look as beautiful as ever."

"It wonderful to see you, old friend. I've missed you." Sophia smiled warmly.

"Matt," Dean said sternly, taking a step between him and Sophia.

"Dean," Matt replied stiffly.

Sophia could see the alpha male in both of them ready for competition and she rolled her eyes. Stepping between the two of them, she placed a hand on each of their chests. "Shake hands, boys. High school was thirty years ago."

They did as she said and everyone went back to their individual conversations.

"Matt, did you say hello to Mindy?"

"No," Mindy answered for him. She stepped forward to give him a hug. "I've been watching your travel show. I tape it and catch up on it when I have time."

"That's the way to do it," Matt chuckled.

"We have an open seat at our table," Sophia said. "Join us."

"If you have the room, I'd love to."

"Mindy didn't bring a date," Demi blurted. "You can sit with her."

"Subtlety is Demi's middle name," Amy whispered in Sophia's ear.

"We didn't ask you if you brought someone," Sophia said. "I'm sure we can squeeze in an extra person at the table."

"No worries. I'm on my own."

"We're going to get something to eat," Michael announced. "Who's coming?"

"I'll hold the table," Mindy offered. "I'm not hungry right now."

"I'll sit with Mindy." Donna rested her handbag on her seat.

"Oh, no you don't." Demi lifted her by the elbow and dragged her toward the buffet table. "You need to eat."

"I've been following your career also, Mindy." Matt and Mindy were seated at the table alone while the others stood on the buffet line. Very few people were in their seats. Most of the crowd was either on the food line, at the bar, or flitting from one person to another, reminiscing.

The room was energized by old memories and shared experiences. Absent was the pretense of past reunions, where impressing each other with how far one had gone in life had been the point of their attendance. This night was for recalling a time long past, and momentarily transporting back to a carefree time when they still had their entire lives ahead of them.

"You know what I remember the most about you?"

"No. I wasn't sure you remembered me at all. You only had eyes for Sophia."

"True, I can't deny that. But I was very observant and had an eye for detail." Matt leaned in toward her, resting his elbows on the table. "If I recall correctly, you never wore the same thing twice. It was astounding. I wondered how you pulled it off."

"I made a lot of my own clothing."

"And now you're a famous designer."

"I don't know about famous. Successful might be a better word."

"Modest." He looked her up and down. "One of your creations?"

In a one-shouldered, sequined, sage green, tea-length dress, her red hair stood out, and the thigh high slit up the side accentuated her lean legs.

"Yes, it is."

"And your personal life? A husband, children?"

"No, and no. You?"

"Ex-wife. No kids."

"What happened? With your wife, I mean?"

"Ah. She couldn't deal with me being away all the time. I didn't have the show then, but I was writing for a travel magazine and I was gone more than I was home."

Mindy nodded, understanding.

"She got tired of waiting for me and eventually she met someone else and asked for a divorce."

"I'm sorry."

"Don't be. It was a long time ago. It was as much my fault as hers. I put work before my marriage."

"I understand that. I put my career ahead of someone I loved. I don't think I ever really got over losing him."

Matt cupped his hands over Mindy's. "The saying 'you can have it all' is bullshit. Somehow it always comes down to choices."

"You're right, Matt. And somehow our gut tells us what the right choice is. Even so, we beat ourselves up for years over it."

"Hey! Listen." Matt held out his hand to Mindy as he stood.

"'Stairway to Heaven.'" Mindy stood at his invitation to dance.

"It wouldn't be a seventies high school dance without it."

"That's true," Mindy agreed. "You know, I have never danced with anyone to this song. I felt it was the ultimate couple's song, but I never went out with anyone in our high school."

Matt pulled her close on the dance floor. "Did you ever really listen to the words? It speaks of more than one path and that you can always choose to change it later."

"Hmm, I like that. Second chances. New beginnings."

"Yes. A climb to fulfillment," Matt whispered softly.

Demi elbowed Amy and Donna. They were sitting on either side of her slowly making their way through the food they'd piled onto their plates.

"Am I good or what?" Demi watched Mindy and Matt in a distance and from what she could presume from their body language on the dance floor, the two of them were engaged in dialogue of an intimate nature.

"Is that why you made me get all this food?" Donna complained.

"That and you really need to eat. I'm looking out for everyone's best interest."

"You're such a *yenta*," Amy teased.

"Actually, technically, I'm a *kotsobolos*. A Greek gossip, which I am not, because I am always looking to help, never to harm."

"I can't even say, *kotsowhatever*."

"Well so much for your diplomatic relations Madam Congresswoman."

The teenage banter between the girls was back in full swing as though the last thirty years had yet to happen.

"Look at Mindy and Matt, Mr. Macho Man," Sophia ridiculed Dean. "You had to stake your claim on your woman. 'I Neanderthal. I drag woman into cave.'"

"You are asking for it tonight," Dean mocked her.

"Oh, I'm expecting it." Sophia laughed and raised her glass. Her other hand grazed her husband's inner thigh.

"Who the hell are you? I think Ms. Proper has had too much to drink." Amy snatched the glass out of Sophia's hand.

"I only had three sips."

"That's all it takes," Michael chimed in.

Sophia stood up and pulled Dean to his feet. "Dance with me, Dino. You owe me this one. It's been a long time coming."

They joined dozens of couples on the dance floor already rocking slowly to Jim Croce's 'I'll Have To Say I Love You In A Song.'

It was such a high school thing to do, but he didn't care, nor did she. He had taken that from her once and he was giving it back to her tonight. Dean and Sophia made out on the dance floor, in front of all to see, forgetting there was any other soul in the crowded room. "The love of my life," she sighed.

Chapter 49

Sophia

October 2004

Hand over the keys, frat boy." Sophia held her hand out until Dean reached into his coat pocket, dropping the keys in her palm.

"I haven't had a drink in over an hour," Dean argued.

"Better to be on the safe side."

It was two in the morning. The class reunion had officially ended at twelve, but the party continued in the hotel rooms rented by some of the out of town classmates.

"We should have stayed the night," Dean said. "It's a long drive back."

"Too late now." Sophia handed the valet her ticket.

"We should have all gone in the same car," Demi said.

"The day just didn't work out that way. We'll follow each other home." Sophia waved goodbye and slipped into the driver's seat."

"No music. Please, Dino," Sophia said when he reached for the car radio. "That music was pumping so loud all night. I could use a little quiet."

"That's the difference between now and thirty years ago. It would have never bothered you then."

"Thirty years ago I wouldn't have been on the road at this hour. My mother wouldn't have allowed it."

The Long Island Expressway was pretty desolate, only a few sporadic cars passed them on the road.

"The girl with the earliest curfew on Long Island." Dean laughed, remembering. "She sure was strict about it. What was going to happen at two in the morning that couldn't have happened at eleven anyway?"

"Back then there were no cell phones to make sure your kids got where they were going safely."

As Sophia spoke, a bright light reflecting off her side view mirror blinded her. Before she knew what was happening, the car jolted and an odd sensation confused Sophia's senses into thinking the car had flipped over. Upon impact, she heard the screeching sound of tires. The loud crunch of metal. A whopping sound followed by blinding dusty clouds of white.

It might have been nanoseconds, but the thousands of thoughts and emotions that ran through her mind should have taken hours. *These were the last moments of her life. Her children. Her father. She was about to die. Dino. No! No! God protect me.* She witnessed her funeral in her mind's eye. Her grieving children. Her broken father. She pictured her daughters, grown—walking down the aisle in wedding dresses with no mother fussing over them and no father to give them away. *No! No!* She refused to give in to those visions. Stiffening every muscle in her body, she prepared for impact and slammed on the brakes.

It took a moment for it to register that the car had stopped. "Dino!" Sophia screamed, choking on the powder filling her lungs. Punching away the white pillows blocking her vision, she yelled out for Dean again.

"Sophia!" She thought she heard Michael shout. "Open your door!" She was so disoriented. *What was Michael doing on the road? Why wasn't Dean answering her?*

"Dino! Open your eyes. Talk to me."

Struggling to open his eyes, Dean groaned, but his lids remained closed.

Sophia reached for him, but Michael stopped her.

"It's better not to touch him until the EMTs get here."

Demi, who looked panic-stricken after watching the erratic driver crash into her brother's door, helped Sophia out of the car and clung onto her.

"My brother. Get my brother out of there," Demi cried.

The car that hit them had entered the expressway ramp and cut over to their lane, hitting the passenger side of the car at full speed. The front end of the offending car was embedded into the passenger door.

Sirens roared in the distance. "I can't," Michael called out to his wife. "I'm afraid to touch him. What if he has a neck injury?" Michael came around to the other car. "Hey! Stay in your car, buddy," he said to the driver who caused the accident. He seemed out of it but not badly injured.

"Is he breathing, Michael?" There was panic in Sophia's words. "Oh, God, please tell me he is." She tried to break free from Demi's hold. "I need to go to him. He needs me."

"He's breathing, but it's shallow. Stay put. The ambulance is here." Michael ran to where the rescue vehicle pulled up.

"You're bleeding," Demi said.

"I don't care. They need to get Dino out of there. Now!" Sophia's chest began to tighten. She felt as though she would suffocate. Terror ran through her like venom infesting her bloodstream.

Fire trucks, ambulance vans and police cars blocked the three lane expressway. Two policemen had given a breathalyzer test to the driver of the other car and were reading him his rights. A tow truck had pulled the cars apart and the 'Jaws of Life' was being used to pry Dean from the car.

Pain that Sophia had ignored seared through her. Burn marks from the airbags stung, and the discomfort from the cuts and bruises on her face and limbs were causing her to wince when she moved. But the worst of it was her left arm.

An EMT put it in a splint temporarily. "Ma'am, I'm pretty sure it's broken."

"Forget about me. Take me to my husband." Sophia looked over to where Dean was being placed on a stretcher. The uniformed woman who tended to her wounds helped her over to him.

"I'm going with him."

"That won't be possible ma'am. The EMT looked at her sympathetically, but she held her ground. "We need room to work on him."

Sophia nodded. She wanted to throw herself onto him. Wrap him in her love. Tell him it would all be fine. But she was afraid to touch his cut and bruised face, and feared she would harm his collared neck. They inserted a breathing tube down his throat making her husband, who had been healthy and strong only hours before, look fragile and broken.

"Dino, Dino," she cried. Demi came to her and hugged her tightly. She and Michael had been giving statements to the police.

"Ma'am, let's get you into another ambulance," the female EMT who'd helped her earlier ordered.

"No. My sister-in-law will take me there."

"I must insist. You've had trauma to your arm, and possibly your head."

"Go," Michael encouraged. "We'll be right behind you."

After a battery of tests including an EEG and CT scan, the doctors concluded that Sophia had no serious trauma to her head. The cuts on her face were superficial, and the burns from the airbag were attended to. X-rays showed an arm fracture in the ulna bone. Fortunately, surgery was not required and a cast was set in order to keep the area immobilized.

Demi had gone to wait with her parents while Dean was in surgery, and Michael stayed with Sophia.

"Go find out what's happening with Dino. I can't sit here and do nothing."

"I don't want to leave you alone. You've been through a lot tonight," Michael worried.

"Please," she begged. "I'll be much better off once I get word on what's going on."

"Alright. I'll be right back."

Sophia rested her back on the elevated bed. She was so weary, but she needed to stay alert. Closing her eyes, it was at times like this, she wished she had her mother by her side. Ana always had a way of comforting and calming her when she was having a crisis.

Sophia felt a hand gently press her leg and another graze her hair. Startled, she snapped her eyes open to see who was there. No one. There wasn't a soul nearby. Or was there? Overcome by emotion, tears dropped onto the pillow. "Mom." Sophia could feel her.

"Sophia!" Alex entered the draped off section in the emergency room where he found his daughter.

"Dad," Sophia cried.

"I know. Thank God you're okay."

"Dino?"

"He's still in surgery."

"He was barely conscious. Dad, I can't lose him."

"You're not going to. The doctors are doing everything possible to help him."

"Mom was here—I felt her."

Sadness came over Alex's eyes. "She promised she would never leave us."

"Don't tell anyone. They might start checking my head again."

"It's between you and me." Alex kissed his daughter's forehead. "Faith is believing even when there is no proof."

"I need enough faith to know that Dino won't be taken from me."

When the doctors released her, Alex escorted Sophia to Dean's room. The rest of the family was in the nearby waiting room or hovering by his doorway. Only one person at a time was allowed in the room, and when Sophia arrived Soula left her son's side to let her sit by him.

Sophia was in a weakened state herself, and when she saw her husband, she nearly collapsed. Leaning over the hospital bed in the Neuro-ICU, she prayed.

Sophia had been told that Dean had sustained an acute subdural hematoma. Rapid surgery was his best chance for full recovery. In addition, his spleen had ruptured and had to be removed.

"Please, God, don't take him from me now," Sophia begged in an inaudible whisper. "Dino, my Dino." He looked so pale. She leaned over him and caressed his cheek. "Don't leave me. Not after all we've been through. Squeeze my hand. Move your eyes."

Comforting arms wrapped around Sophia. "Sweetie, you need to take a break. Get some sleep. I'll stay with my brother."

She turned to look at Demi, collapsed into sobs, and shook her head. "No."

"Everyone is here," Demi told her. "They'll take you home. I'll stay with Dean."

In the doorway stood Amy, Mindy and Donna. They were there when she needed them—always at her side without question—her oldest and dearest friends.

Weakly she walked to them, and they embraced each other in a group hug. Sophia covered her eyes to hide the tears that were spilling.

"What if he doesn't wake up?"

"Sophia," Amy warned. "We're not going there. You're exhausted and you've had a trauma yourself. Let me take you home and you can come back later."

"The situation won't seem as bleak if you're rested," Mindy added.

"You'll be able to think more clearly." Donna pulled out a tissue from her bag and wiped Sophia's tears. "Isn't that what you've been telling me?"

"If you need more convincing, Ezra and Matt are in the waiting room."

"Maybe later you'll be in the mood to gossip about Matt and Mindy."

"I don't like gossip," Sophia half laughed and cried through her tears.

"I'll tell you everything anyway, and when Dean wakes up you can tell him the whole story. Deal?" Mindy asked.

"Deal." Sophia's lip quivered.

"Come. Michael will take you home. My mom and I won't leave him for a second."

"Where is Aunt Soula?" Sophia asked.

"Over there." Demi flipped her chin upward toward a hallway. "She's speaking with the doctor."

"But what if he wakes up when I'm gone?"

"He wouldn't dare." Demi handed Sophia the evening bag she carried the night before. The dress she'd worn had been covered in blood and torn during the accident. The hospital staff gave her a set of scrubs to wear after they released her and she had asked to be shown where her husband was.

Demi pointed her finger up and down the length of Sophia.

"Besides, I don't think this is the first thing you want him to see when he opens his eyes."

Who did she think she was fooling? Sophia thought. Demi was as worried as she was. The stiffness of her body and the dark circles under her eyes gave her away.

"I can take a shower here. You can bring me fresh clothing. I won't leave his side." Sophia was adamant, even in her weakened state. "I can't."

"Listen to me," Demi demanded, "I'm not giving you a choice. My brother would skin me alive if I didn't do right by you, and I know he would want you to take care of yourself. Go home long enough to shower and nap. You'll be in a better shape to spend as much time here as you want after that."

Demi led her out the door, but Sophia halted abruptly and pivoted in Dean's direction. Walking back over to the bed, she unconsciously clutched her cross, as though by touching it her prayers would be answered.

"I'll be back, *agapi mou*. Very quickly, I promise." She bit her lips together to hold back the tears. The compulsion to take him in her arms was strong, but she was afraid to touch him. With two limbs broken, and simultaneous surgeries on his head and spleen, Dean was bandaged, cast and hooked up to all kinds of monitors. She kissed him gently just below his blackened eye. "We promised each other forever," she whispered for no one else to hear. "We have a long time to go."

Turning, she fell into the open arms of Aunt Soula—her mother-in-law. "*Panayia, Panayia, Panayia mou.*" Soula repeatedly cried. Hugging Sophia, they stood over Dean. In rapid motion and with her three fingers pressed together, Soula made the sign of the cross over her son—praying and crossing. Praying and crossing. "*Doxa tou Theou*—Glory to God."

In the shower, Sophia attempted to wash the nightmare away. The water rained down on her skin, ridding her of remnants of dried blood, but she could not be soothed. With her body backed up against the tile wall, she slid down until she found herself on the shower floor, her knees pressed up against her chest, the water assaulting her as her weary body gave way to exhaustion.

She didn't think she could sleep. She'd been so restless, her mind filled with visions of the night before and the possibility of its outcome. But between the battering her own body had taken and the sedative the doctor prescribed, she fell into a desperately needed sleep.

Groggily, Sophia reached her arm out, only to feel the flat surface of the mattress under sheets that had not been mussed. Awareness jolted Sophia from slumber. Rubbing her eyes with the heel of her hand, she turned to look at the alarm clock. "What?" Sophia groaned. She jumped out of bed. Night had fallen and she had slept far longer than she'd wanted to.

After she slid into a comfortable pair of jeans and a cozy black cashmere cowl neck sweater, Sophia found her keys in her everyday bag and walked into the garage. They'd taken Dean's car the night before. Hers was the only one parked in the garage, the empty space causing her stomach to lurch. His car was now a pile of mangled metal, some of which had needed to be cut away to save her husband's life.

Sophia stepped off the elevator. "Dad." She wrapped her arms around her father's waist and rested her head on his chest.

"Nothing's changed, but his vitals are strong." Alex kissed her forehead.

"He hasn't woken up at all?"

"Not yet. But don't be alarmed. The doctors are keeping him in a medically induced coma. Come."

Through the glass, Sophia could see her two older children standing at their stepfather's bedside. Sophia looked at her father, her jaw slack and the crease between her brows more pronounced.

"I called them." Alex raised his palm. "Before you object, I thought it was only right they knew what happened to the both of you. I left it up to them to decide if they wanted to come home or not. *Entaxi*?"

She nodded. "Yes, it's okay." Sophia called quietly to her children.

"Mom!" Evvie rushed to her. "Thank God you're okay."

"Mom." Nicky kissed his mother. The concern was written on his face. "Are you in pain?"

"A little. Nothing too bad." She hugged them with her one free arm. "How long have you been here?"

"A couple of hours," Nicky answered. He turned to his grandfather. "Pappou? How about we get some coffee and give Mom and Evvie some time together?"

Alex patted Nicky on the back and they walked out of the room. Sophia kissed Dean lightly on the cheek.

"Do you think it would be okay if I held his hand?" Evvie asked.

"Just be careful of the IV. I think he would like that very much."

Evvie took his hand in hers and pulled the chair closer to the bed. From behind, Sophia noticed Evvie's shoulders rising and falling in a quiver.

Sophia steadied her.

"I've been so awful to him." Evvie sat at the edge of the seat and hung her hands over the rail. "Even when I knew he was looking out for me." She stroked Dean's hand. "I never once thanked him."

"He knows you've been through a lot." Sophia brushed the hair away from her daughter's face. "Tell him now. Talk to him. Maybe he'll hear us and ..." Strangled by fear, Sophia's throat tightened.

"Oh, Mom. I didn't stop to think how you're feeling. I'm so sorry this is happening. The whole thing must have been terrifying."

"You can't imagine." Sophia cupped Evvie's cheeks. "My biggest fear every time you get into the car is that what happened to us could happen to you or your brother. That's why when you're out I can never rest until I know you are home safely." Sophia looked over to Dean. "I worry for you and your brother, but I never stopped to think it could happen to me."

"You're going to need help," Evvie said, gesturing to her mother's broken arm. "I'll stay home to help you with Cia."

"No. No my sweet girl. You just began college. This is your time to spread your wings. I have Aunt Soula and Pappou. And Aunt Demi. I'll manage just fine."

Turning her attention back to Dean, a sob escaped from Evvie. "Please wake up. You have to wake up," she said, desperation coating her words. "I need the chance to say thank you, and to tell you how much you mean to all of us." She wiped her nose with the back of her hand and ignored the stream of tears running down her face. "I can't lose another father. Please, please Dad, come back to us."

Sophia hunched over as if she'd taken a blow to the stomach. Evvie had never called Dean Dad. And now, for the second time in her young life, she might lose a father. Losing Will had toughened her daughter in many ways. Yet the possibility of losing Dean had brought out her softer side. No! Sophia cut off the thought. Evvie will not lose another parent! I will not lose my husband! He has to make it. He just has to.

Chapter 50

Mindy

October 2004

Three days had passed since the accident. Mindy stayed on Long Island to help Sophia in any way she could. Matt made his apologies, explaining he had an assignment booked but he promised to be back in a week. Mindy herself stayed as long as she could, but she had commitments of her own. She ordered a car to take her back to the city and offered to drop the twins off at Kennedy Airport. It was time they got back to school.

"I'm only a phone call away," Mindy told them as the twins exited the black limousine. "And I'll call you if anything important should arise. I'll charter a plane for you if I have to," she joked. But her attempt at levity was wasted. Nicky tried to force a smile, and Evvie kept chipping away at her black nail polish.

Mindy waved goodbye as the car pulled away. "Hello?" She flipped open her magenta razor phone. "I'm looking forward to seeing you too," she sighed. "No, I cannot join you in Indonesia. You asked me that yesterday. Take your photographs and write your story. I'll be waiting for you when you get back."

For Mindy, the evening of the reunion had been an incredible night before it all went to hell. Although she couldn't get her mind off Sophia and Dean, Mindy's thoughts gravitated back to Matt—a boy she knew so many years ago, but a man she was only just beginning to discover. It was as though they had met for the first time, and in a way they had. They were two very different people than they had been thirty years ago. Yet, he was still Matt. Handsome, maybe even more so now that maturity had replaced the baby face and the lanky body. And a true gentleman, but when she'd danced with him at the reunion, the heat between them made her pulse race.

They'd talked for hours late into the night, sharing stories of their travels and career experiences. His kisses made her want more, but she had made that mistake before. Not this time. This time she would let the relationship evolve as it should—one step at a time, enjoying the walk with each foot planted firmly on the ground.

Yet, she felt a comfort with Matt that she'd never shared with any other man. Mindy had been reluctant to trust anyone since Apollo. Her own judgment was something that she no longer trusted. But Matt was different. She knew him. His family. His history. Where he came from. There were no skeletons in his closet. He had been a gentleman as a boy and it was evident that nothing had changed. For Mindy, this was the only kind relationship she could trust—one with a man she was sure of. One who had common friends among her own. One who would never intentionally harm her physically or emotionally.

Six days later, Matt found Mindy at her office engrossed in the sketches she'd drawn for next season's line. Focused on matching material swatches and color schemes to each of her designs, Mindy jerked in her seat and let out a shriek when a tall figure leaning on her office doorframe cleared his throat, breaking her concentration.

"Matt! When did you get here?"

"A little over five minutes ago. I was amused by how oblivious you were to anything beyond those little squares of cloth."

"These little pieces of cloth hold the key to my success. One wrong decision and I'm staring down failure." Mindy leaned back in her seat and stretched out her arms. "Are you planning to stand by the door all night?"

She kicked off her metallic bronze colored pumps.

"Not if that's the beginning of a striptease," Matt replied. In three strides he was by her side and pulling her from the chair. Without warning, he kissed her, and she melted in his arms.

"Enough work for tonight." Spotting her trench coat over the arm of the sofa, he handed it to her and helped her into it.

"What time is it?" she yawned.

"Ten-thirty, and I'll bet my forty thousand dollar zoom lens that you didn't eat dinner?"

"Forty thousand?" she mouthed. "Lucky for you I didn't."

"Let's get some food into you and you can update me on Dean's condition." Matt wrapped his fingers around Mindy's narrow waist. "After that I'll take you home and try to convince you to take the day off tomorrow."

Lowering his head, Matt gently grazed Mindy's lips. With a rapidly beating heart and a stirring within her, Mindy's need for Matt grew. Closing the gap between their bodies, she pressed herself to him, deepening the kiss.

"You might convince me before we get out the door." Her words came out breathy as she stared at him, tracing her finger around the outline of his face.

"God, you're beautiful." Matt twisted a finger around a lock of her fiery hair.

"And you are *so* hot. When did you get so hunkalicious?"

Matt's laugh reverberated from his belly. "What?"

"Something I picked up from my assistant."

"How old is she? Fourteen?"

"*He* is twenty-eight, and pretty hunkalicious as well."

"Competition?"

Mindy shoved his chest and eyed him with a devilish expression. "I'm not his type," she grinned. "Let's go." She slung her bag over her shoulder. "I'm starved."

The District Tap House located near Mindy's office offered a late night dinner menu, a variety of craft beer and a lively crowd at any hour.

"This place is impressive." Matt ran his hand along the dark wood, which made up the bar. He cocked his head and folded his arms. Squinting, his attention focused.

"You're thinking how you can photograph this place, aren't you?" Mindy didn't wait for his response. "I can see it. Something in here inspired you." She recognized herself in him at that moment. It was the way she felt when an idea manifested.

"The bar is designed after an old library or maybe an apothecary." He pointed to rows of wooden drawers situated under shelves of liquor bottles.

After being seated in a booth reminiscent of old fashioned church pews, they ordered.

"That's all?" Matt asked.

"Just the salmon and mixed veggies. I don't really eat meat."

"Vegetarian?"

"No. I'm not very athletic. I find exercising a bore, so I try to eat healthy to make up for it."

The server brought out their food and Matt bit into his loaded burger. Rolling his eyes, he groaned. "That's amazing." Melted fontina cheese oozed from the brioche bun.

"Yours does look good." Mindy examined her forkful of grilled fish before swallowing it.

"Here have a bite."

Mindy bit her lower lip.

"Come on, I know you want it."

"You do, huh?" Mindy treated him to a seductively wicked glare.

Matt brought the burger to her lips and she moaned at the flavors as she savored the bite.

"That's so good." She caught the tip of one of Matt's fingers in her mouth and licked off the drippings.

"Check please," Matt joked.

Rain pelting the windows awoke Mindy and Matt the next morning.

"See, the Gods are telling us to stay in bed." Matt ran his fingers down the length of Mindy's back.

She turned to face him and laced her legs between his. "Last night wasn't enough?"

Matt raised one eyebrow. "Was it enough for you?"

Pretending to think about it, Mindy teased him. "No," she finally spoke.

"Good answer." Gently, he bit her bottom lip. "Because I am going to make love to you until the sun shines through that window."

Make love. How long had it been since anyone made love to her? Sex, sure, she'd had plenty of that, but it often left her feeling empty. This man cherished her body with every touch and each kiss, and she had never felt so fulfilled or at peace with a man.

Matt pulled her onto him and guided himself into her. Leaning forward, she kissed him and moaned into his mouth. Mindy began to rock slowly, moving up and down the length of him, savoring every glorious sensation. He played with her breasts, intensifying her pleasure, and she called out his name while he watched her crest into a sensual bliss. His peak came soon after when he flipped her over and lifted her to her knees, taking her from behind. When he came, she came with him, the intensity of his thrusts pulling her over the edge once more.

Panting, their bodies glistened with sweat, and neither made an attempt to leave the bed. "We should probably have some breakfast," Mindy suggested.

"I have a better idea."

"Oh?"

"I think we should both hit the shower."

"We, as in together?" she jokingly feigned ignorance.

"Is there any other way?"

Chapter 51

Sophia

October 2004

Mommy, why can't I come with you to see Daddy?" Cia pushed the scrambled eggs around on her plate with her fork.

"Eat Cia. The school bus will be here soon." Sophia continued packing her daughter's lunchbox. "I told you. Daddy is sleeping. He won't be able to speak to you right now."

"But maybe Daddy will open his eyes if I talk to him and give him kisses."

Layer by layer, Sophia's heart peeled away. The man she had waited a lifetime for lay broken and critically injured in a hospital. Her twins may once again deal with loss, and her youngest, her naive angel believed her kisses would heal her father.

"Let's get your jacket on. Don't forget, you're going home with your friend, Skylar, today. There's a note in your backpack to give to your teacher."

Cia pouted. "Okay."

"Don't you like Skylar?"

"Uh, huh, but I miss Daddy."

"I know." Sophia put her arms around her daughter's tiny frame. "I'm going to do everything I can to bring him home to us. I'll give him hundreds of kisses from you."

"Why can't I give them to him myself?"

Sophia dropped down on her knees and rubbed her forehead. "We've been over this, *koukla*. The doctors will only allow grown-ups to come to the hospital. I'm sorry, but it's their rule. Just like your teachers have rules in the classroom. Understand?"

"I guess so."

"Now let's go before you're late."

Alex, Soula and Stavros were already at Dean's bedside when Sophia arrived at the hospital. Along with them was their parish priest, dressed in a black robe, his golden threaded *epitrahilion* draped over his neck and extending down the length of his garment.

"Ah! We were waiting for you." Stavros came over to Sophia and kissed both sides of her cheeks.

"I needed to get Cia onto the bus." She turned to the clergyman. "Hello, Father." Bending, she kissed his hand in a sign of respect.

"How are you feeling, Sophia?" Father John asked.

"*Ti boro na po?* What can I say?" Sophia turned to Alex and Soula and hugged both of them.

"Father is here with *efhélaio*," Soula told Sophia.

"Holy Unction," Sophia repeated. "Yes, thank you, Father." Sophia turned to her in-laws. "Has there been any change at all this morning?"

Soula's imperceptible shake of her head and troubled expression told Sophia all she needed to know.

"Let us all pray together," Father John said, motioning for everyone to gather around. "Ágios ó Theós, ágios iskyrós, ágios athánatos, eléison imás – Holy God, Holy Mighty, Holy Immortal, have mercy on us."

An anxious feeling settled in the pit of Sophia's stomach as the priest continued with his petitions and prayers for the sick. She recalled her mother receiving the sacrament from her own hospital bed. *Thy will be done,* she thought. The blessed oil may have healed her soul, but her body had taken more than it could bear, and God, in his mercy, had stopped her mother's suffering. She prayed that beneath his unconscious state, Dean was not in pain.

"O Holy Father, physician of our souls and bodies, heal your servant of God, Konstantinos, of every infirmity by the grace of thy Christ and through the intercession of the Theotokos and ever Virgin Mary." Father John dipped a Q-tip into the holy oil and anointed Dean on his forehead, cheeks, chin and both of his hands. "In the name of the Father, Son and the Holy Spirit. Amen."

After Stavros and Soula walked Father John to the elevator, Sophia pumped some moisturizer into her hand and rubbed it carefully over Dean's face. Over a week had passed since the accident and the bruises were slowly beginning to fade.

Leaning over the bed, Sophia kissed him on the lips before she began to rub the cream onto his uninjured arm. "A little incentive to wake up," she whispered in his ear.

"Okay, Dino. I'm going to bend your knee. I don't want you to be stiff when you wake up." Sophia massaged his toes and his calf, and then drew his knee up and down. "The doctor said you'd heal better in this unconscious state." The pitch of her voice rose. "At least you're missing the worst of the pain, but you can't stay like this for long, okay?" Her voice cracked. "I need you to wake up."

Sophia pulled a chair as close to Dean as she could. The urge to crawl into the bed with him and protect him with her body had to be controlled. There were so many monitors and wires attached to him that it wouldn't have been possible. Besides, the nurses would probably scold her and throw her out. Her love for him was so absolute and pure that she felt it had the power to heal him. Sophia needed to press her body to his—he would feel the love pass from her to him and he would awaken—of that she was certain.

She laced his fingers in hers. Pressed her lips to his knuckles. Kissed each fingertip one by one. "Cia has been asking to see you. Your little girl misses you." She watched him, looking for signs of movement—any sign that he might awaken. Sophia sat silently for a long time. She replayed the nightmare over in her head, spoke to God and drifted in and out of sleep.

"I brought you something to eat." Soula put her arm around Sophia's waist.

"I didn't hear you come in."

"I know." Soula studied her expression. "What were you thinking just then?"

"I was praying. Making a deal with God, I guess."

"*O Theos* doesn't make deals." Soula handed Sophia a carryout box and a fork. "Eat."

"What is it?"

"It's a chicken Greek salad," she laughed. "I got it in the hospital cafeteria."

Sophia opened it. She crinkled her nose at the processed chicken over a bed of lettuce. "What makes this a Greek salad?"

"Anytime they put feta cheese on something they call it Greek."

"I'm not really hungry."

"If you don't take care of yourself, you can't take care of my son."

"I'll try." Sophia took a few bites and set the container aside. Silently, Soula and Sophia sat wearily, too drained for conversation.

Both of their heads shot up when they thought they heard a moan. Sophia jumped to her feet. "Dino? Do you hear me?"

A small vibration came from his throat. "Dino!" Sophia took his hand. Dean's eyelids remained shut, but she could see there was movement behind them. She turned to Soula. "Tell the nurse. Call the doctor. Get someone in here."

Soula ran out to the nurse's station.

"Dino, can you hear me? Squeeze my fingers if you can hear me." It was weak, barely noticeable, but he had done it. Dean had squeezed her fingers! Sophia used her sleeve to wipe away the salty drops of happiness that streamed down her cheeks.

"He responded to me," Sophia told the nurse as she walked into the room.

"Let me check him."

Sophia stepped back to give the nurse enough space to do her job.

"Dean," she said in a loud voice. She took his hand. "Squeeze my hand if you can hear me. I'm Rhonda. I've been taking care of you." Rhonda turned to Sophia and shook her head.

"He did! He moaned and then he squeezed my hand."

"It's true. I saw it for myself," Soula confirmed when she returned.

Sophia leaned over the bedrail. "Dino. It's me, Sophia. Show Rhonda that you know I'm here."

"I'll check back on him in a bit." Rhonda turned to walk away.

"No! Wait. Please." Sophia fished into the bottom of her bag for her iPod. The nurse crossed her arms, staring at her impatiently.

Sophia scrolled until she found what she was looking for and turned the music on. Placing the device by Dean's pillow, she hoped their song would stir him. Rubbing his cheek, she sang along softly to 'And I Love Her,' the words holding great meaning for them and so many memories.

Sophia barely noticed the presence of anyone in the room, her concentration fully on her husband—her love. But from the corner of her eye, two figures stood unmoving, watching her—Soula and Rhonda.

"I saw that!" Rhonda hastened to Dean's bed. "He moved his hand. Stand back a minute," she ordered Sophia. "I'm going to check his pupils."

Dean croaked out a sound.

"He's trying to say something. It sounds like he's trying to form a word." Rhonda pulled up his lids and looked into them with a penlight.

Dean groaned out what sounded like an attempt at words again.

Sophia put her hand to her throat. She looked up at Rhonda. "He's saying, 'love you.' I love you too, Dino *mou*." She turned to look at Soula, who had her hands clasped together in prayer.

"What happened?" Sophia asked when Dean seemed to fall back into his previous state.

Rhonda was checking his monitors and IV fluids. "That took a lot of his energy. He's resting comfortably now, but that was a good sign that he's regaining consciousness." Rhonda patted her shoulder. "It's going to take some time, but that was progress." She began to walk from the room then halted. "Mrs. Papadakis, can I say something?"

"Please, call me Sophia."

Rhonda nodded and adjusted the stethoscope around her neck. "In all my years, I've never seen anything so beautiful and loving. You were so sure you could reach him. I get the sense that as long as it took you would never give up on him."

Sophia cupped Rhonda's hands. "No, I never would. For better or worse. In sickness and in health. He's my lifeline. We didn't say those words during our wedding ceremony, but it's understood. We have a ritual where we walk around a table and take our first steps as husband and wife. That's the beginning of the promise of a journey for our lifetime, and a promise I will never break."

"Remarkable."

"Rhonda, before you go, can I ask you a few things? If Dean tried to form words, was he conscious? Is his brain functioning normally since he seemed to know that I was next to him and he was able to force out a word? He didn't open his eyes. What does that mean?"

"These are questions for the doctor. He will be here soon to evaluate his condition. It will take him a while to open his eyes even if he makes sounds and moves occasionally. Don't be concerned. The doctor can give you a clearer picture of his status."

"Thank you."

Dr. Campanelli arrived an hour later. After examining Dean, he spoke to Sophia and his parents.

"Dean's responses were what I hoped for at this point. I've been cutting back slowly on the meds that were keeping him in the coma to see if he regained consciousness on his own. His extremities responded when I pricked him and his vitals and blood work look good so far. He's moving in the right direction, but he's still in a serious condition so I need to monitor him closely."

"Moving in the right direction, meaning he's healing and will be coherent soon?" Stavros asked.

"It will take some time. I can't give you any definite answers as to when he will be fully coherent, but even when he is, he will need physical and occupational therapy."

"Go home now and take a break," Soula suggested. "And tell my Cia yiayiá will come over tonight to read her a story and tuck her into bed."

"What if he wakes up? I want to be here."

"That's not likely. Although I've cut back on the anesthetic, I still have him sedated to reduce pain."

"I don't understand the difference."

"Before, he was completely unconscious. Now that I've changed and reduced his meds, he's semi-unconscious, and more likely to move or make sounds. Little by little he will become more alert."

"But not tonight?"

"Doubtful. You should go home and come back tomorrow. There's little chance he'll awaken again. Even if he does, he won't remember."

Sophia made her way back to Dean's bedside. "Good night, *agapi mou*. When I come back tomorrow I want you to whisper those beautiful words to me again. Tell me you love me."

Chapter 52

Sophia

October 2004

O ctober was coming to a close and for the first time since Cia's first Halloween, Sophia would not be with her as she ran from home to home, stuffing her face with the candy she collected.

"It's okay, Mommy," the child assured Sophia. "Aunt Demi will take me, so you can stay with Daddy and make him better." Cia was such a bright little spirit. Even at Sophia's bleakest moments, her daughter brought a smile to her face, pulling Sophia up from the depth of her sorrow.

"Make sure Aunt Demi takes lots of pictures." Sophia kissed the tip of Cia's nose.

She giggled. "I will. Lots and lots of them."

Sophia waved to the staff at the nurses' station as she passed them on her way to Dean's room. He'd made some progress—a little more movement and some words that were somewhat understandable.

'Hurts' was the word he said more than any other, and when he did the nurses increased his pain medication.

Sophia was grateful to see that no one else from the family had yet arrived at the hospital. While she loved and appreciated each and every one of them, and she knew she couldn't have gotten through this difficult time without their support, she appreciated this rare time alone with her husband.

"Hey, *agapi mou, kardia mou, psychi mou*—my love, my heart, my soul. I need you to open your eyes. You're making progress. Any day, any minute, I know you will."

As she did each day, Sophia began to massage and exercise his arms and legs, even carefully manipulating the cast limbs.

"The night of the reunion, before the accident, do you remember what we did?" She kissed the inside of his palm. "In the shower? I want you to do that to me again. Better yet, I'm going to repeat what I did for you as many times as you want. Just open your eyes."

"Prom-ise," Dean grumbled out, turning his head toward Sophia, his eyes barely open.

Sophia gasped and threw her hands to her mouth. "Dino!" Her breathing became very rapid and it made her dizzy. She grabbed onto the side rail of the bed to steady herself.

"Hurts. What happened?"

Sophia lifted the call button but Dean touched her hand.

"No."

"Do you remember the accident?"

"I-remember-leaving-the-party." Dean breathed out one word at a time. His eyes were only partially open and Sophia thought the light streaming in from the window might be too much for him. Walking across the room, she drew the blinds, darkening the room, leaving only a dim light on.

"Remember getting into the car. You drove."

"That's right, Dino *mou*. I wish I had let you drive. A car hit us on your side."

Dean shook his head, causing him to squeeze his eyes shut and wince in pain. "Then it would've been you in this bed."

"Let me get the nurse. She'll want to call the doctor. You've been out for more than a week."

"Wait—tell you something."

"You're ready to take me up on my offer?" Sophia joked.

"Rain check, but I'll hold you to it." Dean's words were slurred and stretched out.

"I'll be counting the days."

"Your mother."

"Yes?"

"She came to me. I think she saved me."

Sophia felt as though the wind had been knocked from her.

"It was a dream maybe. Very strange. I was walking. Too bright but I saw her in the distance. I called to her." He was having difficulty enunciating the words and Sophia could see he was struggling. "Walked to her. She shook her head. Put up her hand. She said, 'No, you're not ready yet. Sophia needs you.' I wanted to go to her. Hug her. She said I couldn't. 'Walk the other way,' she told me. Her command paralyzed me. 'A kiss from yiayiá. Give my grandchildren a kiss.' That was the last thing she said before she disappeared into the light." He huffed out a tired breath.

"I felt her too. The night of the accident. I was alone in an emergency room bed and someone touched my leg and stroked my hair. I smelled her perfume."

"She's protecting us, even now."

As the weeks went by, Dean improved. He'd been moved out of Neuro-ICU and not long after that transferred to a rehabilitation facility in Port Jefferson. Sophia attempted to regain some normalcy and routine in her life. Each day, after she got Cia off to school, she drove to the rehab center, spent the day with Dean and returned home in time to get her daughter off the bus.

Sophia taught her few ballet classes, worked with her private students and spent time with Cia, snuggling in bed and reading the *American Girl* books her daughter enjoyed so much.

Was Sophia happy Dean was improving day by day? Of course. Was life easy? No. Sophia was trying to juggle much too much, while attempting to keep everyone happy. To make matters worse, Dean was prone to mood swings, and Sophia never knew what she was walking into each morning. She might find him sulking in bed, or sitting up in a chair and beaming the minute she came through the door.

Sophia began to realize a pattern—one that was determined by Dean's therapy sessions. If his PT went well, Dean spoke of plans for the future. "We'll take the kids on a vacation when I'm finished with rehab. Hell! We'll get the whole gang to come."

Oh, but if he struggled with an exercise he couldn't manage, Sophia saw a different Dean altogether. "You may as well leave me here to rot. Why would you want a cripple for a husband?"

Enough was enough. Dean was not a man to let the grass grow under his feet. He was frustrated. Understandable. She would be too, if she were in his shoes. But he was bored, and with nothing to do but therapy and watching TV, Dean had become downright nasty at times.

Sophia stood at the door's edge outside Dean's room. *Grumpy Dean*, she thought.

Sitting in a reclining chair, he was tapping his fingers on the cast of the other arm. Staring out the window, she could only see Dean in profile, but his mouth was pressed in a hard line.

Sophia still had a cast on her own arm, so she needed to be creative when carrying anything heavy. Walking into the room, she wheeled in a carryon suitcase behind her.

The rolling sound from the suitcase wheels got his attention and he turned to find her standing before him. "You moving in?" he asked dryly.

"By the sound of it, I wouldn't be welcomed if I planned to." She threw his indignant tone back at him.

Dean drew his eyes up to meet hers, an irascible expression hardening the face Sophia loved. "I'm not in the mood," Dean scowled.

Sophia kicked the suitcase to the floor; the noise it made when it hit the hard tile sounded as angry as she felt. "I'm not either," she barked back. Bending to her knees, Sophia unzipped the luggage with her good hand while holding it in place with the weight of her cast. Struggling, she lifted the contents out and slammed them down onto the tray table next to the chair where Dean was seated.

"What's all this?"

"Something to keep you from feeling sorry for yourself. You can't go into the office so I'm bringing the office to you."

"What am I supposed to do with all of this without my computer? It will take me weeks to catch up."

Sophia retrieved a laptop from the suitcase. "Here you go. No time like the present," she said with sarcasm. "The Carriage House finances won't take care of themselves and it seems that you have plenty of time on your hands."

"Where are you going?" Dean asked when Sophia turned to walk away.

"Home."

"You're not staying a while?"

"I'll tell you what. When my husband decides to make an appearance, call me and I'll come running. *Yasou!*"

"Oh, my God! What I wouldn't give to have witnessed that." Demi was in the floral refrigeration vault unpacking the day's delivery while she listened to Sophia's story. "And you left? Just like that?" Demi snapped her fingers. "No kiss goodbye?"

"No kiss hello, either. He was in a nasty mood."

"You always did know how to put my brother in his place. Even when we were little kids. Do you remember when Dean ran for seventh grade class president? He wanted to win so badly but Vinny won. Dean got so mad at him for running against him."

"I remember. Dino was mad because Vinny didn't even care about the position. Someone nominated him and he thought he may as well play it out." Sophia opened a box of tea roses and placed them carefully in a bucket of water.

"But my stupid brother wouldn't speak to Vinny or even congratulate him." Demi laughed at the memory. "We were still in elementary school. None of it had anything to do with us but you marched over to my house like you were ready to rip him a new asshole."

"But I didn't."

"No, by the time you got into the house you were totally calm and sweet as pie. I really don't know how you do that. Anyway, whatever you said worked because he went right over to Vinny and Donna's and apologized."

"I remember exactly what I said. I told him Vinny was his best friend and that we should be happy for our friends even if it means we're disappointed. I said that he needed to decide what was more important, a friendship that could last a lifetime if he wanted it to, or a title that wouldn't be important by next year."

"Good advice from a ten year old, but Dean could be so bull headed."

"I know. He didn't like to be pushed or told what to do. That's why I told him we all make our own choices and he needed to figure out the right one for himself."

"You didn't seem so gentle with him this time."

"True. This time required a different approach." Sophia shivered. "How do you stay in here so long? I'm freezing."

"Come on. Let's take a break." Demi led the way to her office.

"Demi, what if this doesn't work? I understand how difficult this is and how hard it must be for him to fight to get his strength back, but

I'm terrified the strong will he's always had is gone for good."

"Give him time. It really hasn't been that long if you consider all he's been through." Demi handed Sophia her navy wool jacket. "We need a change of scenery. At least for an hour. Where would you like to have lunch?"

The next day, when Sophia went to the rehab center, she wasn't sure what she would find. She hadn't called Dean at all after she dumped his work on him the day before, but when she woke up in the morning she noticed a missed call from him on her cell phone.

"I think this is the first time I've seen you stand on your own," Sophia said as she entered Dean's room.

Turning, Dean supported himself with the chair in front of him, the look in his eyes and the smile that reached his dimples read of pure love. Sophia's heart flipped in her chest. She had not seen her Dino for some time.

She stood a distance away from him. "You must have had a good session this morning."

His smile widened. "I did. But the ass kicking you gave me might have been the best therapy I've received." He opened his arms to her and she ran to him. He kissed her deeply. He kissed her like her Dino—from the depth of his soul. This was not the weak peck she had to settle for these last few weeks.

"You've been working, I see," Sophia noted as she observed the neatly stacked piles of papers.

"I have. It took me half the day to take a look at them. I was so pissed off at you." He used his good hand to take her by the waist and pull her close to him. "But you were right. Once I dug in, it felt good. I had a purpose again."

"Sit down." Sophia helped Dean into the recliner and she pulled another chair next to him. "You always had purpose; you needed to recognize it for yourself. You're my husband and I adore you. You have purpose in my life. I know this isn't easy for you, but I'm here. I'll always be here for you."

"When I have a good therapy session, I think, 'great! I'll be back to normal in no time.' Then I have a session where I struggle and I can't do what I used to, and I worry." Dean took Sophia's hand and played with the wedding ring on her finger.

"Worry about what? Once the casts come off I think you'll make quicker progress."

"But what if I don't? What if I never get back to the way I was? Is it fair for you to be saddled with a husband whose less than what you married? Weak! An invalid! That wasn't the life we expected."

"No one on this earth is guaranteed a thing. We are given the life we are given and we make the best of it. And I think we have a pretty damn good life. If you're left with a limp, or you don't regain full strength back, it doesn't change a thing. It doesn't change who you are or how much I love you."

"I love you so much. I only want what's best for you."

Sophia jumped from her seat. "God! Sometimes you are so exasperating. What if it was the other way around? Would you not want me anymore?"

"Of course not!" Dean sounded astounded at the thought.

"Then why on earth would you think I would want to bail on you? You could have died. Do you have any idea how close you came? The fact that you are here is a great gift." She began to pace, taking tiny quick steps. "Do you think my dad loved my mom less when she lost her hair and was ashen-faced from the chemo?" She didn't give Dean a chance to answer. "No. He said she was beautiful because she was on this earth with him. That's all he cared about."

"I think you made your point." Dean looked amused.

"Don't laugh at me. This is serious. If we are going to have a future, you have to fight for it and I'll be right beside you."

"Oh, I'm going to fight alright. I want to get out of this place and go home. Then I want to see some of that fire aimed at me in a different way."

"Well that's one incentive I know you'll work toward."

The cast on Sophia's arm was removed a few days before Dean's casts were removed. She felt as though she'd been freed from restraints and could only imagine how Dean must feel. She could understand how frustrating his confinement was between his injuries and the inability to move freely. She only had to manage with one cast arm. Dean had so many more obstacles.

From the minute his casts were removed, Dean's resolve to heal and regain his strength grew to a near obsession. It was as though he was Prometheus being freed from the chains Hercules had bound him to, only to transform into Hercules himself.

One week before Thanksgiving, Dean was released from the rehab center with the understanding that he must continue physical therapy on an outpatient basis three times a week. Sophia's Dino was coming home and she had so much to be thankful for this season.

Sophia helped Dean from the car. As they approached the doorway, Dean smiled and waved to his daughter, whose hands were pressed against the storm door. Cia began to clap when her Daddy came into view. She'd only seen him a few times in the past month when Sophia allowed her to go to the rehab for a short visit.

Supported by his cane, Dean bent down to greet his little girl. "How is my best girl?"

"I'm good, Daddy, 'cause you're home. I'm so excited. Are you all better?"

"Almost baby girl. Almost."

"Come inside. Everyone is waiting." Cia tugged at her father's free hand.

Dean turned to look at Sophia. "Everyone?" he mouthed.

Sophia lifted her shoulders and shrugged. "I was going to stop them?"

"I had other plans, if you know what I mean."

"They won't be here all night."

They walked into the kitchen and were greeted by the family that had visited, worried about, and prayed for him. Dean tried to look pleased to see them all, but Sophia could see that the crowd daunted him. He kept swallowing nervously and gazing at the floor. They had all come to see him at the hospital, but only a few at a time. The large gatherings of family and friends that he'd been accustomed to his entire life were no longer comfortable for Dean. At least not for the time being. What he needed was the chance to adjust slowly but, with the lively crowd around them, that wasn't possible. Sophia knew they all had the best of intentions and she was grateful to each and every one of them for their love and support.

Demi and her mother-in-law were arguing over how much rice to put into the *youvarlakia* before forming the meatball mixture, Soula was hushing the children quiet and lowering the TV, and the men in the family were having a healthy discussion debating the war on Iraq.

"They all love you, remember that," Sophia told Dean as the entire entourage stopped what they were doing and descended upon him.

Michael handed Dean a beer. "You're going to need this." His wicked glance amused Sophia. "And a few more to back it up," Michael added.

"Try this." Michael's mother shoved a wooden spoon in Dean's mouth.

"*Téleios*—perfect," Dean complimented.

Sophia raised her eyebrows and smirked. "Let's have Dino sit down for a while."

Stavros and Alex rose to help him. Dean took a pull from his beer. "I'm okay. Everyone relax. I can get to the couch on my own."

"We'll help him, Pappou," Evvie said.

"Evvie, Nicky! I didn't know you were here." Dean's smile lit up his face. He extended his arm and pulled them into a hug. "Thanksgiving isn't until next week. I wasn't expecting you."

"We wanted to be here for your homecoming," Evvie said.

"We'll go back to school Sunday afternoon," Nicky added.

"Can I get you anything?" Evvie asked.

"Nothing. I have everything I need. Come sit by me and catch me up on everything you've been doing at school."

Sophia looked on as Dean sat on the couch between her two oldest children. It warmed her heart to see the easy, light bantering between the three of them—something she wouldn't have dreamed possible a few months ago.

"Finally." Dean shut the front door after the last person had gone. "Come on, it's time for bed."

"It's nine o'clock," Sophia protested. "I can't possibly sleep this early."

"Oh, you won't be sleeping for hours." Dean reached his hand behind the nape of Sophia's neck and pulled her in for a slow, deep kiss. She felt her heart plummet into her stomach.

"Daddy," Cia called out as she ran into the foyer, "can I sleep in your bed tonight?"

"How about we let Daddy get a good night's sleep his first night home?" Sophia bent down to her daughter's level. "Besides, didn't Evvie say she wanted you to sleep in her bed tonight and cuddle up to a good movie?"

"Oh, yeah!"

"That sounds like fun, angel, and tomorrow we can spend the whole day together and do whatever you want." Dean rubbed his fingers across her cheek.

"Promise?"

"Cross my heart," he vowed. Turning to Sophia, he elbowed her. "A good night's sleep?" he smirked.

"Let's get you in your pj's, little one." Sophia steered Cia toward the stairs. "Go on up and I'll be there in a minute."

Dean leaned his body into hers and she could feel his arousal building.

"You're relentless."

"Is that a complaint?"

"No. I've missed you."

"The way I see it, all my other muscles got plenty of physical therapy, and so I wouldn't want to neglect one."

"I see. So this is purely for medical reasons," Sophia teased.

"Yes, and we may have to work overtime to get me back into shape."

"Well then, I'll have to rate your progress as we go, and I won't allow you to leave the bedroom until you're back up to a ten. That may take several attempts." Slowly, they inched their way up the stairs and into the bedroom.

"Tough terms. You drive a hard bargain." Dean was already peeling clothing from Sophia's body and she was ready for her Dino. He had a few scars that weren't there before, but he was alive and well and she felt blessed. Very, very blessed.

~Youvarlakia in Avgolemono Sauce~

2 pounds of ground beef
½ cup rice (not cooked)
½ cup fresh parsley
1 large onion, grated
1 egg
2 tablespoons dill
2 teaspoons salt
1 generous pinch of nutmeg
1 to 2 pinches of ground black pepper

Mix all the above ingredients together to form meatballs. A good size is a little larger than a golf ball. Place the meatballs in the refrigerator to set for 20-30 minutes. This way the meatballs will not fall apart when you drop them in the boiling liquid.

In a large pot add:
1 bay leaf
2 cups chicken broth (optional)
2 cups water
* If you don't use the chicken broth then double the water to 4 cups.

Bring the liquids to a boil. Turn down the heat to a high simmer and carefully drop in the meatballs. Cover and cook for 25-30 minutes. My mother would lay a dish directly on the meatballs to hold them down in order to keep them from falling apart.

~Avgolemono Sauce~

I've seen many ways to make this sauce. Basically it consists of lemon juice and eggs, which are beaten together. Some cooks add a tablespoon of flour to thicken it. Others separate the egg whites and whip them until they are frothy, and then add it to the egg yolk/lemon mixture. I've tried both of these methods but I still prefer the method my mother used.

3 eggs
Juice of one large lemon (2 if you like the sauce extra lemony)
Fresh lemon zest (optional)

Put the eggs and lemon juice (and zest if using) in a blender and run on medium speed until frothy. Take about one cup of the hot liquid from the meatballs and slowly add it to the egg-lemon mixture while the blender is still running. This will temper the eggs so they do not scramble.

Remove the meatballs from the heat and pour the Avgolemono over the meatballs. Cover the pot and let it sit for 5 minutes before serving,

Chapter 53

Mindy

December 2004

Cirella's Restaurant at Saks Fifth Ave. in the Walt Whitman Mall was filled with chatty holiday shoppers stopping for a bite to eat before accumulating more packages to lug around.

"I think I'll just have the Saks Salad," Mindy decided.

"I'll have the onion soup, thank you." Sophia handed her menu to the server.

"Mmm. That sounds good. Maybe I should change my mind. No I'll stick with the salad. I don't need all that cheese," Mindy said.

"I'll have the Deluxe Sushi Combo," Demi said, addressing the server.

"Ooh, sushi." Mindy bit her lip.

The waitress stared at her, pen in hand waiting.

Mindy waved her off. "I'm good."

"I knocked off quite a few things from my list today." Demi scratched off items on a small note pad. "How far along are the two of you?"

"I'm almost done. But if I finish too soon, I'll just end up buying additional presents at the last minute," Sophia admitted.

"I'm stuck on what to get Matt. It's still a pretty new relationship, but we are seeing each other exclusively. I'm not sure how personal to go with the gift. Or how extravagant."

"I wouldn't stress over it, Mindy. I'm sure he'll be happy with whatever you choose." Sophia placed her hand over Mindy's.

"I don't want to screw this one up."

Demi leaned in. "You really care about him. Are you in love with Matt?"

Mindy placed her hands over her face. "I am." She was almost afraid to say it aloud. "I really am. I feel like a schoolgirl, but this feels different from the other times."

"He lights up around you. It's so nice to see." Sophia took a sip of her water. "He's a good one. It's okay to trust what you're feeling. This is your time."

"Time!" Demi exclaimed. "Get him a nice watch and tell him it's so he can mark the time until you see each other when he's away."

"I like that, Demi."

The petite, blonde server came back carrying all three platters. Mindy dug into her salad but was eyeing Sophia's onion soup.

"Yes, you can have a taste," Sophia said, feigning annoyance.

"Don't look my way." Demi wrapped her hands around her sushi platter, protecting it from Mindy's roaming fork.

"But you have six pieces. Just let me try half a piece," Mindy begged.

Demi cut one of her sushi rolls in half and placed it on Mindy's salad plate. "I'm surprised we got you out here today. What gives?"

"I'm lacking inspiration at the moment. Maybe my head is in the clouds." Mindy picked off another strand of cheese from Sophia's soup. "I just haven't been able to sketch anything I'm happy with for the summer line."

"Are you going to meet your deadline? Shouldn't you have been past that stage by now?" Sophia asked.

Mindy nodded. Frowning, she added, "I don't know where this is coming from. I'm happier than I've ever been and that usually sparks inspiration."

Mindy looked up at Sophia who seemed to be in deep thought. With her elbows resting on the table, Sophia bit on a thumbnail. In unison, Demi and Mindy put down their fork and leaned into the table, waiting to hear what Sophia was thinking.

"What if you already had drawings to use for your designs?" Sophia asked Mindy.

"But I told you that I don't."

"But you might."

"Sophia! Get to the point," Demi demanded.

"When we were young, you used to sketch all the time. Every year you designed a wedding gown marking the year. Remember?"

"Yeah." Mindy huffed out a laugh. "The joke was on me. I was the only one of us to never get into a wedding dress."

"Do you still have them?"

"What? The sketches? Sure. My mother has them stored at her place. She never threw out any of my drawings."

"How old were you when you started them?"

Mindy shook her head. "I don't know. I think seventh grade."

"That was 1968. You have wedding dress designs inspired by the sixties and seventies. When did you stop drawing them?" Sophia asked.

"I did them for years. Pretty much through the eighties. Until Tyler and I broke up."

"You have over twenty designs, Mindy." Sophia sounded enthused.

"That's brilliant," Demi chimed in. "A line of nostalgic wedding dresses."

"Wait one minute." Mindy brushed her hair off her shoulders. "First of all, I am not a wedding dress designer. And second, I was a kid when I drew those sketches. They're probably ghastly."

"No, they're not. I remember them. The one you drew in 1976 was the one I fell in love with and wanted for myself," Demi told Mindy.

Mindy chuckled. "We'll see how you feel about it when we dig up the drawings. You might wonder what you were thinking."

"I'm not saying that you might not need to tweak them," Sophia said. "But they could be your inspiration. Think about it, those were drawn during the actual time period, not from the memory of that time. You can improve them if you need to, but I'd bet the soul of the designs will come through."

"Well, you've convinced me to at least take a look."

"Great!" Demi popped out of her seat. "Let's pay Mama Bloom a visit."

In Edna Bloom's living room, Demi, Mindy and Sophia were sprawled on the carpet surrounded by sketchpads and drawings.

Edna watched with delight. "You girls look just as you did when you were in high school."

They smiled up at her and continued to pour over the designs. "I'm glad you wrote the date on each one," Sophia commented. "This one looks like it came from the roaring twenties, but it's dated 1974."

"I drew that one after we saw *The Great Gatsby.*"

"And this one?" Demi made a disapproving face.

"Ah, the Madonna year, but I went with *Dynasty* glamour for the following year. Here, take a look." She handed the drawing to Demi.

"You have to admit, these are good," Sophia said.

"You were right. I think I might have something to work with. Maybe it's time for something different. The unexpected might shake things up a bit."

"When the dresses are ready, how about using the Carriage House and the vineyard for the photo shoot?"

"Demi, I think that's a great idea. I can't think of a prettier location."

Mindy gathered up the drawings and returned them to their box before rising to her feet. She held the long forgotten treasures to her chest, excited at the prospect of resurrecting her childhood visions into a reality.

"Thanks, Mom." She kissed her mother's cheek. "I'm heading back to the city right now. I'm anxious to get started."

"Let me walk you girls to the door," Edna said.

"Bye Mrs. Bloom." Sophia hugged her tightly.

"Bye. See you soon." Demi pecked her on the cheek.

"Too bad we couldn't get Donna to come out today. This would have been good for her," Demi said.

"The holidays will be tough for her this year. All we can do is be there when she needs us and not push her before she's ready," Sophia advised.

"Come. Let's get you to the train," Demi said to Mindy. "And I'll expect a call from you the minute you have something to show us."

Chapter 54

Mindy

February 2005

"Are you ready for our date tonight?"

Mindy screamed when she heard Matt's voice and saw him standing in her office doorway. "You're home!"

"I promised I would be for Valentine's Day. I'm a man of my word."

Mindy draped her arms around Matt's neck. "Yes, you are." She closed the space between them and brought her lips to his, savoring the kiss she longed for since he left the month before. The travel show Matt hosted filmed on several locations for its upcoming season and he called Mindy at every stop.

"We have a reservation at the most romantic table Daniel has to offer."

"I know a more romantic spot. I have a beautiful view from my window."

"Let me take you out. We'll have all night after that."

"Okay." Mindy brushed the hair off Matt's forehead.

"So, are you going to show me what you've been working on so secretly for months?"

"Yes. I think I'm ready to let you take a peek." Mindy pulled him into another room. Detailed sketches were resting on easels. Beside each one was a dress form with an uncompleted bridal gown pinned to it.

"Bridal collection?" Matt looked surprised. "I didn't know you had one."

"I didn't. Sophia gave me the idea. When I was younger, I used to sketch one bridal gown each year. I'd completely forgotten about them until Sophia asked if I still had them and suggested that I use them as inspiration for a new line this year."

Matt walked by each one, examining the details of the styles and noting the dates on the sketches. "You did these when we were kids? They're remarkable."

"Well, yes, but I made some adjustments. The essence of each design is there, but my skills and style are more sophisticated now."

"If you were to wear one, which one would you chose for yourself?"

"Myself? That's an odd question."

"Is it? Why?"

Mindy stammered a bit. "I don't know. I guess I haven't thought about that in years. I designed all of these with myself in mind. Each year my tastes changed depending on my age and the current trends. But now, I'm creating them for someone else to wear."

"Which would be your taste now?"

"Well, for the first time in years, I designed a new dress to mark this year, inspired by my friends who convinced me to do this. I will present it in the finale at my show. I guess I would have to say that one. That would be my taste now, just as each of those dresses was my taste at the time."

"You should be the one to model it then."

"Me? Seriously, that's absurd."

"I'll bet no one would wear it as well as you would." He kissed the tip of her nose. "Let's go. The sooner we get to Daniel, the sooner I can get you alone in front of your window."

"Exhibitionist." Mindy slapped him playfully on his arm.

Matt threw his head back in laughter. "Ha! I'm not the one who suggested it."

"When did you say you had to leave again?" Mindy pressed her bare body into Matt's.

"In two days, and I plan to spend it in this bed with you." Matt flipped Mindy onto her back, trapping her beneath his muscular frame. "Reconsider. Come with me. Three more remotes and I'll be done shooting for the season.

"I wish I could, but this is the most hectic time for me. I've been working through the weekends to meet my deadlines." Mindy ran her fingers through Matt's hair. "Besides, hiking in the Amazon is not my cup of tea. Next time you go to … let's say … Monaco, I'll be happy to trail along."

"Hmm. I'm going to get you outdoors and active one way or another. I'm making it my mission."

"I like the outdoors. The pool. The beach. Outdoor cafés."

Matt rolled his eyes.

"Make fun of me all you want, but I don't have to swing from vines in the rainforest to get my heart rate up." Mindy grabbed onto Matt's firm ass, pulling his body into hers. "I'm going to prove that I've got more stamina than you can handle."

"You're on. It's a bet." Matt pressed his lips to Mindy's and as he deepened the kiss a shock of pleasure ran through her. He continued to make love to her as though it were the last time he'd see her.

Mindy savored every touch and each sensation, while in the back of her head she wondered how she'd survive the next two months with merely the memory of his body entangled with hers.

Seated in her office chair, Mindy stretched out her arms and legs. It was March and she'd been working diligently, attending to last minute details and tying up loose ends for the photo shoot she had scheduled. Slowly, she took a deep breath and blew it out in an effort to relax.

Her gaze was drawn to the framed picture of Matt she'd placed on her desk before he left on location. Extending her hand, she brushed her fingers over the glass that protected his image and her lips curved upward at the sight of his face smiling back at her. She missed him, but it was just as well that he was off on his own project. With Matt traveling, she was able to dig her heels into her work and focus exclusively on her collection.

Mindy was both excited and nervous to introduce her wedding gown line. In many ways, these dresses told the story of her career from its earliest inception.

The models were hired, the creative team in place, and the gowns ready to be transported for the photo shoot the next day. For Mindy, shooting the wedding gowns at the vineyard made the story complete. Her friends had encouraged the idea of her bridal line and showcasing them at their breathtaking vineyard was the culmination—bringing together all their pasts and presents.

"I cannot believe your team made this cold winter day look like springtime in full bloom," Demi exclaimed.

"That's their job," Mindy said. "We are always shooting in opposite seasons."

"Those poor models," Sophia commented. "They must be freezing."

"They've been through worse. Bikinis in snowstorms." Mindy shivered.

"Excuse me," Wesley, the creative director interrupted. "We're short one model." He threw his hands up, shaking them in a panic.

"No, we're not. I hired one for each gown. That way for the last few shots we can get all the gowns in one photo along with the finale dress."

"Elsa is in the bathroom throwing her guts up and she's burning up." The pitch of his voice rose.

Mindy put her hands together as though in prayer. Sighing, she said, "Call for the car and get her out of here immediately. We'll just have to pull one of the dresses from the finale shot."

"Hey." Demi squinted her eyes. "Remember when you told me that Matt suggested you wear the finale gown?"

"Yes, when I told you I had a funny story to tell you?"

"Why is that funny?" Sophia asked. "I think it's a great idea."

Mindy opened her mouth to protest, but Sophia shot her hand up. "Hear me out. I've seen it done before. The lady of the designs—that's you, of course—is surrounded by models wearing her dresses, while you wear the pièce de résistance."

"All that white with your flowing red hair." Demi's eyes widened. "You'd be stunning."

"No!" Mindy dismissed the idea.

Wesley put his hands on his hips. "I say, yes. I wish I'd thought of it myself. Go! We'll take a few shots out here, but I want the group shot to be in the ballroom foyer."

"Hello?" Sophia answered her flip phone. "Yiayiá, is that you? *Ti symvaínei?* What's going on?"

Mindy and Demi watched Sophia with concern.

"Go get dressed, Mindy. It's nothing for you to worry about. Apparently my aunt is sick." Sophia pressed her lips together. "Go. I can't wait to see you in that dress."

Chapter 55

Sophia

March 2005

The call from Sophia's yiayiá placed her in the center of a situation she wanted nothing to do with. She had no relationship whatsoever with Irini Fotopoulos Mateus, and the few encounters Sophia had with her over the course of her lifetime always turned out to be very unpleasant. The woman wreaked havoc on anyone who crossed her path. Ana, knowing only too well what her sister was capable of, had made Sophia promise to stay away from Irini at all costs.

But Sophia's yiayiá sounded so distraught when she asked for Sophia's help. She spent the day mulling over what to do. Did she heed her mother's words and stay away? Or did she ease her grandmother's mind and tend to her aunt?

Sophia contemplated as she stared out the window of the Range Rover, chewing on the inside of her cheek. Cia had fallen asleep in her car seat and Dean, who after four months of physical therapy and immeasurable determination had regained most of his strength back, was at the wheel.

Earlier that day, they had an argument over what to do about Irini. "No." Dean was adamant. "I don't care what's wrong with her. Hasn't she put you through enough? You don't owe her a thing."

Once again, Sophia was being asked to show kindness to a person who betrayed her mother. Deciding right from wrong was not always easy. With Jimmy, she'd made the right choice, but her dealings with Irini had always turned out disastrous. So the question was, what was the right thing in this case? She needed advice from those who knew her aunt better than she did and asked Dean to come with her so they could all discuss it together, but in his mind the decision was clear.

"Are you going to ignore me the whole way there?" Sophia crossed her arms.

"I don't know what to tell you. We're adults, not children. Why can't you and I decide what to do about this without involving the whole family?"

"Because it isn't that simple, Dino. If I had it my way, I'd never lay eyes on her again. But for my grandmother's sake, I'm not sure I can ignore her plea to go to her." Sophia closed her eyes and sighed. "Believe me, I don't want this thrown onto me. I need our parents' advice. They know her."

"So, what exactly did she say," Alex asked.

"She said Irini has lung cancer and it's bad. She sounded frantic and said that she didn't think she could get a visa in time to come here. I told her that I thought it was best she stay in Athens anyway."

"I think that's wise," Stavros agreed. "At her age, she doesn't need to travel under such stress."

"That's what I told her. But she doesn't want Irini to be alone. She's upset that she's going through this without anyone."

"That's the bed she made." Soula had little pity for her.

"Dad, I don't know what to do. For Yiayiá, I feel like I should go see her, but the thought of going near her sickens me. She's caused us nothing but trouble."

"It's a tough call." Alex turned to Dean. "What are your thoughts?"

Dean raised an eyebrow. The expression on his face told Alex all he needed to know.

"Mom told me to stay away from her, but if she were here today and she knew Irini was sick and alone, what do you think Mom would do?"

Alex, Stavros and Soula looked at one another, their expressions softening. "She would go to her. I'm certain of it. She was the kindest person I knew." Soula's voice cracked.

"I don't think she would have the heart to let anyone die alone if she knew that would be the case," Alex added.

"Christ forgave the thief nailed to the cross next to him at the eleventh hour and brought him into paradise with him," Stavros preached. "There's a lesson in there for all of us."

Sophia rubbed her hands over her face. "Watching Dino go through what he did, I can't imagine anyone bearing it without a soul to help them get through it. I may not like her, but she's a human being."

Standing, Dean flung his hands from his hips upward to gesture his disapproval. "Dad, this isn't a time to start quoting scripture. And Mom, Ana isn't here to tell us what she would do. We only know what she explicitly told us not to do—not to have anything to do with her!"

"Dino, calm down." Sophia gave him a stern look.

"I can't believe you all think this is a good idea," Dean said.

"Not a good idea, just the right thing to do." Alex laid his hand on Dean's shoulder. "There's a difference."

The train ride into the city was painfully long. On top of it, Sophia missed the subway connection to New York-Presbyterian Hospital by a few seconds. She watched in frustration as the train left the platform. It was the middle of the day and the trains were on an off-peak schedule—it would be a while before the next one arrived.

Pedestrians walked briskly through the city clad in warm clothing, but despite the temperature, Sophia's hands were clammy with sweat. She took a deep breath and tried to shake out her nerves as she entered the hospital. Anxious trepidation grew inside her as she practiced the words she'd say to the aunt she barely knew and paid no regard.

Nervously, Sophia walked down the corridor with a colorful bouquet of flowers draped over her arm, searching for the room number she'd been directed to. The door was open and she was about to knock softly, but she could see that the woman in the bed was asleep.

From afar, it could have been her own mother she was looking at. The sight haunted Sophia and it made her shiver. The monitors, IV bags and the gastric suction pump—it was all too familiar. Aside from the leopard print turban she wore to apparently hide her baldness, the frail figure lying in the hospital bed could have been Ana. Irini and Ana had similar features. Although Irini had always been fuller figured than her older sister, now the cancer had ravaged her body. Gone was the woman who blatantly flaunted her ample breasts and made sure her face was always flawlessly made up. This disease was a plague, sabotaging every cell it managed to invade until it plundered the body of its character. For Irini it was her vulgar sexuality, stripped bare, leaving nothing but skin and bones. Although beauty permeated from within her mother's soul, the cancer had stolen her elegant outward beauty, and as Sophia stared at her aunt, it was solely her mother she thought of.

Sophia could feel the blood drain from her as the painful memories ripped through her. Over six years later and it was still raw. She was here because her yiayiá asked her to be, Sophia reminded herself.

Tiptoeing into the room, she set down the flowers on the tray table. Irini stirred and slowly opened her eyes.

"What are you doing here?" Irini asked with as much bite as she could muster.

"Yiayiá called me. She's concerned for you," Sophia said flatly.

"And she sent you to help me? That's rich."

Sophia tried to ignore the sarcasm. Not sure whether to sit or remain standing, Sophia rocked in place, nervously. "Can I get you anything?"

"Not unless you have a cure."

"I know this is hard. I was with my mother when she had cancer."

"Your mother," Irini spat, "had the world at her feet. I always got her leftovers."

Sophia stiffened and drew in a hard deep breath. *I will not fight with this woman.* She repeated those words to herself.

"You could have had us. You chose not to."

Irini raised her voice. "Did you come here to lecture me?"

"No." Sophia pulled back and closed her eyes. "I brought you holy water from the shrine at St. Paraskevi and I can have the priest come to give you Holy Communion if you like."

Irini coughed out a laugh. "Keep your holy water. And don't be sending me your priests. You think all of that can help me?" Irini pointed an accusatory finger at Sophia. "I don't need fairy tales. I need a cure. Your priests give false hope."

"This water has cured people because they believe. Because they have faith."

"Did you give it to your mother? Where is she? Dead. She's dead."

"You don't need to be cruel. We don't always understand God's will." Sophia's throat was tightening.

Irini pulled herself up with the little strength she had. "Sure! God's will. When something doesn't go your way you explain it with God's will. You're all a bunch of fools. I don't need you, or your God!"

"I'm trying to do the right thing, but you make it impossible," Sophia said angrily.

"For your own conscience. Not for my sake."

"My conscience is clear." Sophia lifted her chin. "I've never done anything to you. You have been nothing but mean and hateful, yet I still came so that you would not have to go through this alone."

"Get out of here," Irini seethed. "I don't need you. I don't need anybody. I especially don't need your pity."

Sophia shook her head in disgust and secured her bag on her shoulders.

"If there's anything left in me, I'll make your life a living hell. I'll haunt you when I'm gone." Irini was ranting breathlessly.

Sophia began to walk to the doorway. Pivoting, she said, "Don't waste your energy. May God have mercy on your soul." *If you have one,* she thought to herself.

When she got outside, Sophia decided to hail a cab and call Dean.

"How did it go?" he asked.

"It went exactly how you warned me it would go."

"I'm sorry, baby. Come home. I'll make it all better."

"I'm counting on it."

"Our parents are waiting to hear from you. Did you call them?"

"No. I really am not in the mood to talk right now, but do me a favor. When you speak to your dad, tell him that for some people there is no eleventh hour. Irini truly is a sociopath."

Chapter 56

Mindy

June 2005

Mindy stood backstage waiting to walk the runway in the dress she had designed for the finale piece. She'd worked tirelessly for months to prepare for this day, and so many concerns and details ran through her mind.

Matt tried to calm her down the night before. "Enjoy the ride. Stop stressing," he insisted. "Your team has everything under control and you've checked all the finer details at least a dozen times."

She had so much riding on this. It was her first bridal collection, but more importantly, to Mindy it was symbolic of her entire creative journey. With the encouragement and inspiration coming from the many influences in her life, this line was more personal than any other.

The room and the runway were decorated in white and antique pink, an idea inspired from Sophia's mother's wedding photo in Thessaloniki. Subtle pops of gold were added for richness, but the enhancements were delicate and in good taste.

In the past, some of Mindy's runway shows were offbeat and colorful, or dark and edgy—this show would be quite different. Her concern was that this new direction she was taking would either destroy her career or propel her to new heights. Mindy was about to find out.

Each bridal dress in the collection was inspired by a design Mindy had created in the past—a bridal gown timeline of sorts—updated with a new millennium twist, combining nostalgic elegance with modern flair.

As the show went on, Mindy's nerves lessened—until the time was nearing for her entrance on stage. The dress she was about to reveal to the fashion world was a new design, inspired by the modern day bride.

Her fiery red hair was pulled off her face by a headband made of two strands of tiny, rose gold peonies. Her mass of curls hung down her back and swayed gently as she began to step on stage.

Mindy squared her shoulders and strutted out onto the runway, the train of the dress floating behind her. Formfitting and ruched in the bodice, the one-shouldered Grecian gown was ethereal. As Mindy walked, the light caught the tiny metallic seed pearls along the waist and neckline.

The crowd oohed and clapped enthusiastically. The other models began to make their second run, each coming out for the finale. The audience rose to their feet. Mindy's collection was a hit!

Backstage, Sophia, Demi, Amy, and Donna, swarmed over Mindy with hugs.

"That was your best show yet!" Demi declared.

"Every show has been unique, but this one ... I have no words." Sophia put her hands over her heart.

"You've never looked so beautiful," Donna said.

"I agree." The women turned to find Matt gazing lovingly Mindy. His hands were dug deep into his pockets.

They greeted him all at once, showering him with compliments over his own attire.

"May I steal my girl for a few minutes?"

"Sure!" Demi said. They all looked at one another with a smirk.

As Matt whisked Mindy away, she turned to ask her friends to wait so they could all go out for a bite to eat together.

"We'll be right here, don't worry," Demi assured her.

Matt escorted Mindy into her private dressing room. "Horny?" she asked.

"For you, always." Matt fidgeted with his hands in his pockets. "I love you."

Mindy tilted her head, her eyes lighting up. "I love you, too."

"I really love you. The kind of love that lasts forever. I'm in love with you." He drew his body close to hers and cupped her chin in his hand. "I want to marry you."

"Marry?"

"Yes."

"But, why?"

Matt's forehead creased. "Because I want to be with you. Live with you. I want to commit to you."

"With our schedules I'm not sure how that will work. You travel and I travel, but not in the same places or at the same time."

"We'll work it out."

"It's so perfect right now when we're together. Why change it?"

Matt ran his fingers through his hair. "Do you have an objection to marriage?"

"No. I always thought I would get married someday. But that time has passed. What's the point now? We're happy, aren't we?"

"Yes. But we can be even happier, married." Matt sighed, soaking in Mindy's bridal beauty. "When I saw you in that dress, I knew that was it. No one else was meant to wear it except you."

"You just thought of this now because of a dress?"

"No, of course not. I've been thinking about it for a while. But when I saw you tonight, I knew I couldn't wait a minute longer." Matt pulled a box from his pocket. "I had this designed for you." He opened it. Inside was a rose gold ring in the shape of a peony. A three-carat asscher cut pink diamond sat in the center of the metallic petals.

Mindy gasped.

"Do you like it?" Matt asked.

"Like it? It's dazzling."

"You'll wear it?"

"Matt, this is all so sudden. I need time to think about this."

"Time to think about us?" Matt sounded hurt.

"No, of course not. I love you with all my heart." Mindy kissed him and laced her arms around him. "I've been so impetuous in my relationships in the past. You mean the world to me, but I owe it to both of us to take my time and do things the right way." She closed the box inside his palm. "You hold onto this for me and give me a little time for it to settle."

"The ring is yours. No strings attached." Matt opened the box to remove it and place it on her finger, but she stopped him.

"No. When you put that ring on my finger it will be with strings attached, okay?"

"Okay." Matt grazed his thumbs over Mindy's cheeks.

"Let's keep this to ourselves until we decide what we're doing. Is that alright with you?"

"Whatever you want. But I'm already certain of what I want."

"I do love you," Mindy confirmed, hoping her words were enough. She thought she detected a hint of hurt in Matt's eyes and that was the last thing she wanted to inflict on him.

"I'd like to say a few words." Dean rose from the table. They were at an upstairs table that seated nine at the legendary restaurant, 21 Club, for a celebratory dinner after Mindy's spectacular fashion show.

"First off, I'd like to congratulate Mindy on her smashing success tonight. Once again, you've amazed us all." Dean lifted his glass. "To our Mindy."

"To Mindy!" everyone repeated.

"It's been a hell of a year, but we're all here in one piece." Dean snickered. "They had to put me back together with tape and glue, but I made it." Sophia took Dean's hand and gave it a squeeze. "Amy and Ezra, you fought for each other and now you have a stronger marriage than before and Amy you now have two sons to brag about. Demi and Michael, I can't thank you enough for seeing Sophia and me through a really tough time. Dem, I know it wasn't easy for you to be the strong one for Mom and Dad. I know if it was you lying in that bed I would have been wracked with worry." Dean turned his attention to Matt. "My new friend. We had a rough start." Everyone laughed.

"That's an understatement," Demi chided.

"I like the way you care for our Mindy. She deserves the best. Stick around, pal."

"I intend to." Matt lifted his glass toward Dean.

"Donna. My sweet Donna. Sister of my best friend. You had the toughest year of all of us. The hole in your heart may never fully heal." Dean put down his glass and moved to her side, resting his hands on her shoulders. Bending down, he kissed her cheek. "We're here for you. Always. Whatever you need. We're your friends and your family. We love you, and we'll do anything to help you make a new life for yourself."

Donna, misty-eyed, turned to embrace Dean. "Thank you. I love you all."

Mindy wanted to bring the levity back. "Hey! Are you sabotaging my night with sap?"

"Since when do you get all—'let's embrace our feelings?'" Demi teased.

"Let him finish, Dem," Michael said.

"Yes," Dean pointed to Demi. "Let me finish. I can't forget the most important person." He walked back to Sophia. "My wife. Love of my life. The reason I live and breathe." He took her hands in his.

"You suffered not knowing if I would live or die. And then, I put you through your paces. I was moody and nasty, but you stuck by me. I've always wanted to be the strong one for you, not the other way around."

"You always have been, Dino. My whole life. It was my turn to do it for you."

A collective "Awww" rang around the table.

"Well, now that you've spoken more than any lawyer I know, myself included," Ezra quipped, "let's order. I'm starved."

"Not so fast." Dean held up a hand. "I haven't gotten to the best part."

A wave of groans made Michael laugh. He elbowed Demi. "You'll like this."

"In honor of my wife's upcoming fiftieth birthday, and it being all of you ladies' fiftieth year I thought I would do something special for all of you. I wanted to give you something you've wanted for many years but could never seem to make happen."

Chatter around the table interrupted Dean.

"As my present to all of you, I am sending the five of you to Greece for the vacation you'd planned over thirty years ago."

The five women looked at each other, speechless.

"We all have obligations, Dean," Amy said. "It's a nice gesture, but I don't know how it's possible."

"We were teenagers when we planned that and we couldn't get it to work out then," Donna added. "How likely would it be that we'd all be free now?"

"Donna, you're off from school for the summer, Congress is on vacation starting mid-July, June weddings are over by then and Demi, your assistant will handle the rest. Sophia, most of your ballet students are in workshops over the summer and Mindy you need a break after working for months on this collection and fashion show." Dean looked around the table. "Does that cover everything?"

"Not quite," Sophia said. "I don't want to be separated from you. Not now. Life has just been getting back to normal."

"Not to worry. You ladies will have ten days together to do whatever bonding you women do and then the rest of us are joining you. Kids and all!"

"Everyone?" Amy asked.

"The whole family. I invited Sam, too."

"And to think there was a time I didn't like you," Amy said.

"Right back at you," Dean chuckled.

While everyone was excitedly discussing logistics, Mindy became quiet. She hadn't been to Greece for years, and the last time she was, she'd left broken in body and spirit.

"Dean?" she called to him over simultaneous conversations. "Dean?"

Dean looked her way and frowned. "What's wrong?"

"Which home? What island?" Her tone was pleading. "Not Chios."

"No," Dean said sympathetically, "Not Chios. Aegina. I've had Sophia's grandmother's beach house renovated and extended." Dean nodded. "Does that work for you, Mindy?"

"Oh, yes." Mindy broke out into a wide grin. "It's perfect. The five of us together at the beach house—just like we'd always talked about. I've been waiting for Aegina my whole life."

"We all have been waiting a lifetime to do this together." Sophia wrapped her arms around her husband.

Mindy was overcome with emotion as she observed her friends around her. Sometime during the evening, it had occurred to her that the year the girls made the plan to someday spend the summer in Greece together was the very same year she drew her first wedding gown sketch.

"I don't know what I would do without you. I couldn't have wished for better friends."
—Anastacia to Soula & Stavros 1956

Epilogue

The Honey Hill Girls'

July 2005

The sun shone down over the clear blue waters of the Saronic Gulf, the gentle waves reflecting beams of light, mesmerizing onlookers who stared out at the beauty of it.

"It's almost mystical," Donna said, seeming more at peace than she had in a long time. "It makes me believe Poseidon is below the surface creating the movement of the seas with his trident."

Reminiscent of years gone by, the five friends stretched out on beach towels sunning themselves. Today, they had better information though. Aluminum foil reflectors and baby oil were replaced with sunscreen SPF 50 and sunglasses with ultraviolet protection.

But everything else had resumed as it should—the banter and light conversation, and the sharing of hopes and dreams. Yes, there were always new hopes and dreams.

"I've decided to start a local outreach and support group for teens," Donna said sitting up and folding her legs under her.

"That's a wonderful idea," Sophia encouraged. "When did you decide this?"

"I've been thinking about it for months and doing some research.

I wasn't sure if I had the fortitude to go ahead."

"I think you do," Amy told her. "It's amazing how we find strength when we need to. I may be able to help you. We can talk about some fundraising and donations when we go home."

"That would be a great help."

"I'm proud of you," Demi said.

"There's nothing to be proud of. I have a choice. I can either drag myself through life as I've been doing, which doesn't bring back my son, or I can honor him." Donna bit her lips together and closed her eyes. "I don't want another child going through the mental anguish Anthony went through. Or to have another mother find her son's lifeless body." She swallowed hard, remembering. "The best way to honor my son is to use what happened to him as an example of what should never happen. If I can save one person then my son did not die in vain."

"That's such a healthy way to look at it," Mindy said with awe.

"It's the only way I can survive this life or I'll sink so far down I won't recover at all."

"Doing something productive and positive will be rewarding," Sophia said. "Do you remember that boy who was murdered back in the early '80s? His father never got over it, but he made it his life's mission to help families find their children."

"Adam Walsh," Amy said. "That was the child."

"That's right. I actually met John Walsh at a charity fundraiser," Mindy said. "He was a determined man, but I could see the sadness in his eyes."

"It never leaves your soul, losing a child," Donna told them. "But look at all the good he's done. I'd like to contribute some good to the world."

"You will," Mindy promised.

"And what about Donna?" Sophia asked. "You're set to take care of everyone else, but what are you doing for yourself?"

"I'm doing it. I have my job and I'll work on the support group. I have RJ and all of you in my life. That's enough for me."

"And Richie? Have you spoken to him?" Mindy wondered.

"I have. He's out of rehab and doing a little better, but we're over."

"Are you okay?" Sophia asked.

"Yes, I really think I am. We haven't been right for each other for a long time. He needs to take responsibility for his own life. I feel bad for him but I don't have it in me to help him."

"Are you interested in dating?" Demi asked.

Donna laughed. "Oh my God, Demi. Only you would ask that question." She shook her head. "No. We were conditioned to believe that we had to be coupled off. I went from my parents' home to a marriage at twenty-one. I was just a baby. I only knew Richie. He was my first and only boyfriend, and I never explored further."

"He was all you wanted," Mindy reminded her.

"What did I know? I never had a chance to find out who I was or what I wanted. I'm discovering that I am not half a couple. I'm a whole person on my own. That's enough for me right now. It's what I need right now."

"I think you're right and very smart to realize that." Amy stood, extending her hand to Donna. "Come, I think we've had enough sun for one day. I think we should go into town."

"That's a great idea," Mindy agreed.

To Dromaki restaurant was crowded with both tourists and locals, but Sophia spotted a table waterside and grabbed it. The sun was just beginning to set, but the heat of the day still hung in the air.

They giggled over *ouzotinis* while deciding what to order. Without warning, Mindy surprised her friends. "I'm going to marry him, you know."

Four pairs of eyes suddenly peered over their menus waiting for more information.

"Yup, I'm going to marry him."

"Matt?" Donna asked.

"No, George Clooney," Demi said sardonically. "I hear he's unattached."

"Did you inform Matt?" Amy asked, ignoring Demi.

"Not yet."

"Okay, sweetie. So you're going to ask him to marry you?" Sophia inquired.

"No, he already asked." The waiter came by and Mindy motioned for him. "I think we're ready to order."

Her friends looked at each other astounded.

"I'll have grilled shrimp with some of that skord—" Mindy tried to pronounce the dish.

"*Skorthalia*," Sophia told the waiter. "I'll have the same."

After they finished ordering, the questions resumed.

"Mindy, can you clear something up for us?" Amy requested. "Matt asked you to marry him but he doesn't know that you're going to marry him?"

"That's right." Mindy sipped her drink.

Donna waved her hands at Mindy, prodding her to continue.

"I told him I had to think about it."

"You what? Have you lost your mind?" Demi gripped the edge of the table.

Sophia patted Demi's hand. "Calm down."

"We have crazy schedules and careers. Plus we're not kids."

"None of that matters. Don't let this one slip through your fingers because of schedules." Demi was adamant.

Softly, Sophia asked, "Do you love him?"

"With all my heart," Mindy replied.

"Then don't let anything get in the way." Sophia spoke from experience.

"That's why I am giving him my answer the minute he gets here."

What was once a cottage on the beach was now a larger home filled with four generations of friends and family. When Spyros Fotopoulos bought this strip of heaven for his little family, he had no idea it would become a place of refuge and reunion.

Dean kept the integrity of the home, extending it in a way that matched the original style. But now, with an ever-expanding family, the once two-bedroom cottage became a five-bedroom summer home. A long, white table separated the kitchen and main living area and the open floor plan allowed plenty of sunshine to filter through the large windows and glass doors leading to the beach.

Ana had once found her answers here when she needed solace, and Amy had come here for contemplation. Even Sophia had hidden herself away at the beachside cottage while deciding the fate of her first marriage. And Sophia couldn't forget the many summers she'd spent here with her grandparents, her mother and her Dino.

Everyone was here, Sophia thought as she looked around her—everyone she loved in the world, plus the memories of those who were gone but not forgotten surrounded her.

Sophia took the time to commit the moments to memory. Walking into the newly renovated kitchen, she saw Yiayiá standing over the stove, stirring a large pot and moving about fluidly like a maestro conducting an orchestra.

Walking through the house, Sophia grinned watching Soula dole out a 'to do' list to Stavros and Alex.

Outside on the balcony, Dean, Ezra and Michael relaxed with a beer while watching the younger generation horse around on the beach.

Sophia stepped down onto the sand and dug her toes into it. Lifting her face to the sky, she soaked in the warmth of the sun. It gave her pleasure to watch the children. Most were young adults now, with the exception of her Cia. She would be her little girl for a while yet.

Away from the crowd, Sophia watched Mindy and Matt in the distance along the shoreline. Sophia smiled widely when Mindy threw her arms around Matt and kissed him. She nearly cried when Mindy extended her hand and Matt slipped a ring on her finger.

Demi and Donna came up on either side of Sophia and linked themselves to her by the waist. "It looks like Matt just gave Mindy a ring," Sophia said. They looked in the direction of Sophia's gaze.

Amy came up behind them. "What's everyone staring at?"

"Mindy and Matt," Donna answered. Amy draped her arm over Donna. No one said anything. They watched and observed, enjoying the blessings before them.

"I'm engaged!" Mindy shouted as she ran toward them, kicking up sand.

"We can see that," Demi said. "Let me take a look at that rock." She grabbed Mindy's hand. "Unique. That's gorgeous," Demi admired.

"I'm so happy for you." Sophia hugged Mindy.

"We all are," Donna added.

They stood together, arm in arm, quietly watching their children play volleyball. "I hope it's always like this," Sophia said, breaking the silence. "I want for them what we have—each other."

The End

Glossary of Greek words and phrases

Agori - Boy
Anastasi - The resurrection service of Christ on Holy Saturday night.
Árrostos - Ill; sick
Doxa tou Theou - Glory to God
Efhélaio - The sacrament of holy unction - holy oil used to heal infirmities.
Egoní - Granddaughter
Éhei éna kryo - He has a cold
Eíne kaíros ya mas na páme - It is time for us to go
Entaxi - Alright, okay
Epitrachelion - The stole worn by priests and bishops as the symbol of their priesthood. This liturgical vestment is worn around the neck with the two adjacent sides sewn or buttoned together, leaving enough space through which to place the head. It is usually made of brocade with seven embroidered or appliquéd crosses.
Fasaria - Noise; commotion
Fasolakia - Traditional Greek green bean dish in tomato sauce, made with or without meat. The meatless version is a popular dish during the Lenten seasons.
Fotia - fire
Frappé - Greek foam-covered iced coffee drink made from instant coffee.
Hárika poli - Pleased to meet you; pleasure to meet you
Horio - Village

Kalá Hristouyienna - Merry Christmas

Kalamatianós - A popular Greek folk dance, which is danced in circle with a counterclockwise rotation, the dancers holding hands. The lead dancer usually holds the second dancer by a handkerchief, this allowing him to perform more elaborate steps and acrobatics.

Karthia mou - My heart

Katse - Sit

Kollyva - Boiled wheat combined with some or all of the following ingredients: powdered sugar, almonds, ground walnuts, cinnamon, pomegranate seeds, raisins, anise, parsley and more. The wheat mixture is formed on a platter and decorated with powdered sugar and edible silver confections. Kollyva is made for memorials - 40 day, 3 month, 6 month, 9 month and annually. It is blessed during the memorial service as loved ones pray for the souls of the departed.

Koritsi - Girl

Kotsobolos - A gossip or nosy body

Koufeta - The white sugar coated almonds used in wedding favors. Koufeta is also placed on the tray with the crowns (stefana), which will be used in the wedding ceremony. The white symbolizes purity. The egg shape represents fertility and the new life, which begins with marriage. The hardness of the almond represents the endurance of marriage and the sweetness of the sugar symbolizes the sweetness of future life. The odd number of almonds is indivisible, just as The Bride and The Groom shall remain undivided.

Koukla / kouklitsa - Doll; little doll. A term of endearment.

Koulouri - Greek sesame bread rings. A popular street food.

Koutali - Spoon. Sometimes referring to the wooden spoon used when cooking.

Loukoumathes - Light and airy fried dough balls drizzled with honey and cinnamon.

Makaria - This is the luncheon after a funeral. Traditionally, the main entree of the makaria is fish. The Holy Gospels reveal to us that after Christ's own Resurrection he shared a meal consisting of fish with his disciples. This meal is a symbol of the Resurrection in that it displays the belief in the power of God who triumphed over death. Offering **Paximathia** and **Metaxa** also have become a custom upon arrival at the makaria. **Paximathia** is similar to the biscotti. It is considered appropriate for the somber occasion because of its dry texture and low sugar content. **Metaxa** is a Greek brandy.

Mastiha - A resin obtained from the mastic tree, which is indigenous only to the island of Chios. In Greece, mastiha is known as the "tears of Chios." Originally a sap, mastiha is sun-dried into pieces of brittle, translucent resin. When chewed, the resin softens and becomes a bright white and opaque gum. The flavor is bitter at first, but after some chewing, it releases a refreshing, slightly pine or cedar-like flavor. It is used to make liquors, gum, baking flavoring, and is known to relieve stomach ailments.

Mayiritsa - Traditional Greek Easter soup. After the midnight resurrection service it is customary to break the Lenten fast with this rich lamb soup flavored with Avgolemono. Traditionally, the organs and intestines of the lamb are included in the soup. (Some people opt to omit this part of the recipe)

Melitzanosalata - Traditional eggplant dip

Meze /mezethes - Appetizer / appetizers. Small plates of food similar to tapas. A variety of beginner foods on a platter.

Mnimosino - A memorial service performed at the end of liturgy in the Greek Orthodox Church. This service can take place anywhere from forty days after death to several years.

Opa! -This is one of those words you can use any way you wish. It's a common Greek expression used frequently during celebrations. It can express shock or joy. One might shout it while dancing or breaking plates.

Pappou - Grandfather

Panayia - One of the titles given to Mary, the mother of Jesus. Translated it means "all holy."

Presbytera - The Greek title of honor that is used to refer to a priest's wife. In the Greek Orthodox Church, a priest can be married as long as he was wed before he was ordained. A married priest cannot become a bishop.

Prosforo - The name given to the bread that is offered during Holy Communion. In Greek the word means "the offering." The bread is stamped with a seal before baking. Within the circular seal is a cross and symbols, which are representative of the Body of Christ and the church.

Psychi mou - My soul (pronounced psee-hee moo)

Skáse - Shut up

Skorthalia - Traditional Greek garlic dip or puree made with potatoes or bread as the base.

Spanakopita - Spinach pie made with phyllo dough, spinach and feta cheese.

Téleios - Perfect

Theía- Aunt

Theíos - Uncle

Theos - God

Theotokos - Mother of God

Then katalavaíno - I don't understand

Ti boro na po? - What can I say?

Ti symvainei? - What's going on?

Xenos - Stranger. Often, the Greeks refer to anyone other than a Greek as a xenos.

Yasou - A Greek expression used as a greeting or a toast. It means 'to your health'. Formally, yassas would be used and when making a drinking toast you could say yamas – to our health.

Yemista - Traditional Greek dish made of stuffed peppers and tomatoes.

Yerásei - I've aged; I've gotten old.

Yiayiá - Grandmother

Youvarlakia - Greek meatballs made with rice and herbs. Avgolemono sauce is most commonly poured over the youvarlakia, but they can also be cooked in a simple tomato sauce.

The Gift Saga

For information on *Evanthia's Gift, Waiting for Aegina,* or updates on the release date of book three of The Gift Saga follow Twitter@EffieKammenou & Effie on Facebook: www.facebook.com/ EffieKammenou

For additional recipes follow cheffieskitchen.wordpress.com

If you enjoyed *Waiting for Aegina,* please leave a review on amazon.com